P9-DDB-665

THE OTHER MERLIN

THE OTHER MERLIN

ROBYN SCHNEIDER

VIKING

VIKING
An imprint of Penguin Random House LLC, New York

First published in the United States of America by Viking,
an imprint of Penguin Random House LLC, 2021

LIBRARY OF CONGRESS CATALOGING-IN-PUBLICATION DATA
Names: Schneider, Robyn, author.
Title: The other Merlin / Robyn Schneider.
Description: New York : Viking, 2021. | Series: Emry Merlin ; book 1 |
Audience: Ages 14 and up | Audience: Grades 10–12 |
Summary: "Emry, the daughter of the famed wizard Merlin, must disguise herself as her twin brother to learn magic in Prince Arthur's court, where she finds scandal, danger, and romance"—Provided by publisher.
Identifiers: LCCN 2021020455 (print) | LCCN 2021020456 (ebook) |
ISBN 9780593351031 (trade paperback) | ISBN 9780593351048 (epub)
Subjects: CYAC: Merlin (Legendary character)—Fiction. | Camelot (Legendary place)—Fiction. |
Arthur, King—Fiction. | Magic—Fiction. | Fantasy.
Classification: LCC PZ7.S36426 Ot 2021 (print) | LCC PZ7.S36426 (ebook) | DDC [Fic]—dc23
LC record available at https://lccn.loc.gov/2021020455
LC ebook record available at https://lccn.loc.gov/2021020456

Printed in the United States of America

ISBN 9780593351024 (Hardcover)

1 3 5 7 9 10 8 6 4 2

ISBN 9780593463796 (International Edition)

1 3 5 7 9 10 8 6 4 2

CJKV

Design by Opal Roengchai
Text set in Garamond MT Std

To the girls who dream out loud,
want too much, and refuse to give up.

PROLOGUE

The Crooked Spire isn't remembered in any history books. No important documents were signed at its tables, no heroes rode into battle fortified by its ale, and no revolutions began in its back room. The drinks were watered down, the barkeep turned a blind eye to gambling (how he'd injured it was a constant source of speculation), and the barmaids made no secret that they were willing, for a price. And yet, the Spire does have a place in history—by the pure coincidence of its location—which is, perhaps, why it goes unmentioned.

If you stood with your back to the Thames, just north of St. Paul's Cathedral, you'd need only walk down the narrowest alleyway that borders the churchyard to arrive at the steps of the tavern. The sheer nerve of such a place to set up shop alongside the greatest cathedral in London raised more than a few eyebrows. But the Spire endured, largely because no one could remember which had come first. The only part everyone agreed on was that the magic sword in the courtyard between them had been there since, well, *forever.*

It stuck there, buried to the hilt in a block of veined marble, waiting. Occasionally, a knight riding through on his way to Castle Camelot would stop to try his luck. Or a dockworker might stumble out of the tavern, flexing his muscles and calling to his friends, *Hey, come and watch this!* But the sword stuck fast, and the words chiseled into the stone wore smooth over time.

> *Whoso pulleth out this sword of this stone*
> *is rightwise king born of all England.*

Now there was an idea. Anyone could tell you that, ever since the Saxons invaded and mucked things up, there had been half a dozen kingdoms of England. Sure, the borders shifted on occasion, whenever a restless royal rode off and conquered a neighboring castle. But a *united* kingdom? The thought, although far-fetched, was intriguing.

Yet no knight came who could pull the sword from the stone, and no great hero arose to unite the Britons. The sword had been waiting for hundreds of years, and to be honest, it was bored.

CHAPTER 1

Arthur Pendragon was drunk. Enormously, blissfully drunk. He slouched down in the booth of the Crooked Spire, enjoying the gentle way the tavern had begun to spin.

Everything about the place fascinated him: The arched stone ceiling that gave the impression of an underground cellar. The iron chains that served as handrails to the back staircase. The fat purple candles that dripped wax indiscriminately over floor and table. And then there was that odd sword in the courtyard. If the rumors were true, the last knight who'd attempted to pull it free had strained so hard that he'd actually soiled himself.

Arthur would have laughed if he'd been there to see it. But then, he hadn't seen much of anything lately. Tonight, however, he was free of the castle's oppressive gloom, if only for a few hours. And he intended to savor his freedom.

He drained his mug of ale and glanced across the table, where his friend was fiddling with a deck of cards. Lancelot shuffled them with a practiced snap, sifting them into a bridge. He did it a second time, and then a third.

"Please tell me you're going to do a magic trick." Arthur smirked, and Lance shot him a look.

"I was *going* to make the ale disappear," Lance retorted, "but you already did that yourself."

"Well, we *are* in a tavern."

"Stop looking so pleased with yourself. *I'm* the one who snuck us out."

That part was true: Lance had conjured some absurd excuse that sent Arthur's guards back to quarters, tossed him a shabby cloak, and announced they were going for a drink. It was bold and reckless, but it had worked.

And for that, Arthur was immensely grateful. He hadn't realized how badly he needed to be somewhere else until they were hurrying through the maze of London streets, the night thick with the promise that they could spend it as they pleased.

"I guess I owe you one," he said.

"You owe me six hundred and twenty-three," said Lance, "but who's counting?"

Arthur reached for his ale, finding his mug empty. He glanced hopefully toward the bar. "Another round?"

"Bad idea."

"Terrible," Arthur agreed.

"But how will we learn from our mistakes if we don't make any?" Lance's eyes danced with mischief as he climbed to his feet.

"My thoughts exactly." Arthur offered up some pennies, but Lance waved them off, scooping some petty coins from his vast pile of winnings and sauntering over to the bar.

Lance had left the cards faceup on the table, and the King of Cups stared back at Arthur, bearing more than a passing resemblance to his father. He sighed and pushed the cards away. Of course the great Uther Pendragon would commission his likeness on something so trivial. The king wasn't even the highest card in the deck. And worse, there were *four* of them. Arthur would have laughed, if it wasn't so depressing.

He glanced toward the bar, where Lance was leaning forward, a flirtatious smile on his lips, turning his charms on the barmaid. The girl blushed from the attention, and Arthur snorted, knowing Lance would just as happily flirt with the barkeep, or, probably, the barstool.

It was nights like this he wished he could make a girl smile and laugh, and know it was for real. These days, too much of his father's court treated him like a prize to be won, or a piece of clay they intended to mold. He wasn't sure he'd ever get used to it. Especially when, for most of his life, they couldn't dismiss him fast enough.

It was the end of September, and he was supposed to be at university, dividing his time between the library, the laboratory, and whatever dark watering hole everyone crammed into, just another scholar in the crowd. But that dream was long gone, replaced by a future that was never supposed to be his.

He tried to put it out of mind as Lance sauntered back to the table with two frothing mugs of ale, sending one in his direction with a practiced slide.

"These ones aren't stale," Lance bragged, nodding his chin in the direction of the barmaid. "I think she likes me."

"She likes your purse," Arthur said. "Anyone can see you've won half my coin."

"Consider it charity." Lance swallowed a mouthful of ale. "Guard's pay is a joke." He paused, calculating. "Hold on, was that only half?"

Arthur shrugged, pushing the cards the rest of the way across the table. In truth, Lance had almost cleaned him out, but he wasn't about to admit defeat. He just needed to bluff a hand or two, let his friend get cocky, and wait for his moment. Or else get so drunk that he didn't mind staggering home with an empty purse. Honestly, both were solid options.

Lance gave the deck an elaborate shuffle and started to deal, just as the bells over the door jingled. A blast of cool night air rushed into the tavern—along with a rumpled, nervous squire whom Arthur recognized immediately.

"Everyone, come quick!" the squire urged. "Sir Kay is about to pull the sword from the stone!"

Arthur stiffened. This was bad—very bad. He shot a panicked look across at Lance, who'd slid low in his seat, his hood shadowing his face. Arthur did the same, just as a stout man at the bar let out a booming laugh.

"Sure he is," said the man. "Just like the sop last night, and the night before that."

Suddenly half the tavern was laughing, and the other half shouting insults.

The squire blanched. And then he held up a heavy purse that clearly belonged to his master. "S-see for yourselves," he stuttered. "For those who b-bear witness, the next round is on S-Sir Kay."

"Why didn't ye say that in the first place?" someone called.

The tavern emptied in an instant, its patrons stampeding eagerly toward the door. Arthur slid lower in his seat, but no one paid his table any attention. Games of cards and dice sat abandoned, the tavern empty of all but Arthur and Lance, and one old drunkard snoring contentedly by the hearth.

"Sard." Arthur groaned. "It had to be Sir Kay."

The knight was Lance's uncle, and would enjoy nothing more than dragging the two of them back to the castle and throwing Lance under the horse for their unsanctioned adventure.

"I'm dead," Lance murmured, rubbing a hand over his face. "Speak kindly at my funeral."

"There's still a chance he won't spot us," said Arthur. "Come on. We'll slip through the crowd. Just keep your head down."

"It's not *my* head I'm worried about," Lance grumbled.

Arthur adjusted his hood. His cloak was old and far too short for him, revealing boots of polished calfskin. Even worse was Lance's sword, the unmistakable blade of the royal guard, which he'd refused to leave behind.

Sloppy. They wouldn't make the same mistake next time, if there even *was* a next time.

Arthur yanked open the door, and his last scrap of confidence fell away.

The courtyard was packed. Sir Kay had obviously sent his squire to the cathedral first, gathering a sizable audience there. It was impossible to push past the steps of the tavern, much less through the tightly pressed crowd.

They were stuck.

Lance swore under his breath.

"At least we'll get to watch," Arthur whispered, trying to make the best of it. They had a decent view, and no one would spot them all the way back here.

"I guess." Lance bit his lip as he surveyed the crowd.

"Maybe he'll shit his armor." Arthur was mostly joking, but Lance brightened considerably at the suggestion.

The crowd, growing thicker by the moment, buzzed with whispers, and coins changed hands as hasty bets were placed. The well-heeled church-goers huddled together, shooting apprehensive looks at the unsavory tavern folk who had joined them, most with drinks still in hand.

And at the front stood Sir Kay, with his fair skin, ice-blue eyes, and pointed beard the same honeyed color as Lance's curls. The knight's crimson cloak flowed behind him, and his armor, although dusty, was gold-plated—designed for tournaments rather than combat. The young, fumbling squire saw to his master's horse and equipment. From the amount of it, Arthur surmised that Sir Kay had ridden directly from the tournament in Cameliard. Where no doubt he had triumphed again in the joust.

Sir Kay preened, motioning for cheers from those pressed against the gate, and then the onlookers in the alley, letting the excitement build.

If they had any chance of sneaking away, this was it. Lance jerked his chin toward the alley, and Arthur nodded grimly. They shoved into the crowd, keeping their hoods low. They just needed to get to the gate, and then they could make for the Strand.

Deeper in the crowd, a man bellowed for more beer, waving an empty flagon in the air.

"Comin' through!" a barmaid shrilled, shoving past Arthur with a pitcher filled to the brim.

She slammed into him—hard. Beer slopped down the front of his cloak, and he tented his soaking tunic with a grimace. She must have spilled half the pitcher.

"Don't stop," Lance urged, his expression tense. He kept a hand on his sword as he wrenched his way between two thick-necked dockworkers.

Arthur followed, beer dripping onto his boots. Coming to this tavern had been their worst idea in a long time. And that was saying something.

"Where do you think you're going?" the barmaid accused.

With every step and push, the crowd protested and glared. And then Lance stopped short, and Arthur bumped into him. They were stuck.

"You! In the cloak! You better pay for that," the barmaid snapped, laying a rough hand on his shoulder.

Arthur whirled around in disbelief. "You're the one who spilled on *me*," he accused.

He expected at least a mumbled apology, but none came. Instead, she shot him a fierce glare. And then her eyes went wide.

"No, please—" Arthur begged, but it was too late.

"I didn't r-recognize you," she stammered, and he held his breath, as though that would prevent her from ruining everything. "Your R-Royal Highness."

Goddamn it, Arthur thought. *This evening was just determined to go terribly.*

The barmaid sunk into a panicked curtsey, and Lance shot Arthur a horrified look. This was the *opposite* of sneaking away quietly.

"Get up," Arthur whispered urgently. "It's all right."

It wasn't all right. Already, a ripple was going through the courtyard, and heads were turning in their direction.

"My friends, what distracts you?" Sir Kay boomed.

"It's the sardin' prince of Camelot," someone called, making the churchgoers gasp at both the news and at such a coarse swear.

Arthur wanted to disappear. But that wasn't happening, so damage control would have to do. He painted on a smile and pushed back his hood.

"Your Highness," said Sir Kay, with a small bow in Arthur's direction. "Lance," he added, barely hiding his disappointment. "I didn't realize you'd been at church."

Lance grimaced, but Arthur's shoulders stiffened at the barb.

If Sir Kay wanted a verbal sparring match, then so be it. Lance wasn't getting in trouble for this. Not if he could help it. So Arthur lifted his chin, squared his shoulders, and tried to summon a semblance of his father's stern command.

"And I didn't realize you wished to be High King of England," Arthur returned.

The knight's smile faltered. "You misunderstand me, Your Highness," said Sir Kay. "I aim only to prove a point."

"That winning is your greatest ambition?" Arthur suggested, earning some snickers from the crowd.

"That it's impossible for *any* man to pull this sword from the stone," said Sir Kay.

"So you've assembled us here to watch you fail?" Arthur asked with a frown.

"I—well—no," said Sir Kay.

"I see," said Arthur, surprised he'd managed to gain the upper hand. "By all means, continue."

No one was cheering now. Still, Sir Kay stepped forward, dramatically wrapping both hands around the hilt of the sword.

The courtyard was silent as Sir Kay pulled. And pulled. Sweat dripped from his brow, and he groaned from the effort. But the sword didn't budge.

Of course not, Arthur thought. *It takes more than brute strength to overpower magic.*

Sir Kay let go, and a disappointed murmur rang out.

"Knew he couldn't do it," someone complained.

"As I said, impossible," the knight repeated, trying to save face. It was obvious he'd believed he would succeed.

"What a waste!" someone called.

"Oi! Make the prince try!" someone else yelled.

Arthur stiffened.

"Let's see *him* pull the sword from the stone!"

More people shouted in agreement.

"Well, Your Highness?" Sir Kay challenged.

Arthur desperately wanted to refuse. But of course he couldn't. Because this was what it meant, being heir to the kingdom. He was supposed to lead the people. To listen to them. And they were calling for him to pull the sword from the stone.

"Why not?" he said with a shrug, as though he hadn't just agreed to humiliate himself.

He could feel the press of everyone's stares as he made his way through the churchyard. They weren't stares of encouragement. He was the boy who would be king, and it was clear on their faces: they didn't want him.

But he already knew that. He'd spent his whole life as the embarrassment of the realm: King Uther and Queen Igraine's bastard son. Even though he wasn't, technically, a bastard. Born five months after his parents' wedding, he was merely a scandal. And there was no law against putting a scandal on the throne.

Still, the courtiers had whispered. And King Uther had hastily made it clear that, although firstborn, Arthur would be raised as a spare. When the queen produced a rightful heir, the Royal House of Pendragon would have its crown prince. Except their next two children were stillborn. Then there was a daughter so weak that she had lived only a few hours. The queen had grown frail, but still Uther held out hope. A few months ago, it had seemed a grand celebration was in order. But neither mother nor child had survived the birth. Which meant Arthur was, well, *it*.

The funeral was barely finished before Arthur was summoned before his father's advisors, who declared him utterly lacking. He was, they
accused, deficient in every subject that a royal heir of eighteen should have
long since mastered. No matter that his French was fluent, his Latin excellent, and his knowledge of medicinal herbs first-rate. He knew nothing of
hunting, hawking, or combat. And even more troubling, he preferred the
company of Sir Ector's bastard, Lancelot, a lad so questionable that his
own uncle had refused to take him on as squire.

And now he was going to embarrass himself over a magic sword. Perfect.

He stumbled a little, unsteady from the drink, but his gaze stayed fixed
on the sword. It was buried to the hilt in a block of stone, just like in the
stories. If he squinted, he could make out the engraving: *Whoso pulleth out
this sword of this stone is rightwise king born of all England.*

Fair chance. He wasn't even rightwise prince born of Camelot.

The crowd was keen for his defeat, and Sir Kay was eager for Arthur's
failure to eclipse his own.

He could sense everyone's scorn bubbling up around him. They didn't
think he could do it. They just wanted to have a laugh at his expense. He
was never going to be enough. For his father, or for Camelot.

"Get on with it!" someone shouted.

Arthur closed his hands around the sword's cool iron hilt, feeling foolish.
Here goes nothing, he thought, as he squared his shoulders and pulled.

The sword came loose as easily as if it had been resting in a well-oiled
sheath.

He stumbled backward in surprise, gripping the blade in both hands.

The crowd stood frozen and silent, their eyes wide with shock. For a
long, shuddering moment, no one reacted. And then a tremendous cheer
rippled through the courtyard, and the alleyway beyond.

He'd done it! He'd pulled the sword from the stone! But—but how?
His head spun, and he realized belatedly that Sir Kay wasn't cheering.

"You all saw that I loosened it," the knight claimed. "It's only fair that we try again."

Before Arthur could protest, Sir Kay had fitted the sword back into the stone, his smile wide. The knight eagerly clasped his hands around the hilt and pulled. And pulled again, harder this time, grunting loudly from the effort.

But the sword stuck fast once again.

Sir Kay finally stepped away, bidding Arthur try with a mocking sweep of his hand.

The courtyard fell silent. No one dared to jeer after what they had just seen: the king's bastard, all of eighteen, skinny and bookish and so drunk he could barely stand, had pulled the sword from the stone like it was nothing. While the famous Sir Kay, tournament champion, had failed—twice.

Arthur's heart hammered, and he wondered if he really *could* do it again. The whole thing felt like a dream—surreal and dizzying—or maybe that was the pitcher of ale he'd downed.

He once again stepped up to the sword, grasping it with a single fist. This time, when he pulled it free, he didn't stumble. Instead, he held the gleaming blade high.

The crowd went to their knees.

Here was their one true king, a leader who would unite the Britons, the king to defeat all kings.

"Hail, Prince Arthur! Rightwise King of England!" someone cried.

Arthur grimaced. He didn't want to be King of England—to be honest, he didn't even want to be King of Camelot. And he certainly didn't want any of this.

All he'd wanted was to slip away from the castle for one night. To kick back and down a few drinks with a friend, shedding his troubles and his responsibilities—not gaining *more* of them.

But it was too late. The crowd took up the cheer, and as Arthur surveyed them, he felt sick.

He'd set something in motion, something he didn't know how to take back. He looked for Lance, expecting to find him leaning against the side of the tavern with a smirk, but his friend had taken a knee along with the rest of the courtyard.

Arthur stared out at the sea of bowed heads and deferential faces, at the people who, for the first time, truly wanted him as their leader, and his stomach heaved with alarming force.

Oh no, he thought, as he turned and vomited all over Sir Kay's gleaming armor.

CHAPTER 2

Everything was going to be fine.

Emry Merlin staggered out the back door of the theater and gulped down the warm summer air. It wasn't much cooler outside than backstage, but at least it didn't stink of unwashed armpits. She hunched forward, hands on her knees, willing her heart to stop pounding.

There was no reason to be nervous. She'd filled in for a missing player plenty of times before. Besides, Pell's was a small part. A few lines, a skirmish of swords, a quick death halfway through the first act. And it was only the town theater—it wasn't as though they were performing for their patron, the Earl of Brocelande, at his manor.

And yet, it *was* dangerous. There was nothing wrong with employing a girl to help with the special effects—so long as Emry stayed backstage. But the theater troupe would be in trouble if anyone discovered she was also their understudy.

At eighteen, she was tall and skinny enough to play a boy's part, provided she flattened her chest and tucked her long black hair under a cap. Thankfully, most people assumed it was her twin brother onstage, a mistake Emmett was all too willing to encourage—especially when the mistaken party was a pretty girl.

A bead of sweat ran down her temple, and Emry wiped it away with the back of her hand. It was a scorching afternoon in June, and any sensible person would be indoors, wearing as few layers of clothing as possible.

Unfortunately, Emry wasn't sensible.

"Smart as spades, but foolish as hearts," her father used to say. Whenever he'd turn up, which wasn't often, he'd give Emry a pretty ribbon for her hair and take Emmett out to the woods to learn magic. Emry found this arrangement enormously unfair, and campaigned to be included.

When Father refused, Emry made her twin teach her everything he'd learned. The next time their father had shown up, Emry had tucked her hair under a cap and switched places with her brother. Their father quickly realized he had the wrong twin, because Emry learned twice as fast.

She was included in the lessons from then on, although Father never failed to remind her that she was learning things she could never use, which was both impractical and foolish.

Emry didn't care. She just wanted a chance to prove herself before being told no. She couldn't help being a girl any more than she could help having magic, but she'd be damned if she sat home with a box of hair ribbons, letting boys have all the adventures.

It was the same with the theater. At sixteen, she'd bullied the property master into letting her handle their special effects. Flammable powders and pig's blood were expensive, messy, and no longer necessary. Not if he hired her to conjure illusions of fire and blood. Even better, illusions wouldn't need to be scrubbed out of the costumes between performances. Marion, the dresser, had insisted her father hire Emry immediately, and the two girls had become fast friends. When one of the players was struck ill, it was Marion who had pointed out that Emry would fit into his costume, and Emry who had promptly lowered her voice and reeled off his dialogue with a devilish grin.

Screw being sensible, Emry thought. *Being trouble is* so *much more fun.*

Still, she could have done without Pell's coat, which was not only far too warm, but stunk of flop sweat.

That, at least, was something she could fix.

Emry closed her eyes and focused. Rosemary, she decided. With a hint of lemon. She didn't have her wand, but no matter. She pictured the wretched coat, mentally issuing the command that would fix it: *Extergio.*

Emry gave the coat a tentative sniff. Much better. Everything was very nearly perfect—except for the play itself, which stunk even worse than the backstage.

Ronda and the Elf King. It was supposed to be a comedy, but really, the whole thing was a tragedy. Perhaps one day the troupe would have license to perform in the city, where the latest playwrights supplied better fare. But until then, the earl demanded comedy, and so long as he footed the bill, comedy he would get.

She muttered Pell's lines, which didn't take long, and walked through the choreography for the sword fight. She was going over the lines again when a royal messenger rode up the lane.

Knights and their squires passed through Brocelande more and more these days, and a messenger was nothing *too* out of the ordinary. The town was half a day's ride from London, with a bustling market and a farrier who knew his way around a horseshoe.

The king's messenger was sunburnt and dusty, and his horse was lathered with sweat, but his crimson livery blazed in the hot sun. The golden wyvern on his chest shone so brightly that it had to be made from the precious metal itself.

Emry stared down at her own costume, threadbare with a sloppy yellow stencil of a rising sun. It would look impressive enough onstage. The theater held its own sort of magic, which was, perhaps, why she was so drawn to it.

She glanced back at the royal messenger, expecting him to urge his horse down the hill to the inn, or up the lane to Brocelande Hall. Instead, he slowed outside the bakery, leaning down to ask a question of the baker's boy. With only a moment's hesitation, the boy pointed a plump and sticky finger toward the theater—no, not toward the theater, toward *Emry*.

Well, this isn't good.

She pulled the brim of her cap low across her face, trying to quell her nerves as the royal messenger approached.

"Afternoon, good sir," he called, sliding down from his horse.

Emry inclined her head in response.

"I'm looking for Master Merlin," said the messenger.

"My father?" Emry frowned. "You're about eight years too late."

Seven years, ten months, and three days, actually. Father had left exactly as he always did, slipping away in the middle of the night without so much as a goodbye. Except he'd never returned. Not to Brocelande, or to Castle Camelot, or to anywhere else.

"Then it's a good thing I'm looking for his son." The messenger removed a scroll from his belt and held it toward Emry. "Master *Emmett* Merlin, His Majesty King Uther Pendragon of Camelot requires your presence at court."

Oh no.

Emry stared at the scroll, trying not to panic. The messenger thought she was her brother! And she didn't dare confess the truth now. Not while she stood outside the theater in a *costume*, for god's sake. She couldn't betray the performance troupe, especially to an agent of the king.

With a trembling hand, Emry reached out and accepted the parchment, bowing deeply. "Thank you, sir," she murmured, pitching her voice low. "It's an honor to receive a summons from the king."

"His Majesty will expect you two days hence." The messenger wheeled his horse around and clattered across the courtyard before Emry could say another word.

◗ ◗ ◗

"Why would a royal messenger give this to *you?*" Emmett asked, frowning suspiciously at the scroll.

He was sprawled at the kitchen table, boots up, jerkin loose, and a goblet of wine at his elbow. With his fair skin, black hair, and pirate's grin, he was devastatingly handsome, and what's worse, he knew it.

"He got mixed up," said Emry, taking down some bowls for their supper. "I was at the theater, and I didn't look particularly, well, *ladylike*."

"One day you'll get in trouble for that."

"Tell me something I don't know." Emry sighed, ladling out their stew. She passed a bowl to Gran, who was knitting by the hearth, and set theirs on the table.

"King Yurien invaded Northumbria again," Emmett said, draining his wine goblet. "Bet you didn't know that. Overheard it at the Prancing Stag."

"What were you doing at the Prancing Stag?" Like she even needed to ask.

"Kissing the innkeeper's daughters and betting at merils," Emmett said innocently. "The usual."

Emry shook her head. Not over her brother's rakish ways, which she'd accepted long ago, but over the news about King Yurien. "Northumbria's pretty far away," she said.

"It's not *that* far," Emmett insisted. "And it's just as before. He took control of an unfortified castle along their border and burned the neighboring village. If he goes for Cameliard next, they'll call for Camelot to intervene."

He swallowed a mouthful of stew and started coughing.

Emry cautiously licked her spoon, making a face.

Not *again*.

"Gran?" she asked. "Did you add salt to the stew?"

"Yes, dear," Gran murmured dreamily, knitting another stitch into a long grayish thing with a glove on one end and a sock on the other. "The weather *is* very nice."

"*Salt*," Emry insisted. *"How much?"*

"All of it, from the taste," Emmett muttered, pushing away his bowl. "If you fix the stew, I'll tell you what King Uther wants."

"It's a simple spell," Emry grumbled, reaching for her wand. "I don't know why you refuse to learn it."

"My father was the greatest wizard who ever lived. Why should I bother with basic household spells?"

Because they're useful, Emry thought, *unlike you.*

She aimed her wand at their supper.

Abdere.

She took a cautious taste. Spicy, which tended to happen when you magicked your meal. But no longer inedible.

"Ha!" Emmett cried triumphantly, flinging the scroll to the floor. "I'm going to be knighted!"

Emry let out a sharp laugh. "I didn't realize sarding the innkeeper's daughter counted as a noble deed," she retorted.

"Well, I'm *practically* going to be knighted," Emmett amended, shoveling a spoonful of stew into his mouth. "Ugh. Why does magic ruin the flavor of *everything*? Anyway, King Uther wants me to live at the castle and train to be the next court wizard."

Emry's spoon clattered into her bowl. She'd imagined a handful of reasons the king had summoned her brother to Castle Camelot, but nothing like *this*.

"That's—that's wonderful," Emry said, wishing she truly meant it.

"It's about time Father's legacy came in useful," Emmett went on. "I bet half the ladies at court will take one look at me and drop to their knees." He grinned wickedly. "Openmouthed."

Emry blushed. "Don't *say* things like that in front of Gran," she scolded.

Or me, she almost added, even though, between Emmett's miscreant friends and the theater troupe, she'd heard far worse.

"Well, it's true." Emmett shrugged. "Probably. I've heard Prince Arthur's nothing special. And we all know King Uther's bald as my arse."

"Keep talking like that, and you'll find yourself in the castle dungeons," Emry warned. "Or worse, the gallows."

"Two days," Emmett muttered, ignoring her. He scanned the scroll again, making a face. "I should probably brush up on some magic. What'd you do with Father's books?"

"Next to my bed," Emry said. "Help yourself."

Emmett yawned, leaning back in his chair. "Maybe later. The innkeeper's daughter wore me out."

Of course she did, thought Emry.

It was all so enormously unfair. *This* was why their father hadn't wanted to teach her. Why he'd brought her dolls and ribbons and had frowned when she'd mastered spells faster than her brother. He'd known this would happen.

Their father had served at the royal court. When he was alive, kings had trembled in fear of the great kingdom of Camelot, ruled by the powerful Uther Pendragon and protected by the formidable Wizard Merlin. And now Uther wanted to continue that legacy, with Merlin's son standing alongside his own.

Well, good luck with him.

Emmett drained his second glass of wine and rambled on about his day, but Emry had stopped listening. All she could think was, *Emmett's going to London, to live in a castle and learn magic. And not because he's smarter than me, or older, or more talented. Because he's Merlin's son, and I'm just his daughter.*

CHAPTER 3

Emry sat up in bed, her heart pounding.

Someone was hammering on their front door. It was the middle of the night, a completely unreasonable hour. She fumbled for her bedside candle, wondering what on earth was going on.

Ignium, she thought, and the wick burst into flame.

The knock sounded again, hard and impatient.

"OPEN UP!" a gruff male voice insisted.

Emry pushed aside the curtain around her sleeping quarters. Her brother stood by their old wooden table, awake and fully dressed.

"Don't answer it," he instructed as Emry reached for her shawl, wrapping it around her shoulders.

"Why not?" She frowned. "What's wrong?"

"Just stay out of it," Emmett warned, taking out his wand. His eyes were wide and scared, and his pirate's grin was nowhere to be found.

"Whose daughter was it this time?" Emry asked tiredly.

Emmett's face scrunched the way it used to when they were little and he'd done something truly terrible.

The knock sounded again, rattling the windowpanes.

"MERLIN!" their would-be visitor roared.

"It's a gambling debt," Emmett confessed, slumping into a chair and putting his head in his hands. "I—I made a huge mistake. I thought I'd be gone by the time they came to collect."

Out of everything her brother could have done, that was the last thing Emry wanted to hear.

"You're unbelievable!" she fumed. "We're barely scraping by as it is."

Another powerful hammering shook their cottage.

"OPEN UP OR WE'LL BREAK DOWN THE SARDING DOOR!"

Emry didn't doubt it.

"Help me," Emmett begged. He looked terrified.

"How?"

"Remember what Father taught us about Corperus magic?"

Of course she remembered. It hadn't been a lesson so much as a warning of what *not* to do. No matter how dire the circumstances.

"We could make them forget why they're here," Emmett went on.

"You mean mind control," she said flatly.

"More like memory manipulation."

"Absolutely not!" Emry bristled. "You *know* how dangerous that is! The last time you tried it—"

"I got knocked unconscious for a week. I know." Emmett eyed the door nervously, talking fast and low. "But I have much better control now. And if you have another idea, I'm all ears."

"Murder?" Emry suggested.

Emmett's jaw dropped. "There's *three* of them," he spluttered.

"I meant you."

That was when the door crashed open with a tremendous bang.

Emmett had been wrong; there were only two of them. Two enormous, dangerous-looking brutes, with muscles like boulders and knives that glittered in the candlelight.

"*Merlin!* You sarding *snake!*" the bald one thundered.

The other was too busy leering at Emry in her linen shift. She scowled, folding her arms across her chest.

Emmett raised his wand.

"Don't!" Emry cried, but she was too late.

"*Damnatio memoriae! Damnatio memoriae!*" Emmett bellowed, desperately sweeping his wand between them.

The spell dropped from his wand like rancid fruit, polluting the air with its wrongness. Emmett slid to the floor. His eyes rolled back in his head, and his body convulsed in violent waves.

Emry screamed his name and crouched down beside her brother, trying to hold him steady. In a few moments, the convulsions stopped, and his body went limp. His eyes closed, and his heartbeat slowed from its frantic pounding to a faint but steady thump.

"Wake up!" Emry pleaded, her throat tight. "Please!"

But she knew he wouldn't. Magic couldn't be cured with magic. At least, not *this* kind of magic. There was nothing she could do, which was almost worse than seeing her brother laid out on the floor, catatonic from the blowback of his own misfired spell.

She looked up, surprised to find that the thugs were still there, gaping at the scene before them.

"Get out!" Emry howled.

"Well now, miss, we can't do that," the bald one said, rotating his neck with a sinister crack. "We came to get payment, and we 'ent leavin' empty-handed."

"Sorry," the other one added. His back was pressed against the wall, and his eyes were fixed on Emmett's wand as though it might come alive and attack him.

"How much?" Emry asked warily.

"Two pounds," said the bald one.

Emry sucked in her breath.

A fortune.

It was more than she earned in a year. They didn't have it. Not even close. What had Emmett been thinking, racking up so large a debt and hoping to get away with it? Or rather, she realized, to *run* away from it.

"I could pay you in magic," she offered hopefully.

Baldy shook his head. "The debt 'ent to us. We've only come to collect. And like I said, we 'ent leavin' empty-handed."

Emry took a deep breath, trying to think. If she magicked some pennies to look like gold . . . no, they'd only come back once they realized what had happened. And then they'd be after her as well as her brother.

A hand pressed against Emry's shoulder, giving her a fright.

But it was only Gran.

"Go back to sleep," Emry said.

But Gran shook her head. Her eyes were sharp, and her chin jutted stubbornly. "No, child," she said. "Let me help."

"Gran—" Emry began, wondering how the old woman could possibly help. But Gran shot Emry a severe look and, with shaking hands, twisted off her wedding ring.

"Take this and leave us in peace," Gran snapped, holding out the gold band, its small ruby glinting in the candlelight.

Baldy was so surprised that he stared at the ring for a moment before realizing she meant him. "Y-yes, ma'am," he said.

After the men left, Emry turned to Gran, her eyes still brimming with tears. She threw her arms around the frail older woman.

"Oh, Gran," she breathed. "Thank you."

"Thank me all you want," said Gran, "after you get this enormous oaf into bed."

CHAPTER 4

The next morning, Emry hoped for a miracle, but the covers were tucked up to Emmett's chin just the way she'd left them. He hadn't so much as rolled over in his sleep. His pallor was frightening, and his breathing wasn't the easy rise and fall of slumber, but a shallow hitch.

Oh, Emmett. Why did you have to go and do something so reckless?

They'd been fourteen the last time he'd tried a similar spell. He'd slept like the dead for a week, and had very nearly convinced Emry that he was. At the end of seven days, she'd expected to find a corpse, but had instead found her brother sitting up in bed, rosy cheeked and ravenous.

He'd promised never to work magic like that again—spells that twisted someone's mind to your will could snap back as easily as they could bend forward. And Emry had foolishly believed he meant it. The gambling was bad, but the way he'd tried to deal with it was worse.

Especially when he was expected at court *tomorrow*.

Failing to answer a royal summons would land him in prison. Emmett had known that, and he'd *still* cast that risky spell.

Even if she could send word to the castle that her brother was indisposed, who knew if the king would receive it, or if he'd extend another invitation?

Magic was uncommon, like green eyes or red hair, but it still ran deep in the old families. Surely, between the Ninianes and the Dulacs, there was another boy eager to take her brother's place . . .

"Chamomile, dear? Or lavender?" Gran called over the whistle of the kettle.

At least Gran was herself again, which was a relief.

"Trying to calm me down?" Emry asked suspiciously.

"Chamomile it is," Gran sang. "You'll need it."

Emry shook her head, but accepted the mug, breathing in the fragrant herbs. She picked up the royal scroll, scanning the parchment as she sipped her drink.

An apprentice position at the castle under Master Ambrosius, the now-ancient court wizard who had trained their father. Room and board. Payment of three pounds per month—Emry let out a gasp at the sum. No wonder Emmett had joked that he was going to be knighted.

So that's *where Emmett expected to get the money to pay his debts.*

"Don't worry, your father tripped over his own spells more than once in his day," said Gran, patting her on the shoulder. "He'll sleep it off."

"He'd better sleep fast," said Emry. "He's expected at Castle Camelot tomorrow."

"Tomorrow?" Gran frowned. "I could brew some vervain tea . . ."

"That *never* helps!" Emry didn't mean to be shouting, but suddenly, she was. "You can't cure magic with *tea*! All of this"—Emry thrust the scroll at Gran— "just *handed* to him because of Father! I don't know which is worse, that he didn't realize how lucky he is, or that he was stupid enough to ruin it! If King Uther had summoned *me* . . ."

Emry trailed off, because of course that was impossible. And dwelling on it only made her more infuriated.

"Are you done, dear?" Gran asked calmly. "One can never tell."

Miserably, Emry nodded.

"Let's hope your little tantrum didn't knock anything out of place," Gran said, plucking the teacup from Emry's hand and peering down at the dregs.

"Don't you dare predict I'll marry the blacksmith's son," Emry warned.

But Gran merely pursed her lips, studying the cup.

Emry was used to Gran's fortunes, which always sounded like vague nonsense. Gran peddled them in the market for extra coin, but her predictions weren't magic. They were just educated guesses.

"You look so much like your brother," Gran mused. "A stranger would be hard pressed to tell the difference."

"Wait, what?" Emry asked. The old woman couldn't be saying what Emry thought she was saying.

"The leaves predict a journey ahead."

"A journey?" Emry echoed with disbelief. "Am I supposed to show up at the castle claiming to be my brother?"

But as she said it aloud, she realized that, actually, she *could*.

Emry bit her lip, considering. Emmett would likely be up and about in a week's time. She could keep her head down in court for that long. After he woke up, he'd set off for London, and they'd trade places before anyone realized a thing.

Being the court wizard was Father's legacy, and they had so little of him left. And there was no denying they needed money. The roof was half made of spells and charms as it was, and Emry doubted it would last through another winter.

Emmett may have inherited their father's estate, but without income to run it, they were quickly sliding toward ruin. They had already sold off the silver and rented the land to tenant farmers to make ends meet, and it still wasn't enough.

Three pounds a month. They couldn't lose this. Not if she could help it.

"We'd switch back in a week," she mused, and then stopped, shaking her head. "No, I can't just leave you here."

At this, Gran scoffed. "Child, I'll be *fine*." She arched an eyebrow. "It's high time the women in this family did something more than get left behind while the *men* leave their mark on history."

Emry rather agreed. She *would* like to see London. And to study magic

again, properly. All she had to do was take on the role of an understudy.
Except this wasn't the theater. It was the royal court. And she'd be playing
a living, breathing person, which wasn't at all the same as reciting someone
else's lines in a play.

Not to mention, her magic wouldn't help make the masquerade any
more believable. Spells could only be cast outward, not inward. And while
there were potions she could brew to change her appearance, she didn't
have enough time.

She stared down at her brother, weighing their similarities and their dif-
ferences. He was broader through the shoulders, but some padded clothing
could mimic that. His height was close enough. They both had the same
wide mouths and strong chins, the same dark eyes and raven hair.

And if they could fool their father, surely a doddering old wizard could
be deceived. It wasn't as though she'd have any reason to interact with the
royal courtiers.

But if she *was* found out, she shuddered to think of the consequences.
Of the king's legendary temper, and what he'd do to a girl who had deceived her way into a position at his court.

She could do this. She *had* to do this. Or else she'd spend the rest of
her life trapped in this too-small town, scrambling to keep a roof over their
heads, cursing Emmett's foolishness and her own lack of nerve.

She was going to Castle Camelot as her brother. And when he came to
his senses and learned what she'd done, he'd thank her for it.

She realized she had been silent for too long, and Gran was frowning
at her.

"Well," Gran prompted. "Were my tea leaves wrong?"

Emry shook her head. "I'll be careful," she promised. "No one will
suspect a thing."

"I should hope not," warned Gran. "The king has ordered men executed for less."

Emry swallowed nervously, knowing her grandmother was right. But what other choice did she have?

"I'll ask Marion to stop by often," Emry promised.

She bent down to kiss Gran on the cheek, and then straightened, trying to look brave. Gran was watching her again, with a sharp eye. Emry wondered what was the matter now, when her grandmother *tsk*ed.

"You'd better cut your hair," the old woman said decisively. "This isn't the theater, dear. A hat won't fool anyone."

◐ ◐ ◐

"If it isn't the fairest maiden in Brocelande!"

Marion blushed furiously as she saw her friend's handsome brother sweep into the theater, flashing his pirate's grin.

"Evenin', Emmett," she said. "Your sister 'ent here."

He made a face at the news and slouched against the wall. "You're sure?" he asked. "I was hoping to say goodbye."

"I—" Marion began, but then she narrowed her eyes, realizing. *"Emry?!"*

"Good, isn't it?" Emry beamed, pushing off from the wall. She looked every inch her brother, from the unruly mop of black hair to the unbearably smug expression of an eighteen-year-old boy who had never in his life been told no.

"Very." Marion gave her a closer inspection. "How'd you make your shoulders that wide?"

"Padded the doublet," Emry explained. "Lifted the insides of my boots, too. I had to try three different spells until it worked."

"I'm almost afraid to ask," said Marion, "but *why* exactly are you dressed as your brother?"

"I'm going to Castle Camelot in his place," Emry admitted, recounting the entire story.

When she'd finished, Marion blinked in shock. This was far beyond whatever silly amusement she'd been expecting. There was no question Emmett had gone and thrown himself arse over elbow, the way he'd been threatening to do for a long time, but Emry's plan was a lot to take in.

"Say something," Emry begged.

"The royal court," Marion spluttered. "Dressed as your brother."

"It's only for a week," said Emry. "Besides, I'm hoping the food will more than make up for having to magic a bulge into the front of my hose."

Suddenly, the two girls couldn't stop giggling.

"Is *that* what you did?" Marion asked. "I'd thought it indelicate to ask."

"Stage tricks," Emry assured her. "I didn't have much time."

"I can tell," Marion said, reaching for the scissors on her sewing table. "Your hair's uneven in the back. Sit."

Emry flashed her friend a grateful smile and climbed onto a stool, straddling it in a most unladylike manner. "Just practicing," she said innocently.

Marion shook her head and began to snip.

"Do you think you'll meet the prince?" she asked.

"Arthur?" Emry made a face. "I suppose so."

"You could at least *try* to sound more excited. He pulled the sword from the stone!"

"Almost a year ago!" Emry returned. "And I still don't see why it's so impressive. He hasn't done a thing since."

Marion rolled her eyes. What did Emry expect? For a nineteen-year-old boy to ride off and unite England in a fortnight? "Doesn't matter," she insisted. "Crown prince. Magic sword. And I bet he's gorgeous."

"Not according to Emmett. Besides, I'll be dressed as a lad," Emry reminded her.

"Good. Then you can tell him all about your beautiful friend Marion." She ruffled the back of Emry's hair. "Done."

"How do I look?" Emry asked, leaning forward to peer into the ancient looking glass. "Devastating? Emmett-ish?"

"You're practically his twin."

Emry shook her head over her friend's terrible joke. But Marion bit her lip, suddenly serious. This entire plan wasn't just foolish—it was dangerous. But danger came with the territory when you had a wizard for a best friend. And Marion had learned long ago that once Emry set her mind to something, there was no talking her out of it.

Marion leaned forward, throwing her arms around Emry. "I'm going to miss you."

"Of course you are. You're going to be so tired of washing pig's blood from the costumes that you'll weep tears of joy upon my return."

Marion groaned. The costumes! How had she forgotten?

CHAPTER 5

The sun was melting toward the rooftops by the time Emry reached the city gates. She was exhausted and stiff, and she definitely smelled like the back of the tanner's wagon she'd hitched a ride on, but London made her forget all of that.

Wherry boats glittered with lantern light as they cut across the Thames. Market stalls snaked along the river's edge, merchants calling out their wares in a dozen different accents, selling everything from fortunes to fresh-caught fish. Timbered buildings rose four stories high, pressed so close together that Emry could hardly tell where one ended and another began, and the spire of St. Paul's soared high above it all.

She craned her neck, staring up at it. Prince Arthur had pulled the sword from the stone in that very churchyard, she knew. When news of it had reached Brocelande, she'd waited for everything to change, for Arthur's action to *mean something*. But nothing had happened, other than the towns-folk suddenly singing the praises of the prince they'd grumbled over only a day before.

Maybe it was like Gran's tea leaves. A prediction of what might happen, rather than a prophecy of what would. Well, fate better hurry up, because even predictions have an expiration date.

In a week's time, she'd meet her brother in the tavern next door to switch back. But she pushed the thought from her mind, because there was so much to get through before she could even think of her adventure's end.

She kept going, following the river so she wouldn't get lost. London was both larger and smaller than she'd imagined, the kind of place you could easily cross on foot, but which could still swallow you whole without warning.

"'Ent you a handsome lad?" a woman in a low-cut dress purred from a dark alleyway.

Emry blushed, hurrying past.

The buildings grew shabbier, and the merchants' wares became more suspicious. She spotted more than one dubious seller of cure-all tonics, and a man in a soot-stained cloak with a sharp dagger in each hand selling, well, Emry wasn't exactly sure.

Maybe following the river wasn't the best idea.

She took the next turn, following a narrower road that seemed to wind and twist for an eternity, through a rough neighborhood that smelled like the city ditch. Dirt-smeared faces peered out from unglazed windows, and a racking cough echoed from an open doorway.

Emry clutched her belongings tighter. Just as she was about to turn back, the road spilled open into a large and colorful market square.

Jugglers, buskers, musicians, and merchants jostled for space around an ancient stone column. Roads shot off in all directions, most looking far more agreeable than the one she had stumbled down. And beyond the column, at the end of a long lane lined with stately townhouses, sat Castle Camelot.

As she got closer, she could feel the hum of old magic swirling through its walls. The castle wall was forged from ancient spellcraft: impenetrable to conquering armies, and enchanted to prevent siege. Thanks to the wall, the castle was no remote military fortress. Instead, it was an impressive collection of buildings, some made from decorative brick and others from smooth stone, with paned glass windows and gothic spires, all arranged in neat squares around a series of courtyards. There were more chimneys than she could count, turrets with weathervanes, turrets with gargoyles, and atop it all, a single crimson flag, its golden wyvern catching the sun.

Emry approached the timbered gatehouse, her heart pounding.

This is it, she thought, taking a deep breath to quell her nerves. *Act I, Scene I: Enter Emmett Merlin, an overconfident country lad with a talent for magic.*

Two guards slouched outside, sweating under their metal helmets in the summer heat. When they spotted Emry, they snapped to attention, crossing their halberds to block her path.

"I'm Master Ambrosius's new apprentice." She held out the scroll for inspection, and one of the guards snickered.

"*You're* a wizard?" he asked, not very nicely.

"What else would I be?" Emry raised an eyebrow.

"A stable boy? You're certainly dressed like one," the guard said, making his friend laugh.

"At least I'm not strong as a mule but only half as clever," Emry retorted, taking back her scroll and glaring until the guards stepped aside to let her pass. "Now if you'll excuse me, I hate to keep the king waiting."

◑ ◑ ◑

Emry had arrived later than she'd hoped. The receiving courtyard was empty, and she didn't know what to do. She finally managed to track down an annoyed-looking page, who couldn't have been older than twelve. He led her through an opulent hallway and bade her wait as he vanished into the Great Hall, closing the doors behind him.

As the seconds ticked painfully by, Emry glanced around the anteroom, jittery and filled with dread. The castle was far grander than she'd imagined—the wood-paneled walls were not only carved, but hung with elaborate tapestries, and the ceiling beams were painted with delicate swirls of gold. It made Brocelande Hall seem plain by comparison.

She stared at the doors, swallowing nervously. Any minute now, she would stand before Uther Pendragon, the King of Camelot, disguised as her brother.

Please, she hoped, *let this work*.

Finally, the doors opened, and the page emerged, looking even more put-upon.

"King Uther will see you now," he reported sourly, as though he'd hoped the king would refuse.

The Great Hall was the most lavish room Emry had ever seen. Her stomach clenched as she took in the size of the crowd that filled it. And she could feel every one of them staring curiously at her.

This is a performance, Emry told herself. *They're just the audience*.

It didn't help.

The timbered room was stifling. *No wonder*, she thought, noting the fire that blazed in an enormous fireplace, and the dozens of candelabra that lined the walls.

At the far end of the hall, on a raised dais, sat King Uther. He canted languidly across a wooden throne, chin propped in his hand, his expression inscrutable.

He looked older than she'd imagined, and weathered, as though there had once been a lot more of him. Like Emmett had said, he was bald, but his black eyebrows were surprisingly thick, and his expression was stern and disapproving. A heavy golden crown encircled his brow, and despite the heat, he wore an embroidered velvet robe trimmed with white fur that was the finest thing she'd ever seen.

Here was the king at whose side her father had ridden into battle. A ruler who kept peace with neighboring kingdoms that he could easily conquer, even as King Yurien flexed his might in the north. A king whose laws were so strict and unyielding that she often wondered if everyone felt as stuck as she did.

Emry took a deep breath and walked forward, stopping in the open space before the throne.

Don't curtsey, don't curtsey, she thought as she sunk clumsily to one knee, doffed her cap, and stayed there.

"Emmett Merlin, Your Majesty," announced the herald.

"Stand up straight, boy," ordered the king.

Emry rose awkwardly, all too aware of the king's scrutiny. She held her breath, waiting for him to declare her unsuitable, or worse, to see through her hastily cobbled disguise.

She'd been so focused on helping her brother that it hadn't occurred to her to wonder what to do if she was caught.

Well, it was certainly occurring to her *now.*

Why wasn't the king saying anything? Emry's heart felt like it was in her throat. She stood as still as she could manage, not daring to meet the king's gaze, instead staring at a courtier's jeweled shoe clip.

"The very image of your father," the king pronounced, and Emry let out a sigh of relief.

"Thank you, Your Majesty," she said, making her voice low.

"But that doesn't qualify you to become our next court wizard."

Emry's mouth went dry.

"I require a demonstration of your magic," demanded the king.

"A demonstration, Your Majesty?" she echoed, horrified.

"When you're ready," the king said, making it clear he meant her to give this demonstration *now.*

She hadn't prepared a thing. And yet the courtiers' faces all turned eagerly in her direction, and the King sat up straighter on his throne.

She couldn't think. Every spell she knew had emptied from her head.

It was far too warm. Even the ladies in low-cut gowns were fanning themselves. Between the blazing fire and the candelabra and the endless wood paneling, the heat was oppressive. Sure enough, the king, in his heavy ermine-trimmed robe, had beads of sweat on his brow.

Why not? she thought. She closed her eyes, concentrating. Pride kept her from reaching for her wand. It was much more impressive without—if she could pull it off.

"*Nivis*," she whispered.

For a moment, nothing happened. And then snow drifted down from the ceiling. It fell in soft, fat flakes that vanished as they landed. It was just an illusion, one she'd performed at the theater many times, but the courtiers still gasped in amazement.

The crowd fell to murmurs, then silence as King Uther slanted her a look of approval.

"Most impressive," he declared, reaching out to catch a falling snowflake. The illusion stopped on contact, and his mouth twisted in disappointment. "Pity it isn't real. Or cold."

The courtiers tittered.

"I still have much to learn, Your Majesty," Emry said, casting off the spell with a wave of her hand.

"And Master Ambrosius has much to teach," said the king. "Mark him well, so that you may serve my son as your father did me, Apprentice Wizard Merlin."

"Yes, Your Majesty," Emry murmured with a bow.

The king motioned for a serving girl to come forward and show her to her room, and Emry practically sagged with relief.

◐ ◐ ◐

This room had to be a mistake.

There was a four-poster bed hung with silks and bolstered with a small battalion of pillows, a washbasin that looked to be made of real silver, a wooden desk, and a chair. A grand fireplace took up an entire wall, and a tapestry depicting a unicorn in the forest occupied another.

Emry frowned, confused. She'd been expecting servants' quarters, not a lavish bedroom with a private garderobe attached.

"It was your father's," the serving girl explained, bobbing a curtsey. "No one was using it and—"

"It's perfect," Emry interrupted, hardly daring to believe her luck.

"Is that my new apprentice?" a gruff voice called from what sounded like the top of a stairwell.

The serving girl blanched.

"Best go and see what he wants," she said, eyes wide. "You wouldn't want to keep Master Ambrosius waiting."

Her words seemed ominous, but the girl escaped before Emry could ask what she'd meant.

Emry's heart hammered as she stepped into the hallway, pausing at the base of the narrow stone stairwell that led to the wizard's workshop. There were so many ways this could go wrong, she thought. Just because she'd fooled the king didn't mean she could deceive his wizard. What if he was disappointed in her abilities? Or saw through the spells that enhanced her disguise? Still, up she climbed, until she was dizzy from the spiraling staircase.

The top of the tower was an odd, pungent space, with herbs drying from the ceiling, cages full of twittering birds, and shelves bursting with glass apparatus. It reminded Emry of a cross between an apothecary and her father's disorganized study, and instead of finding it strange, the room felt unexpectedly like home.

Emry hesitated in the arched doorway, taking it all in, and waiting for the walls to stop spinning.

"Come closer, boy." Master Ambrosius reached for an elaborate pince-nez, settling it on his nose. "Let me get a look at you."

Practically blind. Excellent.

"Hmmm," Master Ambrosius said, his eyes hugely magnified as he peered at Emry through his thick lenses. "I taught your father a very long time ago."

"Yes, sir, I know," said Emry.

"I was old even then," the wizard said with a cough that might have been a laugh.

Emry believed it. Master Ambrosius was tall and thin and so pale that Emry wondered if he ever left the tower. White hair puffed wildly around his wrinkled face. His eyes were bright green, and his nose was very red, and he wore an unfashionably long tunic in a faded shade of yellow.

Father had favored expensive court fashions, worn a flashy gold earring, and been almost as much of a rake as Emmett. But Master Ambrosius was like a wizard from a storybook, or perhaps an absentminded scholar, the kind who was forever misplacing his inkpot. And Emry desperately wanted to impress him. Being here, in her father's old workshop, with his former teacher, was everything she'd dreamed of.

And yet, it was only hers by deception.

"I assume you have a basic foundation in Mechanical magic," Master Ambrosius continued, removing his pince-nez, which dangled from a gold chain around his neck.

Emry nodded, recognizing the term, which referred to the casting of spells and charms on inanimate objects.

"Good," Master Ambrosius said. "What is your limit?"

Emry frowned, confused by the question. "I don't know, sir," she replied.

His expression sharpened. "And why not? Do you practice magic that infrequently?"

"I wasn't aware wizards had limits," she admitted truthfully.

"Of course we do. I myself can cast a dozen spells in a day before I begin to misfire, half that if I'm also maintaining any long-term enchantments. Your father could produce significantly more than I, although—"

Behind him, a thick-bottomed kettle began to bubble ominously, emitting a worrying stench.

"Sir, the potion!" Emry interrupted.

"Sard it all!" Master Ambrosius whipped his wand out of his sleeve. *"Refrigescant!"*

He squinted, pointing his wand in the general direction of the kettle. Emry winced as the old man's spell missed its mark.

"Blast," he murmured, fumbling to untangle his pince-nez.

The concoction was still bubbling over, and Emry reacted without thinking. *Extinguo*, she thought, aiming her magic toward the fire. The flames went out, and the liquid calmed immediately.

Master Ambrosius blinked at her through his glasses. "What did you just do, boy?" he demanded.

"I—um—" Emry said nervously. "I figured removing the heat wouldn't affect the potion, so . . ."

She trailed off. It was a poor excuse, and she knew it. She shouldn't have intervened with someone else's spellwork. Especially when she was unfamiliar with the potion. She stared at her boots, waiting for the reprimand.

"You didn't use a wand," the old wizard accused. "You didn't cast a spell."

"I did, sir," she said. "I just didn't say it aloud."

"Hmm." Master Ambrosius tilted his head to the side, inspecting her more sharply this time. Just when she thought it might go on forever, he nodded, as though having found the answer to an unasked question.

"Did your father teach you to do that?" he asked.

"Not exactly," Emry admitted. She'd discovered the skill by accident, when she'd stayed up late practicing and hadn't wanted to wake anyone. She'd figured out she could *spell* the words in her head. While she explained, the old wizard peered at her with fascination.

"Useful," he pronounced. "But foolish. As long as you're under my tutelage, see that you cast your spells aloud. I can't instruct what I can neither see nor hear."

"Yes, sir."

"Silent spells, and evidently no limit to how many of them you can rattle off." The old wizard heaved a sigh. "Heaven help me. Your father wasn't exaggerating when he boasted of his son's great talent with magic."

Emry offered up a weak smile, even though she was furious that her father had never boasted of his *daughter's* great talent.

"What's that?" she asked instead, noticing a lumpy cot in the corner, half hidden behind a screen.

Surely the old wizard didn't sleep here, not when her own chambers were so lavish.

"The infirmary," he explained.

Emry frowned. "I thought there was a royal physician."

"There is," Master Ambrosius replied gravely. "And he is quite skilled with both leeches and bloodletting. He is also a terrible gossip." Emry couldn't tell whether the old man was joking or not, and before she could make up her mind, he added, "Not everyone wishes their maladies to become common knowledge. Sometimes it's an ill-gotten black eye, but others, it's a matter of the utmost discretion. Sir Kay once got himself into quite a lot of trouble with a gerbil." The wizard shuddered. "Retrieving the poor fellow wasn't pleasant."

Emry hoped she'd misunderstood where, exactly, the gerbil had gotten stuck.

"But you're talking about Corperus magic," she protested. "My father always warned not to work spells on people unless you're willing to risk the blowback."

Emmett's accident had been an extreme example, but Emry still couldn't forget the time she'd tried to mend Marion's sprained ankle and had blacked out from the effort, earning herself a splitting headache that had lasted for days.

Master Ambrosius gave her a look. "And how old were you when your father issued this warning?" he inquired.

"Ten, sir," Emry admitted.

"I wouldn't trust a ten-year-old boy with a blunted practice sword, much less a real blade." Master Ambrosius raised a bushy eyebrow. "There is, of course, a technique to it. One that takes finesse, knowledge, and strength."

"I'd be interested to learn that," Emry said.

"Even despite your father's warnings?"

"I'm not a child anymore," she replied, lifting her chin. "Besides, I came here to learn."

The old wizard went to a shelf, plucking down a bundle of dried herbs. "Belladonna. What would you use this for?"

"Insomnia?" Emry suggested. "My gran brews it into a tea."

"If you'd answered poison, I would have said your father was right not to teach you. A corrupt mind breeds corrupt magic."

Emry thought of Emmett's misfired spell, and of what he'd been trying to do when he'd cast it. Had Father scared them away from such spells because he'd suspected what Emmett would use them for? Or had he truly thought them too young to learn?

Whichever it was, Emry's heart sped up with excitement at the thought of learning an entirely new discipline of magic. One that went far beyond household spells and illusions.

It's only for a week, she reminded herself. But a week was better than nothing.

The old wizard reached for a quill and a scrap of parchment, scribbling down a few lines. "Come back here first thing tomorrow. You'll need the *Corperus Magicarum* and *A Practical Herbalist's Guide*, third edition. Fortunately, there are copies of both in the castle library."

CHAPTER 6

Emry's jaw dropped as she pushed open the double doors of the library. Not from the chessboard marble floor, although that *was* impressive, nor the long wooden tables and velvet-upholstered chairs. Not even from the crests of the noble houses that bordered the ceiling, painted in what had to be real gold. She'd never seen so many books. They stretched two stories high, the second level bordered by a slim balcony with an iron railing and narrow spiral stair. It was a library in the same sense that a cathedral was a church.

And while it was undeniably wonderful, it was also a little bit of a disaster. She had no idea how she was going to track down Master Ambrosius's books before supper. And then she spotted the pale, brown-haired librarian slouched behind a stack of books, a quill and inkpot at his elbow.

He was tall and lean, with wavy chestnut hair, dark, intelligent eyes, and high cheekbones. He couldn't have been older than twenty, and he was dressed plainly, in a blue tunic with the sleeves rolled, brown hose, and worn leather boots. He was, overall, an outstandingly handsome young man.

Not that she noticed. Much.

He tapped his quill against the table, thinking. And then, with a satisfied smirk, bent his head over a piece of parchment and began to write.

Emry waited for him to look up, but he kept scribbling. "Excuse me," she finally broke in.

"Did you need something?" he asked, eyes still on his parchment. "Or do you just enjoy disturbing those who are otherwise occupied?"

Emry bristled. He had no call to be so rude. She wished she could march right out of the library, giving the door a satisfying slam behind her, but she knew better than to fail her first errand as Master Ambrosius's apprentice.

"I'm looking for some books," she persevered.

"Whatever for?" he mused, dipping his quill into his inkpot.

"Baking into a pie," Emry snapped, losing her patience.

The young man finally glanced up, regarding her coolly. "I believe you're supposed to eat your own words, not someone else's."

He made as though to go back to his writing, but Emry leaned forward, sliding the slip of paper across the table.

"I need these," she said. "Tonight."

"And what do you expect me to do about it?"

"You're the librarian," Emry said, exasperated. "Either help me or don't. But I'll be gone faster if you do."

"An excellent point." He took the slip of paper and set down his quill. "In that case, I suppose I had better assist you."

She'd thought him handsome slouched over his books, but standing up, he was so much more than that. There was an unstudied elegance to the way he moved, and she realized belatedly that she was staring. Thankfully, he hadn't noticed.

"So Master Ambrosius finally has a new apprentice," he deduced, striding over to a shelf on the far wall and plucking down a volume without even checking the spine.

"This is the fourth edition," Emry protested, showing him the title. "He said the third."

"You'll want the fourth. Someone's ripped whole chapters out of the third, and it's the only copy. You should remind him about that, by the way."

"Can I have the third as well?" Emry asked. "Just in case."

"Whoever tore out the pages also did some truly ghastly drawings."

"You're mocking me," she accused.

The librarian shrugged. "Don't say I didn't warn you."

He pulled down another volume and flung it in her direction. Emry hastily caught the book. The whole thing was warped, and the first few chapters were completely missing. As she flipped through, her mouth fell open at the pornographic doodles.

"Wow." She grimaced at a detailed sketch of a lusty man chasing a horrified sheep. "You weren't joking."

"Like I said, the fourth edition." The librarian sounded smug.

"What's going on in here?" boomed a cheerful male voice.

A tall, strapping blond boy sauntered into the library, his hand resting absently on the pommel of a gleaming sword. He was freckled and tanned, as though he spent a lot of time outdoors. His short scarlet cloak and livery marked him as a member of the Royal Guard. Emry thought nervously of the coarse, rude guards she'd encountered at the castle gates, and steeled herself for ridicule. But he merely tossed her a polite nod, his attention on the librarian.

"I thought you'd be done by now," the guard said, making a face.

"Just helping the new wizard's apprentice find some books," the librarian explained with a lopsided grin.

The boys exchanged what was clearly some sort of silent communication, and Emry narrowed her eyes, wondering what was going on.

"You know, I've never been that desperate," said the guard, nodding toward a rather large drawing in Emry's book.

"Maybe you've just never seen a sheep that attractive," Emry suggested before she could help herself.

The guard laughed and picked up the book, flipping through it.

"We should commission a painting," he suggested. "His Excellency the King, tending to his flock."

"Good luck finding the artist," Emry said.

"You mean this isn't your work? I'm disappointed."

"Even if it were," said Emry, "I'd never admit to defacing a book in front of the royal librarian."

The guard stared at his friend, who shrugged with considerable elegance.

"As well you shouldn't," the guard continued, looking entirely too amused.

Emry's stomach grumbled, loudly. For a moment she was horribly embarrassed, but then she remembered that everyone thought she was a boy. "I'm starved," she complained. "And I still need one more book."

"The *Corperus Magicarum*," said the librarian. "It's on the upper level."

He sauntered off to retrieve it, and the guard slouched against a shelf, making it clear he meant to wait.

"Do you have a name?" Emry asked.

"Oh, sorry." He offered a large, calloused hand. "Lancelot Debenoic."

"Emmett Merlin," she said.

She tried to make their handshake as brief as possible, since his hand was nearly twice the size of hers.

"Ah, Merlin," he said, brightening in recognition. "You'll serve the prince. What do you think of him?"

"I haven't met him yet," Emry confessed.

Lancelot grinned, as though hoping she'd say that. "Watch out. He's spoiled rotten."

Emry's stomach sank. "Is he really?" she asked, disheartened.

"Oh, beyond repair," Lancelot went on. "Insufferable company. I pity his guards."

"As do I," said the librarian, handing over a slim volume bound in green leather. "Lance is right. The prince is a pompous, sniveling fool."

"His head is so far up his own arse that his royal decrees are farts," said Lance.

"He has no friends, only acquaintances who wish they were better strangers."

"The only throne he's fit to sit on is a privy," Lance returned.

Emry laughed, delighted over the boys' clever insults. And then she realized it was her turn. "It's a shame acting like a cock won't make his any bigger," she suggested.

She grimaced, worrying the joke had crossed a line. To her relief, Lance laughed so hard that he nearly fell over.

"Well," he gasped, clapping a hand to his friend's shoulder. "Better get changed before supper. See you around, boy who claims he didn't draw those very attractive sheep."

"I didn't!" Emry called, as the boys strolled off without her.

☾ ☾ ☾

The banquet hall was not nearly as resplendent as the Great Hall or the library, and for that Emry was thankful. Instead, it was merely functional, designed to seat everyone at court.

Emry froze in the doorway, staring at the long tables that lined each wall, realizing she had no idea where she was meant to sit. She tried to spot the boys from the library, but no luck. Finally, a page put her out of her misery, directing her toward a table in the back.

"Thank you," she muttered, hurrying toward the table.

"Excuse me!" another page called, when she unwittingly walked past what turned out to be a hand-washing station, where young nobles training to be knights held linen cloths and bowls of perfumed water.

"Sorry," she mumbled, hastily copying the man who stepped next to her, and hoping her cheeks weren't as pink as they felt.

She had no idea what she was doing when it came to court etiquette. Thankfully, the real Emmett wouldn't have fared any better. Still. She had better stop drawing unnecessary attention.

"You're late, boy," scolded Master Ambrosius as Emry hastily joined him.

Actually, she was just in time. She had no sooner sat down than the musicians began to play. "I got held up in the library—" Emry started to explain.

"The library will still be there in the morning," the old wizard assured her. "But unlike books, supper has a tendency to disappear."

Emry grinned at his joke. And then supper arrived, and she stared openmouthed.

There were heaping platters of pheasant with toasted almonds, roast and stuffed chickens, fine white rolls, mushroom pie, and bottles of French wine. This wasn't supper—it was a feast.

Emry happily dug in, remembering the joke she'd made to Marion about the food. It really did look delicious. She took a bite—dear god, had the pheasant been drizzled in *honey*?

"This is only the first course," Master Ambrosius warned, as though he'd guessed she was considering another slice of pie.

"The first course? But it's already more than enough."

"The platters go next to the servants' tables, and after that, to the deserving poor," said the old wizard. He paused before adding, "Queen Igraine insisted on the last part. She said she never wanted to feast in ignorance while her people starved."

Queen Igraine had been beloved for her kindness, even though much of Camelot had disapproved when the king chose her as his bride. The widowed Duchess of Tintagel was a rare beauty, but she'd been well into her twenties at the time, and barely out of mourning for her late husband. It had been both a relief and a scandal when Prince Arthur came along five months later.

"My father spoke well of her," Emry said.

"And of the king too, I hope," the old wizard said.

"Of course," Emry assured him, biting off a big mouthful of bread. More often than not, her father had complained loudly about the king, whose fearsome temper was as well-known as his wife's kind heart.

A few seats down, a group of bearded men in fine tunics laughed up-roariously at a coarse joke, and Emry startled, having forgotten about them entirely.

"... better lock up your codpiece, then!" the loudest advised as he mer-rily poured another round of wine.

"Oh, she's already done it for me," said his friend, raising his goblet in mock salute to a scowling, olive-skinned brunette in a crimson gown.

Even though they sat at the same banquet table, Emry couldn't have felt further apart from this drunk and bawdy crowd. She was relieved they hadn't tried to include her in their merriment.

Everyone here, it seemed, gave the old wizard a wide berth. True, his robes were shabby and stained, and he smelled of herbs from his workshop and, faintly, of magic. Emry wasn't sure anyone else picked up the scent, but they definitely sensed something. She knew from experience that magic made many people uneasy.

This could work to her advantage. If the other courtiers avoided her as they avoided Master Ambrosius, she'd make it through the next week in a snap.

"Who's that?" Emry asked as a lovely young woman with fair skin and a cascade of blonde curls entered the dining hall, her lateness clearly cal-culated to garner attention. The girl's gown was exquisite, pale pink silk trimmed with gold lace that shimmered in the candlelight. Her hair was twisted with pearls and jewels. Emry slouched down in her seat to better hide her own drab doublet. The soldiers at the gate had been right: even in Emmett's best clothing, compared to everyone else at court, she *was* dressed like a stable boy.

"Ah, Lady Elaine. I think you'll find her a most pungent flower," said Master Ambrosius. "You'll have heard of her father, Lord Howell.

Emry nodded. Lord Howell held one of the highest positions on the king's council. She watched as Lady Elaine sailed toward the royal banquet table, chin lifted high.

"Which one is he?" Emry asked.

"At the right hand of the king." Master Ambrosius nodded toward a short, plump, sour-looking man with white-blond hair and a pointed goatee, who was deep in conversation with King Uther. It was clear Elaine didn't get her looks from her father's side of the family. "And beside him is his wife, Lady Howell," Master Ambrosius went on.

Lady Howell was still very beautiful, despite the gray that streaked her chestnut hair, and she looked as though she knew it—and so did the king.

Emry snuck another glance at Lady Elaine, feeling sorry for the girl.

"There's the Countess of Agravaine, the king's cousin," Master Ambrosius said of a pale, elegantly dressed older woman with auburn hair and an aquiline nose. She wore an expression of polite interest as she watched the trio of musicians.

"And her husband, Lord Agravaine." Master Ambrosius nodded toward a tall, imposing man with dark brown skin and close-shorn black hair. "One of the king's most trusted advisors."

There was a shrewdness to the man's expression, as though he missed nothing, and Emry decided she'd prefer not to catch his attention if she could help it.

"They have two sons around your age, though both are away at school," said the old wizard. "And of course, to the king's other side is Prince Arthur."

Emry glanced over.

And nearly choked.

He wore the same rumpled tunic and hose, hastily topped with a fine red jacket that he hadn't bothered to button. A slim golden circlet glinted against his dark hair, and Emry realized that she'd made a terrible mistake.

He wasn't a librarian at all.

How had she been so stupid?

The clever insults the boys had traded, daring her to join in—they hadn't been making fun of the prince, they'd been making fun of *her.*

Emry boiled with fury. At that moment, Arthur looked in her direction and caught her staring. He raised his goblet with a wide grin, as if to toast her humiliation.

Emry didn't toast back.

Oh, this was a disaster. She'd meant to lay low, not torment the crown prince and his guard.

Emry ate the rest of her meal without noticing. She was too busy sneaking glances toward the royal banquet table, where King Uther bent Arthur's ear for the rest of supper.

Whatever they were discussing must have been serious, because the prince's grin was gone, replaced by a deep frown. He didn't even glance over as the Lady Elaine deliberately upset her goblet of wine and dabbed at the front of her low-necked gown with a borrowed handkerchief, even though a few men old enough to be the girl's father certainly looked interested.

After supper, Emry loitered in the hallway. A gaggle of court ladies lingered as well, obviously keen to throw themselves at the prince. One of them caught Emry staring and giggled.

That was the last thing she needed.

Suddenly, she had an idea. "I do hope you're not waiting for the prince," Emry said, inspired. "He left with the Lady Elaine."

The blonde looked positively scandalized. "That *witch*!" she declared, and clapped her hand over her mouth. "Excuse me."

Emry tried not to grin as the girls hastened away, skirts rustling. So her guess had been right about Elaine, who hadn't been able to take her eyes off the prince for most of supper.

Finally, Arthur strolled around the corner, hands thrust in his pockets.

He frowned, confused, as though he'd been expecting the court ladies. Then his expression brightened.

"Ah, Merlin," he said. "So we meet again."

"So we do, Your Royal Highness," Emry murmured with a bow.

"What's this?" Arthur asked, bemused. "Only an hour ago, you demanded I drop everything to help with your apprentice duties. I wonder what's changed?"

Emry glared. "You should have said something," she accused, unable to help herself.

"And ruin such a delightful misunderstanding?" The prince's eyes glittered with amusement, and his golden circlet glinted in the torchlight.

"You mocked me," said Emry.

"I would never," Arthur protested, putting a hand to his chest. "I assisted you. Very selflessly, I might add. If memory serves, *you* were the one who mocked *me*."

Emry's jaw dropped.

"You may apologize, if it would make you feel better," Arthur went on. "For insulting my personality, and my cock."

Emry spluttered, wishing more than anything that she'd never made the joke in the first place. Arthur raised an eyebrow, as though daring her to make it worse, or else atone for what she'd said. She wasn't sure which was the better option, but she had best choose one, and fast.

Thankfully, Lord Howell stepped into their path with a practiced bow, sparing her. "Excuse me, Your Highness," he cut in with an oily smile. "I was hoping to have a word."

The prince sighed, his amusement gone. "My father has already had several," he said, "and my opinion hasn't changed."

"Of course not," the man persisted. "I only hoped that—"

"—I'll be in attendance at tomorrow's high council meeting?" Arthur interrupted. "So that I may further elaborate the reasons for my refusal?"

"Um," said Lord Howell, who clearly had not been hoping anything of the sort. And then, realizing he was outmaneuvered, "Indeed?"

"You may look forward to it," Arthur confirmed. "Please forgive me, I won't keep you any longer."

The man tried to resist the dismissal, and Emry bit her lip to keep from smiling at the indignity. So it wasn't just her. It seemed the prince had a habit of treating conversations as though they were fencing bouts. She had to admit, it was a neat trick, and a useful one.

Arthur flagged down an attendant, asking for two glasses and a carafe of water to be brought up to his rooms immediately. The man bowed deeply before hurrying away. When Arthur turned back to Lord Howell, he looked entirely too pleased with himself.

"As you can see, I'm unfortunately quite busy this evening."

"Then I'll leave you to your . . . company. I'm sure the matter will come up tomorrow."

"I'm sure it will," Arthur said with a sigh.

Lord Howell delivered an insincere bow before hastening away.

Arthur raised an eyebrow at Emry. "Still here?" he asked.

"You haven't yet dismissed me," Emry pointed out. "Although I assume you're about to, seeing as how you're expecting company in your chambers."

The prince cocked his head, as though surprised to find his own maneuver used against him.

"Not bad," he acknowledged, rooting his hands back into his pockets and striding down the corridor with that infuriating grin.

◑ ◑ ◑

Emry sat in the window of her bedchamber, staring up at the night sky. She wore her brother's nightshirt, the unfamiliar fabric a reminder that she couldn't even be herself here, alone in her room.

But it was worth it. The deception, the risk, the gamble she was taking that she'd get away with it. Because beyond the castle walls, she could just make out the dim peaks of London's rooftops, the serpentine stretch of the Thames, the far-off shadow of the cathedral's spire.

It was all here, just like she'd dreamed. And she was here at the center of it—somewhere the history books wrote about—finally. Not helping Marion mend threadbare costumes so they wouldn't have to beg their patron for more coin. Not cooped up in her run-down cottage, terrified of living a life she hadn't chosen in a town she was afraid she'd never leave.

She was the apprentice wizard at the royal court. Just like her father.

Well, *Emmett* was the apprentice wizard. But she was here now, and that was enough. It had to be.

No matter that the king had been terrifying and the prince had been obnoxious—she doubted they'd cross paths many more times before the week was through—between the books and her supper, she'd never been anywhere so wonderful.

And yet, it was all so bittersweet. Because it was borrowed. Temporary. A lie that could come crashing down at any moment. Which meant she couldn't truly enjoy it. Especially not while Emmett was recovering from his miscast spell, and Gran was left alone to look after him. She didn't know how to stop worrying, about either of them.

This was Emry's first time away from her family, and she hadn't realized it would be so lonely. She'd believed for a while that she'd outgrown Brocelande and her life there, but now, at the castle, she didn't feel nearly so brave about having left.

So she gazed out at the rooftops, summoning happy memories of home. Of Gran teaching her to bake honey cakes and twisting her hair into braids while it was just the right amount of damp. Of her father, with his tired smile and elegant clothes, swinging her into the air and threatening to let go and see if she could fly. Of Emmett, climbing trees and boasting he'd be able to see all the way to London, to Father, if he just went high enough.

But those memories were old. Stale reminders of the way things had once been, not of what she'd truly left behind. These days, Gran was forgetful, Father was gone, and the only things Emmett boasted about were women and gambling.

She was the only constant, the one piece of the family that had stayed the same while everything else changed with the years and the seasons: a girl who wanted to learn magic, and who felt there had to be more written in her stars than she could see from her narrow bed in her small village.

But now that she was miles from that bed, and from everything she knew, the sky was no more clear on what she was supposed to do with her life, or how she was supposed to do it. Because the stars still looked the same from London, and her questions were all still there, and all just as unanswered.

CHAPTER 7

"Well done, Your Highness!" Lance pronounced, lowering his broadsword as though it weighed nothing.

Arthur tugged off his helmet and lowered his own blade. His shoulder ached from the heavy weapon, and he rotated it with a grimace.

"Lance," Arthur warned. "The truth."

"You're getting worse." Lance pushed his sweat-dampened hair out of his eyes. "I didn't know that was even possible."

"Thanks," Arthur grumbled.

He'd spent the better part of an hour trying and failing to block Lance's blows, and he knew his friend was going easy on him. Arthur could hold his own with a foil, since fencing was more strategy than muscle, but he absolutely despised the broadsword. And it was almost like the weapon could *tell*.

Still, these practice sessions were helping. Even if they did mean sneaking into the armory before the rest of the castle was awake.

Arthur crossed to a table, where he'd set out a carafe and two glasses of water. He poured a glass for Lance and bolted down the other, trying to catch his breath.

"You should come train with the guard," Lance suggested, draining his in one long gulp. "That'll whip you into shape."

"I can't." Arthur sighed. "They'll stare."

"No, why would they do that?" Lance protested, and then he grinned. "Oh, right, you *did* pull a sword from a stone."

"Which is why everyone expects me to be able to swing one. The weapons master thinks I'm hopeless."

"What did you expect? Until this year, the heaviest thing I saw you lift was a book."

Lance absently hefted his sword, executing a complicated pass with ease.

"At least *I* never hung around the stables just to watch Master Raymond take his shirt off," Arthur retorted.

Lance turned briefly scarlet, but then he shrugged. "Beauty is beauty. I admire it where I find it."

"You find it too often. And in the worst places."

"And *you* request two glasses of water at night with no one to warm your bed," Lance returned. "Not that I'm complaining about staying hydrated. But everyone *is* wondering who you're bedding."

Now it was Arthur who turned red. He didn't want anyone knowing about their early morning practice sessions. It was bad enough disappointing Lionel, the castle's weapons master, but getting caught practicing extra and still being so terrible at it? The thought was too depressing. He'd rather suffer the court gossip.

Especially since he knew how badly he needed the practice. News from the north was getting grimmer by the day. And now that everyone thought he was this prophesied hero, he had to live up to their expectations. Somehow.

"Same time tomorrow?" he asked hopefully.

"Fine, but you have to disarm me one more time before we're through."

Lance rammed his helmet back on and hefted his sword.

Arthur groaned. He was beyond exhausted. And yet he somehow managed to raise his own blade and square his stance.

Lance's blow came too quickly, and he wasn't ready for it. He stumbled backward, the blade narrowly missing his exposed side.

"Sard," Lance swore, raising his visor. "I could have killed you!"

Arthur's heart pounded under the thin sheet of practice armor, but he played it off with a shrug. "Go again," he insisted, clenching his jaw and raising his weapon, arms trembling. He was a better swordsman than this. He had to be.

Lance shook his head. "No way. Not unless these things are blunted."

"I'm not going back to wooden practice swords," said Arthur, making a face at the humiliating thought. They weren't twelve-year-old pages.

Lance's eyes lit up. "Hold on, what if you asked the wizard to make us something?"

"Merlin?" Arthur pulled off his helmet. "Can't you strike *him* with a sword instead?"

Lancelot let out a hearty laugh. "That poor lad had no clue."

"Honestly." Arthur sighed. "Do I *look* like a librarian?" Off Lance's grin, "Don't answer that."

"Wasn't going to. Although if you want some advice, I think you should befriend the kid." Lance lowered his blade and leaned forward on the hilt. "He's useful, he's surprisingly entertaining, and you're stuck with him."

"Don't remind me," Arthur muttered. "Bringing him here was in no way my idea."

"Exactly. Let your father think he's won. But show the kid that he should be loyal to you," Lance advised. "Otherwise, he's in the perfect position to become your father's spy."

Lance was so obviously right. Arthur couldn't believe he'd missed it earlier.

Tormenting the boy had been a terrible idea, even if it had been amusing, and even if the wizard *had* been asking for it. Life at court was lonely, and besides the guards and squires, Arthur rarely came across anyone his age other than calculating young noblemen and desperately flirtatious court ladies. So he supposed he could do far worse than show a little kindness to the sarcastic wizard whose family name carried power in his father's court.

"You make a good point," said Arthur.

"I have my moments," Lance acknowledged. He glanced toward the window, where the sky was just beginning to lighten with the first streaks of sunrise. The guard had started to assemble for morning training in the courtyard below.

Lance sighed. "I should get back," he said without enthusiasm.

It was obvious how much he was hurting, despite his brave face. Almost two years ago, Lady Agravaine had caught Lance in a compromising position with her youngest son, Lord Jereth. The boy had been too cowardly to own the truth about their relationship. Instead, he'd insisted Lance's attention was unwanted, and things had blown out of proportion.

Assaulting a member of the royal family was a serious crime, and one that needed no trial. Jereth was the king's cousin, a blood relation, and Lance merely the illegitimate son of a minor knight. It was all Arthur could do to save Lance being stripped of his family name, or worse.

Thankfully, it had not gone so far as all that. In the end, King Uther had banned Lance from becoming a knight. Four grueling years spent as a page for nothing. Dark whispers followed Lance through the castle corridors, and instead of squiring for Sir Kay, as everyone had expected, he had moved from the comforts of the castle to the barracks in disgrace.

Arthur was well aware that his friend had only become a guard because of him. That Lance had stuck around waiting for him to leave for university before facing down his suddenly uncertain future. But after Arthur was named heir to the kingdom, there was no way his father was letting him go.

"The last thing you need is more *books*," Uther had snapped. "You're going to be a king one day. Now *act* like it."

What his father had really meant was: act like someone you're not.

Selfishly, Arthur was relieved that Lance had stayed. At least they were stuck together.

Although it didn't make Lance's predicament any less unfair. Nor did the fact that Jereth had received no reprimand at all. Instead, he'd been hustled away to boarding school, where he'd continued to raise hell and stir trouble. His life had gone on unaffected, while Lance slunk through the castle he'd once called home, wearing a guard's uniform and acting as though he wasn't devastated by the stares and the whispers. The whole thing made Arthur furious.

"You're wasted as a guard, you know," Arthur said, not for the first time.

Lance gave him a sad smile, the way he always did. It was a subject they never quite addressed head-on, at least, not in a way that truly mattered.

"Oh, I know." Lance gazed out the window for a moment, looking genuinely upset. But then his self-deprecating grin was back. "Honestly, I'm worried they might kick me out. I'm too good at standing in front of a door. I'm giving the other guards a complex."

"And how are you at standing in front of a gate?"

"Magnificent. My Latin tutor would weep to see it."

They were both silent a moment, wishing for a different world. A different past. A different future. And then Lance picked up his helmet and slipped away into the quiet dawn.

CHAPTER 8

Emry stifled a yawn.

She slouched at the old wooden table in the wizard's workshop, an empty mug of tea at her elbow, and the *Herbalist's Guide* open to chapter four. The room was cloyingly warm, and it was dreadfully early, and she could barely keep her eyes open.

"Have you finished the chapter yet?" called Master Ambrosius.

"Nearly," she mumbled, blinking down at the book.

She wished someone had warned her that the castle rose before dawn—like a godforsaken *farm*. The royal guard had been running drills directly under her bedroom window, and while the view was certainly worth admiring, the noise was unbelievable. Like four dozen roosters. With swords. No wonder such a lavish room had been empty.

Focus, Emry urged herself. *How many days will you have to study magic?*

The answer, of course, was not nearly enough.

Even though this wasn't magic at all. Just an ordinary book on herbs. Which was probably why she found it so tedious.

"Pay close attention to the section on tinctures," the old wizard called. "You'll be mixing one after you finish."

Emry nodded. And very nearly nodded off.

"Morning, Master Ambrosius."

Her eyes flew open at the sound of a boy's voice.

It was the prince. Emry slid down in her chair, wondering what on earth he wanted, and why he was awake so early.

"Ah, Arthur, have a seat," Master Ambrosius said, sounding unsurprised by the prince's appearance.

He must be here for the infirmary, Emry thought.

But then Arthur flashed a honeyed grin and joined her at the table. He set down a mug of, well, Emry wasn't sure, but it smelled fantastic, and leaned forward to get a look at her book.

"Tinctures?" He made a face. "Dull."

"Don't you have somewhere you're supposed to go and . . . prince?" Emry mumbled.

"Not really." Arthur shrugged. "My father rarely rises before eleven."

"I envy him," Emry said through a yawn. "Did you know the guard trains at dawn? Loudly."

"Ah, so you're on the south side of the castle. Beautiful rooms. Shame about the noise."

Why is he even here? Emry wondered. *And why is he being so . . . not horrible?*

She shook her head and slogged through the rest of the section on tinctures. Arthur sat there fiddling with a sprig of dried lavender and nursing his drink.

Emry sniffed, trying to place the scent.

"What *is* that?" she finally asked.

"Coffee," he said smugly.

"Never heard of it."

The prince grinned. "Well, I don't suppose Ottoman traders make it to—where are you from again?"

"Brocelande," Emry supplied.

Arthur slid his mug across the table. "Have some," he urged, as though it was the most normal thing in the world, to share his drink with a wizard's apprentice. "You look like you need it."

"Thank you," Emry said, surprised at the offer. She raised the mug and inhaled the fragrant steam, taking a gulp of the warm liquid, and then another. The drink was bitter, but quite pleasant. Miraculously, it seemed to wake her up. "What is this sorcery?"

Arthur laughed. "Combats the effect of early mornings. There's plenty in the kitchens, just ask."

Emry took another gulp, and then glanced up guiltily.

"Keep it," Arthur said. "It's my second mug this morning."

"How long have you been awake?" she grumbled, but the prince merely shrugged.

He was dressed for sport, she realized, in a tight, plain tunic with the sleeves rolled up, and even tighter cream-colored breeches. Her own clothes were worn and unfashionable, but at least she was wearing a suede jacket with silver buttons. She couldn't imagine walking around the royal castle dressed so informally. He wasn't even wearing his circlet, which seemed to be a habit. Slouching there in the wizard's workshop, picking apart a sprig of herbs, it was easy to imagine that he wasn't the crown prince at all, but a handsome, clever, obnoxious boy who was barely a year her senior.

Marion had been so right about him.

Sard it all, she couldn't concentrate on the book. But at least she wasn't in any danger of falling back asleep.

"Finished," Emry called.

"Talking or reading?" the old wizard asked mildly.

"My fault," Arthur said before she could apologize. "I'm very distracting. Occupational hazard."

Emry took another sip of coffee, wondering what was going on. The prince was acting nice. Too nice. Which wasn't necessarily a good thing.

"Book closed," Master Ambrosius said, fumbling with his pince-nez as he joined them. His wand was tucked into his belt, and there was a fresh dusting of ash down the front of his olive-green robes.

Emry closed the book and stared at the old wizard, wondering if anyone was going to explain why the prince had turned up acting like this was routine.

"All tinctures are extracts," Master Ambrosius prompted.

"But not all extracts are tinctures," Arthur finished, not missing a beat as he quoted back the First Rule of Concoctions from memory.

"Good, Arthur," the old wizard said, and then frowned at Emry. "Merlin, keep up."

Emry sank even lower in her chair. Surely they weren't supposed to be . . . lab partners?

Oh, but they were. After Master Ambrosius was thoroughly convinced they knew what they were doing, he set them to bottling tinctures that alleviated stomachache.

Soon, the table was spread with a mess of fennel seeds, ginger root, and dried peppermint. On the other side of the workshop, the old wizard busied himself stirring powders into a large glass alembic, which emitted the occasional burble.

Emry stared down at the ingredients, overwhelmed. She'd never done anything like this before, working with herbs instead of magic. But it was clear Arthur had.

The prince chewed his lip as he measured out the seeds on a little brass scale, and Emry shook her head. *This* was what he was doing a year after pulling the sword from the stone? Waking up early to bottle tinctures in his sportswear?

Emry glanced down at the mortar and pestle, wishing she could just use magic. She'd pounded the ginger down to a pulp, and it was making her eyes water.

Arthur cleared his throat.

"What?" Emry whispered.

"You were supposed to grind that, not pound." Arthur nodded toward the ginger root. "Here, I'll show you."

"I can do it," Emry snapped, but Arthur had already wrapped his hand around hers, correcting her grip on the pestle.

"Twist," Arthur instructed. "Hard. Like this."

Emry swallowed. His hands were very warm. Or maybe hers were just very cold.

Master Ambrosius glanced up from his cauldron.

"You lads better be grinding," he warned.

Emry exchanged an amused glance with Arthur, and tried not to snicker.

"Yes, sir," Emry said, grinning broadly.

"My favorite is when he says to 'pound one out,'" Arthur confessed.

Emry choked.

"Don't correct him, it's too good," Arthur said, and Emry realized that the prince was fond of the old man.

"So, you come here a lot," she observed, reaching for the dried peppermint.

"When I can." Arthur passed her the scale. "It's not university, but it's something."

"What about your tutors?" Emry asked, measuring out the peppermint.

"They instruct me in every suitable subject of my father's choosing," he said with a thin smile.

"But not in the unsuitable subjects," Emry finished.

"Definitely not," Arthur agreed, combining their dry ingredients into a bowl.

Emry watched him, knowing all too well how frustrating it was to have your days shaped by someone who didn't have to live through them. How powerless she'd felt, watching her father take her brother out to the woods to learn magic while she was left behind with the washing and the cooking.

But then she remembered she was supposed to be Emmett, and her spoiled arse of a brother wouldn't have understood the prince's frustrations at all. Or his decision to do something about them.

She bit her lip, wishing she hadn't said anything. She should keep her distance from the prince, she knew. He was too sharp by half, and not at all what she'd expected. She snuck another glance in his direction, admiring the sharp angle of his jaw, and the way a lock of hair fell over his right eye as he worked.

"Looks about right," Arthur said, taking up a pinch of their dry ingredients.

"You've done this before," Emry observed. It wasn't a question.

"My mother was often ill." He hesitated before elaborating, "I used to come up here and ask Master Ambrosius if there was anything I could do to help. A tonic I could brew. That sort of thing." He shrugged, offering Emry a sad smile. "I guess I never stopped coming."

He reached for a glass vial, his arm knocking against the bottle of vinegar. The bottle wobbled and tipped, a wet stain spreading across the table.

"Sard," he cursed, reaching for a rag to mop it up.

"*Reponere*," Emry muttered without thinking. The stain disappeared, and the bottle refilled and tipped back upright.

Arthur blinked at it, as though he'd forgotten he was in the presence of a wizard.

"I drank your coffee." Emry shrugged. "Now we're even."

When they finished the tincture, Master Ambrosius inspected the vials and nodded his approval.

"Well done, lads," he said.

Emry beamed at the praise, but Arthur merely looked embarrassed. He pulled out a gold pocket watch and consulted it with an apologetic frown.

"Off with you," Master Ambrosius said, flapping his hands at the prince, who took his leave with a neat bow.

Emry's stomach grumbled, and she stared at the wizard hopefully.

"You," he said, "may get something to eat from the kitchens. But then you're right back here to learn the spellcraft for this."

Her mouth fell open. "You mean I could have *magicked* that?" she asked.

"Not without first knowing how to make the tincture," said the wizard.

"To effectively and safely work magic on a living person, you must know more than just the words to the spell. You must understand what you're asking of the magic."

"Or else the magic could refuse." Emry finished, thinking of what had happened to her brother. The old wizard nodded, looking pleased.

"So you see, Arthur learns what he can, and you learn what you must, and if the two of you work together?" The wizard shrugged. "Well, it's good practice for the future."

"Right. The future," Emry echoed. Too bad she wouldn't stick around long enough to see it.

CHAPTER 9

The council meeting was never going to end.

Sir Bors rambled on about the Lothian court rejecting another request for an exchange of ambassadors, and Arthur resisted the urge to sigh. Between his practice session with Lance and his morning in the wizard's workshop, the day had already stretched on for what felt like a week. At least.

He reached up to run a hand through his hair, remembering just in time that he was wearing his circlet. No wonder he was getting a headache.

Lance had been right, though, about befriending Merlin. The young wizard wasn't nearly so bad as he'd feared. And Arthur had expected the worst, since his father had chosen the lad. But Merlin had turned out to be surprisingly decent company. And from all accounts of yesterday's demonstration before the court, he had quite a talent for magic. It was a rare occasion his father managed to get something right, and in this case, Arthur was pleasantly surprised.

He glanced at his father, who sat at the head of the table, more interested in his goblet of wine than in Sir Bors's report.

When was the last time he'd seen his father without a drink? Not for a while, that was certain. Ever since the queen's funeral, his fleeting moments of kindness were gone, replaced by unpredictable dark moods and fits of anger. It was as though he'd lost his drive to be a good ruler. Or maybe he'd simply lost the one person who had kindled that desire.

These days, he made no secret of taking Lady Howell to bed, and had executed a bishop who had dared to sermonize against adultery in his presence. He denied an audience to most of his petitioners, played obvious favorites within his court, and had delegated far too many of his responsibilities to Lord Agravaine.

While Arthur found Lord Agravaine tiresome and overbearing, the man was undeniably good at what he did. Probably thanks in large part to the network of spies he was rumored to lead on Camelot's behalf. The incompetent Lord Howell, however, was a blustering fool from a well-connected family, who did little more than fawn over the king.

Perhaps the only subject the two advisors agreed on was that Arthur was preferable to the alternative: King Uther's younger sister had been married off to the ruthless Duke of Cornwall, in an attempt to bring the king's greatest opponent into the family. Princess Clarine had died of the coughing sickness years ago, but their son, Maddoc, a spoiled, coddled boy of thirteen, stood next in line after Arthur. And if Maddoc ascended the throne before he came of age, the duke could rule as regent.

Arthur frowned at the map spread across the table, staring at the tiny but formidable duchy of Cornwall at the bottom left. His eyes couldn't help but sweep up to wealthy Camelot, then proud Cameliard directly to the north. Beyond that sat rocky Northumbria to the west, and the small kingdom of Lothia to the east, where King Yurien ruled from his ill-gotten throne. And he couldn't forget the seafaring kingdom of the Isles, whose royal family was desperate to marry off their large brood of royal children.

He had known these borders and kingdoms for so long. Yet the sword in the stone told another tale. Of a united kingdom. One that *he* was destined to lead.

"Enough," growled the king, raising a hand to silence Sir Bors. "I grow weary of King Yurien. Is there further news, or will we continue rehashing his secretary's letter?"

"My apologies, sire," said Sir Bors.

"Lord Agravaine will draft my response. And affix my seal."

Lord Agravaine bowed. Arthur frowned, wondering when his father had stopped composing his own correspondence with the neighboring kingdoms.

"What's next?" Uther demanded, draining his wine goblet. "And it better not be more tiresome news of Cameliard's endless jousting tournaments."

Lord Howell cleared his throat. "There is still the matter of the prince's marriage."

Arthur winced. He'd hoped they'd forgotten about that. "No, there really isn't," he said wearily.

His hand went to his hair. The circlet slipped backward, clattering to the floor. It rolled, hitting the wall with a clang. A servant gingerly retrieved it, handing it to Arthur with a slight bow.

When he looked up, the entire council was staring at him. Not to mention his father. And the guards. And the young attendant who'd retrieved his circlet, and who was trying very hard to become wallpaper.

"You object?" Uther asked, an edge to his voice.

"Of course I object," said Arthur. "Nineteen is far too young to think about marriage. Besides, with all of my responsibilities, and tutors, and training, I don't have the time to romance a potential wife."

"Which is why I've found the ideal candidate," said the king. "Her mother is a princess of Portugal in her own right. Her father holds the largest kingdom in France."

Arthur frowned, trying to discern which eligible princess they were discussing. And then it clicked, and he snorted, because surely his father wasn't serious. "Very funny," he said.

Except no one was laughing.

"To be perfectly honest," said the king, "I wasn't expecting such a match. I doubt you'll do better."

Arthur shook his head in disbelief.

"Princess Anne is a wonderful choice," insisted Lord Agravaine.

"Princess Anne is *seven years old*," Arthur said. "I'm sure she would rather have a pony than a fiancé."

"I'm told she already has several, Your Highness," said Lord Howell.

"Fiancés?" Arthur asked, deliberately misunderstanding.

"Ponies," Lord Howell corrected, looking flustered.

"The wedding wouldn't take place until the princess is at least fifteen," said Lord Agravaine. "As you said, you're too young and busy right now."

Sard. He *had* said that. Lord Agravaine was sharp. But Arthur was sharper. And he knew just how to make the members of his father's council squirm.

"Eight years *is* a very long time," said Arthur mildly. "Shall I assume producing some illegitimate heirs in the meantime isn't out of the question?"

Uther coughed into his wineglass, and Arthur held back a smile.

"Actually, Your Highness—" began Lord Agravaine, but whatever the man had to say on the subject of illegitimate heirs, Arthur really didn't want to hear it.

"It's a ridiculous match," Arthur interrupted. "I refuse."

"I doubt an opportunity such as this will come again," said King Uther. "France does not offer alliances lightly. But the king is convinced you'll one day rule as High King of England."

Uther shook his head, acknowledging the absurdity of such an event ever occurring. More than a few members of his council smiled as though amused at the idea.

"This is about the sword, isn't it?" Arthur asked.

Evidently, no one had expected him to come right out and say it. Lord Agravaine coughed, and King Uther twisted the stem of his wineglass. Lord Howell was suddenly fascinated by the crenellated ceiling.

"Seriously?" Arthur muttered.

"It has been nearly a year since you pulled the sword from the stone," said Uther. "And while I'm relieved you finally did *something* to prove yourself, with every passing month, it becomes far less impressive."

The council members nodded their agreement.

"Wow," Arthur said softly. "Better lock in the child bride now, huh? Before everyone figures out I'm such a massive disappointment." He pushed to his feet. "My answer remains no. *Especially* to Princess Anne."

Arthur strode from the room, his chest tight. He wasn't going to lose it in front of his father and the entire council. They may have humiliated him, but he wouldn't give them the satisfaction of seeing it.

The corridor seemed to stretch on forever, flanked by guards who insisted on bowing as he passed. His own guards trailed behind him, silent and impassive. Even at a distance, Arthur found their presence stifling. The whole castle pressed in on him, making it hard to breathe.

Finally, he pushed open the doors to his chambers, collapsing onto his bed. The sarding sword was mounted on the wall over his fireplace, and he eyed it with hatred.

"What are you even *for*?" he wondered aloud. "What am I supposed to *do*?"

Whatever it was, agreeing to marry Princess Anne was out of the question. He couldn't believe his father had suggested it. At first, Arthur had assumed his father was only humoring the French king. That he wasn't truly considering such a match. The girl was *seven years old*.

He shook his head in disgust. The way his father had announced that an offer so advantageous might never come again. In front of the entire council.

Was he *truly* such a disappointment? Arthur grimaced, wishing he had evidence to the contrary. But after so many years being called a bastard and a spare, how could he be anything else? He wasn't anyone's first choice—except for the sarding *sword's*.

When it came to love, he wasn't quite ready to let go of the possibility.

He'd given up practically everything else, being made his father's heir. He hated to surrender his heart, too. An arranged marriage was starting to seem inevitable. But still, he hoped it might at least be with someone . . . desirable.

Except his father's advisors were set on bartering the position of future queen to the highest bidder, using the sword in the stone as leverage. Which was absurd, because the High King of England thing was nothing but an old story. The kind that minstrels sang on market days while passing around a hat to collect coins. The kind meant to entertain children.

But the most unbelievable part wasn't the legend. It was that, somehow, by pulling the sword from the stone, he'd managed to fail his father all over again, because no matter what he did, he was still himself.

Arthur was half convinced that his father had secretly kept a tally of all the times he'd brought a book to the table, or had been caught sneaking off on some misadventure with Lance, or had cheerfully skipped out on an archery lesson, only to turn up in the castle gardens with pockets full of herbs for Master Ambrosius. And he was pretty sure that no sword, prophetic or otherwise, would transform him into the successor Uther truly wanted—a son who would rather wield weapons than ideas.

And Arthur would never be that. No matter how much he tried. It was in his nature to question the king's advisors, to believe the word of an honorable friend over a dishonorable royal, and to confront hard truths about how closed-minded the aristocracy could be. Ever since he was a child, he'd tried to use his status to help in any way he could, no matter how low or undignified the task.

But that wasn't how a king behaved. King Uther was feared and respected. There were few who dared to cross him, and even fewer who would refuse an alliance with such a formidable ruler. And when the day came that Arthur inherited his father's throne, he needed his people to see him as a symbol of power. Of strength.

The only thing he symbolized now was weakness.

Here he was, the pathetic prince who had surprised everyone by pulling the sword from the stone. He had prevailed where far greater warriors had failed, but not in a way that truly *mattered*.

His cheeks burned with shame as he remembered the scene. The cheering. The way people had knelt in respect. And how he'd been sick in the middle of it, in front of everyone.

A true king never would have done that.

He wished his mother were still alive. Wished she would ask him to pull up a chair and read to her while she rested. Wished she'd lift a cool hand to his cheek and smile softly, like she saw something in him that was steady and reassuring.

Not like his father, who had always looked at him as though he couldn't quite work out what had gone so terribly wrong.

CHAPTER 10

Supper had ended hours ago, and Emry was sprawled across the foot of her bed reading a book she'd borrowed from the wizard's workshop. There was a faint scratching at her door, and she glanced up, wondering if she'd imagined it. But then she heard the noise again.

"*Merlin*," someone whispered. "Merlin, you awake?"

It couldn't be. But oh, Emry had a sneaking suspicion that it *was*.

She glanced down at her clothes to see if she was decent.

Nope.

She hastily retrieved the tight band of fabric she wore around her chest, and slid it on under her tunic.

"What?" she whispered, tiptoeing to the door and opening it a sliver.

The prince grinned back at her. Lance hovered behind him, and they were both carrying broadswords.

"We're here to see the wizard," Lance said with a winning smile.

"Seriously?" she muttered.

So inappropriate.

But of course it wasn't, Emry realized, at least, not to them. They thought she was a boy. And by that logic, the crown prince turning up at an apprentice's door should have been an honor, not an inconvenience.

"We have a request," said Arthur. "May we come in?"

He looked even more exhausted than she felt, and Emry remembered something about a council meeting. No wonder he'd spent the whole of supper looking ill, and refusing to make eye contact with his father. Uther had consumed an enormous amount of wine, Emry remembered, but Arthur hadn't touched his.

"Fine," she said, opening the door the rest of the way.

"Nice space," Lance said, glancing around. He was the sort of boy, Emry discovered, who touched *everything*. And sure enough, he was already running a hand over the tapestry on her wall.

Arthur peeked at the page Emry had been on. "Potions for hair growth," he read aloud, sounding amused.

Claudo, she thought, and the book slammed shut. Arthur frowned, as though trying to decide whether the book had done that on its own.

"Okay, what?" Emry asked, quickly losing patience.

This was the opposite of keeping to herself. She needed to make the prince leave before this went horribly wrong, but she couldn't exactly kick him out.

Arthur hefted his sword, which looked absurdly heavy. "Any chance you can blunt these?" he asked. "Or something where, if they strike an opponent, they won't cause as much harm?"

"Don't you already *have* a magic sword?" Emry asked, not very nicely.

"Common misconception." Arthur sighed, looking askance to his friend.

"The spell was put *on* the sword. The sword itself isn't magical," Lance explained, taking a seat on her bed.

"That must have been disappointing," Emry said with a smirk.

"You have no idea," muttered Arthur.

Emry frowned at the prince's broadsword. "Where do you strike? Not just with the tip, like fencing?"

"Sides of the blade, too," called Lance, who was actually lying down on her bed at this point.

"Do you mind?" she complained.

"He really doesn't," Arthur put in.

"Leg day," Lance groaned. "We did drills all afternoon. In this heat."

Lance went on, describing the drills, which admittedly did sound terrible, but Emry had stopped listening. She picked up Arthur's broadsword, grimacing at the weight. And then she had an idea.

"If I make the sword blunt, you'd just have a metal club," she said. "But what if I alter the metal so it bends harmlessly on contact?"

Arthur considered it. "That might work."

Lance nodded his agreement. "They'd be rubbish for combat, but perfect for training."

"I'll have them back to you in a month," Emry said, and the boys' jaws dropped. "Joking. Give me a moment."

Emry reached for her wand. Illusions and cleanup spells were one thing, but she didn't dare attempt a permanent magical transformation without it. Hers was a polished holly branch, which her father had made for her tenth birthday. He'd gifted her and Emmett matching ones, a rare moment when they'd been given the same thing. Emry rolled the wand between her fingers until it felt like an extension of herself. Until she was confident she could draw enough of her magic up and through. Because the last thing she needed was to faint in the prince's company.

She pointed the wand at Lance's sword, which he'd propped against the wall, and envisioned its edges bending on contact.

"στροφή," she commanded.

The sword trembled, and then promptly fell over. Lance heaved himself off the bed and retrieved it.

He thrust the blade forward, attacking Emry's tapestry. She winced, anticipating damage, but the blade bent as easily as a tree branch, and the tip left no mark.

Emry sighed in relief, and Lance laughed.

"Impressive," he said.

The spell had been easy. Emry let out a slow, long breath, her confidence returning. She did Arthur's sword next. The prince hefted the blade with considerably more effort, trying a pass that nearly knocked a book off her desk.

"Sorry," he said, having the good sense to look embarrassed while he hastily straightened the stack of books.

Emry shook her head. No wonder she'd mistaken him for a librarian.

"There you are, two magic swords," she said, sitting down on the bed and yawning loudly. "Now, with all due respect, Your Highness, go away."

The boys slunk from her room with a chorus of sheepish thank-yous.

Emry changed into her brother's nightshirt and crawled into bed, remembering just before she closed her eyes to mumble a muffling spell at the window.

And a locking spell on the door.

CHAPTER 11

"How's your magic sword?" Emry asked.

It was the next morning, and she and Arthur were gathering the ingredients for pain tonics from the wizard's stores.

"A vast improvement. And since the swords are matched, it's still the same effect when—"

"I don't actually care," Emry interrupted, reaching for a bottle of powdered tansy. "I was just being polite."

"How's your noise issue?" Arthur asked innocently.

"Fixed it with a muffling spell." Emry smirked, tossing him the jar.

"You're supposed to say 'catch,'" he complained, fumbling it.

Fleoges, Emry thought. A bottle of yarrow floated off the shelf and started nudging Arthur in the shoulder.

"Catch?" she suggested, and he shot her a disgusted look.

They brought their ingredients back to the table. Master Ambrosius looked them over before nodding his approval.

"Oh, and Merlin?" The old wizard lifted an eyebrow. "What did I say about silent spells?"

"Not in your workshop?" Emry recited with a sigh.

"So you *do* remember. Which means you actively chose to disobey me."

Emry's stomach twisted at his sharp tone. She hadn't meant to break the rules. And she certainly hadn't intended to infuriate the old wizard. Which, judging from his irritated expression, she clearly had.

"I didn't mean—" Emry began, but Master Ambrosius waved off the rest of her apology.

"To get caught?" Master Ambrosius pursed his lips. "I was going to give you thirty minutes to brew a pain tonic, but as punishment, I'm giving you fifteen. Both of you."

Arthur's jaw dropped.

"Sorry," Emry mumbled, feeling terrible.

The prince glared, and Emry shot him an apologetic look. She hadn't meant for him to be reprimanded as well. To be honest, she hadn't thought Master Ambrosius would react the way he had.

It had been a harmless joke. But then, she supposed, she probably shouldn't have cast a silent spell that launched an attack on the crown prince. Even if it was just a bottle of herbs. Even if he *had* been asking for it.

Neither Emry nor Arthur said anything else for the next fifteen minutes, as they frantically worked on the tonic, trying to ignore the tiny hourglass on the hearth.

"Sloppy," commented the old wizard, inspecting their work. "Looks like you could have used some more time."

"Yes," Emry acknowledged through clenched teeth. "We could have."

"A shame." Master Ambrosius took up their cauldron and slopped it out the window. "Magic is a privilege, not a secret, and certainly not a *joke*. When you misuse it, those around you suffer. I've asked you to follow my rules, and I won't ask a second time."

His tone was mild, but Emry could tell that he was quite serious.

"I'm sorry," Emry said, her cheeks flushed with embarrassment. "I promise it won't happen again."

"There, you see? Lesson learned." The old wizard beamed. "And now all that's left to do is brew up another batch of the tonic, properly this time."

☾ ☾ ☾

Once again, Emry found herself waiting outside the banquet hall for the prince after supper. A pretty blonde serving maid caught her eye and blushed, and Emry's own cheeks grew warm from the attention. Swaggering around the castle corridors in imitation of her brother had some decidedly awkward side effects.

Under ordinary circumstances, she would have been quite pleased at the girl's interest, and would have flirted back. A person's gender made no difference to her. But Emry knew that any girl who smiled in her direction at Castle Camelot did so because they thought she was a boy, which utterly ruined it.

No matter what she did, no one ever seemed to like her for her. A problem her rake of a brother didn't seem to share. Everyone loved a handsome, powerful wizard, but who *wasn't* intimidated by a girl who was magic?

A boy who is going to be king, a small, traitorous voice whispered in her head, just as the prince rounded the corner.

"Wizard," he said, as though surprised to find her there. "Were you waiting for me?"

She stared at him, flustered. He looked well that evening, in a brown suede jacket with shining gold buttons and a high collar that emphasized his chiseled jawline. The color brought out the chestnut tones in his windswept hair. He smelled faintly of horses, as though he'd been riding.

"Um, I wanted to apologize again," she blurted. "For this morning."

Arthur frowned, as though he'd entirely forgotten about it. "Oh, it's fine," he said. "Master Ambrosius can be tough sometimes."

"You could have warned me," Emry said.

"And you could have warned *me* that you can *think* magic," he retorted as they fell into step down the tapestry-lined corridor. They passed a trio of court ladies, whom Arthur favored with a brief bow, before accusing, "You did it last night, too, with that book."

Emry winced. The prince was far too observant.

"I thought I was imagining things," Arthur admitted. "I never saw your father cast a spell like that."

"Neither did I," Emry said.

It felt so strange, these constant reminders that her father had lived here. That these hallways and the people in them were new to her, but had belonged to the life her father had led when he was away. A life she had known so little about.

"Although," she added with a frown, "you probably saw more of him growing up than I did."

"Lance and I terrorized him." Arthur sounded pleased. "I believe we once begged for a horse, but green, and could he please make it breathe fire."

Emry snorted. "You couldn't have just asked for a dragon?" she asked.

"In our defense, we were four," said Arthur. "Actually, Lance was five. He should have known better."

Arthur grinned, but Emry just shook her head. After last night's demands for two magic swords, she could picture it easily.

"Arthur! There you are!" called Lance, hurrying to catch up to them.

He looked awful. A faint bruise stood out against his cheek, and he held his left arm stiffly. His knuckles, Emry noticed, were scraped and bruised, as though he'd punched something solid. There was blood on his collar, and his uniform was damp with sweat.

"Do I want to know?" Arthur asked mildly.

"I had to run laps through supper. A punishment that in no way fit the crime." Lance grimaced as he flexed his battered hand. "I swear I was defending my honor, not 'going around starting brawls.'"

Arthur sighed, and a silent moment of understanding passed between the two boys.

"I'll have some food sent up to my room," said Arthur, and Lance shot him a grateful look.

"You're truly in pain?" Emry asked, remembering that afternoon's lesson.

"Yes," Lance said. And then, to Arthur, "Why does he look so pleased about it?"

"Because I just learned a spell to fix that," said Emry.

Lance and Arthur exchanged a look. Lance shrugged. Arthur shook his head.

Emry glared at the two of them. It was so annoying when they did that. "Well?" she said.

"This is a *very* bad idea, isn't it?" Lance asked.

"Terrible," Arthur agreed, holding back a grin. "But I want to see if he can do it."

"Of course I can," Emry boasted with more bravado than she felt. Even though she'd only done it twice. On Master Ambrosius' canaries. But still.

"To the royal bedchamber," Lance announced grandly, and Emry winced.

How on earth had she gotten herself invited to Arthur's *bedchamber*? She sighed, wishing she'd kept her mouth shut. Still, the opportunity to attempt a healing spell on a real person . . . the temptation was too much.

They rounded the corner and ran straight into the Lady Elaine.

Emry had admired the girl's dress at supper, but it was even more exquisite close up. Dark blue satin and stitched with pearls, with sleeves trailing yards of cream-colored silk. The neckline was so low that Emry couldn't help but stare. And that, she suspected, was the desired effect.

"Your Highness," breathed Lady Elaine, "what a pleasure running into you here."

She bent forward into an overly deep curtsey, and Lance coughed.

Emry didn't blame him. Another inch, and the girl would come disrobed. Arthur gallantly took her hand and raised it to his lips.

"The pleasure's all mine," he said, flashing her a winning smile. "That dress is lovely on you."

Emry stared at Arthur in surprise. She'd thought him immune to Lady Elaine's charms—and obvious ambitions. Apparently not. Judging from the look on Lance's face, he was similarly confused by the prince's behavior.

"You don't find the shade of blue too dark for my coloring?" Elaine purred.

"*Eryngium planum* is a favorite of mine," replied Arthur. Lance coughed into his fist, and Emry smothered a grin.

The girl blinked at him, confused.

"There's a fresh bloom in the castle gardens," Arthur went on. "I was admiring it just the other day. A pity you weren't there to distract me."

Lady Elaine preened, pleased. "Have you heard the news, Your Highness?" the girl forged on. "It's terribly exciting!"

"There's news?" Arthur asked.

"Lord Gawain is returning from Paris!" Lady Elaine announced triumphantly.

Lance stiffened, horrified. Arthur's smile faltered.

"He arrives in just a few days," Elaine continued, unaware that no one seemed to share her enthusiasm. "I overheard my mother discussing it with his, and I thought you'd want to know, since he *is* your dear cousin."

From Arthur's pained expression, Emry had the distinct impression that he wouldn't exactly call his cousin *dear*.

"And is his brother returning as well?" Arthur inquired.

"Jereth?" Elaine's nose scrunched. "I'm not sure . . ." She glanced in Lance's direction and bit her lip.

Lance fidgeted, and Arthur's frown deepened. Emry had no idea what to make of it.

"No doubt he'd rather spend time at his boarding school," Arthur said coolly. "He always did prefer the company of other boys."

Elaine looked suddenly uncomfortable at the turn in the conversation. Emry wondered what on earth was going on.

"Aren't you supposed to be guarding the door?" Elaine asked Lance.

"What door?" He shrugged. "It's a hallway."

"Any door," she said sweetly.

"I could guard yours?" Lance suggested.

"That won't be necessary," Elaine said frostily. She glanced up at Arthur through her eyelashes. "And besides, it would prevent visitors."

Arthur choked. "We'd, uh, better be going," he said, with a hurried bow.

When the girl was out of earshot, Lance turned to Arthur with a frown. "Not her," he said.

"Why not?" Arthur asked, with the smirk of someone who absolutely knew why not.

"If you're that desperate to warm your bed, you should try a hot water bottle," Lance retorted.

Emry snorted, enjoying the direction their conversation had turned. But then Arthur's smirk turned to laughter.

"You should have seen your faces," he said gleefully.

"That was a *joke*?" Emry spluttered.

"An amusement," corrected Arthur. "If I don't encourage her every once in a while, she'll stop spilling wine down her dresses at supper."

Lance cackled. "That's awful," he said fondly. "Also, I approve."

Thank goodness, Emry thought, even though the prince's love life was no concern of hers. And then she realized she'd let the silence drag on a moment too long.

"I can't believe you compared her to a thistle," she admonished. "In *Latin*."

Arthur shrugged, slanting her a grin. "I was wondering if you caught that, wizard."

"I've never heard botany used as an insult," she replied.

"What can I say? Plants are infinitely useful." Arthur's grin stretched wider.

"Well, I hope she picks a whole bouquet of them," declared Lance. "Barehanded." He winced, cradling his wrist.

"Come on," Arthur said, "let's get you fixed up."

◐ ◐ ◐

Two cheerless guards stood at attention outside the prince's rooms. They opened the double doors with a crisp bow, and Lance slunk inside with a sheepish expression, as though he wasn't meant to be there, which surprised Emry. She'd assumed he was Arthur's personal guard, the way they were so often together. But clearly she'd assumed wrong.

Arthur's bedchamber wasn't quite what she was expecting. It was twice as large as her own, and the bed was more elaborate, with rich velvet drapes and intricate carvings. The ceiling was painted with constellations, and a handsome tapestry of an enchanted forest hung across one wall.

The rest of it was pure Arthur, from the overlarge desk piled with books and papers to the windowsill crammed with potted plants. A trailing vine sat on top of the wardrobe, hastily discarded riding gear littered the floor, and an extremely battered leather chair had been dragged next to the fireplace. Over the carved mantel, with zero fanfare, hung the sword in the stone.

Emry stopped short, staring at it. "This is the sword?" she asked.

"This is the sword," Arthur confirmed.

She stepped closer, examining it in fascination. The sword wasn't magical, but it was far from ordinary. The blade was laced with the faint traces of faded spellwork, almost like a scar. The only time Emry had ever seen anything like it was at the gates of the castle. It took a truly powerful piece of magic to leave behind an echo like that, and she made a mental note to ask Master Ambrosius about it.

"They even got the vomit off," said Lance.

"Don't," Arthur said tiredly.

But Lance, who had already flopped onto the prince's bed, grinned. "Come on, it's a great story."

"Well, now I have to hear it," said Emry, taking pleasure in Arthur's scowl.

It *was* a great story. Especially the way Lance told it, with the two of them sneaking out of the castle to get drunk, only to find themselves cornered by the arrogant Sir Kay.

The food arrived midway through, and Lance cheerfully stuffed his face with cold meat and bread while he explained about the barmaid spilling beer all over Arthur and ruining their disguise.

"Sir Kay is your uncle?" Emry cut in.

"Unfortunately. Behold the family resemblance." Lance raised his chin and puffed out his chest, adopting a pompous, sneering expression.

Emry had only seen Sir Kay from a distance, but now that Lance mentioned it, they *did* have the same golden hair and oversize build.

Which meant Lance was wellborn. And Arthur had said they'd grown up together. He certainly didn't act like a common guard, especially the way he was lounging across the prince's bed, getting crumbs everywhere. But then . . .

"Why aren't you a knight?" Emry blurted.

"I was a page," Lance said with a sigh. "It didn't work out."

Both Lance and Arthur had gone stiff and awkward, and when Lance didn't bother to elaborate, Emry sensed that she shouldn't push. She watched as he polished off the last of the bread, and climbed to his feet, dusting crumbs off the coverlet.

"Weren't you going to fix me up?" he asked.

"He was going to try," challenged Arthur. He was draped across the worn, comfortable-looking leather chair by the fireplace, pulling off his boots. His jacket was flung aside, and the ties of his tunic were loosened.

Emry swallowed, looking away. She was in the prince's bedroom, and he was *getting undressed*. And it turned out that Lance wasn't any kind of chaperone at all, but a delinquent noble. If she were smart, she'd head back to her room immediately. But since she was already here, there was no harm in trying the spell. Just to know if she really could do it.

Emry dug out her wand, and Lance blanched as though she'd pulled out a jar of leeches. "Last chance to take a pain tonic like everyone else," she warned.

"I'm not giving the royal physician the satisfaction," said Lance. "You'd better not turn me into a frog."

"How about a fire-breathing horse, but green?" Emry asked, which made Arthur laugh.

"That would be an improvement," said the prince. Lance threw a heel of bread at him.

"Stay still," Emry snapped.

"Sorry," Lance mumbled.

Emry took a deep breath, picturing the ingredients that went into a pain-relief tonic and focusing on Lance's swollen wrist.

She pointed her wand, closed her eyes, and whispered, "*Angsumnes.*"

The spell released like a shot, and she staggered backward from the force, steadying herself on the corner of Arthur's desk.

Master Ambrosius had warned her that the spell would take as well as give, but the blowback of working controlled, precise magic on another living person left her surprised.

Sard. Was she supposed to feel so light-headed?

"Amazing," Lance marveled, rotating his wrist with a grin. "It really worked."

He sounded strangely far away. But maybe that was because the room had begun to spin . . .

Emry wobbled, and a pair of warm, steady arms caught her before she fell.

It was the prince. Barefoot. In his half-laced tunic.

"All right there?" he asked, peering down at her in concern.

He thinks you're Emmett, she reminded herself woozily.

The prince's arms were still around her. She could feel the steady thump of his heart. Did he always smell so good? Like herbs and old books and leather?

"I'm fine," she retorted, despite her dizziness. "Obviously."

"Never doubted you could do it," said Arthur, with a smile that made the room spin all over again. Her stomach fluttered in a way that definitely wasn't blowback from the spell. The prince's bed was right there, and she couldn't help but imagine pulling off his tunic and pushing him back onto those soft pillows and—

No, Emry told herself. *Not him. You know why not.*

"I, um, I should go," she said, twisting away and hurrying from the room.

◖ ◗ ◖

Emry had no sooner left the prince's rooms than she heard a cold voice call, "You there. Boy."

She turned to find a glowering Lord Agravaine. He was wearing a dressing gown and carrying an armload of scrolls, and he looked unhappy to have run into her.

"My lord," Emry said, with a brief bow. She was dizzy enough to botch it, and nearly lost her footing. The corridor spun as she straightened. "Er—did you need help with something?"

"This is a private wing of the castle," Lord Agravaine accused, as though he suspected she was poking around where she shouldn't. "What are you doing here?"

"I—" Emry swallowed nervously.

Lord Agravaine cut an imposing figure, but more than that, his whole demeanor was intimidating. The way he watched everything, as though he hoped people would forget he was there and say something they shouldn't. As though he trafficked in secrets.

For some reason, she didn't want him to know where she'd really been, or what she'd been doing. Lance had clearly gotten in trouble for *something*, and anyway, she wanted to attract as little attention as possible. Not rouse the suspicions of one of the king's closest advisors.

But if he thought she was sneaking around where she wasn't supposed to be, that was even worse.

Lord Agravaine was still glaring at her, as though he had caught her rifling through his personal effects. For all she knew, she was literally standing outside the door to his rooms.

Sard.

"Spit it out, boy. Unless you would rather explain yourself to the king," Lord Agravaine threatened.

"I was looking for the, um . . ." Emry said, casting around for a suitable lie.

Don't say toilet.

"He was with the prince, my lord," interrupted the younger of Arthur's guards, with an obsequious bow. "And Lance."

Lord Agravaine's expression soured. "You were looking for?" he prompted, raising an eyebrow.

"The way back to my room, from His Highness's," Emry finished smoothly.

"Indeed."

Emry scrambled down the corridor, her heart pounding from the confrontation. She could feel Lord Agravaine's watchful gaze with every step.

CHAPTER 12

The rest of the week fell into a routine. Emry spent her mornings in the workshop with Arthur, brewing draughts and tonics. And she spent her afternoons working with Master Ambrosius on spells that had once intimidated her. She ate her suppers with the old wizard, trying not to glance too often toward the prince at the royal banquet table and failing miserably. Evenings she spent in her room, reading as many books on magic as she could get her hands on, and sighing in relief when no knock sounded on her door before bed.

The sharp way Lord Agravaine had looked at her—as though he would be all too happy to unearth her secrets. It made her uneasy.

She supposed it was for the best that she was leaving. Things had gotten far too complicated. She'd meant to keep her head down, but after she'd met Arthur, that plan had gone out the window.

Emmett was going to kill her when he found out she'd gone around conjuring magic swords and casting healing spells and nearly fainting in the prince's bedchamber. But then, none of this would have happened if he hadn't gambled more than he could pay and tried to fix it with a terrible spell. So really, he could only blame himself.

She hadn't *wanted* to pretend to be her brother at court. But in the moment, she hadn't seen another choice. Besides, *she* was the one who'd had to prove herself as an apprentice. She was the one who had to chop off her hair and trade her airy linen dresses for a stifling jacket, doublet, and trews in the peak of summer heat. She had ensured Father's legacy was kept alive, instead of letting it pass to some unworthy stranger, along with money they so desperately needed.

Emmett *should* be thanking her. Not that her brother ever admitted that he was in her debt. He was too proud. Like Father had been. Or maybe all boys expected the world to bend to their desires, while Emry was wise enough to know that, as a girl, she needed to prove herself twice over just to be offered a chance.

At least it wouldn't be any trouble to slip away and switch back. Arthur's cousin Gawain was due to arrive at the castle the same night she was swapping places with Emmett. And with all of the excitement over the arrival of Lord and Lady Agravaine's eldest son, who stood third in line for the throne, it would be easy to disappear unnoticed.

Still, when that final evening came and Emry took one last look at her room, she wished leaving didn't hurt quite so much. She wouldn't have the chance to say goodbye. To Master Ambrosius, or to Arthur, or even Lance.

It was going on sunset when she approached the gate guards with a conjured pass from Master Ambrosius that granted her an evening's leave.

The guards glanced at her pass and moved aside, and she shifted her pack, her hands trembling.

It's over, she told herself. *It's already done.*

She was going home to Brocelande. Home to Gran, and Marion, and the theater. Home to slip back into the life she'd always had, so her brother could take possession of the one she'd temporarily borrowed.

It was never yours, she told herself. *You always knew that.* And yet, leaving the castle felt wrong. Like walking away from something important before she'd even gotten started.

Leaving should have felt like a relief. She'd gotten through the week without anyone discovering her secret. She'd fooled the royal court into believing she was her brother, and here she was, having lived to tell the tale.

Except it wasn't only relief she felt. It was also regret. Her chin quivered, and she sucked in a deep breath, trying not to cry, because crying wouldn't fix anything. She couldn't go back and write her name onto the

king's summons any more than she could go back and make her father want
to teach her magic along with her brother.

She only hoped Emmett didn't make a mess of it. That he applied
himself, for once, and became the great wizard she knew he could be if he
only *tried*.

Emry tried to think of all the things she missed back home. And when
that didn't work, she studied the city instead, marveling at how much of
it there was, and how many wonders it held, from the grand townhouses
along the Strand to the colorful mix of people crowding the taverns and
churches and merchants' stalls, which were closing up shop for the night.
She took in the sound of distant bells chiming the hour, and the scent of a
bakery selling its last loaves as she walked past. She loved being part of it,
and only wished she'd had more time.

She plunged onward, through the darkening London streets. She passed
alongside the river Thames and the tilting timbered houses of Cheapside.
The spire of St. Paul's beckoned sharply nearby, like the point on a com-
pass, guiding her to the tavern next door.

The tavern, when she reached it, was hardly more than a narrow sign,
and an even narrower door.

She pushed it open, surprised at how much larger the tavern seemed
on the inside. Even though the place was crowded, she spotted Emmett
immediately.

He was slouched down in a booth against the far wall. A week's worth
of stubble shadowed his jaw, and dark circles hung under his eyes. His hair
was limp and greasy, instead of pushed back in its usual swoop. A collection
of wine jugs littered his table, along with an eel pie that he'd barely touched.

Emry frowned. She'd *never* seen her brother like this. She hoped—oh
sard, she hoped it wasn't because of *her*. Because he'd woken up to find
she'd gone off to the castle in his place, and left Gran alone, and put her life
in danger by deceiving the royal court.

"Hi," she said guiltily, sliding into the booth across from him. "Have you been waiting long?"

Emmett stared at her, blinking slowly. His eyes had a glassy, unfocused sheen, and it took Emry a moment to realize he was drunk. *Very* drunk.

"You look like Father," he said. "Dressed as a boy. Don't know if I've ever—told you."

He hiccupped at the end, and Emry winced.

"I look like you, you idiot," she said. "Twins, remember?"

"And you're the good twin," he went on balefully. "You must be. Because I'm definitely—*hic*—the bad one."

Something was up, Emry realized. Something big.

"What's going on?" she asked.

Emmett shifted in his seat. Looked everywhere except at her. "I'm not going to the castle to study magic."

Emry's stomach twisted. "What are you *talking* about?"

Of *course* he was going to the castle. She'd never seen him more delighted than when he'd read the summons from the king. But he certainly didn't look delighted now.

Emmett dragged a hand over his face. He seemed . . . haunted.

"I *can't*," he said, his voice breaking. "Because of Jane." Off Emry's frown, he explained, "The innkeeper's youngest daughter. She's with child."

Emry stared at her brother, unsure whether to congratulate or console him. "Oh, Emmett," she said, which seemed to cover both.

"She sat by my bed waiting for me to wake up. Waiting to tell me. And I—I can't just . . ." He trailed off, picking up his cup and taking a long, sad gulp. "I'm not abandoning her and the baby. I'm not going to be Father."

Emry could see that he meant it. The way their father had left them behind to seek fame and fortune at court, expecting Gran to raise them. Their mother had died in childbirth, and their father had never once acted as though he was expected to shoulder any additional responsibilities because of it. Emry had always wished things were different, but she'd never considered that their father could have chosen otherwise. That the great and powerful Merlin could have brought his children to court, or else stayed home in Brocelande and raised them himself.

Maybe, if he *had*, he'd still be alive.

Emry stared at her brother, who never meant to screw things up. And yet he always did.

"You're not Father," she said softly.

"You're right about that," he said. "I'm not one-*tenth* of the wizard that he was. But you are."

Emry bit her lip. "You just need *practice*," she insisted. "A couple of weeks with Master Ambrosius and—"

"It won't work," he interrupted, shaking his head.

"What if Jane came with you?" she said desperately. "I'm sure—"

"Em, you don't *get* it. I'm not out of practice. I can cast three spells before I start to misfire. Four, on a good day."

Emry stared at him, positive that couldn't be true. She tried to remember the last time she'd seen her brother do any serious magic . . . and realized she couldn't. He swaggered, and he boasted, and every once in a while, he made a show of casting some flashy spell. But when it came to practical, necessary spellwork, he always forgot, or claimed he'd do it later, until Emry got frustrated enough to do it herself.

"It's all bragging," he continued softly. "And I'd rather impress everyone at home than let down everyone at court." He reached for his wine, gulping down the rest of his cup. "Especially now they've seen what *you* can do. So, I'm not going."

"I can't just go back and pretend to be you *forever*," said Emry. "It was nerve-wracking enough doing it for a week!"

"I know," Emmett said, his dark eyes serious. "An indefinite stay at court would be a huge risk. And if it's one you don't want to take, then go back and tell them that I quit. You quit. Whatever."

Emry bit her lip, picking at a loose thread in her tunic. She wished there was another way. Disguising herself as her brother was always supposed to be *temporary*. A role she'd play for a week, and then she'd be herself again. The timeline was something she'd held close, repeating it whenever Master Ambrosius referred to her as "boy," or when she caught sight of her reflection in a serving platter and had the strangest impression she was seeing someone else. Pretending to be Emmett was harder than she'd imagined, in so many small ways she never could have predicted.

But she'd be lying if she said she didn't want to keep learning magic. And continue seeing the prince dressed in his sportswear, smiling at her across the big wooden table in the wizard's workshop. She was overwhelmed by how much she wanted to unpack her things and climb the stairs to Master Ambrosius's tower tomorrow morning, and the morning after that. Despite what might happen if she was caught.

Emmett was giving her his shot. And she didn't know if she dared to take it.

"Em," her brother pressed. "You're wasting yourself at the theater. Someday soon, Camelot's going to need a wizard. A good one. And when they do, they're not going to care that you're a girl."

She hadn't even thought of that. But Emmett was right. Master Ambrosius was old and frail. If something happened, if King Yurien threatened their borders, if Arthur—kind, brilliant Arthur—had to ride into battle to defend their kingdom, then she wanted to help. And the best way to help was to learn all she could. Not sit at home magicking stains out of costumes.

Yes, it was risky, but she'd already gotten away with it for this long. Which meant it could work. And if it did, she'd earn money that she could send home to Gran and Emmett. Money that was sorely needed, especially if Emmett was going to have a wife and child. Their house, technically, was his. Everything that had been their father's belonged to him.

Except, perhaps, a life at the castle. Studying magic. The lie didn't have to be forever. Like Emmett said, eventually she'd reveal the truth. She'd figure it out. Somehow.

Her brother nudged a bundle across the floor with his boot.

"What's that?" Emry asked suspiciously.

"Hair ribbons," he said, rolling his eyes. "What do you think? My second-best tunic and hose. Father's books. And Gran altered one of Father's old coats."

"She did?"

"She said old castles get drafty, and she didn't want you to freeze." Emmett made it sound as if it were already decided. But then, she supposed it was. Her father's words came back to her then: *Smart as spades, but foolish as hearts.*

"This is a terrible idea," Emry muttered.

"Of course it is." Emmett's lips twitched as he held back a smile. "But when has that ever stopped you?"

◐ ◐ ◐

Gawain wasn't impressed. So this was the tavern where his boring, bookish cousin had pulled the sword from the stone? He'd expected more. Or, better wine, at the very least.

He glanced around, curious what sort of patrons wasted their coin here. Dockworkers mostly. And rough-clothed laborers. There was just the one other lad by himself, slouched in the next booth. He had an interesting face, handsome and fine-featured, but it was the tragic slant to the lad's shoulders that snagged Gawain's attention.

Gawain reached for his sketchpad and charcoals, in no hurry to reach the castle. He'd sent his servants on ahead, conjuring a lie about an errand for his father. But really, he wanted a moment to himself before stepping back into the life he'd gladly left behind two years earlier.

When he arrived at the castle, he just knew there was going to be fanfare. And some wretched supper where the courtiers would scrutinize every inch of him. At court, his father demanded perfection, and perfection was exhausting.

There wasn't even a point to it, because no matter how hard he worked, he was always behind Arthur. He could best his second cousin at fencing, at archery, at dancing, it didn't change the fact that his blood ran less royal. That even now, he was a spare to a spare. But there was no way to make his parents listen, and so he'd eventually stopped trying.

It was easier just to be elsewhere.

He'd left Camelot believing that if he remained, he'd only watch himself slip further down the line of succession. But the queen had died in childbirth, and Arthur had performed an unlikely miracle, and he'd read his father's letters with a curious sense of detachment, feeling as though, so long as he wasn't there to witness it, it was all happening in a different life.

Still, a small part of him wondered how different things might have been if he'd stayed. If *he'd* pulled the sword from the stone. But there was no use dwelling on alternate histories, because when it came to the past, there were so many things he wished he could change.

He put charcoal to paper, setting down the first lines of his sketch before the boy could move. He lost himself to his work, sipping absently at his wine as the rough portrait bloomed onto the page.

He missed Paris already. He'd been happy there, with his easel, and his apartment overlooking the Seine, and his French staff who didn't know Camelot from Cameliard. There had been ballets, and balls, and music that had made him feel alive, nights spent weaving drunkenly through the gardens of the Chateau de Saint-Germain in the company of beautiful women, and stumbling into brothels with his sketchpad under arm.

While he wasn't wholly immune to the prostitutes' charms, he mostly paid the girls to let him sketch. There was a thrill in signing his name to a scandalous drawing, instead of a stuffy court document. It made signing his name to the letters he sent home detailing the comings and goings under the dauphin less distasteful.

His family were courtiers. Politicians. Cold, calculating men of power. They found others' weaknesses and exploited them to their advantage. They gained information by any means necessary. Gawain didn't want to be like that, but sometimes he wondered if he had a choice. Wasn't it what his brother had done, saving himself while dooming Lance? Wasn't that same ugliness coiled within himself, waiting to strike?

He wished, for the thousandth time, that his father hadn't insisted he return home so soon. But when the great Lord Agravaine said jump, the only acceptable answer was to ask how sarding high.

It was cover, he knew, so his parents could quietly send for Jereth and drill some sense into the lad. What was it his younger brother had set on fire this time? The school chapel? No, the scriptorium. *Merde.*

Yet this offense was being quietly swept away, along with the rest of them. It felt as though, while Gawain was expected to do no wrong, his brother could do nothing right.

Their mother coddled the lad. True, he'd nearly died of influenza as a boy, yet Jereth had found a way to turn even *that* to his advantage, complaining of cough or chill to get out of whatever he wished.

Gawain couldn't remember the last time he'd been allowed to refuse anything. Even these few years of so-called freedom in Paris had been in exchange for his "diplomacy" at court. It wasn't spying, exactly, but his weekly letters, written in code, certainly weren't voluntary.

And now even *that* arrangement had been yanked out from under him. He doubted he'd be granted half as much freedom in Uther's dull, conservative castle.

Gawain sighed and considered his sketch. Not bad, although he'd gotten the hands wrong. He flipped the page over, starting again. A bell jingled over the door, and he noted with surprise that the lad who entered was *identical* to the subject of his drawing. Now *this* was interesting.

The lad sat down across from his brother, and Gawain leaned forward, curious.

"You look like Father, dressed as a boy," said the drunk one.

Dressed as a boy? Did that mean the lad who'd just turned up was a *girl*? That was illegal, of course, as was dressing above one's station. The king's sumptuary laws were strongly enforced, from colored dyes only nobles could use to the types of fur allowed to trim a commoner's coat. If this girl was pretending to be a boy, there had to be a good reason.

A round of cards at the next table erupted into a loud argument, and Gawain frowned in annoyance. He couldn't *hear*. He needed somewhere closer . . . like the bar.

He picked up his goblet of wine, slamming the distasteful swill back in one gulp. And then he sauntered over to the barmaid for a refill.

He slowed as he passed their table, angling for a better look. She *was* a girl. Around his age, with hair as dark as his own, and the most magnificent warm brown eyes.

"I'm not going to the castle to study magic," said the boy, and Gawain had to force himself to keep walking and not openly stare.

The *castle*? *Magic*?

He signaled for a mug of ale, sliding onto a stool. Ordinarily, he would have avoided such a conspicuous seat—between his dark skin and his expensive, French-cut clothes, he was practically asking for trouble—but he *had* to hear the rest of this.

So he sipped his drink, his eyes growing wide as he pieced together the situation.

The girl had temporarily gone to Castle Camelot in the boy's place, and now the boy was refusing to switch back. He'd gotten some girl pregnant and—*merde*—Gawain choked as he realized why the boy had caught his attention.

He was the spitting image of his father. As a child, Gawain had been thoroughly intimidated by the elegant court wizard, who seemed to crackle with magic. And it seemed Merlin's wand hadn't fallen far from the family tree.

The girl pleaded with her brother, and Gawain's eyes grew wide as the boy confessed that his powers were nothing compared to hers. As they made arrangements for the boy to return home, and the girl to remain disguised at court—indefinitely.

Had no one discovered her deception?

Well. Gawain grinned, filing away this fascinating information. After all, there was a time and a place to barter secrets, and he wasn't yet sure of this one's worth.

CHAPTER 13

Emry hurried through the fog-thick London night, hardly daring to believe she was headed back to Castle Camelot. She didn't know whether to laugh or to cry.

Maybe both, she thought, overwhelmed.

Her shoulder ached from the weight of her pack, and with every step, she felt the sharp edge of a book dig into her ribs. She still couldn't believe Emmett had given her their father's magic books. No—more than that. He'd given her his future. And she was terrified by what that meant. At the lies she'd have to maintain, and how much she stood to lose if she was caught.

Smart as spades, but foolish as hearts.

Father had known her so well.

And yet, she hadn't known Emmett at all. His boasting and swagger, his reckless behavior, all of those nights she'd wished he would just *try*. She'd thought him lazy, but it turned out he was playing a part. That he'd decided long ago that it was better to live a lie than reveal a disappointing truth.

She wished he'd confided in her.

There was a loneliness in keeping secrets. One that Emry knew well after a week at the castle.

In the theater, everyone on stage was playing a part. But at the castle, she was the only one in disguise, and she felt the weight of what that meant. A weight she'd have to carry with her going forward—as the apprentice court wizard. Even if the title was based on a lie, it was still hers. For a little while longer, at least.

A rat skittered across the cobblestones, making Emry jump. London was different at night. Colder. Lonelier. It grasped at her from the shadows of dark alleyways, making her skin prickle whenever she came upon a blind corner, or heard the yowl of a street cat.

The normally colorful storefronts were closed for the night, the street vendors had packed their wares, and the craftsmen had boarded up their stalls. The sheriff's men had rounded up the poor souls with nowhere to go, casting them outside the city walls so the gates could be safely locked until dawn.

London was still a fortress, even when it pretended to be a city.

She knew the quiet was supposed to be reassuring, but the emptiness unnerved her. She clutched her thin jacket tighter around her shoulders as the neighborhood grew rough and the alleys narrowed around her. She was already past the docks, and almost to the square where, earlier in the day, there had been dozens of market stalls. It wasn't so much farther to the castle gates. And once she was through, she'd be able to breathe a sigh of relief—a small sigh—before figuring out how she was going to make this work long-term.

Suddenly, she heard footsteps behind her. She could see his shadow in the thin moonlight. She chanced a look back, spotting a boy with brown skin and an expensive coat.

She'd seen plenty of opulent fashions at court, enough to know that his coat, a sky-blue brocade trimmed with gold, must have cost a small fortune. Which meant he was someone important. And snagging the attention of someone important was the last thing she needed right now.

Because as far as everyone at the castle knew, she was still in her room, not wandering the city streets with a suspicious amount of luggage and a forged pass in her pocket. She didn't know what excuse she'd give if she were caught, and she'd prefer not to find out.

If she went much farther, her destination would be obvious. She spotted an alley up ahead, and darted into it, curious if the boy would follow.

The alleyway was rougher than she'd expected. She passed a ruined building, its timbers singed black, its windows boarded shut. Next door, a tavern's wooden sign swung overhead, yet there was no name, only a grim picture of a bird of prey, its talons outstretched.

Emry swallowed nervously, forcing herself to keep going.

Cutting through this alley had been a terrible idea. She had her pack slung over her shoulder, heavy with Emmett's additions, and she knew it made her an easy mark.

Footsteps echoed softly behind her, and Emry's heart thudded against her chest. The boy had followed her after all.

"Can I help you?" she called, making her voice as deep as she could.

"It's a dead end!"

She suspected the boy was right. "Then why are you following me?" she demanded, just as two tall, sneering figures stepped from the shadows, blocking her escape.

Their clothes were rough spun and stained, and the men reeked of ale. The bigger one was missing half his teeth, and the smaller had pallid skin, and blond hair that hung in rattails over his greasy jerkin. Their daggers glittered in the moonlight, and Emry didn't doubt for a moment that they knew how to use them.

Sard.

Icy fear shot through her veins as the men sized her up, sensing her distress.

"You must be lost," said the first with a rotting grin.

"'Ent anyone ever tell you cities are dangerous?" lisped the other.

"Give us your pack," said the first, "and we might let you live."

He stepped toward her, his dagger held low, as though he meant to gut her like a fish.

Emry swallowed nervously. She didn't have a knife. Didn't have any weapon on her except her magic, and she'd never used it to defend herself before. She took a step back, which only seemed to encourage them.

"Nowhere to run," said the grinning man, menacing toward her.

Was her magic faster than their daggers? She didn't know. And she *hated* that she was about to find out.

"Two against one hardly seems fair," someone called.

It was the boy in the beautiful coat, calmly unsheathing a knife from his boot and brandishing it against her attackers.

"I don't need your help," Emry snarled. *Honestly.* Why couldn't he just leave her alone?

Yet when the men turned to leer at the elegant stranger, the distraction gave her a precious moment to reach for her wand.

Fleoges, she thought, sending her attackers' weapons flying from their hands. The knives embedded themselves in the nearest wall, handles vibrating.

Emry smirked as the men stared at their daggers, brows knitting in confusion, unable to work out what had happened.

"Not so tough now, are you?" she goaded.

The men merely exchanged a look, then reached down to pull spare knives from their boots, their horrible grins returning full force. Emry's stomach sank.

"Not so confident now, are you?" one of them taunted, slashing his knife in threat.

Fear rippled through her.

The man with the rotting grin slashed his knife again, and Emry scrambled back, the blade narrowly missing her abdomen.

"Drop yer pack an' go," he growled.

But Emry wasn't giving up her father's books and coat. Not to these thick-skulled thieves who didn't even recognize magic when they saw it. *Perhaps,* she thought, *I haven't shown them magic enough.*

"How about you drop your knives," she retorted, lifting her chin. "Or else I'll do it for you."

"Gonna fight us with that stick?" his friend asked, leering at her wand.

"Actually," Emry said, with as much confidence as she could manage, "I'm going to *burn* you with it."

Ignis, she thought.

A wall of fire roared to life between Emry and her attackers. They stumbled back, eyes wide with fright, cursing loudly.

"*Amplius,*" she hissed. The fire crackled higher, flames licking up the walls of the buildings, eight and then ten feet high.

It was only an illusion, a stage trick, but the men didn't know that. The color bled from their faces.

"*Fleoges,*" Emry snarled. Two crumbling bricks rose into the air and knocked heavily into her attackers, cracking one in the nose, and the other in the chin.

Blood ran down their faces, and the men moaned in pain. Emry didn't care. She levitated two more bricks, letting them hover in front of her.

"Get out of my sight," she ordered.

The men listened. They scrambled back down the narrow footpath, cursing loudly.

Emry watched them run, her heart pounding. Her hands were shaking as she cast off the spell.

It had worked. She was safe.

From them, at least.

She stared down at her wand, hesitating to put it away. The boy in the beautiful coat was still there, eyeing her appraisingly.

"Not bad," he said, bending to tuck his knife back into his boot. "The fire was a clever touch."

His reaction to her magic wasn't one of fear, but of curiosity. It was as though he'd known she could do it all along, and approved of her demonstration.

Emry grudgingly tucked away her wand. After all, the boy had stowed his knife.

"It was an illusion, right?" the boy went on. "Because there wasn't any smoke. Unlike the bricks."

"Why are you following me?" she demanded again, instead of answering his question.

"Who says I'm following you? Perhaps we're just headed to the same place."

He let that sit there a moment, as though daring Emry to ask where he was headed. But she wouldn't give him the satisfaction.

"There are only so many roads to the castle," the boy continued. "Although, as I warned you before, this isn't one of them. Shall we?"

He motioned for Emry to walk with him, and she scowled, reluctantly falling into step. He was tall and athletic, with liquid brown eyes and an infuriating smirk that only accentuated his soft lips. And he seemed familiar, which was maddening, because she would have remembered him.

"How do you know I'm going to the castle?" she asked.

The boy's smirk deepened.

"An educated guess. Gawain d'Orkney at your service. Although actually, I believe it's the other way around."

She should bow, she realized a moment too late. So this was the prince's cousin, the young royal whose arrival was expected that very night.

Suddenly, she felt silly, imagining she was being followed. Of course he was headed to the castle. Emry belatedly dipped into a bow, which seemed to please her companion.

"And you're Apprentice Merlin, I presume," Gawain went on. "You look very like your father."

Gawain smiled, as though enjoying a private joke. He had a hint of Arthur's wide grin, she realized, and the same deep-cut cheekbones as his father. That's what had made him seem familiar. He couldn't have been more than nineteen. For some reason, she'd imagined him older.

"What are you doing wandering around London, Lord Gawain?" she asked.

"Avoiding the horrible banquet that's no doubt being held in my honor. And you?"

Emry forced herself to match his light spirits, even though she was still reeling from the attack. "Arriving to the same banquet, fashionably late," she said.

"Fashionably? Are you sure?" he drawled, nodding at Emry's clothing.

Oh, he was infuriating. Everything she'd expected of the prince and worse.

"Shall we claim we were attacked by bandits?" Gawain went on. "That we valiantly fought off three each? You with magic, of course, me with just my knife and my wits."

Emry snorted. But Gawain wasn't laughing. "Oh, you're serious?" she asked.

He shrugged. Elegantly, of course. "It was just a suggestion. Might get us out of that dreadful supper entirely. If it did, I'd be in your debt."

Dangerous, a small voice in the back of her head warned. He wanted something. That's why he had followed her down that alley. And why he was watching her so closely now. But she couldn't figure out what.

She should be careful, she knew. Lord Agravaine had already caught her leaving the prince's bedroom, and she had no good explanation for what she was doing wandering the streets of London.

Emry lifted her chin. "I'll pass, thanks. As it stands, you're already in my debt."

"How so?"

"For my silence," she said. "I *did* save us both, after you so foolishly followed me down an alley you knew was a dead end. So whatever story you tell to explain the late hour of your arrival, and your apparent lack of guards or servants, I won't contradict it."

Gawain stared at her, considering. "You think your word is worth as much as mine?" he asked, sounding every inch the spoiled royal.

"I don't know," Emry admitted. "But I'd be interested to find out."

She watched with satisfaction as he wrestled with what to say next.

They were fast approaching the castle. The gates loomed in front of them, and suddenly Emry had an idea.

"I'll take my leave now, my lord," she said with a brief bow. "The servants' entrance is around the back."

"But you're not—" he began, confused. And then the gate guards got a look at him, and it was all "My lord Gawain! The whole castle has been waiting!" which was exactly what Emry had been counting on.

CHAPTER 14

When his father sent for him the day after his cousin's arrival at court, Arthur wasn't surprised, just resigned to whatever it was he'd unknowingly done wrong this time. Perhaps one of his tutors had a complaint, or he had annoyed Lord Agravaine with his questions regarding land grants in the latest council meeting.

Or maybe it was nothing at all, and Gawain's arrival was simply making him paranoid. As children, they'd been pitted against each other so often that it had turned them into enemies instead of allies.

Though they weren't children anymore, Arthur still couldn't forgive his cousin for all of those years he'd gloated over small, useless victories. And he certainly couldn't forgive him for staying silent as his younger brother betrayed Lance, taking away everything his friend had worked for as well as his future.

He was dishonorable, Arthur thought. And a man without honor was as morally bereft as his word.

At least Gawain had no interest in the wizard's workshop. For that, Arthur was thankful. The tower room was the one place in the castle where he could still find peace.

Even if he wished Merlin would snap out of his funk. He supposed the lad was embarrassed from nearly fainting after performing the healing spell. It was nothing to be ashamed of. That was a piece of risky, impressive magic, and Arthur hadn't quite believed Merlin would dare, much less manage it on his first go. But he had. And whenever Arthur remembered catching the young wizard in his arms, he felt his own cheeks go warm.

So he didn't talk about it. Even though he really did want to say thank

you. The way Merlin had helped Lance—at his own expense—it meant a
lot. There weren't many in the castle who would have done the same.

Arthur paused outside the door to his father's rooms, taking a moment.
It wasn't often these days that he came to visit this corridor of the castle.
His mother's old chambers were just down the hall, cloaked with a sense
of disuse.

He glanced away, swallowing thickly. Trying not to think of her. Because if he started, he didn't think he'd be able to stop.

It was just a room now. Just another empty space.

Even so, the lack of guards outside made him ache with loss.

Steady, Arthur told himself, taking a deep breath. *You're the crown prince of
Camelot. You should be able to handle seeing a door.*

"Enter," called his father, and his guards crisply flung open the doors.

Uther was neither in his bedroom, nor his sitting room, nor his private
dining chamber. Instead, Arthur found his father at his desk in his study, a
mess of parchment before him, a pair of tiny spectacles on the end of his
nose. Arthur knew his father hated the spectacles, which was why he'd devel-
oped the trick of demanding members of his council deliver reports aloud.

Uther removed his glasses and gave Arthur a thin, tired smile. "The
weapons master says you're improving," he said.

Arthur bowed his head, surprised by his father's praise.

"There might be some hope for you yet," mused the king.

"Don't tell Gawain, he'll be so disappointed," Arthur deadpanned, the
words tumbling out before he could stop himself.

"I believe that childhood rivalry has played itself out," said Uther. Before Arthur could respond, the king went on, "If there is any threat to the
crown, it will come from beyond our kingdom."

No doubt his father meant the Duke of Cornwall or King Yurien.

"I trust your wisdom on such matters," Arthur said cautiously. "But
I hope I was clear: I'm not agreeing to marry a seven-year-old."

He waited for a reprimand, but his father only shook his head.

"Perhaps that wasn't the best idea," the king allowed.

"It was an alliance worth considering," Arthur said diplomatically, sinking into the chair across from his father's desk. It was horribly stiff, yet somehow too springy. A devil of a chair. He knew his father kept it there on purpose.

"The day we need to call on help from the continent is not one I want to see in my lifetime," said Uther.

"Nor mine," Arthur agreed.

"Although that isn't to say that a more suitable marriage prospect would be out of the question," the king added, shuffling through the mess of scrolls atop his desk.

Outmaneuvered again, Arthur realized. "No," he agreed grudgingly, "it wouldn't."

The king smiled, and Arthur suddenly had a very bad feeling about why he was here, and his father's unexpected praise, and how he'd been quietly disarmed by it. He shifted in his seat, thinking that he'd never hated a chair more.

"You must remember King Leodegrance's daughter, Guinevere," the king went on.

Arthur tensed, sensing where this was headed.

"Barely. I was ten the last time I saw her."

And Guinevere had been nine, with a penchant for purposefully whacking him in the shins while they'd played croquet. She'd drawn in one of his favorite books, and her apology had been forced and terrible, and Arthur still hadn't forgiven her.

"I've arranged things with her father, and she'll be staying with us for the remainder of the summer," said King Uther.

"For any particular reason?" Arthur asked, trying to stay calm. Perhaps it wasn't what he thought. Perhaps . . .

"I assumed you'd be thanking me," said his father. "You said you wished for the opportunity to romance your future wife. But if you'd prefer, I can have her remain in Cameliard, and you'll meet on your wedding day."

"When might that be?" Arthur asked, an edge to his voice.

"When I command it." His father glared. "King Yurien also has a son. Would you rather Cameliard makes their ties with *his* kingdom?"

"Of course not." Arthur sighed.

He couldn't deny the logic. He just hated that he hadn't seen this coming.

"Your marriage will assure a continued alliance between our kingdoms," Uther said.

Arthur grimaced inwardly.

"So would signing a peace treaty," he pointed out, even though he knew it was a move his father would never consider. Not without benefit. Especially now, when they could find themselves dragged into a conflict against King Yurien on Cameliard's behalf.

The king's jaw clenched, and Arthur knew his father was struggling to master his temper.

"You *will* do this," growled the king. "I'm counting on you to show the princess what Camelot has to offer."

Arthur sighed. First Gawain, and now Guinevere. This castle was becoming far too crowded with people he'd prefer to avoid. He needed to get out. To do something other than grit his teeth through supper and bow to every passing courtier and suffer through his father's endless council meetings.

Or else he was going to lose it.

He clearly wasn't getting out of this mess with Princess Guinevere. But perhaps he could gain something in return. And then he thought of something so obvious he couldn't believe he hadn't come up with it sooner.

"I'll do what's expected of me," Arthur said smoothly, "after I return from my quest."

"Quest?" his father said with a frown.

"Well, I was thinking about what you said. About the sword I pulled from the stone. And you're right," Arthur said carefully.

He had to sell this exactly if it was going to work. He paused just long enough for the praise to sink in, but not so long that Uther would have time to realize it was meaningless.

"I can't figure out what I'm meant to do now that I have it," Arthur continued. "And I'm afraid it's starting to reflect badly on my potential as the future king."

"Go on," said King Uther, his voice stony.

"I should have done this ages ago, to be honest," said Arthur. "I want to visit the Lady of the Lake. On the Isle of Avalon."

"Avalon?" His father's frown deepened. "That's practically in Cornwall."

In truth, the isle was in the lake that separated their kingdom from the duchy. It was claimed by neither, holy from the days when magic dwelled more strongly through the whole of England.

But most of the magic was gone, no matter how many stone henges— or sacred sites—remained. Now magic only surfaced if it was already in your blood, and many of the old families had died out.

Apparently wizards were more likely to blunder into danger than to settle down and raise children. Cornwall's wizard was little more than a charlatan, and Cameliard had none at all, though that was more out of religious preference.

Arthur was reminded suddenly of the terrible apprentice who had come to Castle Camelot a few years back. He'd defaced the library's magic books before admitting he barely had the ability to light a candle.

With the exception of young Merlin, that was how magic ran these days—in trickles rather than streams. Enchantments like the one on the sword in the stone were a thing of the past. Which was why he'd thought of Avalon. The tiny isle was home to an ancient order of priestesses, led by a direct descendant of the sorceress who had set the sword in the stone in the first place. Or, if the rumors were true, by the very same sorceress, having lived for centuries.

"It's a four-day trip at least," said Arthur. "And if I don't go now, I can't imagine when I'll have another chance. As you said, I'll need to show Princess Guinevere how much Camelot has to offer."

Arthur stared hopefully at his father. Perhaps it was too much, to ask for this. But he couldn't stand the thought of doing nothing. Of politely welcoming Princess Guinevere, whose imminent arrival felt entirely like a reprimand for his refusal of Princess Anne. He assumed he had Lord Agravaine to thank for it.

"You'd go straight there and back," said Uther.

"Of course, Father." Arthur couldn't believe what he was hearing.

"And you'd travel with a company of guards."

Arthur opened his mouth, but before he could say anything, his father added, "Not Lance."

"Dakin and Brannor, then," Arthur allowed, naming his two humorless guards. "And Lance."

Uther nodded his agreement. "And take that wizard with you," said the king. "Merlin's boy. What's his name? Emric?"

"Emmett," said Arthur, hardly able to believe his good luck. "So I can go?"

"You can go."

◑ ◑ ◑

"Focus," warned Master Ambrosius.

"I'm trying," Emry grumbled.

"If you're complaining, you're most certainly not," the old wizard retorted.

Emry barely resisted the urge to sigh. It was early evening, and Master Ambrosius had her working on a sleeping spell. He'd hung birdcages the length of his workshop, and was determining the farthest distance from which Emry could accurately put his canaries to sleep.

She'd been at it all afternoon, and she was exhausted. Master Ambrosius was pushing her, making her fight to master the magic. And while she wanted dearly to fall into bed and sleep for a week, she could feel herself improving. So she supposed it was worth the effort.

She took a deep breath, trying to gather her remaining strength. *Sleeping draught*, she thought. *Ingredients? Valerian. Lavender. Not too much valerian.*

"*Mætan*," she whispered. The spell shot from her wand, leaving her light-headed and panting. She held her footing, though, with just the slightest wobble.

"Well?" she gasped. The canary was so far away that she couldn't even tell if the spell had landed.

"Bull's-eye!" The old wizard applauded, and Emry grinned with relief, swiping the back of her hand under her nose.

It came away red with blood. If she wasn't so drained, she would have laughed, because she'd always thought a bloody nose from spellwork was an old wizards' tale, and not an actual thing that happened.

"Again?" she asked warily. She wasn't sure she could manage it, and the last thing she wanted to do was overtax her magic and pass out.

"No, you've earned a break," said Master Ambrosius. "And from the look of things, you need one."

She sank gratefully into the nearest chair, trying to shake off the dizziness. She swiped at her nose again, but the bleeding had stopped.

There were footsteps on the stairs, and then Arthur poked his head through the doorway. He was wearing his circlet, she noticed. And a fine blue jacket with gold embroidery. His dark hair was freshly combed, and he looked even more handsome than usual. Gawain was definitely getting to him. It was amusing watching Arthur brood over the arrival of his arrogant cousin.

"Merlin?" he called uncertainly, taking in the stack of books on the battered wooden table.

"Over here," Emry groaned.

Arthur's shadow fell over her. "Wild night at the tavern?" he teased, lips twitching as he held back a smirk.

"The brothel, actually," Emry replied.

Arthur arched an eyebrow in disbelief.

"For your information, I've been driven to the brink of exhaustion casting *sleeping spells*," Emry said hotly. "On *canaries*."

Arthur snorted.

"It's not funny," she scolded.

"It's *hilarious*," Arthur corrected, grinning.

Master Ambrosius handed Emry a mug of warm, pungent liquid.

"Drink this," he instructed. "All of it."

Emry took a sip of the bitter drink and made a face. It tasted even worse than it smelled.

"Holy basil," Arthur hazarded. "And roseroot?"

The old wizard nodded.

"Show-off," Emry muttered, taking another traumatizing sip. "Ugh. This is foul."

"So is the headache you'll have if you don't finish it," warned Master Ambrosius.

"Well, bottoms up," Arthur said cheerfully, pausing for effect. "Tomorrow, we undertake a great quest."

"Do you have to be so dramatic?" Emry swallowed down another terrible mouthful.

"A quest?" asked the old wizard curiously.

"To Avalon," said Arthur.

"The Isle of the Blessed?" Master Ambrosius sounded impressed. "Your father agreed to that?"

"He did," Arthur said, entirely too pleased with himself. "It was *his* idea for me to take Merlin along."

Emry almost dropped her mug. Somehow she'd missed that part. "Wait, what?" she said, horrified. "You mean an *actual quest*?"

"How else am I supposed to get answers about my sword?" Arthur grinned. "Lance is coming, too. It'll be a proper adventure."

"How far is it to Avalon?" Emry asked, trying to tamp down her panic. Maybe it was a day quest. The kind where they packed a picnic and were home by nightfall.

"Two days either side," said Arthur.

Emry choked. Posing as her brother at the castle was one thing, but holding her disguise for four days on the road? Or more? Where was she supposed to pee? And what about sleeping arrangements?

Oh, this was a nightmare. Couldn't she just stay here and learn magic and sleep in her comfortable bed with its en suite privy and wake up every morning to fresh cups of coffee and warm bread in the kitchens?

"You'll have to go without me," she said, sagging back in the chair and playing up her fatigue. "I'll never recover in time."

"Nonsense," protested the old wizard. "You'll be fine by supper."

Emry shot him a murderous glare.

"Then it's decided," Arthur said happily. "We leave at dawn."

CHAPTER 15

Arthur couldn't stop grinning as he rode through the castle gates the next morning. Free at last—for a few days, anyway.

Still, a sliver of freedom was better than none at all. Even so, he felt certain that, at any moment, one of his father's messengers would catch up with them, claiming there had been a terrible mistake and they were to return to the castle immediately.

But no messenger came, and the pale light of early morning gave way to clear afternoon sunshine. The timbered houses turned to thatched cottages and pastures and rolling hills, and just like that, London and the castle were far behind.

His two guards rode at the front, chatting amongst themselves. About what, he had no clue, since they fell silent whenever he was around. He wished they were more like Lance—friends with swords who could hang—but after he'd been declared heir to the kingdom, his father had chosen his guards personally.

Dakin, the youngest, was all muscle and little brain. According to Lance, he frequently boasted of his outlandish sexual exploits in the guard's mess, despite spending all of his spare time lifting weights. Then there was gray-haired, battle-hardened Brannor, who, if he'd ever had one, had lost his sense of humor long ago. Arthur hated having an experienced soldier stuck standing outside his bedchamber, and wished he could trade them both for some of the younger, friendlier guards he'd seen around the castle. But, as with most things, his father got his way.

Thankfully, having Lance and Merlin along on the journey was far more enjoyable.

Lance rode alongside him, and the young wizard trailed behind, letting out a steady stream of expletives at his horse. They were all dressed plainly, so as not to attract attention. Not even their saddles bore the stamp of the castle armory. It gave Arthur a thrill, but Lance, without his uniform, looked distinctly uncomfortable, as though he wasn't sure which role he was expected to play: friend or guard.

The last time they'd traveled together was three years ago, on a visit to Lance's family home, just before his half brother Sir Hector had inherited the estate. They'd been two young nobles then, both with disapproving fathers, both with a penchant for finding trouble and a knack for pretending trouble had found them first, both on the cusp of choosing their own paths: Arthur a scholar, and Lance a knight.

Funny the difference a few years could make.

Behind them, the wizard let out a particularly colorful swear, and Lance grinned, his shoulders shaking with silent laughter.

Merlin clearly had little experience riding. He kept jerking the reins and muttering foul curses, and if it wasn't so entertaining to see the lad fail at something, Arthur might have advised him to use a softer grip.

Except it *was* entertaining, which meant he wasn't saying a word.

"Hey, wizard!" Lance called over his shoulder. "Are you *trying* to choke your horse?"

"He's plotting against me," Merlin insisted.

Arthur bit back a snicker. He'd chosen the mounts himself. They were slim gray palfreys, bred for their smooth gait and ability to cover great distances. The most manageable and docile beasts in the royal stables. "I thought every country lad could ride a horse," he said.

Hadn't the boy grown up on his family's estate? Or perhaps not, he realized, taking in the wizard's plain, worn clothing. Even so, Merlin was acting as though he'd never sat astride a saddle.

"I'm from a *town*, not a *country farm*," Merlin retorted, lifting his chin.

"Until a few weeks ago, I was a member of the Lord Brocelande's Men."

"You belonged to a theater troupe?" Arthur said, recognizing the name. "You never mentioned that."

What an odd place for a wizard. But then, nothing about Merlin was as he'd expected.

"You never asked." Merlin loosened his grip on the reins unconsciously, paying more attention to their conversation than to his riding, and his horse ambled cautiously forward.

"You played the girls' parts, right?" Lance asked airily.

Merlin stiffened at the assumption, but Arthur saw immediately where Lance had gotten the idea. The wizard was slight of build, with delicate, almost feminine features. And he was certainly dramatic enough for the stage.

"Sorry to disappoint, but I did the special effects."

"With actual magic?" Lance asked, falling back to ride alongside the lad and eagerly peppering him with questions about conjuring blood and rain.

Every so often, Lance corrected the boy's grip on his reins, and by the time they reached the forest of Lansdowne, Merlin's riding was much improved, and Lance's spirits seemed lifted.

They stopped briefly for lunch in the forest, and reached the other side just as the sun was beginning to set. A small, picturesque village nestled below, its thatched-roof cottages and modest church spire a welcome sight after hours of nothing but trees.

Brannor grimly surveyed their sweat-lathered horses and frowned at the darkening sky. "We'll rest in the village tonight," he declared. "I know a decent inn there."

"Yessir!" Dakin sang out, as though they were riding into battle, and not to soft beds and supper.

"Hold here a moment," Arthur called.

"Is something wrong, Your Highness?" Dakin asked with a frown.

Arthur sighed. He'd asked his guards not to call him that while they were traveling discreetly, but they kept forgetting. Dakin especially. The lad wasn't exactly the sharpest blade in the armory.

"No," said Arthur. "I just . . . wanted to take in the view for a moment." It sounded silly after he said it aloud. But the view really *was* something.

From their vantage above the village, rolling hills and meadows stretched in every direction. The sinking sun bathed everything in a soft, golden light.

Camelot. He forgot sometimes how far it extended beyond London. How the kingdom itself wasn't suffocating or unbearable. It was just his father's castle, and his future, that felt so oppressive.

A future that now included marriage to a complete stranger. His heart squeezed at the thought. Perhaps she wouldn't be so bad. Perhaps, like with Merlin, his father would have accidentally stumbled onto exactly the right choice.

He unfortunately doubted it. But there was no use worrying about it now. So he tried to put it out of mind and drink in this moment of absolute freedom. To reserve some of it within himself so that, on the next particularly grim day, he would remember. Sky. Horses. His best friend by his side. His clothing unadorned and comfortable, his evening clear of royal responsibilities. A life that, even in small part, still felt like his.

Merlin's horse nudged up next to his, breaking his train of thought.

"Surveying your kingdom?" the lad asked with a knowing smirk.

"Savoring my freedom," Arthur admitted, an embarrassed smile rising to his lips.

Merlin smiled back, and Arthur found himself staring at the delicate, soft pink of the boy's mouth. His pulse quickened, and he cleared his throat, glancing away, and urging his horse into a trot.

CHAPTER 16

The inn was a welcome sight, even though the building tilted forward precariously, and the windows were so slender that Emry wondered if they were any use at all. Not that she cared. The place could have been a windowless hovel, and she would have been overjoyed to see it.

She was dusty and sore after a long day's ride. Not to mention annoyed that the prince had picked up on her clumsy riding. It had been easier to feign inexperience on a horse, rather than have him guess the truth: that she had only ridden pillion or sidesaddle, as anything else would have caused a scandal and, apparently, done away with her virginity.

Well, that ship had departed a year ago, thanks to a troublesome playwright who'd neglected to mention his wife and son back in Warwick. And it had been nothing at all like sitting astride a saddle, so she had no idea what the fuss was about. In either case.

Emry had expected the inn to be quiet, but the main room was full of travelers. Men in dusty cloaks hunched over their cups, and a rowdy table in a corner had a game of dice going.

Thankfully, no one seemed to pay them much mind. After a long day of riding, their company looked just as unremarkable as everyone else.

Still, Arthur put up his hood, and Emry saw Lance's hand go to the sword concealed beneath his cloak.

"Popular place," said Lance, glancing around uneasily.

"A day's ride exactly from London," Brannor grunted. "We 'ent the only travelers who rest at nightfall."

"All of the tables are taken," Dakin complained.

"There's one, in the corner," Arthur said, pointing out a small round table crammed up against the hearth.

Lance went to make arrangements for supper and some rooms, and Emry followed the rest of them toward the terrible table. At first the guards balked to sit with the prince, but Arthur shot them a look.

"If you want to draw unnecessary attention, by all means, keep standing," he said mildly.

The guards gingerly took their seats. Emry had no such qualms. After all, she'd been sharing a table with Arthur most mornings in the wizard's workshop, often with him carrying up a second cup of coffee unasked. It was easy to forget who he was sometimes. That this brilliant, rumpled, dreamy-eyed boy was the crown prince of Camelot. That the sword casually belted around his dusty tunic was *the sword in the stone*.

Even though this quest was exhausting and stressful, and she'd probably have nightmares about peeing in the woods for months, it wasn't every day you went to Avalon.

Her gran had occasionally spoken of the Isle of the Blessed, and how she'd been a priestess there as a young girl. Emry could almost picture the wildflowers that bloomed year-round, the ancient stone caves, and the pale cloisters where the young priestesses lived, tending to the sacred waters and making soap.

The soap part had always made Emry laugh. "Making *soap*?" she'd repeated, stifling giggles.

And Gran would sigh, her patience lost, the story ending before it had even begun.

Emry sat gingerly in her chair, aching from a long day in the saddle.

"You'll get used to riding," Arthur said, looking far too amused at her discomfort.

"Or I'll figure out a way to magic the horse," she threatened.

Arthur shot her a dark look. He was about to say something back, but Emry never found out what, because a peal of coquettish laughter sounded from the bar.

"That would be Lance," Arthur said, nodding.

Emry glanced over, and sure enough. She watched, bemused, as Lance flirted shamelessly with a sour-faced woman of fifty who had to be the innkeeper's wife. By the time the woman took his coins, she was giggling girlishly and patting him on the shoulder.

Arthur shook his head, and even Emry bit back a smile at the woman's transformation.

"What?" Lance asked innocently, joining them.

"He always does this," Arthur told Emry.

"Because it always works," said Lance. He dangled a single brass key. "See? We've got the last room."

One room. For the *five* of them.

Everyone collectively groaned, and Emry slid down in her seat, wishing she could disappear under the table, or perhaps sleep there. She'd thought riding was bad, but at least she hadn't had to *share* the horse.

It'll be fine, she reassured herself as she dug into her stew. It wasn't as though they were stripping naked to bathe in a river. All she had to do was curl up on the floor with her coat as a blanket and her pack as a pillow. Still, as they hauled their things up the rickety staircase, Emry's stomach churned with dread over the close quarters.

The room was small and spare, with two narrow beds and a chair. The floor was covered with rushes, and a tiny window sat high on the far wall. There was a lone chamber pot beneath, and zero privacy with which to use it.

"Guess we're all usin' the jakes," said Dakin.

Lance snorted at the crass term for the outdoor privy. Arthur paled a little, but put on a brave face.

"Better than camping," he pronounced.

"Equivalent to camping," Emry corrected.

"I'm gonna agree with the wizard," said Lance.

"Nobles," Dakin grumbled, and Emry was about to protest that she was in no way a *noble*, when Brannor interrupted, taking charge.

"We'll have to leave at dawn to make Avalon before nightfall. The prince sleeps there." He pointed at the bed furthest from the door. "I'll take the floor. Dakin, you're on first watch."

Dakin looked betrayed.

"Wake me in a few hours and we'll switch," Brannor went on, unfastening his cloak.

"What about me?" Lance asked.

"You 'ent one of the prince's guards," Brannor reminded him. "You and Merlin can split the other bed."

Emry was already spreading her coat on the floor, and she glanced up, horrified.

"But I—" she began.

Dakin snickered meaningfully.

"Something you'd like to share?" Arthur asked the young guard, his tone sharp with warning.

"Nope." Dakin tried to stifle his amusement. Badly. "Nothing I'd like to *share*."

"I'll sleep on the floor," Lance mumbled. "It's fine."

"Absolutely not," Arthur said. "If you're not part of my guard, then you're here as my guest."

"*I'll* take the floor," Emry volunteered desperately.

"I don't blame you," smirked Dakin.

Lance's expression clouded with pain, and Emry wondered why he was so upset. Was he truly that intent on taking a watch?

"Merlin, would you just *share the sarding bed*?" Arthur hissed through gritted teeth.

"I'd prefer the floor," she insisted.

It was a mistake, and she realized that as soon as she'd said it. There was an awful, heavy silence. She couldn't figure out what had gone wrong.

Arthur looked like he wanted to punch her. Lance looked like he wanted to punch the wall. Dakin, for some reason, was *living* for it. Brannor let out a sigh, making it clear that he was too old for this, whatever *this* even *was*.

The prince's eyes blazed as he aimed a glare in her direction.

"That wasn't a suggestion," he said, quietly furious. "You're an inexperienced rider. If you sleep on the floor, you'll be too sore to get back on the horse tomorrow. Do I make myself clear?"

His expression dared her to argue any further. She'd never heard him speak like that before. As though he was issuing a command, and expected to be obeyed.

"Perfectly, Your Highness," she said, hatefully eyeing the narrow bed.

"So," chirped Dakin. "Now that we've all got our cozy bedfellows, who's first?" He kicked the chamber pot into the center of the room with a wicked grin.

Nope.

"I'll take my chances with the jakes," Emry retorted, bolting from the room before anyone could lower their hose and go first.

She officially *hated* this quest. She hated how sore she was from riding, and how Lance had behaved as though she'd insulted him terribly, and how Arthur had nearly lost his temper, and she still had no idea what she'd done wrong, or how to fix it. And on top of everything, she had to share a *bed* with an enormous, sweaty *boy*.

He better not snore. Or worse, *cuddle*.

When she returned to their room, only Dakin was awake, slouched wearily in a chair.

He smirked and mouthed, "Have fun!" at her. If Emry didn't already dislike him, that would have done it.

She stepped over Brannor, who was loudly snoring on the floor, and tried very hard not to stare at the sleeping prince, but failed miserably. He looked younger in his sleep. His features were softened, and his hair ruffled across the pillow. His lashes were two dark fans against his pale cheeks. He seemed troubled. Or maybe just sad. But it was a beautiful kind of sadness, and it looked well on him.

Emry tore her gaze away and sat down gingerly on the edge of her bed, peeling off her boots in the dim light from the room's sole candle.

Extergio, she thought, that familiar old spell from the theater. If she was going to sleep in her clothes, at least they'd be clean. She cast the spell on Lance's as well, as a sort of apology, and he mumbled in his sleep.

He was curled on his side, on the very edge of the bed, holding tight to his sword. Like Arthur, Lance looked even more troubled in his sleep.

"No, Jereth, don't," Lance murmured. "I love you . . ."

Jereth? Where had she heard that name before? And then she remembered: Arthur's youngest cousin. The one the boys had been so strange about when Lady Elaine had mentioned his return to the castle.

Ohhh, Emry thought as she eased herself onto the vacant sliver of bed. *That certainly explains things.* Like why Dakin was being such a smug arse about their sharing a bed. No wonder Lance had been so hurt and Arthur had been so furious when she'd insisted on taking the floor.

They thought her refusal was because Lance liked boys.

What a *disaster*.

She wished she could explain that she hadn't known, and even if she did, it made no difference. Half the boys in the theater troupe preferred each other's company, and at fourteen, Emry had found any excuse to walk past the smithy, in case the blacksmith's daughter Kira was at the forge.

She was pretty sure, however, that not all of the courtiers and guards at Uther's court were accepting of such things. Still, a preference for lads shouldn't have gotten Lance banned from becoming a knight. Something terrible must have happened.

That fight Lance had gotten into, defending his honor, and being punished for it. How everyone at court said his name as if they wished they could change the subject—well, everyone except Arthur.

And she trusted the prince's judgment. No wonder Arthur was so protective of his friend. The way they were so often together; it wasn't because Lance was protecting Arthur, it was actually the opposite.

She should have realized something was going on that night Lance had injured his wrist. It was obvious, in retrospect. She felt like a fool for stirring up trouble when they were all exhausted from a long day's ride. She'd been so terrified of her secret being discovered that she hadn't thought about anyone else.

She pulled up the blanket, her eyes adjusting to the dark. It wasn't so bad, sharing the bed. She was ashamed she'd made such a fuss over it. She curled onto her side, her back toward Lance, which of course meant she was staring across the short expanse at the sleeping prince.

The distance between them was so small that, if she reached out, she could touch his cheek. A hint of stubble shadowed his jawline, and she imagined running a finger across it. Imagined Arthur opening his soft brown eyes and smiling at her. Imagined the rest of the room, and its occupants, melting away, until it was just the two of them, alone.

Her stomach fluttered at the thought.

No, Emry scolded herself, *stop catching feelings for the prince*.

Nothing good could come of this.

She had better get ahold of herself, and fast.

CHAPTER 17

They left the inn at dawn, and made good time to Bedwynn Forest, not that Arthur was paying much attention to the road. He was more concerned with Lance, whose expression was downright tragic.

"Just say it," Arthur insisted midway through the morning.

"Why did you even invite me?" Lance sighed, and Arthur didn't blame him for being hurt.

"I thought it would be like old times." Arthur cringed as he heard the words come out of his mouth.

Lance leveled him with a glare. "Yeah, just you and me. And your magic sword and company of *assholes*." And then he urged his horse forward, riding between Arthur and his guards.

Arthur shook his head. He'd thought—well, Dakin's stance was no surprise, but Merlin? Ugh. He'd expected better. He had half a mind to give the lad a verbal thrashing for how he'd behaved.

But when he dropped back, he was surprised that Merlin looked even more miserable than Lance.

"Rough night?" Arthur asked, not very nicely.

"It's not what you think," the wizard said, ducking his head in embarrassment.

"Isn't it?" Arthur said coolly.

"I don't share beds. With *anyone*." The boy deliberated before adding, "Sometimes I, um, accidentally cast spells. In my sleep."

"In your sleep?" Arthur said curiously.

"You can't always control magic," Merlin retorted. "Anyway. I feel horrible. I was so panicked about my own problem that I never even thought about anyone else. I only realized afterward how bad it sounded."

Arthur could see that the lad was sincerely sorry. So all right, maybe he *hadn't* meant to cause such a terrible scene.

"You could have *said* something," Arthur said harshly.

Merlin shot him a skeptical look. "Right. And if I confessed that I *might* accidentally set fire to the curtains, your guards *wouldn't* have made me sleep in the stables?"

The wizard had a point. Brannor probably *would* have put him out with the horses.

"I'm not the one you owe an apology," said Arthur.

"I know."

"Well, I am, and I'll gladly take one," Lance called, falling back to join them. "Or three. Is the casting spells in your sleep more like a fart, or more like—"

"*Lance*," Arthur cut in.

"Like you weren't thinking the same thing."

"Definitely not," Arthur protested, shaking his head. Although he certainly was *now*.

At least Lance seemed to be in better spirits, Arthur thought. There was never a dull moment where Merlin was concerned.

"Wait. I've smelled like rosemary all morning," Lance accused, turning to the wizard. "Did you *magic my clothes clean* last night? In your sleep?"

"No, I did that on purpose," Merlin said. "You smelled like a horse."

◐ ◐ ◐

They reached the lake as the sun was beginning to dip below the horizon, and Emry suspected the priestesses knew they were coming. A small and ancient rowboat was waiting at the dock, along with a young woman in a long white dress, who promised to see to their horses.

Brannor eyed the girl suspiciously, as though she might be a threat, while Dakin preened, hoping to impress her. The girl soundly ignored him, much to Emry's delight. She caught Lance's eye, and he shook his head over Dakin's ridiculous strutting.

Thank goodness she'd been able to straighten out their misunderstanding. Even if it *had* meant telling yet another lie. Well, more of a stretch than a total fabrication. She really *had* set fire to the curtains in her sleep one time. Of course, she'd been twelve, and just starting to go through puberty. She hadn't realized she'd also bleed *magic*.

But it had been a convenient excuse, and one that Arthur and Lance had readily accepted for her panic over their sleeping arrangements. Maybe now she'd get a bed to herself. Although sharing with Lance wasn't the worst. Especially if it proved a point to Dakin.

Earlier that afternoon, while they rode, Lance had finally explained how he'd become a guard. She couldn't imagine having her heart broken *and* having everyone believe such a terrible lie at the same time. Emry felt awful for him.

"Well, you have a wizard in your corner, if you ever need one," she'd said.

"Better there than in my bed," Lance had teased. "You hog the blankets."

"You talk in your sleep!"

"At least it's just words, not spells."

"*Enough*," Arthur had scolded, but he was smiling.

Now, as they squinted across the misty lake, none of them were smiling. Because suddenly their destination felt all too real. There it was, faint but unmistakable in the distance: The Isle of the Blessed. *Avalon*.

Just as Gran had described in her stories, a thick swirl of mist hovered just above the surface of the water. It was a miracle they could even see the island.

Not a miracle, Emry realized. *Magic*. The mists of Avalon were magic.

Emry had heard many legends about the Isle, and she doubted even half of them were true. But apparently the one about the magic mist wasn't an exaggeration. Good to know.

"The boat is ready for you," the girl said, gesturing toward the rickety rowboat, which was equipped with a set of falling-apart oars.

They weren't all going to fit, Emry realized.

"You sure this boat's safe?" Brannor asked doubtfully.

"No one ever said passage to the Isle of the Blessed is safe," the girl retorted. "Only that it's possible."

"Well, that's not ominous," Lance muttered.

"For those staying behind," said the girl, "there's an inn just over the hill. You'll find your horses stabled there."

The girl clicked her tongue softly at the horses, which followed eagerly after her.

"So," Arthur said doubtfully. "I suppose we climb aboard."

No one made the first move.

"Oh, for goodness' sake," Emry scoffed, climbing into the boat. She hadn't come all this way to *not* see Avalon.

Arthur squared his shoulders and stepped in after her.

"I'm coming, too," Lance said, but before he could, the boat shot out from the dock of its own accord.

Emry's heart pounded in alarm. She stared down at the oars, still at the bottom of their boat.

"*Merlin*," Arthur warned.

"It's not me," Emry protested.

"I 'ent signed up for enchanted boats," Brannor exclaimed from the shore, which was growing smaller and smaller in the distance.

"We'll wait at the inn!" Lance called desperately, and then the shore was swallowed by the fog, and it was just the two of them. Alone. In an enchanted rowboat in the middle of a lake. A very *small* enchanted rowboat.

Emry glanced at the prince. He looked pale. He was clutching the side of the boat with one hand, and his sword with the other. She hoped he wasn't going to be sick.

"It's just a little magic," she said.

As disorienting as it was, at least they didn't have to row.

"That's—not—the problem," Arthur said through gritted teeth. "My sword's—well—look!"

His sword was trying to *escape*. As Emry watched, the blade wrenched itself loose from Arthur's scabbard. He surged to his feet, grabbing for it. The boat rocked precariously, but Arthur caught hold of the hilt. The sword vibrated harder, its tip pointing toward Avalon.

What on earth was happening?

"*Claudo*," commanded Emry, but her spell didn't work.

"Can't you—" Arthur asked.

"I'm *trying*!" Emry snarled. "*Prohibere!* Come on! Stop it, sword!"

Still nothing.

"I didn't realize 'Stop it, sword!' was a magic spell," Arthur said wryly.

Emry shot him a glare.

They were still zipping across the lake. The sword shook so intensely that the boat rocked side to side, sloshing water into the hull. Arthur didn't look like he could hold on much longer. And neither did the poor boat.

He dug in his heels, still keeping a grip on the sword. The boat rocked dangerously, and Emry had a sudden vision of them tipping.

Her disguise definitely wouldn't hold in wet, clinging clothing. Or worse, in none at all.

"Let go! We'll capsize!" Emry warned.

"Help—me—hold—it," he grunted back.

Emry grabbed the prince around the waist. But they were no match for the sword. It dragged them both forward, inch by inch.

The boat was beginning to tip . . .

"*Stabilis!*" Emry tried, but her magic had no effect. "You have to let go!"

The prow was nearly in the lake.

"I can't!" he cried as the sword twisted free from his hands.

They fell backward, landing in a heap. The boat rocked madly, but righted itself, to Emry's intense relief.

The sword hovered in the mist, its pommel inches above the surface of the lake. As they watched, a pale, seaweed-covered hand shot out of the water, grabbing the sword.

The hand and sword disappeared into the lake, and a rough churn bubbled up, stopping a moment later.

Emry blinked, confused as to what had just happened, but relieved it was over.

Arthur was still on top of her. Sard, he was heavy.

"You can get off me now," she complained.

He did, looking miserable. "It's gone," he said quietly, as though he couldn't believe it. "I've lost the sword in the stone."

"I'm sorry." She knew what the sword had meant to him. What it had represented. But there was nothing more they could have done.

Her magic didn't seem to work here, which she hadn't expected. In the past, there had been a few times when her magic was blocked, but she'd always been ill or injured. The only explanation was the mist. Gran *had* called Avalon an isle apart. Emry had always assumed she'd meant geographically.

Arthur put his head in his hands. And then he sat up, his expression cautiously optimistic.

"We've stopped moving," he said.

They had. They were floating where they'd lost the sword. Emry squinted toward the shore. They were in the middle of the lake, and the sun was sinking fast.

"I guess we row?" She offered him an oar.

Arthur leveled her with a look that plainly said, *Not happening.* He bent down, tugging off his boots.

"What are you doing?" she asked.

"Going after my sword," he said, as though it was obvious. He pulled open the neck of his tunic, and Emry flushed scarlet. "By all means, just sit there."

Emry rolled her eyes and dug her wand out of her coat. "*Erigo*," she said, pointing it at the water.

The lake emitted a rude noise that sounded remarkably like a wet fart.

"I don't think it's coming back," she said.

"It has to," Arthur said desperately, wrenching his linen tunic over his head.

He was very shirtless. Like a skin statue.

Emry glanced away, but not before Arthur unbuckled the scabbard from around his waist.

"You're not going in—naked?" she gasped, horrified.

"We both are. Clothes off, wizard."

Arthur folded his arms across his bare chest, waiting for her disrobe.

Oh no. There had to be a way out of this. She just had to think of one—fast.

Emry hoped the panic didn't show on her face. She reached for her boots, tugging one off as slowly as she could manage. She couldn't take her clothes off, but she couldn't very well go in with them *on*.

When she glanced up, Arthur was unfastening his codpiece.

Emry's panic flared.

Help! she thought. *Boat! Why aren't you moving?*

As if it understood her, the boat lurched forward, speeding toward Avalon once again.

She was so relieved that she almost laughed. She had no idea what she'd done, but it had worked, which was all that mattered.

"No!" Arthur cried, twisting over the side, looking for his lost sword. "Stop!"

Don't you dare, thought Emry.

At that, the boat actually went faster.

Good boat.

This was much easier than riding a horse. Or, for that matter, rowing a boat.

Magic didn't work on magic, but apparently *asking* the magic to do what she wanted wasn't out of the question. Good to know.

She snuck another look at Arthur, still barefoot and shirtless, standing at the prow of the boat. She swallowed thickly, managing to wrench her gaze away.

"Better get dressed," she said, tossing him his tunic. "Unless you want to greet the Lady of the Lake wearing nothing but your hose."

🌑 🌒 🌓

A tall, ethereal woman waited for them at the water's edge. The gossamer white of her dress shone against her copper-brown skin. Her face was ageless, and her dark hair, which hung in loose waves to her waist, was dressed with leaves and flowers. She stood still as a statue, her eyes the pale gray of morning mist.

Even though Emry had never seen her before, she knew immediately it was the Lady of the Lake. And so, apparently, did Arthur.

"My Lady," he said, sinking into a bow the moment he stepped ashore.

Emry bowed as well, having a bad feeling about this. Surely this sorceress would see through her disguise?

"I expected you sooner, Arthur Pendragon," said the Lady. Her voice dripped like honey, sweet and golden and wonderful. "And I see you have not come alone. The wizard suits you."

Emry straightened, staring at the Lady in surprise. But the Lady merely smiled back at her, although those mist-gray eyes seemed to convey a warning.

"Thank you, my Lady," Arthur said, his manners more formal than Emry had ever seen them. She watched as he stepped forward and took the Lady's hand. He knelt, bringing her hand to his lips. He seemed very much like a prince here, on this strange isle in the swirling mist, and not at all like the annoyed boy from the castle library.

"The great and powerful Merlin," the Lady went on, looking back and forth between them. "This was foretold. You have a destiny—both of you. You will be a great king with this wizard by your side."

Emry frowned. Surely the Lady knew that she was a girl? That Arthur had the wrong twin?

"Nothing would bring me more joy," Arthur said, his head bowed. "But my Lady, I came here with a sword. And that sword is now lost at the bottom of the lake."

"Then you have done your duty. You brought the sword home," she explained. "It was never meant to remain yours. It was only proof of your destiny for those who would demand such a thing."

"Is *that* why the sword wasn't magic?" Emry asked, forgetting herself. "Only enchanted?"

The Lady nodded. "You are clever, wizard," she said. "And cleverer still that you did not give chase to the sword. What the lake takes as payment for safe passage is beyond my control."

Emry shot Arthur a smug look, implying that she'd known it was a bad idea to jump in. Arthur rolled his eyes in return.

"Come," said the Lady, beckoning for them to follow her up the shore. "We will find you another sword, Arthur Pendragon. A better sword." She cut a knowing look at Arthur. "One day soon, you will usher in a golden age of peace and tolerance. An era of great learning and great understanding."

"But how will I?" Arthur pressed.

The Lady merely smiled. Then she held out her hand. "And you, child of the wizard Merlin," she said, her eyes boring into Emry's, as if to say, *I have chosen my words carefully.*

I'm sorry for deceiving you, Emry thought.

I am not deceived, the Lady's voice said inside Emry's head, as clearly as if she'd spoken aloud. *Your truth is not mine to tell.*

Thank you, Emry replied in her head, somehow not at all startled by this strange turn of events. After all, she'd already conversed with a boat.

"Perhaps," continued the Lady, "you would like to see our famous soap?"

Emry barely caught herself before laughing aloud.

CHAPTER 18

As Emry followed a young priestess through the cloister, she tried not to worry about Arthur, whom she'd left with the Lady of the Lake. Instead, she forced herself to concentrate on what the girl was saying.

". . . which is why our waters here are sacred. Any injured traveler that the lake allows across may bathe their wounds and take their cure."

The priestess threw a lingering glance over her shoulder at Emry.

Really? Emry repressed a sigh. The girl couldn't have been older than fourteen.

At least it meant her disguise was holding, despite the mysterious magic of the isle. With nearly every turn through the vaulted corridor, Emry caught clusters of young girls peering at her curiously, whispering and giggling behind their hands. So she acted as her brother would have, and adopted a cocky grin as though enjoying the attention.

"So the magic water heals them," Emry summarized, with that maddening confidence boys always seemed to have toward subjects they knew nothing about.

The girl hesitated. "Not exactly," she said, her hand on an elaborately carved knob to a wooden door. "The waters do little to ease their suffering, as they only heal physical wounds."

The room was arched and made entirely of stone, like an ancient treasure vault, and the air was thick with steam. In its center sat a dark, thick oblong pool of water. The pool smelled faintly of minerals, but also of deep, pungent spices and ancient magic. Ribbons of mist curled from its surface, beckoning her nearer.

Emry stared down at the smooth surface, feeling a strong urge to walk closer, to look closer . . . *no*. That was the magic pulling her. She shook her head, clearing it, and took a step back, trying to remember what the priestess had just said. Something about suffering.

"What—um—what wounds can't the water heal?" Emry asked.

"To brush so close to death, to undertake such a desperate quest to live, many never recover," the girl went on. "They find themselves . . . haunted . . . by their own minds."

Emry followed the girl to an enormous wooden cabinet, which was carved with stags and flowers. The girl solemnly opened the doors, revealing stacks of translucent soap. The bars were rectangular in shape, and they gave off the unmistakably spicy scent of magic.

"Wow," Emry said politely. "Lots of soap."

"We ask the travelers to bathe with it, as it eases suffering of the mind."

"Oh, so it's magic soap," Emry said, thinking of the healing potions Master Ambrosius had promised she'd start learning next week.

"Enchanted," the girl corrected. "It makes them forget their troubles—what they have seen, what they have done, what they have lost. When the travelers are strong enough, they leave. But many become accustomed to having their demons be kept at bay. Many come back, desperate for more soap. Desperate enough to trade their daughters for a life's supply."

Emry stared at the girl in horror. Her grandmother had never told her *this* part. "Is that how *you* came to live here?"

The girl bowed her head. "If you stay too long on Avalon, the mist won't let you return home," the girl said, her voice small. "You become bound to the isle and its magic. Some girls still hope to pass through when they're of age, but I came here as a baby."

Emry shivered. So the girls—the priestesses—were stuck here. All because their selfish fathers had struck desperate bargains with the sorceress. They weren't magic, not like the Lady of the Lake. Which made sense, because her gran hadn't been magic, either.

"My grandmother was a priestess here," Emry said, realizing.

"Yes, we know that story well. It's why the Lady keeps us away from the travelers," the girl said. She hesitated before adding, "Your father was born on Avalon."

Emry gaped at the girl.

Her *father* had been born here? Her grandmother had been sold to the Lady of the Lake? Emry felt as though her brain was breaking from all of this new information.

"Perhaps," the girl suggested gently, "you have seen enough of the soap?"

◖ ◖ ◖

Arthur followed the Lady of the Lake through the forest, feeling entirely disarmed without his sword and his traveling companions. Merlin had been led away by a blushing maiden under some ridiculous pretense concerning soap. And now the young wizard was probably lounging in a perfumed bath, being attended by beautiful priestesses. Meanwhile, he was trailing through the woods after a powerful, terrifying sorceress, without so much as a sword.

You chose this, he reminded himself. *This quest was your idea.*

Whether it was a good idea or a bad one remained to be seen.

Right now, he was thinking bad.

A keening wail that started off like a teakettle and ended as a scream rattled through the trees. Arthur stiffened, feeling the hairs on the back of his neck prickle. It might have been the wind, but then again, it might not. The Lady didn't seem to notice, so Arthur tried to pretend he hadn't, either.

The island felt . . . not quite haunted, but not *not* haunted. It was uncanny. And most uncanny of all was the Lady herself. Arthur couldn't imagine *her* using the jakes at a travelers' inn.

She probably didn't even pee.

Stop thinking about pee, Arthur ordered himself, which of course made him think about it more. He wished the Lady would say something to distract him. But she walked in silence, leading him deeper into the forest.

The trees here were so ancient and thick that their branches twisted together overhead, blotting out the sky. Leaves crunched beneath his feet, yet there was no birdsong, and no presence of animals. It was almost as though the forest was holding its breath, either out of fear or anticipation.

Finally, they reached an enormous cave, hewn into the side of a mountain. The cave seemed to glow from within.

"Come, Arthur Pendragon, and we shall see about that sword."

He couldn't very well return home without one, so he steeled his nerves and followed her inside. The ceiling dripped daggers of glowing ice and rock, and the stone floor echoed with every step he took. The Lady's feet moved soundlessly, because of course they did.

"What is this place?" he asked.

For a moment, he thought the Lady might not answer, but then she said, "The tomb of an ancient king, whom history has forgotten. A king from a different world. This isle exists because of his blessing, and endures because of his curse."

Nope, not creepy at all, Arthur thought.

The Lady ducked through an arched doorway, and Arthur followed. In the center of the room sat a raised tomb. As Arthur stared at it, he became convinced that the space they were standing in had been carved away, and that the tomb was part of the cave itself, like a statue hewn from a block of marble.

"Step inside," said the Lady. "And the king will judge whether you are worthy."

At first Arthur thought she meant the room, but then he realized she meant the *tomb*.

She wanted him to lie down inside the tomb. And be judged. What would happen if he *failed*? His stomach twisted with fear, and his feet felt frozen in place.

But there was no turning back now. So he forced himself to take a tentative step forward, and then another.

The tomb was covered with unfamiliar symbols, and he could feel a strange magic rising from within, first in a crackle, and then in a steady, throbbing pulse that deepened as he approached.

The magic set his teeth on edge as he lay down on top of the cool, ancient stone.

The Lady stood over him, and a cold, bright glow rose from the edges of the tomb. She murmured something too low for him to hear, and traced a mark upon his forehead that burned like ice.

And then he was falling.

He was no longer in the tomb, or the cave. That much was clear. He sat up cautiously, squinting into the pale, swirling light.

Not light, he realized. *Mist*.

The mist cleared, and he was surprised to find he knew this place: his mother's bedchamber. She was alive, but barely. Weak with fever, her dark hair stuck damply to her forehead. She looked up at him with glassy eyes. His heart twisted at the sight of her after all this time.

"Arthur," she whispered through cracked lips. "My medicine. Please."

"Of course, Mother," he said, spotting two elixirs upon a silver tray. One was stoppered with iron, and one with gold.

"Which one is it?" he asked helplessly.

"Hurry," his mother whispered, closing her eyes.

So—he'd have to choose. They didn't look like medicine. This was a test, he realized. An ordeal.

He opened the iron-stoppered bottle and sniffed. Clear. Odorless. It could be medicine, or water, or the worst kind of poison.

And then he opened the gold. It was exactly the same.

He didn't know which to give her.

"Hurry, my child," his mother said with a weak cough.

He couldn't chance it. Couldn't give her something that would make her suffer. But he had to do something. And then he noticed a humble carafe of water and a wooden cup.

With a heavy heart, he brought the cup of water to his mother.

"Your medicine," he told her.

"Thank you, my son," she said as he held the cup to her lips. "I'll be better soon."

"I know you will," he lied as her eyes fluttered closed. He couldn't save her. Not even here, in this moment that felt like a memory crossed with a dream.

The room melted away, changing into the castle's weapons room. He was on the floor, gasping as he clasped at a sharp pain in his side. His cousin Gawain stood over him, the tip of a wooden practice sword pressed against his throat. Gawain's cheeks were round with baby fat, and he looked perhaps eight years old.

Arthur remembered this fencing match. He had slipped in a puddle of melted candle wax and broken two ribs from his fall. He could feel the wax now, warm and sticky against his leg. They had been tied for blows until then, but Gawain had shamefully taken a false victory, and had bragged to the entire court that he was the superior swordsman while Arthur was stuck in the infirmary. Arthur had lost his taste for weapons after that match. In the weeks that followed, he'd recovered in bed, reading stack after stack of books to escape the humiliation and the pain.

"Do you yield?" Gawain asked haughtily, glaring down at Arthur.

Yes, he thought. *I'm done.*

"No," he choked out, rolling onto his side. He climbed painfully to his feet, splinting his ribs with his left hand. "En garde."

"You can't win like that," said Gawain.

"Doesn't matter," Arthur said through gritted teeth. "The question is whether *you'll* fight me like this."

Arthur raised his blade. Gawain stared at him, conflicted.

"Which is it?" Arthur asked his cousin. "A dirty fight, or an honorable draw?"

Again, the scene melted away.

He was in the courtyard behind the Crooked Spire, his hands clasped around the sword in the stone. No matter how much he pulled, it didn't come loose.

The crowd laughed and jeered at him. But instead of strangers, they were his father's courtiers.

"Give up!" Lord Howell bellowed, throwing a rotten tomato.

The foul fruit hit Arthur on the cheek, its sour juice dripping down his face. He winced, but didn't let go of the sword.

Come on, he thought. *Come loose.*

"You'll never do it!" The crowd parted to let the speaker through, and Arthur saw it was his father. "Be honest, Arthur. You don't want this."

His father was right. *Had* been right. At least, Arthur had thought so at the time. But he didn't feel that way anymore.

"Maybe not now," Arthur allowed, "but the sword wants me. The sword *chose* me."

"Mistakes happen." This from Lord Agravaine. "Perhaps if you refuse, the sword will choose again. Rightly, this time."

Arthur froze. He had the same fear—that all of this was a mistake, and if he just admitted it, he could have his life back. But the sword *had* chosen him, and the only thing standing in his way was—well—himself. His father's courtiers could think what they wanted. They didn't know the future any better than he did.

Still, they stared back at him, waiting.

"It's not a mistake," said Arthur. "Just because I don't understand it doesn't make it less true. The sword was right to choose me. This is my destiny."

As he spoke those final words, they rang out across the courtyard, and the sword came loose.

The scene melted away.

The mist swirled around him once again, except this time no new scene unfolded. Instead, there were faint echoes within the vapors. Arthur strained, realizing he could see himself in those echoes. Was this his future?

There he was, leading men armed to fight, with Lance at his side. Staring down at a tiny baby in a cradle. Kissing Merlin—no, that couldn't be right—he tried to see better, but the image twisted. He was sailing on a great boat, standing next to a girl with dark hair. He was in a dungeon. Injured. Dying. He was—wait, no—not yet.

With a lurch, Arthur was once again lying in the tomb. Or perhaps he had never left. His body felt strangely stiff and disused, and his heart thundered against his rib cage.

His hands grew heavy, and when he looked down, he found he was holding a sword. A scabbard he'd never seen before was buckled around his waist, its leather blackened with age, the runes etched down its length worn illegible over time.

He sat up, marveling at the blade. It was thin and impossibly light, with a golden cross guard that swept back dramatically toward the pommel, featuring intricate carvings of knots and branches. The sword glowed from within, filling the dark cave with what almost passed for warm, golden sunlight. He had never seen a blade like it. Losing the sword in the stone didn't feel quite so awful anymore.

"Does this sword have a name?" he asked the Lady.

"It is called Excalibur," said the Lady of the Lake, "and those who wield it are unbeatable in battle."

Excalibur.

It couldn't be.

Like everyone else, he'd grown up on tales of the famous blade, lost centuries ago. Of the legendary sword used to defeat monsters in an age of magic, a glowing weapon that brought entire armies to their knees. A sword that many believed had been destroyed by Saxon conquerors, or hidden where it would never be found.

It was the sword of a warrior, not a teenage boy who read too many books and kept potted plants in his bedroom window. But it was more than that: it was the sword of the one true king.

"I shouldn't have this," Arthur protested. He wished there were somewhere to set it down, but the tomb was lacking in convenient side tables.

"It is yours," said the Lady. "The sword in the stone chose you. And Excalibur recognizes that choice, of its own free will."

Arthur stared down at the sword, which continued to glow.

"You have proven yourself to the sword. Its glow shows that you are worthy to wield such a blade," said the Lady. "But I find it curious you don't ask about the scabbard."

"The scabbard?"

"It carries a most valuable enchantment: any who wears it is unkillable in combat."

"*What?*" Arthur yelped, forgetting himself. He knew of no magic that could create such an enchantment. "How is that possible?"

"The scabbard belongs to the King of Anwen," said the Lady. She caught sight of Arthur's frown and added, "You might know it as the Otherworld. A place where magic is wild and monsters are bold. Such enchantments are possible there. The wall between our two worlds is thin on Avalon. Occasionally things travel through the stones, but they cannot remain here forever. Nor are they meant to. The King of Anwen will call back what is his, once it has served its purpose."

The Lady paused, as though expecting Arthur to ask what that purpose might be, but he bit back his question, knowing she would give him no true answer.

As Arthur climbed from the tomb, the Lady gave him a long, hard look. "I did not expect that scabbard to come with Excalibur," she said. "Remember that it did, the next time you doubt your destiny."

◑ ◑ ◑

Emry woke to the sound of screaming.

She sat up in the small, windowless bedchamber, her heart pounding as she fumbled for her bedside candle.

"*Ignium*," she ordered, but the stubborn thing remained unlit.

Come on, Emry thought crossly, *any light will do.*

The room flooded with a bright glow that came from, of all places, the tip of her wand.

That worked. She squinted as her eyes adjusted to the glare. The noise sounded again. It was more howl than scream, and it was coming from outside.

What if it was Arthur? Or something that had *caught* Arthur?

Emry shivered at the thought. She hadn't seen the prince since they'd arrived on Avalon. And she worried about him, especially without a sword to defend himself.

She tried the doorknob. It was locked, of course, from the outside.

Open, please, she thought, and to her surprise, the thick wooden door swung open.

She stepped into the cold night air of the cloister's inner courtyard, wishing she had a thicker cloak. Her breath fogged, and she clasped her cloak more tightly around her shoulders. The stone building rose up around her like a fortress, its endless arches ghostly pale in the moonlight. Emry held her wand out in front of her as though it was a weapon, but the cloister was dark and silent.

She was alone.

Except for the creature that sat motionless in the courtyard. It was smaller than a fox, but with a spiked, sinuous tail like a dragon's, which was covered in iridescent scales. Its fur was pure white, its face sleek and beautiful, its eyes ancient and knowing.

Emry stared at the creature, transfixed. She'd never seen anything like it.

"What are you?" she whispered.

The creature didn't answer. Again, the scream sounded from deep within the forest. The creature lifted its nose, and then darted through the arch that led out of the cloister.

Emry knew she had little choice but to follow.

The soft glow from her wand barely illuminated her path, and she stumbled over rocks and roots as the forest rose up around her. But she kept following the sleek white beast that bounded effortlessly through the trees.

Eventually, they came to a clearing, trees giving way to moss and brambles, and Emry startled at where the creature had led her.

An ancient arch made of immense stone slabs sat in the middle of the clearing, still and waiting and pale as alabaster in the moonlight.

A henge. Built hundreds, perhaps thousands of years ago, they were meant to hold open the doors between worlds, and to keep them from closing for good. She had never seen one before—not a real one.

She couldn't believe it was still standing. Well, most of it. Emry stared at the ancient stones, some leaning, some fallen, others cracked in two, wondering if it still worked. If it had *ever* worked.

Growing up, she'd loved these bedtime stories best, the ones about heroes who traveled through the stones and found themselves in a strange land full of monsters and magic. She had begged Gran for them, and for many years she'd fallen asleep dreaming of Anwen.

The creature leapt nimbly atop a stone at the center of the henge. It sat and watched her with knowing eyes, as if waiting for something.

"Did you bring me here on purpose?" Emry whispered.

The creature didn't answer. Instead, it bowed its head, giving her permission to come closer. Emry approached it gingerly, her hand extended. Its fur was soft as silk, but shockingly cold. Emry gasped, pulling away as though she had plunged her hand into a bank of snow.

Help me.

The words were as clear in Emry's mind as if the creature had spoken them aloud.

"How?" she asked.

Send me home. To the world beyond the stones.

"I can try," Emry promised. She had never seen its like. How lonely it must be, all by itself in a strange place.

She thought back to Gran's stories, remembering the soft, rhythmic words that had long ago lulled her to sleep.

So the girl pricked her finger, and her blood dripped forth onto the stones, each precious drop containing iron, from the world of man, and salt to ward away the monsters that thirst for such a place.

Emry smiled as she spotted the tangle of wild berries, thick with thorns. They would do. She pressed her finger to a thorn, watching a bead of blood gather at the tip.

Carefully, she smeared a drop of blood to either side of the stone doorway.

The creature blinked at her, watching. And Emry reminded herself of the next part of the story:

But what the girl had given was not enough. And so she cut deeper into her flesh,

until it was not just blood that flowed, but magic. As her magic dripped onto the altar,
she bid the door to open in the language of the ancients.

Emry dragged her palm across the brambles, hissing from the pain.
The creature jumped down from the stone where it had been sitting.

Here, it seemed to say. When Emry pressed her bleeding hand against
the stone, she felt a deep vibration that thrummed through her, setting her
teeth on edge.

Gran's stories had never included the words she would need to open
the doorway. But no matter: this was why she had learned not just spells,
but the languages they came from.

She cleared her throat and spoke the words that would open a door.
"Aperi ianuam."

Nothing happened. Emry made a face and tried again. *"Openian duru,"*
she ordered.

There was a sharp crack, as though a branch had snapped underfoot.
But it came from deep in the forest.

Emry shook her head. Perhaps it had been just a story her Gran had
told. Or perhaps sending the creature home took more magic than she had.
Still, she hated to walk away after coming this far. She could figure it out.
She had to.

"ἄνοιξε την πόρτα," Emry said, the Greek low and lovely on her tongue.

For a moment nothing changed, and then the henge began to
tremble. The stone beneath her palm pressed back, and Emry gasped as
magic flowed out of her, flooding into the stone.

She struggled to blink back the dizziness. It was like the healing spell
she'd performed on Lance, only worse. The air between the standing stones
shimmered, then began to glow. Emry could just make out a faint landscape
forming beyond it, one that wasn't the forest.

A cliff the color of bone. A beach of strange pink rocks. A wine-dark sea.

The creature arched its back and padded through the doorway, silent and graceful as a cat. The air rippled behind it, and the creature stared back at Emry from the other side of the doorway, just for a moment.

Then it bounded away, toward the cliffs. Emry watched, pleased.

She should get back. This doorway frightened her, as did the screaming forest.

Emry tried to lift her hand from the altar, and found that she couldn't. The stone was still sucking at her magic. The beach on the other side of the doorway grew more solid. Now Emry could smell the salt water, and hear the crash of the waves. She could see the stars that powdered the sky with unfamiliar constellations.

But more than that, she could sense the magic on the other side of the doorway, calling out to her.

Something you want?

Something you wish?

Something you desire?

Emry stared, transfixed, as the pink rocks on the beach began to glow with an otherworldly light. She could take one. Or two. Just a flick of her hand should do it.

Emry licked her lips, imagining the warm, solid weight of the stone. Imagining the power it contained, and what she might do with such magic.

No. She pulled, trying to wrench her palm from the stone, but it was stuck. Panic flared in her chest as she pulled again.

On the other side of the doorway, the pink rocks chattered like teeth.

"*κλείσε την πόρτα*," commanded a harsh voice from the edge of the clearing,

The Lady of the Lake.

The stone released, and Emry stumbled backward, catching her balance just in time to watch the doorway fade.

Now they were just stones. Emry was breathing hard, as if she'd been running. Though the night air was cold, she found she was damp with sweat.

"What are you doing?" the Lady of the Lake demanded, a lantern held high, her expression fierce.

"My Lady," Emry said, with a short bow that had become second nature after the time she'd spent at court. "I'm sorry. I—"

"Your chamber was locked, was it not, Child of Merlin?"

"It was," Emry said, not quite daring to meet the Lady's gaze. "I heard screaming. I thought Arthur might be in trouble."

"The prince is in no danger here," said the Lady. "Avalon recognizes its future king. My forest screams because its magic was taken without permission. Taken by one who would open a doorway through any means possible."

The Lady stared at Emry, as though wondering whether she had been planning the same thing.

"I have no interest in taking magic that doesn't belong to me," Emry said.

The Lady's expression turned grave. "That's not what it looked like."

Emry winced, hating that the Lady was right. For a moment, she had been tempted. For more than a moment.

"I was only trying to help," Emry insisted. "A creature led me here. It was small, like a fox, but so strange. It asked me to send it home." She lifted her chin. "It seemed so lost, I figured I had to try."

The Lady stared at her in surprise. "What happened to the creature?"

"It went through the henge," Emry said. "But after it did, the stone wouldn't let me go. I—thank you, for coming when you did."

The Lady of the Lake considered her. "That was the Questing Beast," she said. "Many men have wasted their lives in pursuit of that creature. Its blood can bring someone back from a freshly dug grave, but its bite is a pain worse than any mortal wound."

Emry swallowed nervously. She'd knelt down and petted it like a puppy. "I didn't know," she said.

The Lady of the Lake's expression softened. "Be careful, child," she warned. "Your heart was in the right place, but you were foolish to open something you didn't know how to close. Such doors go both ways."

"I'm sorry," Emry mumbled again.

The Lady was right, she *had* been foolish. Her palm stung, and when she stared down at it, she saw that her wound had closed, replaced by a thin scar that shone bright silver.

"You showed great strength, to resist the temptation of Anwen's magic," said the Lady. "Perhaps I needn't have locked your door after all."

Emry frowned. But the Lady didn't say anything else. She merely motioned for Emry to follow her back to the cloister.

Emry fell gratefully into bed, exhausted. While she slept, she dreamed of strange animals in the forest, and of her father, trapped in a slab of stone. And then the dream shifted, and it was no longer her father who was trapped in the stone.

It was her.

● ● ●

When the Lady knocked at her bedchamber door the next morning, Emry was waiting, her belongings already packed. She had slept fitfully, plagued by nightmares after her encounter with the Questing Beast. At least she'd brought a book, which she'd read by wand light, trying very hard not to think about the strange creature, or how unwise she had been to chase it, or her confusing dream.

As they walked through the cloister, the Lady floated ahead of Emry, as though daring her to break the silence.

"My Lady?" Emry said tentatively. "One of the priestesses said my father was born on Avalon. Did he come here often?"

"On occasion. But he kept his own counsel, as wizards and men do. I was surprised to learn he had children."

"I think everyone was," said Emry before she could help herself. She mustered her courage before asking, "Do you know what happened to him?"

The Lady gave her a long, hard look.

"The sorceress Morgana took his life."

Emry closed her eyes, her throat tight, willing back tears. Willing back all the hope she'd held on to, even after the rest of her family had moved on. Her father was gone. She had known it for a long time, but she hadn't truly accepted it. Not while there was still a chance, however slight. Now there was no hope left. Just stale grief. And anger. Whoever this Morgana was, she had killed Father. The greatest wizard Camelot had ever known.

Well, if she couldn't have her father back, at least she could have some answers.

"But why?" Emry insisted. "Who was she?"

"Like you, she was born gifted in the ways of magic," said the Lady. "But she craved power. Revenge. Magic beyond what is possible in this world." The Lady gave Emry a piercing stare. "She demanded knowledge that was not mine to give. And power that was not hers to take. I warned your father, yet he did not heed my warnings and took her as his pupil."

His pupil? That didn't sound like Father at all. Emry had barely convinced him to let her share her brother's lessons. But apparently Morgana was so talented that Father had taught her magic, despite the Lady of the Lake's cautions. It was hard not to feel resentful.

"Is she . . . the reason why your forest screams?" Emry asked.

The Lady nodded gravely. "Terrible things happen when magic doesn't consent. Someone—or something—must suffer." She laid a hand on Emry's arm. "But do not concern yourself with Morgana, child. You have troubles enough without her."

Emry stared at the Lady, her head spinning from what she'd just learned.

"So she's still al—" Emry began, but the Lady held up a hand.

"She is nothing to you. A cautionary tale. While yours is a legend that is barely begun."

"Thank you, my Lady. I think," Emry said, confused.

"You care very much for the boy who will be king."

Emry considered denying it before she realized the Lady already saw what was in her head. "Too much," she admitted. "I don't know how much longer I can lie to him. To everyone."

"Your truth will reveal itself. The right moment will come soon enough. And so will the wrong one."

Emry almost snorted. It was like talking to living, breathing tea leaves.

"Before you shed your disguise, you must protect Arthur from those who would stand against him," the Lady went on.

"How, my Lady?" Emry pressed.

"The how I cannot see. Nor the whom. Even the future keeps its secrets," said the Lady. "Arthur has the potential to become a great king, but he does not know his value. Compassion is his greatest strength. The king who rules with an iron fist exerts his own will, not the will of his people."

"Do you mean King Uther?" Emry asked.

"Uther exerts no will at all. Soon he will fade into obscurity. But Arthur is destined for greatness." The Lady's eyes flickered, going momentarily white. It was almost as though they had filled with mist. "You will return here together. There will be blood and sorrow and pain."

Emry stared at the Lady, unnerved. But the Lady didn't seem to realize she'd said anything.

They had reached the dock. The boat was waiting, along with a yawning, tousle-haired Arthur, who had an unfamiliar sword belted around his waist, and looked extremely ready to get the hell out of Avalon.

CHAPTER 19

Arthur fiddled absently with his magic scabbard as they sailed away from the Isle of the Blessed. He still didn't know what to make of the visions he'd had in the tomb. They unsettled him, deeply. And he didn't feel as though he'd gained any knowledge by coming here. If anything, he had even more questions.

The Lady of the Lake had confirmed his greatest fear: That it was no mistake he'd pulled the sword from the stone. That this High King business was real.

Which was terrifying. But not unexpected. At least, not after what he'd experienced in the tomb. He was just now coming to terms with what it meant to one day become King of Camelot. With all of the ways his future belonged to the kingdom, to be spent in its best interest.

And he had a terrible suspicion that best interest was war. Because what use were a magic sword and scabbard except to kill people? The stories he knew of Excalibur were of great battles won, or horrible monsters slain. Excalibur and its scabbard were the sword and sheath of a killer who couldn't be killed in return.

He didn't want that to be his fate. Surely there was some other path. One that didn't lead to blood-soaked battlefields, where he'd always be amongst the few left standing, his blade stained red and his path home littered with corpses of men who had fought under his command. Men who had left families and friends and unfinished lives behind, never to return.

He'd never pictured himself at the head of an army. He'd imagined so many other things: the hushed calm of a university library, the merriment of a tavern full of drunken scholars. The girl he might have met, who came to know him as a person before discovering he was a prince.

He'd certainly never imagined he had any great destiny. It had been a relief, being told he was a spare. Being given that freedom, and that measure of control over his future. And it had been difficult, watching it all vanish, and realizing he would need to lead the kingdom after all.

But nothing had prepared him for the fear that the course of history rested squarely on his shoulders. That he would need to do more than any King of Camelot had done before.

He sighed, wondering how everything had gone so sideways. When he'd undertaken this quest, he'd thought the Lady of the Lake would tell him what to do with his existing sword, not give him another *actually magic* one.

But just as curious as this extremely magic sword was what the Lady had said about Merlin. She'd told Arthur he would be a great king with the wizard by his side. And then, what he'd seen in the mist . . . the two of them *together*.

What? He didn't—he'd never felt that way about another boy—and yet, something within him stirred at the thought of pressing his lips against the young wizard's. Which was the last thing he needed with his future wife arriving at the castle within the week.

"Okay, what?" Merlin asked, interrupting Arthur's thoughts. "You're staring at me weird."

"I wasn't staring at you." Arthur protested, even though he had been. "I was staring pensively into the mist."

"My mistake." The wizard smirked and took out a book. It was borrowed from the castle library, Arthur noticed. He craned his neck, trying to get a look at the title.

"You're *definitely* staring at me now," Merlin accused.

"Because you're reading a book. In a boat."

"I'll put it away if you tell me about that sword you're wearing," the wizard bargained.

Well played, Arthur thought. He'd wondered if Merlin would notice. He stared down at the worn leather scabbard helplessly, unsure how to even begin.

"Well, it's magic," he tried.

"Obviously." Merlin looked smug. "So it all worked out. You lost one sword, and the Lady of the Lake had a better one waiting for you."

"How do you know this one's better?" Arthur asked, curious.

"It has a vibe," Merlin insisted, waving a hand airily. "Like, 'Hello, I am ancient and very magic, please tremble in fear.'"

Arthur snorted. "Yeah, that's Excalibur all right."

Merlin's eyes went wide. "Wait, you mean *the* Excalibur? The unbeatable sword that's been lost for centuries?"

"So you've heard of it," Arthur said with satisfaction.

"And she just *gave* it to you?"

"Not exactly."

Arthur explained about the cave and the tomb, and Merlin's eyes grew even wider. It *was* a hell of a story, Arthur had to admit. And telling it made him feel a little more worthy of wearing the ancient blade.

"You had to face your insecurities," the wizard summarized, looking thoughtful.

"Something like that. Highly not recommended, by the way."

"I'll bet." Merlin hesitated, as if deliberating whether or not to say something.

"What?" Arthur prompted.

The wizard grimaced and looked down, tracing a silvery scar on his right palm that Arthur hadn't seen before. "The Lady of the Lake says that my father is dead," Merlin said quietly. "I mean, I knew that. I'd just—I'd just hoped."

"It never gets easier, does it? Losing a parent," Arthur replied with a ragged sigh. Some days he missed his mother so much that it was unbearable. On others he forgot to be sad, which felt even worse.

"Try losing both." The young wizard offered him a pained smile.

Arthur was suddenly very glad that Merlin had come with him. That they had both faced the strange magic of Avalon. That, for once, he wasn't alone on his journey, but traveling a parallel path with a friend.

"Now how about you show me this extremely magic sword?" prompted the wizard.

Arthur unfastened the sheath from around his waist. "The Lady of the Lake said the blade glows for any who are worthy," he warned, holding out the scabbard.

Merlin hesitated a moment, then drew the sword. The blade flashed bright as sunlight.

Interesting, thought Arthur. Somehow, he'd expected as much.

"It really does glow, like in the stories." Merlin let out an incredulous laugh, high and clear as a bell.

He looked well, holding the sword. His slim shoulders curved forward, and his dark hair ruffled in the breeze off the lake. There, in the mist, he was like something out of a legend.

Sard. Arthur had never *noticed* anyone like this before. His gaze was constantly drawn to Merlin's smile, and to the wicked glint in the lad's eyes, which he was starting to suspect was magic bubbling to the surface.

Magic. That *had* to be what was drawing his attention. The wizard was made of magic, radiating it even in his sleep. It was probably the magic Arthur couldn't stop noticing. The magic that had made his heart beat faster when Merlin had grabbed him around the waist to stop his sword from jumping ship. The magic that made him want to protect the lad, even before the Lady of the Lake had hinted he might need to.

◐ ◐ ◐

"Finally!" said Lance, when the prince and the wizard turned up at the inn. "Dakin was convinced you'd capsized."

In truth, Lance had nearly been convinced of it himself. It had been agony, waiting and not knowing. He'd never been so relieved to see anyone in his life.

"What are you talking about?" Arthur asked, confused.

"We were gone one night," Merlin added.

Lance frowned. How could they not know? "It's been *four days*," he told them.

Arthur's brow creased with concern, and Merlin looked absolutely horrified.

"Four days?" the wizard yelped, turning toward Arthur. "Why didn't you *tell* me time moves differently on Avalon?"

"I didn't know!" Arthur said, shaking his head in disbelief. "Sard, has it *really* been four days?"

"If I was messing with you, I would have come up with something a lot worse than *four days*," Lance pointed out.

It was no wonder the island stood apart, belonging to no kingdom, if it couldn't keep time with the rest of the world.

"Fair enough," said Arthur. "Listen, before the others realize we're back, there's something I want to show you."

"Is it a hangover cure?" Lance asked hopefully. "Because I could really use one."

His head was *killing* him. Freed from their guard's duties, Dakin and Brannor had gone hard the last three nights, and he'd foolishly tried to keep up. There had been glasses of something called whiskey, and a fiddle, and Brannor on the table belting out the filthiest sea shanties Lance had ever heard. Dakin had miraculously seduced a barmaid, and that morning, Lance had woken up in the rosy-cheeked stable boy's bed, wearing his tunic back to front, and unable to remember how he'd gotten there, or even the lad's name.

"Why would he have a *hangover cure*?" scoffed the wizard as Arthur sheepishly rooted through his pack, pulling out a small cloth pouch.

"Dried fennel. Needs to be steeped in hot water."

Thank god for Arthur.

"You're an absolute prince," Lance said, clapping his friend on the back. "Now what was it you wanted to show me?"

"Not here," Arthur said, slanting Lance a look he knew all too well.

Something was up. Something *big*.

"Follow me," Lance said, setting off toward the woods and dumping the fennel seeds into his water pouch. "Hey, wizard, want to heat this for me?"

Merlin rolled his eyes, but muttered the spell, and the pouch grew warm in Lance's hands.

As they walked, he chugged down the tincture. He *never* should have matched Dakin drink for drink. He'd just wanted the smug arse to stop smirking at him, clearly thinking, *You may play at being a guard, but you'll never be one of us.*

As though he wasn't painfully aware. Even disgraced, he was still the son of a knight. He'd still grown up with tutors and banquets and jackets lined in the finest silk, granted more than his fair share of luxuries as a favored playmate of the young prince. He still knew the castle's shortcuts and secret passages far better than the cramped barracks.

Now the barracks were all he had. He was the son of his father's mistress, not his wife, though Sir Ector had claimed him all the same, so he could become a knight. Instead, he'd become a disappointment.

Arthur had warned him that Jereth was trouble, but he hadn't listened. Instead, he'd followed his foolish heart and fallen in love with a beautiful boy who loved only himself.

They'd shared so many stolen kisses, so many afternoons swimming in the cool river, and borrowing horses from the royal stables to ride to a secluded spot in the woods. Lance had thought Jereth just needed time. That eventually, they'd stop hiding. Instead, they'd gotten caught. He'd never forget the fear in the other boy's eyes when his mother had opened the door. How roughly Jereth had pushed him away.

How dare you assault me so, page? I merely asked for help unclasping my cloak.

When Jereth had lied about what they were to each other, Lance's heart and dreams had smashed into a million pieces. There was nothing he could do to scrub out the dark rumor that followed him through the castle, the lie of what he had done.

Sometimes, when he trained with the guard, he imagined competing in a tournament, the stands chanting his name. And then he remembered that he would never be allowed—that tournaments and jousts were for knights—and his heart broke all over again.

The courtiers were scandalized at the sight of him fallen so low, and he worried his fellow guards would never respect him enough to follow his command. Not everyone acted that way—handsome Percival and cheerful Tristan usually saved him a seat in the soldier's mess—but Dakin was far from the only guard who made no secret of his views, or his distate.

The only cure for Lance's despair was Arthur. His brother in all but blood. If Arthur hadn't come back from Avalon that morning, Lance had been planning to find a boat and row across himself.

Which, judging from the ferocity of his headache, wouldn't have gone well.

They reached a small clearing, and Arthur glanced around nervously, checking to make sure no one was around.

"Don't freak out," he warned.

"Why would I fr—" Lance started as Arthur unsheathed his sword.

The clearing filled with a blindingly bright light, and Lance doubled over, moaning. "Aghhh! What the *hell*?" he complained. "I *told* you I'm hungover."

"This is worth it, trust me," said Merlin.

Lance swallowed down his nausea and squinted into the light. The horrible glow was coming from Arthur's sword. "What is it?" he asked.

"Excalibur."

Lance nearly fell over. "Shut up," he said. *"Where? How?"*

Arthur explained about losing the first sword in the lake, and the Lady taking him to the tomb, and how the sword only glowed when its bearer was worthy.

"Anyway," Arthur finished, "the blade makes you unbeatable, but the scabbard makes you unkillable in battle."

"This ratty old thing makes you *unkillable?*" Lance said, gaping at the worn scabbard. "No offense, but you need that."

"It's not funny," Arthur said miserably. "It's looking more and more like this whole High King thing isn't a joke."

"Well, yeah," Lance said. "I could have told you that."

Arthur sighed, his expression pained, and Lance didn't blame him: if the Lady of the Lake had given *him* the legendary Excalibur in some creepy tomb and told him he'd become High King of England, he probably wouldn't be very pleased, either.

But you know what he *would* do . . .

"We should test it," Lance said, breaking the gloomy silence.

"Now?" Arthur stared at him in surprise.

"Why not? If the scabbard doesn't work, Merlin can magic away any injuries. Right?"

"Um," said Merlin.

Lance forged on before the wizard could protest. "When else are we going to have a chance? That thing's clearly getting locked in the vault the moment King Bummer realizes what it is."

Arthur's lips twitched at their childhood nickname for his father. "I don't *love* wearing a sword I've never used," he allowed.

That was all Lance needed. Screw being hungover, he was going to see Excalibur in action.

"All right." Lance held out a hand. "Give me the scabbard. Wizard, get your wand ready for that healing spell, just in case."

"No," Arthur said firmly, before offering him the sword. "If we're testing Excalibur, we're testing it on me."

Lance's mouth fell open. "But," he spluttered, "but you're—"

"—the one who will put his life in danger trusting this scabbard? I don't want to know that it works for someone else. I need to know that it works for me."

Lance looked askance at the young wizard. "Merlin, come on," he pleaded.

"I agree with Arthur," the traitorous wizard said.

This was just perfect. Stabbing the unarmed crown prince with a legendary magic sword *definitely* wasn't what he'd meant when he'd suggested a test run.

He wouldn't even have dared back when they were two young lads stirring trouble in a castle where no one paid them much mind. But even though the courtiers may have written Arthur off, Lance had always seen his friend's talents more clearly.

Arthur was a strategist, not a warrior. Now that he had Excalibur, instead of eagerly rushing to test its abilities, he'd handed the sword to his friend, strapped on the magic scabbard, and designated himself the first victim.

It was so . . . Arthur.

"I trust you," Arthur said, his eyes locked with Lance's.

"Well, I don't trust either of you," the wizard remarked. "Not that anyone's asking."

"Will you shut up?" Lance called. "I'm trying to run our future king through with a sword, so I should probably concentrate."

He took a deep breath, and the proffered sword. The blade glowed brightly, and Lance stared down at it in surprise.

His hangover was gone. He felt like he could take on an army without breaking a sweat. He tried a few passes, the sword remarkably light in his hands. Arthur gave him a small nod, the way he did when they practiced broadsword, telling him to go ahead.

It was now or never.

Lance lunged forward, the tip of the sword slicing high and shallow on the prince's forearm.

Arthur flinched, stumbling backward and clapping a hand to the wound.

"Well?" Lance asked nervously.

Arthur peeled his hand away. A slash of red blood darkened the sleeve of his tunic.

"I hardly felt a thing," he said with a small, incredulous laugh.

He rolled up his sleeve. The cut on his arm had already faded into a thin pink line. As they watched, it turned translucent, becoming a silvery scar, and then disappeared entirely.

It had really worked!

"That's amazing," Lance proclaimed, and then, to Merlin, just to make sure, "That wasn't you, right?"

"Not me," said the wizard, who, for whatever reason, had turned crimson.

"This time, go harder," Arthur said, tugging off his tunic and tossing it aside. He squared his stance. "I want you to really strike me."

Lance groaned. Of course Arthur wouldn't stop at just the one test. He hefted the sword, executing a complicated pass.

"Should I aim for the left nipple or the right?" he asked.

"They're not targets," Arthur said severely.

Merlin quietly had a coughing fit.

"Wait," said Lance, taking off his own sword and offering it to Arthur. "At least attempt to block me."

The prince grinned as he hefted the blade of a royal guard.

Their swords clashed, Excalibur ringing with a bright, clear twang. Lance gathered his nerve as their blades came together again. And then he feinted to the left, twisting around and aiming for the prince's side.

The sword gleamed as it slid through Arthur's flesh, and the prince cried out in pain. Lance watched in horror as he dropped to his knees, doubling over and clutching at his rib cage. Blood seeped from beneath his hand, and he went still.

Lance stared down at the glowing blade, its light a ghoulish red from the prince's blood, and felt as though he might collapse on the spot.

"What did you *do*?!" Merlin accused, rushing to the prince's side.

"He told me to! *Sard!*" Lance said, his eyes wide with fright. He knelt down, shaking his friend. "Arthur! Arthur! How bad is it?"

Merlin hovered nervously, wand out, muttering curses.

Arthur wasn't moving. And he looked pale.

Please, Lance thought. *Please, no.*

He picked up Arthur's crumpled tunic, pressing it against the wound.

"Say something," he begged, a sob rising in his throat.

And then Arthur looked up at him, his lips quirked, his eyes dancing with mischief. "Nice to know you care," he said, standing up and brushing himself off.

"That was a *joke*?!" Lance roared.

"You said you were going to slay my nipple!" Arthur retorted. "With *Excalibur*!"

"So you pretended I *killed* you?!"

Lance let out a frustrated shout and shoved into the prince, sending them both rolling. They'd done it all the time as boys, fighting over the last sweet from the kitchen, or whatever book Lance had grabbed away when Arthur was ignoring him for too long.

But things were different now. Arthur was different. He was . . . the one true king.

Lance hesitated for a fraction of a second, which was all Arthur needed to pin him. They were breathing hard as they rolled to a stop. Arthur grinned down at him triumphantly, his cheeks pink, his hair falling into his eyes, the picture of perfect health.

"You let down your guard," Arthur accused, surprised.

"Because you were wounded," Lance protested.

"Actually, you both let down your guard," Merlin interrupted, casually hefting the glowing sword. "You left Excalibur lying in the dirt."

"We probably shouldn't call it that," said Arthur. "Someone might overhear."

"Fine, you left *Aunt Matilda* lying in the dirt," said the wizard, which made Lance howl with laughter. And then grimace with pain. Without the sword, his hangover had returned. With a vengeance.

"Ugh," Lance moaned, clutching his head. "I wish you *had* capsized in that magic lake."

"You do not," Arthur said cheerfully, sheathing the sword.

"We should get back," said Merlin. "Before those annoying guards come looking for us."

"Sard. How am I going to explain this?" Arthur tented his torn and blood-soaked tunic with a grimace.

"Abdere." The wizard waved a hand as though shooing away a mosquito. The prince's tunic unwrinkled itself, the blood and rip disappearing.

"That itched," Arthur complained. "You could have warned me."

"You could have *not* pretended to be *mortally wounded*," Merlin retorted.

"I can't help the itching. I'm only an apprentice, you know. Some things are beyond my power."

"Like riding a horse?" Arthur suggested.

"Gahhhh!" the wizard roared.

The three of them didn't stop laughing until they reached the inn.

CHAPTER 20

The last gasp of daylight was fading into darkness as they approached the gates of Castle Camelot. Arthur had been trying to slow his horse ever since the city walls had come into view, but it was no use delaying the inevitable.

He was home. His quest was over, and his freedom was dwindling fast. Princess Guinevere would be arriving at the castle within days. And he doubted he could conjure up another good excuse to spend a week riding horses, playing cards, and drinking ale with Merlin and Lance.

Beside him, Lance let out a sigh, as though he wasn't much looking forward to their return, either.

Arthur slanted his friend a knowing look. "End of the road," he said sadly.

Lance groaned. "Don't remind me. Tomorrow I'll be back to running drills at sunrise."

"And I'll be back to sleeping in my own bed and riding no horses," Merlin announced gleefully.

Arthur glared. "Aren't wizards supposed to be all about magical quests?"

"I like what I like. Besides, I miss coffee."

Arthur shook his head.

Wizards.

Or maybe just this one.

Ahead of them, Brannor said something to Dakin. Both guards' posture straightened as they proudly urged their horses toward the castle's outer gates.

Please, no, Arthur thought, realizing a moment too late what they meant to do.

"Make way!" Brannor announced loudly. "For His Royal Highness Arthur Pendragon, Prince of Camelot!"

The gate guards snapped to attention, banging their halberds. From deep within the courtyard, a trumpet blared.

Arthur winced. "Did they have to?" he muttered. He'd been hoping they could slip around the back and avoid the literal fanfare.

"I know, I'm desperate for a piss," said Lance, fidgeting.

"You're the one who told them about *Aunt Matilda*," Arthur accused.

"It was an accident!" Lance protested.

"They were bound to notice," added Merlin. "The sword has a *vibe*. Also, it glows."

Arthur supposed the wizard was right. Still, he wished his guards hadn't reacted quite so strongly.

At first sight of the legendary blade, Brannor had taken a knee, attempting to pledge fealty on the spot. Arthur had urged the old guard to please get up, but ever since, Brannor had been taking his job far too seriously. Dakin, meanwhile, kept shooting the sword anxious looks, as though unnerved by its presence.

At least the quest had been a success, Arthur reminded himself. He was returning home with *Excalibur*. He'd never gotten something right before. Not on purpose.

Somehow, without his noticing, Lance and Merlin had dropped back, letting him ride through the castle gates alone. He wished he'd asked the wizard to do that clothes-cleaning trick. But too late now. The fanfare had done its job: courtiers were streaming curiously into the courtyard to witness his arrival.

Well, he *was* returning from a great quest. One that had lasted longer than expected, thanks to the strange progression of time on Avalon. It was only just occurring to him that anyone might have begun to worry. After all, it wasn't as though his father's court had much confidence in his abilities.

Arthur sighed and tried to brush the dirt from his rumpled traveler's clothes. He had just twisted round to signal to the wizard to do the thing when his skin began to itch, and the wrinkles disappeared from his tunic, replaced by an over-strong scent of cloves.

Merlin smirked, pleased. Arthur shook his head. The wizard had made him smell like a church altar.

As they entered the inner courtyard, King Uther burst through the castle doors, his advisors and their families not far behind.

"My son," cried the king, a little too loudly, "I'm relieved to see you returned safely home!"

Sard, was his father *drunk*? Lord Agravaine gripped the king's elbow, his lips tamped into a disapproving frown as King Uther staggered forward.

Definitely drunk.

Which was either going to make this better, or so much worse. Arthur was thinking worse. Gawain stood off to the side, a bored smirk on his lips. His coat was ridiculous, crimson velvet with ornate balloon sleeves, and his embroidered velvet heels were even more absurd. At his side was the arrogant Sir Kay, a cloth tucked into his collar to protect his doublet from food splatter.

He'd interrupted supper, he realized. The king had risen from the table, causing the entire hall to empty out.

Maybe it was better this way, Arthur told himself. Excalibur was meant to be a spectacle, and for a spectacle, you needed an audience.

"Father," he said, dismounting his horse. A groom materialized, leading the beast to the stables.

"I trust your journey went well?" said the king.

"Very." Arthur dropped to a knee at his father's feet, well aware of their sizable audience. "I've returned with a great prize."

He unsheathed the glowing blade, which lit the darkened courtyard as though it was suddenly the afternoon.

"Behold, the sword Excalibur," said Arthur, laying the blade flat across his palms. He bowed his head and lifted the sword.

The courtiers gasped, whispering amongst themselves as a ripple of excitement passed through the crowd.

King Uther stared at the sword in disbelief, and even his advisors looked shocked. Lord Agravaine's mouth had fallen open, and Lord Howell's expression was even more incredulous.

"I thought Excalibur had been lost for centuries," called Sir Kay, who no doubt felt *he* should have been the one to recover the sword.

"Not lost," said Arthur. "Waiting. At least, according to the Lady of the Lake. For the one true king."

Those words rang out as he held Excalibur, making the sword glow even brighter in his grip. His heart beat faster, from the stress and the attention, but he kept the blade, and his posture, steady.

The courtiers stared at him in awe. Arthur knew he didn't look like much: travel worn and dressed as plainly as his guards, and barely nineteen. But he needed them to look beyond all that. To see their future king with a glowing sword in his hands, who would lead them into a new and better Camelot.

He needed them to believe.

Or else he didn't know how he'd find the strength to try.

The sword's glow illuminated the deep lines in his father's face. Uther blinked again, shocked that his son hadn't merely returned demanding his supper. That once again, the boy he'd long called an unfit spare had managed to prove himself.

"Excalibur," breathed the king, unable to tear his gaze from the blade. "May I?"

Arthur bowed his head and lifted the sword higher. As it passed to his father, its glow dimmed, and then went out entirely.

Fortunately, the king didn't seem to realize Excalibur had slighted him.

"Extraordinary," he marveled, examining the blade. "This relic will be kept under guard in the castle vault."

Lance had been so right about that.

"As you wish, Father," said Arthur, with a stab of disappointment. It wasn't as though he wanted to wear Excalibur to the library, but still. It seemed a shame to lock the sword away when it had only just been recovered.

"Did you bring back anything else?" Lord Agravaine asked, his expression shrewd.

Arthur hesitated. "Just the sword," he said, shooting a nervous look at his guards, who thankfully had no idea about its equally magical sheath.

The scabbard he'd keep to himself, for a little longer.

"Come," said Uther, clapping a hand to Arthur's shoulder. "Supper grows cold."

The courtiers whispered as he walked past, and he knew they were talking about him. About the crown prince they had grudgingly accepted, and then quietly begun to doubt.

But not anymore.

Arthur squared his shoulders, knowing their whispers meant he had done well, that he should be proud, but if anything, all of this just made him feel more alone.

You're not *alone*, he reminded himself. *You have Lance, and Merlin, and Master Ambrosius. You have friends who will tell you when you're being an idiot, and who will travel with you beyond the edge of the kingdom.*

And those friends would be waiting on the other side of this night.

What he needed to do was be the prince his father's subjects had always wanted. He could do that. For one night at least.

So he followed his father to the banquet hall, and smiled broadly as the king commanded music and dance and wine in his honor, and forced himself to enjoy it.

For his people. For his kingdom. For the future.

At the end of the night, he tumbled drunkenly into bed still wearing his boots and his scabbard.

◐ ◐ ◐

In his dream, Arthur was running.

Merlin was in trouble, and he wasn't going to get there fast enough. But he was sure as hell going to try.

Arthur's chest heaved and his lungs burned as he careened through the London streets, Excalibur sheathed at his side. Somehow, he knew exactly where he was going. And in an instant, he was there, in the churchyard of St. Paul's, staring down at the block of stone that had once held a surprisingly ordinary sword.

Except now it held something else.

His wizard was trapped inside. Dying.

Arthur drew Excalibur, trying to force the glowing blade through the stone, but it was no use. Merlin continued to scream soundlessly, fists pounding against the stone, as though trapped beneath ice in a frozen lake.

Arthur watched, useless, no hero at all, as Merlin choked and went still. Not still. Dead. The wizard was dead.

The dream shifted, and suddenly, they were in a dark, dusty crypt that Arthur somehow knew was beneath St. Paul's Cathedral. Merlin's body lay atop a stone tomb. Arthur knelt before it, overcome by loss. He had failed, where the Lady of the Lake had told him he must succeed. He hadn't been at the wizard's side. He was here now, but it was too late.

He placed Excalibur in Merlin's hands. The sword sat there, a dull, lifeless blade. It hadn't worked.

Arthur reached over to take back the sword. Before he could, it began to glow . . .

Arthur woke suddenly, feeling as though he had just fallen from a great distance. He gasped in the darkness, unsure where he was, or if the events in his dream had really happened. And then he took in the familiar curtains drawn around his bed and breathed a sigh of relief.

He was in his room, and he'd fallen asleep on top of the covers, fully dressed. His empty scabbard was white-hot against his thigh, as if in warning.

It had been a dream. A nothing. A fiction.

And yet it had felt like so much more.

◑ ◑ ◑

Emry eagerly climbed the stairs to the wizard's workshop the next morning, thrilled to be back. She set down the mug of coffee that she'd begged from the kitchens, swallowed a mouthful of brioche, and looked expectantly to Master Ambrosius.

She hadn't seen the old wizard at supper the night before. To her surprise, she'd been surrounded by courtiers eager to hear the tale of their quest. The attention had made her so uncomfortable that she'd begged exhaustion, and had crept back to her chambers. But not before seeing Arthur resplendent at the royal table, the entire court raising their goblets in his honor.

The sarcastic boy from the library had vanished. Last night, he had been every inch the future king.

At the start, their journey had seemed more like an excuse for a road trip than a true quest. But something had changed after they'd returned from Avalon. They had visited somewhere few others had gone, and had encountered strange and powerful magic. Not to mention the Lady of the Lake herself.

"Well," said Master Ambrosius, rising from his chair by the fire. "I'm glad to see my apprentice has returned in one piece."

He was watching her carefully. Too carefully. Emry frowned, wondering what was going on. She pasted on a smug expression and slouched against the table.

"Of course I have," she boasted.

"Should I assume no one discovered your secret?" the wizard asked mildly. "I have to say, it's impressive you managed to masquerade as a boy for a whole week on the road."

Emry stumbled, nearly losing her balance. Panic flared white and hot in her chest. She'd thought she had been careful. She'd thought no one knew. And yet the old wizard was staring at her expectantly, clearly harder to deceive than he'd let on.

She looked down at the wooden table, not daring to meet his eye. "When did you guess?"

"I don't believe your father ever spoke of his son casting silent spells. Only his daughter."

"You knew this whole time?" Emry asked, shocked. "But you never said anything!"

"It's not my secret to tell."

"That's what the Lady of the Lake said."

"You accompanied Arthur to the Isle of the Blessed?" The old wizard sounded surprised. "The boat let you cross?"

"It did," she said, wondering how he knew about the boat.

"What else did Nimue say?"

She didn't recognize the name, but she knew he meant the Lady of the Lake.

"That Arthur will become a great king with me by his side," said Emry, nervously meeting the old wizard's gaze. "I'm sorry. I never meant for it to go this far."

"And yet it seems fate means for it to go even further," said Master Ambrosius. "The Lady of the Lake speaks true, although her words are not always plainly understood."

"She was pretty clear about the it being me part," said Emry, "and not my brother. If that's what you were asking."

The old wizard nodded slowly. "Forgive me," he said, "but what *has* happened to your brother?"

Emry winced. "It's a long story," she said, starting with Emmett getting knocked unconscious from the blowback of his own spell.

Master Ambrosius frowned. "It couldn't have been a very nice spell," he said. "What was he trying to do?"

"Memory wipe. On two people at once. He was in trouble over some gambling debt."

The wizard shook his head, looking unspeakably disappointed. "So you came in his place."

"It was only supposed to be for a week," said Emry. "Until he recovered. But Emmett refused to switch back. He said it should have been me all along."

"Do you agree?"

Emry bit her lip, considering. "I think so. I want to help Arthur, and I want to learn magic. And if I have to pretend to be my brother to have the chance, then it's a price I'm willing to pay. For now." Emry looked up, the thought occurring to her. "So long as it's all right with you, having me for an apprentice."

"King Uther will never accept a woman as his court wizard," said Master Ambrosius. Emry winced, knowing the old man was right. "But Arthur, perhaps, might feel differently."

Emry stared at him, hardly daring to hope. "I think so, too," she said. And then, before she could lose her nerve she added, "The Lady of the Lake said my father had a student. A woman named Morgana."

Master Ambrosius inhaled sharply.

"It has been a long time since I've heard the name Morgana le Fay," said the old wizard.

"So you know her?" Emry pressed.

"Only by reputation," said Master Ambrosius. "She was a very ambitious young sorceress."

"She's why my father didn't want me to learn magic, isn't she?" Emry went on. "Because he thought I'd turn out like her."

The old wizard's mouth twisted into a frown, as though he found the subject distasteful. "Your father knew what she was when he agreed to teach her. He had hoped she might overcome her anger. That he could set her on a different path."

"What happened to her?" Emry asked.

Master Ambrosius shook his head, his gaze growing unfocused as he considered the past.

"I have heard nothing of her for years. Perhaps her ambitions got the best of her."

"Because a corrupt mind breeds corrupt magic," Emry said, remembering what the old wizard had said to her the first time they met.

"Exactly." Master Ambrosius stared at her intently. "A very long time ago, Nimue told me my destiny was to instruct the great and powerful wizard known as Merlin. Naturally, I had not come to her seeking any such destiny."

"You didn't go to see her about the soap?"

"I wanted to save the man I loved," he admitted. "But Archimedes didn't survive the journey. Still, I pleaded with Nimue. She told me she couldn't bring back what I had lost, but she could instead give me something to live for. A purpose. I had thought that purpose was to instruct your father." The old man hesitated before adding, "Until recently."

"What changed your mind?" Emry asked curiously.

"You did," said Master Ambrosius. "Arthur pulled the sword from the stone long after your father could help him. Perhaps, if he had done so as a boy, things would have been different. But history runs how it must, not how we will it." The wizard sighed. "I have lived a long life, and seen many whom I cared about die. But there is still hope to be found in this world. And I believe it rests with Arthur. And with you."

"No pressure," Emry joked. She smiled gratefully at the old wizard, who was looking at her as though he saw her truly, and was proud to have her as his apprentice. Not her brother—her. She wanted to hug him. To thank him for teaching her, even though she wasn't the pupil he'd expected. And for keeping her secret. And for so many other things.

But before she could, Master Ambrosius clapped his hands together and said, "Now I think I'd better start you on potions. They can be quite useful in an emergency."

"What constitutes an emergency?" she asked curiously.

"With you?" replied the old wizard. "I'd say every day that ends in the letter 'y.'"

CHAPTER 21

Emry hurried down the castle corridor after supper, feeling Gawain's eyes on her.

The prince's handsome cousin slouched next to an antique suit of armor, wearing yet another ridiculous coat, this one embroidered with silver serpents. His brown skin glowed richly in the candlelight, the shadows illuminating the chiseled hollows of his cheekbones. His sketchbook was tucked under one arm, and he was soliciting volunteers for private portrait sessions in his chambers, so he might better study the female form.

Emry rolled her eyes. A surprising number of court ladies were vying for the honor, though she didn't spot Lady Elaine amongst them. Gawain tipped his chin in Emry's direction, and she nodded back.

She'd sensed Gawain watching her during supper that evening, and had often felt the pressure of his gaze even before she'd left for Avalon. Well, he *had* seen her chase off two bandits with flying bricks and a wall of fire, she reminded herself. But still. There was something probing about the way he watched her, as if he was looking for something.

Or maybe, Emry thought with a disparaging sigh, it was simply that he wished her to feel inferior, dressed as shabbily as she was in the royal court. Well, shabby would have to do, because she wasn't wasting precious coin on a set of fancy boy's clothing.

She'd spent the afternoon working on a particularly potent potion, and no matter what spells she tried, the spicy scent of magic wasn't coming out of her doublet. She stared at the girls who encircled Gawain, with their glossy hair twisted into intricate plaits, dressed in delicate silk and perfumed like flowers.

Must be nice, smiling at a boy and having him smile back in appreciation.

She let her imagination wander, wishing she were here at the castle as herself, that she had dressed for supper in a fine gown, braiding her hair and dabbing rose salve on her lips. But even then, she still wouldn't belong. She never did.

She forced herself to look closer at the courtiers, taking in the painful lacing of their gowns, the desperation in their charms. The way they tripped over each other to vie for Gawain's affection. Perhaps they weren't as content as she had assumed, either.

"If you're trying to catch a girl's attention, there are more effective ways to do it than lurking pensively in corridors," Arthur said mildly, coming up behind her.

He looked even more handsome than he had from afar. His circlet glinted in the candlelight, and up close, Emry could see the golden threads woven through his sleeves. He shot her a teasing grin, leaning one shoulder against the wall.

"Oh, *please* give me dating advice," she said. "I'll pay special attention to the part about being royal and waiting for girls to shove each other out of the way."

Arthur shrugged, but didn't deny it. "Listen, we need to talk."

Emry's stomach twisted. "Is—is something wrong?" she asked, trying not to sound alarmed.

Arthur glanced around at the crowded hallway. "It's a matter best discussed in private. Walk with me to the library?"

Emry swallowed and nodded, trying to slow her racing pulse.

It was a short walk, yet the entire time, her heart felt as though it might leap from her chest. She kept replaying Arthur's ominous words over and over. *We need to talk.*

She doubted it was about anything good.

What if he had discovered her deception? Was it possible he'd waited until their return from Avalon so that he could confront her in private? She watched him carefully, trying to gauge his mood.

He looked exhausted, and frustrated, and overwhelmed, but that could mean anything.

"Well?" Emry asked nervously after they'd settled into the library.

The prince sighed. "I meant to talk to you about this sooner," he began.

He'd guessed. He had to have guessed. That final night at the inn, when she'd won two shillings off Lance at cards, and had shrieked in pleasure, forgetting to lower her voice.

Her hands were shaking, and she barely dared to breathe as she blurted, "So did I."

"You already know?" Arthur looked surprised. But not upset.

Emry frowned. "What are we talking about?" she asked carefully.

"The weird nightmare I had last night," he said.

Emry laughed. *This* was what Arthur had needed to talk about. In private? Ugh. It figured he'd nearly given her a panic attack over nothing.

"Why? What are *you* talking about?" Arthur asked.

"Nothing," she said quickly. "Please tell me everything about your weird nightmare. This is clearly of the utmost importance. Have you checked your horoscope recently? Or your tea leaves?"

Arthur's eyes narrowed. "You're mocking me," he accused. "If you dreamed of *my* death, I'd expect you'd tell me about it."

That had Emry's attention.

"Oh," she said, embarrassed. "Go on, then."

Arthur explained about how he'd found her trapped in a block of stone. How he'd tried to rescue her . . . but couldn't.

Emry slouched back in her chair, nibbling her lower lip. "I had that same nightmare," she said. "Back on Avalon."

She'd dismissed it as nothing. But now Arthur had dreamt the same thing. They were both quiet a moment, thinking.

"That's not normal, is it?" Arthur asked, breaking the silence. "Us having the same nightmare?"

Emry bit her lip. "I don't think so," she allowed.

"When I woke up, my scabbard was warm," Arthur confessed. "I'd just assumed it was random. But what if it's not? What if it's a warning?"

Emry frowned at the scabbard hanging below Arthur's waist. And then averted her gaze, cheeks burning, because of course she hadn't *just* been staring at the scabbard.

"If I see any magic stones, I'll try not to get trapped in them," she promised.

"Good plan." Arthur rolled his eyes.

"I wish we knew more about your scabbard." Emry drummed her fingers against the table, thinking. "You're sure it didn't come with instructions?"

"All the Lady of the Lake said was that it carried an enchantment that makes the wearer unkillable in combat, and that it was on loan from the King of Anwen."

Emry stared at him accusingly.

"You're just mentioning that *now*?"

"I'm sorry, wizard, do I report to you?" the prince retorted.

"You do when it's about *magical enchantments*," she replied.

So the sword and scabbard had come through the stones. That made sense. Of course it took magic from the Otherworld to produce an enchantment that let the wearer defy death.

Emry remembered the pull of Anwen's magic. How it had called to her. She ran her thumb across the scar on her palm, thinking how strange it was that she'd had the same dream as Arthur back on Avalon. That the dream had *followed* them.

"Fine," Arthur conceded. "I promise to inform you the next time my scabbard gets warm."

Emry coughed. "Wow," she said, holding back a smirk.

"Shut up," Arthur muttered, his cheeks going pink. "I didn't laugh about your creepy soap."

"No. You did not."

Sard. She hated that she was lying to him. She hadn't realized how terrible it would feel to keep up the lie that she was her brother.

She wished she could tell him that she was really Merlin's daughter. That she had come here in Emmett's place, and that no one else could know. But it was unfair to ask Arthur to lie for her. To ruin all of the ways in which he trusted her. It had been bad enough to ask Master Ambrosius to keep her secret, even though he'd been doing so all along. And the old wizard was just her teacher. Arthur was more than that. He was—he was—

The door slammed open, the unexpected noise making them both jump. Gawain strolled in, taking no notice of them.

He sauntered toward the French language section, hands in the pockets of his absurd brocade jacket, whistling a tune under his breath.

"Do you *mind*?" Arthur asked his cousin, annoyed.

"Oh, sorry." The whistling stopped. "Didn't realize I was doing it."

He ran a hand over the spines of a couple novels, pulling one from the shelf and reading the title aloud.

"This any good?" he asked.

"I'm not a librarian," Arthur said tightly.

Emry quietly had a coughing fit.

Gawain studied Arthur, eyes narrowing.

"You've read it, though," he announced. "I can tell. And you *hated* it."

The whistling started up again, and Gawain put the book back on the shelf.

"You'll like the one with the green spine," Arthur said with a sigh. "Fourth shelf. It has pirates."

"Merci beaucoup, cousin," said Gawain, tucking the book under his arm. He traipsed to the door and then stopped short, as though knowing how desperate they both were for him to leave. "Did you know you're wearing an empty scabbard?"

"It's a—er—fashion statement," Arthur said stiffly.

CHAPTER 22

"What do you know about Anwen?" Emry asked Master Ambrosius, wiping the sweat from her brow.

The old wizard had her working on magical elixirs, which she didn't know how anyone had the patience to brew. She'd been boiling mineral water for the past hour, and had collected only the barest amount of magnesium salts.

Master Ambrosius arched an eyebrow. "Does this have anything to do with elixirs?"

"No," Emry admitted.

"Anwen is lost to us. Not even stone henges could keep the doors from closing."

Emry frowned. "But what if they could be reopened? The Lady of the Lake said Morgana le Fay was able to force the magic to—"

"Watch out!" Master Ambrosius scolded as Emry's cauldron boiled over, scalding water spilling over the sides.

A few droplets splattered against Emry's wrist, and she hissed in pain, cradling her hand against her chest.

The old wizard motioned for Emry to hold out her arm. When she did, his eyes went wide at the silver scar on her palm. "How did you get this?" he asked roughly.

He backed away from her, alarmed.

"I—it was an accident," Emry said.

Master Ambrosius gave her a hard look, and Emry realized that he knew exactly how she'd gotten that scar.

"If what I have to teach isn't enough for you—" he began.

"It is," she promised, muttering a spell to clean up the mess. "I want to be a court wizard. Like my father. I-I'm sorry."

Master Ambrosius nodded, some warmth returning to his expression.

"Healing salve?" Emry asked, holding out her wrist.

"That salve takes three months to make," said the old wizard. "And I won't see it used up because you couldn't keep your mind on your cauldron."

Emry sighed and fetched a jar of chamomile instead, which was what her Gran always used.

Master Ambrosius grunted his approval.

"Not all problems need to be solved with magic," he said. "I don't want to see you ignoring what's in front of you, especially when you have everything you need."

"Sorry," she apologized again, realizing it had been a mistake to bring up Anwen. Her question had clearly unnerved Master Ambrosius. Whatever it was Morgana had been after—and whatever strange, beguiling magic she'd encountered by opening that doorway—she wouldn't get her answers from the old court wizard.

But maybe she could from her father's books.

☾ ☾ ☾

Later that night, as Emry sat in her room with the slimmest, most worn volume in her lap, she was surprised to find herself blinking away tears.

Holding her father's books in her hands *here* made her heart ache with renewed loss. She traced her fingers over his rushed, terrible handwriting, wondering if he had sat at this very desk.

She missed him so much that even the sight of his notebooks cut through her like a knife, her memories of him dripping onto every page: his fondness for spiced almonds, the absentminded way he patted his coat pockets whenever he'd misplaced his wand. The infectious rumble of his laugh.

But no matter how closely she held his notebooks, she couldn't bring him back. She could only watch as he drifted further into the past.

So she steadied herself and pored through the pages, searching for anything that might be useful, and trying to ignore the pain in her chest.

Finally, on Thursday evening, she found what she was looking for:

> *I believe that the legendary sword Excalibur is a weapon forged of Anwen, for I have found no magic of this world that would allow for the creation of such a blade. The more I study Anwen's magic, the more I become convinced that the accepted rules of magic do not apply. If this is true, then Anwen's magic will work on other magic—on enchantments as well as naturally magical objects and persons. It is overwhelming to imagine the ability to cast spells inward as well as outward. To face no limits, or fear of blowback. Yet without proof—*

Emry turned the page, but whatever came next had been torn roughly from the book. As had the next three pages.

Had someone removed them on purpose? Emry frowned down at the book and barely held back a sigh. A crude drawing of a boy wizard in a flowing cloak and ridiculous hat stared up at her. Beneath it were three smudged games of X's and O's.

"Emmett," she groaned.

Still, it was the first reference to both Excalibur and Anwen that she'd been able to find, and she thought Arthur might like to see it.

The prince hadn't been to visit the workshop since they'd returned from Avalon, and whenever she'd caught glimpses of him in the castle, he'd looked overwhelmed and exhausted.

Emry checked her reflection in the mirror before going to see the prince. Not that it mattered. To him, she was a shabbily dressed boy. A friend. Nothing more. Still, she sighed as she caught sight of her cropped hair and drab doublet.

He was probably either in his bedroom or the library, Emry decided. The library was the closest, so she tried it first.

Except when she poked her head inside, it wasn't Arthur she found, but Gawain.

He was dressed more lavishly than usual, in a purple velvet coat embroidered with opulent goldwork, and a matching silk-lined cape knotted over one shoulder. His feet were propped on the table, displaying a pair of ridiculous heeled shoes, and his chair was balanced on just the back legs.

Across from him sat a miniature version of Lord Agravaine, with dark curls and an even darker scowl. He was about her age, but his haughty expression made him seem older. So this was the infamous Jereth. She'd been wondering when he'd turn up. He twisted a quill between his fingers, looking as though he wanted to stab someone with it.

"I don't see why I have to memorize all of it," he complained.

"Because you're annoying me," Gawain said. "And there isn't a tutor in the castle who will put up with you, so you have to do what I say."

Jereth grumbled, returning to his text.

"Ah, the elusive Merlin," Gawain said, looking up at her over the top of his book. "Que fais-tu?"

His smirk was infuriating. As was the smug way he was waiting for her response, one eyebrow raised, as though expecting she hadn't understood a word.

"Rien, milord," she said crisply, turning to go. "Je suis désolée de vous déranger."

"You speak French?" Gawain sounded surprised.

"And Latin, and Greek, and a fair bit of Old English," Emry replied, annoyed. "Did you think wizards recite spells without knowing what the words mean?"

"Actually, I figured you just waved your wand and magical walls of fire appeared," Gawain said.

It took Emry a moment to realize he was joking. "That's only on Fridays," she corrected. "Tuesdays it's roast beef sandwiches."

Gawain's mouth twitched with what might have been a smile. "Sounds pretty good right now, if you're offering," he said.

"To make you a sandwich? No." Emry scowled.

Gawain snorted, and then motioned toward an empty chair. Jereth shot him a tortured look and let out a pointed sigh.

"I was actually looking for Arthur," Emry said, and then, to be polite, added, "But, another time?"

She tried Arthur's bedroom next. Thankfully, his guards were stationed outside.

"His Highness is expecting you?" Brannor asked crisply.

Emry rolled her eyes. Hadn't formality gone out the window after spending a week on the road together? Apparently not.

"Yeah," Emry lied. "He requested help with a, uh, magic thing."

Thankfully, the door opened, and Arthur poked his head out, all nervous energy.

"Is the pr—ah, Merlin! Come in."

She followed after him, and surveyed the room with a frown. She'd never seen it in such a state. Every surface was covered with clothes and books. A mountain of embroidered silk and velvet worth a small fortune was piled onto the bed.

"When did Jereth arrive?" Emry asked, politely ignoring the mess.

"Yesterday, I think? Sorry, a lot's been happening." Arthur shook his head and held up a yellow silk court shoe with a high heel and a pearl-encrusted buckle. "Have you seen the match to this?"

She hoped he wasn't actually planning to wear those ridiculous things. "Um." Emry glanced around, wondering why his wardrobe seemed to have exploded.

"Found it!" Arthur plucked the shoe off his desk chair, wedging it on with a grimace. Emry watched as he took a few tentative steps in the uncomfortable-looking shoes. Even though they were absurd, she had to admit, they *did* make his legs look shapely.

But she wasn't here to stare at the prince's legs, she reminded herself, tearing her gaze away from the gentle swell of his calves.

"So, I found some stuff about Anwen in one of my father's books," Emry said while Arthur rooted through his desk drawers.

"Sorry, what?" Arthur replied. Now he was digging around in an elaborately painted trunk that seemed to be entirely filled with books, and the occasional piece of armor.

"Is this a bad time?" she asked, not very nicely.

"Sort of, yeah," Arthur said, frowning down at his trunk. "I can't remember what I did with the sarding thing."

"Your brain?"

"My best circlet," said Arthur absently. He crossed to a door Emry had previously taken for a garderobe, but was apparently a solar, and bellowed, "Lucan? Luc!"

When no one answered, he yanked on a thick silken cord. Moments later, a well-dressed manservant appeared with a crisp bow.

"Sorry, er—any chance you've seen my emerald circlet?" Arthur asked. "I can't find it anywhere."

"I believe you had it sent to the vault, Your Highness," said the valet.

"Why did I do that?" Arthur asked, furrowing his brow.

"You ran out of room for your books."

Emry stifled a laugh.

"Oh. Right." Arthur looked defeated.

"I can send someone to retrieve it?" asked the manservant.

"There's no time," said Arthur. "My usual one will have to do."

After the valet left, Arthur cursed under his breath.

"Big occasion?" Emry asked, remembering that Gawain had been dressed up as well, even more than usual. Maybe it was someone's birthday. Oh, hell, she hoped it wasn't *Arthur's* birthday.

He slanted her an incredulous look. "Princess Guinevere arrives within the hour," he said.

Emry's eyebrows shot up in surprise. That was *today*? No wonder he was in such a state.

She remembered vaguely that King Uther had invited the Princess of Cameliard to stay at the castle for the remainder of the summer. Arthur had grumbled about it on their journey to Avalon, but she'd been so stressed by her own predicament that she'd hardly paid attention.

And now the princess was about to arrive, and Arthur was clearly losing it. Which was somewhat entertaining to watch.

"What's she like?" Emry asked, trying to sound casual.

"No idea. We haven't seen each other since we were children."

That didn't sound like he was in love with her. Which was—none of her business, she reminded herself.

He shrugged on a tomato-red waistcoat with balloon sleeves and fur trim, and Emry coughed.

"What?"

"Nothing," she said. She hadn't even known he owned such a ridiculous thing.

"It's too much, isn't it?" Arthur said, his shoulders sagging.

"Just a bit."

"*Sard*," he swore, sitting down and putting his head in his hands. "I'm sweating through my tunic. I can't do this."

"You can absolutely do this," Emry promised. "She's just a girl. They're not that scary."

"Clearly you've never bedded one, then heard humiliating gossip the next morning."

"Actually, I have," Emry said, lifting her chin. "People talk. About princes, but also about wizards."

"At least you know where you stand," Arthur pointed out. "The girls at court behave like I'm some object to win so they can become queen."

So that was why he didn't keep company with any of the ladies who so eagerly vied for his attention. She had wondered.

"Maybe Guinevere will be different," Emry said, trying to make him feel better. "People can surprise you, but you have to give them a chance."

Arthur's gaze met hers, and for a long moment, neither of them looked away. His eyes were really something. Deep and brown and endless. She wanted to let go of everything holding her back and drown in them forever. Instead, she wrenched her gaze away, and slouched against a bedpost in imitation of her brother.

"Well, I have plenty of advice," she said, "on how to get girls to like you."

"This should be good," said Arthur. "Go on, wizard."

Sard, she had really done it now.

"First, you compliment her hair, or something she's wearing," Emry advised. "*Don't* be bawdy about it. Or gape at her bosom. Even if it's on display."

"Okay. Then what?"

"You should talk about your feelings," Emry went on.

"My feelings?"

"Just enough so she knows you're vulnerable and sensitive. And don't hog the conversation. There's nothing worse than listening to a boy boast for hours. You should ask her about herself, and listen attentively when she answers."

Arthur burst out laughing. "Now you're screwing with me," he said, shaking his head. "Talk about my *feelings*. Ask her about herself. What do *you* know about girls, wizard?"

Emry's cheeks heated. "Far more than you," she snapped, her temper flaring. She didn't know why she'd even bothered. "Fine. Wear those ridiculous heels and brag about your magic sword for all I care."

She glared at him, expecting a sharp retort. Instead, he just sighed, defeated.

"You'd think Excalibur would make a difference," Arthur said sadly. "But no. I've tried arguing it every which way. My father still insists we go forward with the wedding."

"Wedding?" Emry yelped. Before, she'd thought Arthur was overreacting at the princess's arrival, but now she wondered how he wasn't in *more* of a panic.

"It's a good alliance," Arthur said diplomatically. "We do share a border. Cameliard's not as prosperous as it once was, but they do have a strong western seaport."

"So sign a treaty."

Arthur grimaced. "It's too late. Our fathers have already arranged it."

"And Guinevere doesn't have a say in any of this?" Emry asked, incensed on the girl's behalf.

"Neither do I," Arthur said, offering her a thin half smile. "Guess we both should have checked the job description before being born."

He turned to the looking glass, surveying his outfit with a frown. He looked like a prince, dressed in the latest courtly fashions. But he didn't look like her Arthur.

"That jacket's all wrong," she blurted. "You should wear your brown suede, it brings out the gold in your eyes."

She wished she hadn't said it, but too late now.

Arthur's eyes met hers in the looking glass, and Emry ached for all the things she wanted to say, and all the things she never would.

"The brown suede," he repeated thoughtfully. "Well, wizard, stop standing there and help me find it."

CHAPTER 23

Guinevere peered out her carriage window as Castle Camelot came into view. For some reason, she'd remembered it being bigger.

The gate guards stepped aside, banging their halberds, and the trumpets began their fanfare, announcing her arrival. Guin swallowed nervously, pressing a hand to her elaborately braided hair. She couldn't believe she was here. Again.

Not for another carefree summer, but to make sure her kingdom was protected should peace give way to war. Their northern border was at risk, and her father, King Leodegrance, didn't have the resources to defend it. Not after last year's lean winter. Their people could barely afford the taxes as they stood. And the increase it would take to fund a war would leave them starving. Cameliard needed an alliance with a richer, larger kingdom. And in exchange, her prideful father had offered King Uther a trade he couldn't refuse: his daughter's hand in marriage.

For her whole life, Guin had known something like this might happen. And yet, as her carriage approached the castle's inner gates, she felt entirely unprepared.

At least she was meant to marry the eligible young prince, and not the widowed king. Her mother hadn't been so lucky. At sixteen, she'd sailed from Andalusia to a country she'd never seen, with just the barest grasp of the language, to marry a king thrice her age.

Which had made Guin's mother entirely unsympathetic when she'd shouted that it was horribly unfair, and she wouldn't go to Camelot, and to make Papa see reason.

"Daughters are currency, and sons are kings," her mother had reminded her. "And you, querida niña, are a rare diamond."

A diamond was a fair metaphor, since the stone needed to be carefully polished to sparkle as it did. And Guin's parents had been polishing her for years. There were music tutors, and dancing lessons, and instructions on everything from arranging guests at a dinner table, to how deeply to curtsey, to the most flattering angles at which to stand when approaching a throne. She avoided sugar for fear of tooth rot, and dairy for fear of indigestion, and every night, a maid combed her curls with the finest scented oils until her scalp ached and she begged for mercy.

Guin stared out at the half-remembered castle, with its turrets and battlements and crimson-cloaked guards marching drills on a distant lawn. Resentment rose in her throat, threatening to spill out as a frustrated, piercing scream. But no tantrum could fill her kingdom's empty coffers, or guarantee a plentiful harvest, so she swallowed down her theatrics.

She tried to recall the boy she'd played with a decade earlier, but her memories were hazy. All she remembered was racing his fair-haired friend to the pond, and drawing in some boring old books, and having to apologize for it like a badly behaved child, even though she was a princess in her own right, and Arthur was just the king's bastard, whom everyone said was an unimportant spare barely worth the title of prince.

That summer, Queen Igraine had been expecting, and the courtiers whispered that the baby, when it was born, would be the heir to the kingdom. So Guin had spent her visit playing in the gardens, and thought nothing of it—or of Arthur—for years. Instead, she'd dreamed of finding love on her own terms. Of winning the hand of a handsome foreign prince. One whom she would dazzle instantly with her beauty and her charm, and who didn't remember her as a bratty child who had shrieked over a skinned knee.

And then Arthur had pulled the sword from the stone, and suddenly an alliance with Camelot was all her parents could talk about.

Yet somehow, her father's plan to pack her off to London with her wedding date all but set had still caught her by surprise. She didn't feel ready. And she was afraid she never would.

She wanted to be young and unburdened forever, racing through Cameliard Keep late at night with wine stolen from her father's vault, and laughing with her friends as they dared each other to jump naked into the lake. She wanted to dance with the silly, eager boys who worshipped her beauty and her title, and order them to bring her impossible presents, and act unimpressed if they actually managed. She wanted to sneak sugared treats into the bath and order silk from Paris and have it made into a dress so scandalous that it gave her father heart palpitations.

Not smile politely and defer to some boy just because his kingdom was richer. Or because he'd pulled some dumb sword from a stupid stone. And the sword wasn't even an important one. If he'd pulled *Excalibur* out of a stone, *then* she'd be impressed.

The carriage pulled to a stop, and Guin's stomach fluttered with nerves. She wished her mother had let her come with ladies-in-waiting, so she wasn't alone.

"What if one of *them* catches the prince's eye instead?" her mother had said, daring her to argue. So here she was, all alone, giving up everything for her kingdom, while her parents and elder half brother sat home and congratulated themselves on their cleverness.

Guin dabbed some rose salve on her lips and adjusted a loose pin in her hair. She'd forced herself to stay awake the entire journey for fear that if she slept even a moment, she'd ruin the elaborate arrangement.

She imagined her mother now, smoothing back her hair and pronouncing her ready.

Be steady, my Guinevere, the queen would have said. *You have nothing to worry about.*

Even though there was plenty to worry about. What if Arthur was awful and ugly? What if some jealous courtier started terrible, unfounded rumors about her pleasuring a horse? What if King Yurien never carried through on his threats of building an empire, and all of this was for nothing?

"I'm not worried," Guin said aloud to the empty carriage. "I'm merely summoning my nerve."

With that, she rapped smartly on the door and picked up her skirts.

◑ ◑ ◑

Arthur raced down the castle staircase, brushing some imaginary dirt from his suede jacket. The wizard had been right; there was no sense pretending to be someone he wasn't. He'd leave the fashionable opulence—or at least the slashed balloon sleeves and jeweled shoe buckles—to his cousin.

The fanfare sounded again, and Arthur quickened his pace. Of course his rooms were on the opposite side of the castle from the main entrance. Behind him, his guards followed noisily, weapons clattering against their mail.

The courtyard was lined with courtiers eager for a glimpse of the princess. The scene reminded him of his return from Avalon, when he'd presented his father with Excalibur, and for one brief evening, all had seemed right and good at Castle Camelot.

Except he'd begun to worry that he'd foreseen Merlin's death, had spent the week stuck in endless council meetings, and now his father was presenting him with a bride he had neither requested nor chosen.

And their first meeting was happening in front of everyone, his potential humiliation on public display, as usual. Yet another perk of being heir to the throne.

Arthur took his place on the steps behind his father, and just in front of Gawain. Jereth lurked in the background, scowling as though he'd prefer to be elsewhere. Arthur would have preferred that as well, to be honest. Lance, predictably, was nowhere to be found. Arthur suspected his friend had requested gate duty just to avoid the castle corridors, and by extension, Jereth.

Sard, it was warm out. He had definitely sweated through his tunic.

"Look lively, cousin," Gawain whispered in his ear. "Or at least try not to look as though you're digesting spoiled meat."

"At least I'm not costumed so it takes three servants to undress me every time I need the privy," Arthur shot back.

Behind him, Jereth snickered. The princess's carriage came to a stop, and a groom placed a small wooden stair under the door.

Arthur swallowed nervously. This was it.

His father stepped forward, his fur-trimmed cloak billowing behind him, and his ruby-laden crown catching the light.

And then a dark-haired girl descended from the carriage in a froth of crimson silk. Before Arthur could get a better look at her, she dropped gracefully into a curtsey.

"I thank you most ardently, Your Majesty," she murmured, "for your kind hospitality. Camelot is exactly as I remember it."

"I am pleased to hear it. Although I think you'll find some things have changed," Uther replied smoothly. "Where is my son?"

"Here," Arthur said, hurrying forward. "I'm here."

The princess rose from her curtsey, and Arthur blinked in surprise.

Gone was the plain, bratty child who had thrown tantrums over games of croquet and demanded the kitchens produce tiny cakes for a doll's tea.

In her place was a singularly beautiful young woman. Her mahogany curls glinted auburn in the sun. Liquid brown eyes blinked up at him from a tan, heart-shaped face. Rosy lips curved into a soft smile, and her ample figure spilled suggestively from the low neckline of her fashionable gown.

Her beauty was intimidating. It poked at him, making Arthur want to fidget, or at least flatten his hair. Instead, he offered the princess a smooth bow, aware that she was examining him in return.

Had she noticed the pimple on his jaw where he rested his hand while reading? And what must she think of his plain circlet? He wished he'd sent Lucan to retrieve his better one after all.

Yet if the princess was disappointed, she gave nothing away. Instead, she stared back at him, her expression coolly neutral.

"What a long time it's been," she said, offering him a small smile.

"Too long," Arthur agreed.

"If you wish a rematch of croquet, you have my word I would not whack you in the shins with my mallet," said Guinevere.

"I wouldn't mind if you did, so long as I had the pleasure of your company," Arthur replied smoothly.

He felt ridiculous, speaking such flowery nonsense, even though he knew it was expected. It wasn't him. None of this was. It was all so insincere and showy. Even with no choice in bride, he hadn't expected to meet like this, with every statement and gesture being watched and judged by his father's court.

Guinevere dipped again into a brief curtsey, which gave Arthur quite the front-row seat to her bosom.

"My company is yours," she said, her eyes finding his, "for as long as you'll have me."

Arthur swallowed thickly. It really had been a while. Since he'd had anyone.

But this was a performance, he reminded himself. Their alliance was valuable enough for her to hide her true feelings. She spoke as he did—formally, prettily, and with caution.

What he needed was time alone with the princess. So that they might drop the pretense and get to know each other truly. There was always a chance that he would find her to be a charming, brilliant ally, with similar interests and a sense of humor as alluring as her bosom. And that she would find him equally wonderful.

"May I give you a tour of the castle?" he suggested. "We have an excellent library, if you are fond of such things."

"I'm afraid I'm not much for books," the girl said politely.

"How about gardens?" Arthur inquired, hiding his disappointment. "Ours are thick with lavender this time of year, and all manner of fascinating herbs."

"Perhaps another time, when the weather is more temperate," she said disinterestedly.

Arthur tried to think. Did girls play chess? He couldn't remember. Riding? No, that was too forward, and she'd been traveling all day. And he dared not invite her to join him for a game of cards. This really was impossible.

He should have arranged something. A romantic picnic, perhaps, or a theatrical performance. But he'd been too nervous to plan a date with a stranger. And now he had nothing, other than an overwhelming urge to laugh at his own stupidity.

"You should show the princess the royal vault," suggested King Uther. "I suspect she'll find it most illuminating."

Arthur's shoulders tensed. Anything but that.

"Why?" the girl asked curiously. "What's in the vault?"

"Nothing," said Arthur, at the same moment his father replied, "The sword Excalibur."

CHAPTER 24

Lance wiped a trickle of sweat from his brow and raised his longbow. The afternoon was scorching, and Captain Lamarc was punishing them all with a double session of target practice.

Some of the boys had gone to an alehouse on Sunday, and Tristan had wagered badly at a game of dice. When none of the guards could lend him the coin to settle his debt, he'd been stripped naked in payment. Of his uniform.

Lance, who was on gate duty, had pretended not to notice as the guards smuggled Tristan back into the barracks wrapped in Percival's cloak and nothing else. The next morning, everyone who had been at the alehouse requested a single replacement piece of their uniform, hoping to hide Trist's problem.

It had been a good plan, but it hadn't worked. The captain had found them out immediately, and had been furious at the situation.

"What would happen," Captain Lam had growled, his graying whiskers twitching with fury, "if an enemy of the crown got their hands on a *royal guard's uniform*?"

He did have a point. And of course the lost clothing was worth three months' pay, far more than the handful of shillings Tristan had owed.

Lance wished he had been asked along to the alehouse. Perhaps if he'd gone, he could have quietly settled Tristan's debt, and they all might have avoided the captain's wrath. But he hadn't been invited. As usual. And it always hurt the same amount, no matter how much he tried not to care.

Concentrating on his training always made him feel better. He notched an arrow into his longbow and sent it flying toward the target.

Bull's-eye. Dead center.

He loosed another arrow, which landed with a twang, splitting his previous one in twain. Curious if he could manage it a third time, he raised his bow again.

"Take a rest, Lance," called Morian, wiping sweat from his brow. "You're making the rest of us look bad."

"Then keep up," Lance goaded, lowering his bow. "If any of you can."

"Is that a challenge?" Percival asked with a competitive gleam in his eyes.

"Only if you find accuracy challenging," replied Lance.

A couple of guards hooted, and Percival reached for an arrow, his jaw set with determination. He rushed it in his haste to prove himself, and it landed at the very edge of the bull's-eye.

Percival grimaced. "I can still split it," he boasted.

"A penny says you can't," called Tristan.

"If you had a penny to wager, none of this would have happened in the first place," someone shouted.

Lance tried not to sigh as the friendly contest devolved into posturing and name-calling and more than a few friendly shoves.

Here we go again.

It was like they wanted to fight for the sake of it, not because they had anything to fight for. Any page behaving with such a lack of chivalry would have been severely punished. Especially for fighting with another noble son. But the guards weren't pages. And with one glaring exception, they weren't nobles, either. There was no code of chivalry here.

He glanced across the training field, where Princess Guinevere was taking a stroll through the rose gardens.

It had been years since he'd last seen her. Since her arrival, he'd only spotted her from afar—due to his Plan To Avoid Jereth. Guin rounded a corner, coming nearer to the archery field. And Lance caught a glimpse of her companion.

Lady Elaine. Ugh.

The two girls giggled loudly, their heads together, and Lance realized—they were spying on the guards for entertainment.

He imagined Guin recognizing him here, now, like this, and he almost cringed with embarrassment at what Lady Elaine would tell her.

Perhaps he could set the guards right.

"All right," he said, addressing the company. "If Percival can split his arrow, then no one should be impressed that I did. If not, then I had a lucky shot. And I'll welcome the challenge to do it again, with any conditions."

"Any conditions?" Percival grinned, waggling his eyebrows.

"Now that you've seen Trist's bare arse, are you so eager to view mine?" Lance teased.

"Are you so eager to volunteer?" Percival asked with a smirk.

"Are *you* so afraid you can't hit the mark?" Lance challenged.

"Oh, my aim is true," Percival assured him. "As is my stamina."

This last comment drew loud hoots from the guards. Their rivalry was well known amongst the company. After Lance, Percival came a close second in most weapons. With his friendly manner and country charm, the others were instantly at ease around him, and he was the obvious frontrunner to be their next captain.

Percival carefully notched an arrow into his bow, sweat glistening against his dark brown skin.

It went so quiet that Lance could hear the birds circling overhead.

Perce adjusted the tip of his arrow, sighting down the shaft with one eye closed, and then the other.

And then a castle falcon dove toward their practice field, its talons extended, heading straight for Percival.

"Agh!" Perce cried, letting loose the arrow in surprise. It went wide. So wide it would miss the target entirely.

And hit another one.

Guinevere stood rooted to the spot as Percival's arrow headed right toward her.

Lance didn't think. He just reacted, reaching for his own bow and shooting as fast as he could. There was a searing pain as the bowstring snapped against his forearm, but he hardly noticed.

"Look out!" he yelled.

◑ ◑ ◑

The arrow was going to kill her.

One moment Guinevere had been watching the jocular guards challenge each other to hit a difficult target, and the next, it was as though she had left her body, and was watching the moment unfold from far above.

Then the golden-haired archer shot another arrow, knocking the first harmlessly aside. And it was over.

Time snapped back into place, and through the deafening beat of her heart, she became gradually aware of Lady Elaine's loud hysterics.

"Princess!" the golden-haired archer called, hurrying over. "Are you all right?"

She nodded, the horrible moment replaying in her mind. She was trembling. She didn't know how to stop trembling.

"Guinevere," he said, taking her gently by the shoulders. "Say something."

His hands felt soft and strong wrapped around her, and they seemed to quiet the thunder in her chest.

There was something comforting about him, and even familiar. He was uncommonly broad and handsome, with honeyed blond curls and the brightest blue eyes she'd ever seen. He stared down at her in concern, thick muscled arms bulging from beneath his mail. She definitely would have remembered seeing *him* around the castle.

But then she took in the rough cloth of his uniform. He was no knight or squire, only a common guard. She could smell the sweat on him, mixed with freshly oiled leather. And his hands were on his shoulders.

"What are you doing?" she protested, twisting out of his grip.

"Helping," he said, "with the shock. And before that, with saving you from a stray arrow."

"That arrow was a menace!" Lady Elaine put in. "I'm going to speak to my father and have the guard who shot it turned out into the streets before supper."

"It wasn't his fault," the blond man protested. "One of the castle falcons attacked."

Elaine sniffed and folded her arms across her chest.

"Come on, Guinny," said the guard. "Surely you saw it."

Just who did he think he was, addressing her like that? "I beg your pardon," she said haughtily. "Do I know you?"

"Sure you do." He grinned amicably. "It's me—Lancelot."

"Lance?" she said, surprised.

The lad she remembered had been Sir Ector's son, a favored companion of the young prince. She'd had the best time with him that summer, chasing frogs out on the gardens, and stealing sweets from the kitchen, and annoying Arthur to put down his books and join in their mischief, which had rarely happened.

They had explored the game forest one weekend, venturing in so deeply to the royal hunting grounds that they'd come across an old church with an ancient tomb beneath, and had made up spells with tree branches as wands to try to wake the dead.

Guin could see it easily now, the shadow of the young boy he'd been. It was there in the mischievous smile that tugged at his lips, and the rebellious glint to his eyes. He'd grown so handsome and tall! If only scrawny, bookish Arthur had done the same.

She was so happy to see Lance that she threw her arms around him, sweat be damned.

Elaine cleared her throat in disapproval. What an insufferable companion she was turning out to be.

"You saved my life," Guin said, drawing out the hug just to make Elaine squirm.

"Ah, that flimsy little arrow?" Lance scoffed. "Wouldn't have done much damage at all."

They both knew he was lying. She squeezed tighter. And he hissed in pain.

"Are you hurt?" Guin asked, pulling away, her eyes wide.

Lance inspected his arm with a grimace. A bloody red welt traveled the length of his forearm.

"Must've snapped it with my bowstring," he said, not particularly concerned.

"Princess, your gown!" Elaine exclaimed. "It's ruined!"

Guin looked down in dismay. Elaine was right. Lance's wound had streaked blood across the silk bodice of her lavender dress. How frustrating! She'd rather liked this one. And she'd only brought four trunks with her, so her wardrobe was quite limited.

"Honestly, Lance," Elaine went on. "Everything you touch, you taint."

His eyes blazed at the insult. "Funny, I don't remember touching your personality," he returned.

"As if I'd let you anywhere near me," the girl said coldly.

Guin blinked at them in surprise. What was going on with these two? Well, whatever it was, she was *over it*. She drew herself up to her full height, lifted her chin, and channeled her mother's imperious manner.

"Enough!" she insisted. "Lady Elaine, how dare you insult Lancelot so? He prevented a terrible accident. He is to be commended, not attacked."

"Of course, Princess," Lady Elaine mumbled with a curtsey.

"And if I hear anything about a guard being turned out into the streets, I'll assume your father has volunteered to take his place," Guinevere added.

Elaine's eyes widened at the threat. Good.

"And Lancelot," Guin said, turning to him. The guard winced, expecting the worst. "I suspect that injury has sharpened your tongue, to hear you say such things to a lady."

"I apologize you heard me say them," Lance replied.

Guinevere's mouth quirked at his response. "The damage to my gown is unfortunate, but I'd rather my dress be this morning's only casualty."

"Actually," said Lance, "I know someone who can fix your dress. And mend my arm."

Fix her dress? "Well then," Guinevere said grandly, "you may lead the way."

But Lance didn't move. "I want your word that the guards will come to no punishment for what happened," he bargained.

"As I said before—" Guin started, but Lance cut her off.

"You said he wouldn't be turned out into the streets," he explained. "Which isn't at all the same thing."

Guin blinked at him. She'd never before concerned herself with the lives of the castle guards. They seemed a trivial, unimportant bother. But she could see that Lance was quite serious. That this *mattered* to him.

"As you wish," she said airily.

Lance grinned. "Well then, let's go and see the wizard."

CHAPTER 25

Arthur stared pensively at the mortar and pestle on the table in front of him. Even a rare morning in the wizard's workshop wasn't serving as a distraction from his problems. Well, it *was*, but not in the way he'd hoped.

Across from him, Merlin flipped through a book of potions, lips slightly apart, dark lashes lowered. Arthur wasn't trying to stare, but whenever the wizard's fingers twitched, the page turned itself. Loudly.

"That's incredibly annoying, you know," Arthur said finally.

Merlin looked up, the picture of innocence. "*I'm* annoying? *You've* been tapping your boot for a quarter of an hour. Master Ambrosius is testing me on potion ratios today. What's your excuse?"

Arthur sighed, scrubbing a hand through his hair. He felt embarrassed admitting it. Yet the young wizard seemed to guess.

"She's not *that* bad," Merlin said.

Objectively, Merlin was right. Yet all he could think about was the look on the princess's face when his father had made him show off Excalibur the very hour of her arrival. As though he was such a poor prize that he needed to sweeten the deal before she called for her carriage. Which, actually, Arthur would have appreciated. At least then she would have been honest.

He couldn't help thinking of the letter she'd written that night, telling her father of the sword. He'd noticed the ink stains on her fingers, and had borrowed the letter off a royal messenger before it could be sent.

He'd told himself he was making certain there was no threat from Cameliard, yet truly, he was looking for a far more painful betrayal.

His cheeks burned as he recalled a particularly damning paragraph:

Camelot is both a valuable ally and a formidable foe, though you would not know it to gaze upon its crown prince. He is not much for appearance, more closely resembling a malnourished scholar than a knight. I believe he would rather marry a library than a princess. Yet he somehow recovered the sword Excalibur, a priceless treasure that glows as a thousand suns when Prince Arthur draws near. Should the old legends prove true, the sword alone would defeat invading armies.

He wished he'd never read it. Afterward, all he could see in the princess's polished smile was her interest in doing whatever it took to protect Cameliard.

To make matters even worse, she'd formed a fast friendship with Lady Elaine, and had ruined Chef's menu for the week after announcing that she ate neither sugar nor dairy. According to Arthur's valet, the mercurial Frenchman had pulverized a cake with a meat cleaver.

"Princess Guinevere," Arthur said, twisting the pestle into his ground ginger, "is none of your concern."

Merlin snorted.

"I have other matters that occupy me," Arthur insisted.

"Tell that to the poor ginger root you've mutilated."

Arthur guiltily loosened his grip on the pestle. He'd needed to do *something* with his hands. And Master Ambrosius was down in the infirmary, having a go at the court physician for using arsenic to treat headache.

"I was pretending it was your face," Arthur told the wizard.

It was then that he heard footsteps on the stairs, along with the echo of voices.

A moment later, Guinevere and Lancelot appeared at the threshold to the wizard's workshop. Arthur wasn't sure who was more surprised to see whom.

"Your Highness?" Guin frowned.

"Did you need me?" Arthur asked, rising from the table.

"Don't flatter yourself," Lance said. "We're here to see the wizard."

"He's with the royal physician," said Merlin.

"Actually, I was looking for you instead," said Lance.

That was when Arthur spotted the angry welt on his friend's forearm. "You're hurt," he accused. "Who did this?"

And how on earth had *Guinevere* gotten dragged into it?

"Snapped it against my bow," Lance said. "Hurts like a bi—" he glanced at Guinevere. "Um, well, it stings."

"Lancelot saved my life," Guinevere piped up. "And injured himself most terribly in my protection. I am in his debt, and I beg you to heal him, Master Apprentice Wizard."

She blinked prettily at Merlin, who burst out laughing.

"I'm sorry," gasped the wizard. "Does she *always* talk like that?"

Guin's cheeks flushed scarlet, and her mouth fell open into an indignant, round O.

"*Merlin,*" Arthur said, his voice low in warning. That was no way to speak to a lady. Much less a princess. "Apologize."

Merlin shot him an incredulous look. "But—" the wizard began.

"*Now,*" Arthur insisted.

"My apologies, Princess Guinevere. I am a lowly commoner, unaccustomed to the flowery language of nobility," Merlin said, eyes glittering sarcastically. Arthur hoped that was the end of it. But the wizard flashed an infuriating grin and instructed, "Also, I'll thank everyone to refer to me as Master Apprentice Wizard from now on."

"If you'd like a nickname, I can think of far more fitting ones," offered Lance.

"And *I* can think of a spell that turns nipples into garden slugs," Merlin replied.

Guinevere looked horrified.

"He's joking," Arthur assured her, daring Merlin to say otherwise. Honestly, the wizard's behavior was appalling.

"Let's make this quick," Merlin complained. "I have a potions exam this afternoon, and I need to *study*."

"And *I* have bloodstains all over my new gown," Guinevere replied, unfazed. "I climbed all the way up this ridiculously steep tower because Lancelot promised you'd do something to fix it."

"All over" was a gross exaggeration, Arthur thought. It was a few streaks at worst. Judging from Merlin's expression, the wizard felt rather the same way.

"He'd be happy to help you with that," Arthur said smoothly, arching an eyebrow in Merlin's direction and daring him to disagree.

Merlin grumbled the spell, and Guinevere's eyes went wide as the stains disappeared, replaced by the overstrong smell of roses.

"Thank you," Guinevere said, sinking into a curtsey. "Master Apprentice Wizard Merlin."

"I'm just glad I could save the day," Merlin replied dryly.

Arthur had hoped Guinevere would leave after Merlin restored her dress, but no such luck. She flounced over to Master Ambrosius's favorite chair and settled her skirts around her.

"Before the wizard fixes you up, I'd like to hear what happened to your arm," Arthur said.

Lance explained about Percival and the falcon. Guin kept interrupting, adding in small, insignificant details, unaware that everyone was glaring at her.

"Was Percival hurt?" Arthur asked.

"Nah, he's fine," said Lance. "Screamed like a little girl, though."

Arthur turned his laugh into a coughing fit.

"Are you quite well, Your Highness?" Guinevere asked, her brow knitting with concern.

"I am," Arthur hastily assured her.

"Well, I'm not," complained Lance. "If anyone cares."

"Right," Merlin said, pausing a moment before adding, "Princess, you should probably leave before I begin. Healing spells can get a bit . . . messy."

"Messy?" Guinevere asked, wrinkling her nose. "How so?"

"It's best if you just take my word for it," Merlin said delicately.

Guinevere blanched, hastily bobbing a curtsey and giving a formal farewell.

After she was gone, Arthur felt the tension ease from his shoulders. Sard, she was exhausting. She acted like—well, like a *princess*, he supposed.

"Finally," Merlin muttered.

Arthur glared. The wizard had no right to undermine him like that in front of his future wife.

"What? I didn't see either of you making her leave," Merlin retorted. "Now shut up and let me concentrate."

Merlin muttered the spell, wand aimed at Lance. Lance's wound faded to a thin pink welt, and the wizard's knees buckled.

Arthur was there in an instant. Merlin stared up at him, eyes wide, cheeks flushed, lips parted. And Arthur was overcome with the strongest desire to press his lips against the wizard's, as though they were both dying, and the only cure was each other. He could feel his heart racing, and wondered if Merlin could feel it, too.

"You can set me down now," Merlin said. "I'm fine."

Arthur released the wizard, who pasted back on that signature smirk. He felt like a fool for rushing over, as though rescuing a swooning maiden, instead of an arrogant ass who had felt the need to insult one.

"You didn't have to antagonize Guinevere like that," he said harshly.

"Are you kidding? She never shuts up, she's offended by everything, and she speaks as if she's reading off a scroll."

Lancelot snorted.

"Merlin," Arthur warned, quietly furious. "I don't want to hear it."

"You don't want to hear it, or you don't agree?"

That was it. He'd had enough of the wizard's mocking. Merlin had hit a nerve, and instead of backing off, had scratched deeper and deeper.

"You forget your place," Arthur snapped, "*apprentice*."

He'd never spoken to Merlin like that before, and he didn't know which of them was more surprised. The room went silent and cold. The wizard stared at him in disbelief, as though the blow had been physical. Lance shifted awkwardly, trying to melt back against the wall.

A storm gathered in Merlin's eyes. The air crackled and fizzed, and the candle flames stretched to an unnatural height. The glass bottles on the shelves trembled and clinked like chattering teeth.

Arthur's stomach twisted, and he wondered for the first time what would happen if the wizard lost control.

Then Merlin took a deep breath, and the crackle of magic disappeared, everything returning to normal. They glared at one another in the uneasy silence. And then Merlin dipped into an exaggerated, sarcastic bow.

"My deepest apologies, Your Royal Highness," the wizard simpered.

Somehow, that made everything worse.

"I think we're done here," Arthur said coolly, jerking his chin at Lance, who followed after him. "Good day, apprentice."

CHAPTER 26

Arthur didn't mean to keep his father waiting. But with Guinevere and Lance's unexpected visit to the wizard's workshop, he'd completely lost track of time.

Even his father's guards shot him a knowing look as they opened the doors.

Late, their expressions accused.

As if he didn't know it.

The king's rooms were dark, the windows tightly guarded against the bright morning sunshine. Arthur sighed, knowing his father would be in a foul mood.

And sure enough, King Uther slouched sourly in his private dining chamber, looking ill and ignoring the army of dishes Chef had prepared for his breakfast. Instead, he nursed a sludgy green drink vaguely reminiscent of pond scum, still wearing his dressing gown.

Lord Agravaine's and Lord Howell's heads snapped up as Arthur entered, and he felt his cheeks burn with shame at his tardiness.

"So," the king said crossly, "you finally decided to grace us with your presence."

Arthur sunk into a bow. "My apologies, Father. I was with Princess Guinevere and lost track of time." He hoped that news would soften his father's anger.

"And how is she?" the king inquired.

Awful, thought Arthur. "In good spirits," he replied instead.

King Uther grunted in response, tipping back more of the green drink.

"What's in that?" Arthur asked curiously.

"Eel, cabbage, and sugar," said Lord Agravaine crisply. "The royal physician's own concoction."

No wonder his father looked so ill.

"I personally swear by the mixture," said Lord Howell, with a smile that was just a little too wide. Arthur didn't blame him for being on edge. The king's mood often dictated his temper. And it was apparent King Uther was in wretched spirits.

Lord Agravaine motioned toward an empty chair with an even emptier smile. "Sit. We were just discussing the king's birthday celebration."

"Right," Arthur said, relieved. "That."

This year, his father was turning fifty, and the plans were lavish. There was to be a full weekend of performances and feasts, culminating in a grand ball. All of Camelot's noble families were to be invited, and so were royal guests from afar.

"You're still planning to invite King Yurien?" Arthur asked.

"Every king and queen of England will be invited," said Lord Agravaine. "Though I assume most will send their regrets."

"But you believe Yurien will accept the invitation," Arthur guessed.

Lord Agravaine didn't deny it.

"It seems wise to get a measure of him in peace," added King Uther.

"And let him get a measure of us as well," Arthur finished, with a sidelong glance at his father's shrewd advisor.

"Precisely," said Lord Agravaine. "A birthday celebration is the perfect opportunity to display Camelot's might without insinuating any threat."

Even though insinuating a threat was exactly what his father meant to do.

Arthur knew very little about the former baron who had muscled his way onto the Lothian throne three years ago. Just that a mysterious fire had wiped out the royal family while they knelt in prayer. The entire chapel had burned to the ground, and Yurien hadn't even waited for the ashes to cool before he'd shown himself to the throne room and begun giving orders.

"Lothia is a small kingdom," said Lord Howell. "One of barren lands, cold winters, and large debts. I have no doubt King Yurien will be thoroughly intimidated by his visit."

"He'd better be," warned the king, "if I am to suffer the man's presence at my birthday celebration."

Arthur braced himself against the sudden unwanted remembrance of his father's previous birthday celebrations. Memories flooded forth, of riding in the carriage at his mother's side, her warm hand squeezing his, her smile bright and happy as she gazed out at her subjects. Of his father, stony-faced and severe, dressed for battle rather than celebration, staring straight ahead, without so much as a wave.

His mother's hand had always squeezed tighter whenever the people lining up to watch the parade looked particularly ragged or hungry. Or whenever the procession stopped, and the guards pressed into the crowd.

One year, his father had held an archery competition, and Lance had tried everything to be allowed to compete against the knights and nobles, though he was only a few months into his training as a page. Another, Arthur had been pronounced old enough to attend the ball, and had danced with the newly arrived courtier Lady Elaine, which, in retrospect, he thoroughly regretted. There had been the birthday he and Lance had snuck bottles of wine onto the roof and nearly fallen to their deaths climbing back in through a window. And the birthday that had come and gone in a somber cloud of mourning for everyone, except the freshly widowed king, who had taken Lord Howell's wife to bed for his comfort, and made a habit out of borrowing his courtiers' wives ever since.

Arthur sighed, thinking of Princess Guinevere, and how he'd be expected to keep to her side throughout the festivities, implying their kingdoms' impending alliance. As if it wasn't a match designed by their fathers, but a choice they had made on their own.

Lord Howell had switched to talking about a sword-fighting contest that would be held as part of this year's entertainment. Arthur was still brooding about Guinevere, but then his father said something he didn't quite catch about Excalibur.

"Sorry?" Arthur said.

"For the competition. So that you may enter the ring wearing it," Lord Howell repeated.

"In the sword-fighting contest?" Arthur said incredulously, hoping he'd misheard.

"It will send a warning that Camelot shouldn't be trifled with," the king said decisively. "In the contest, in front of our kingdom's noble families and our royal guests from afar, you will draw Excalibur—"

Arthur opened his mouth to protest, but the king held up his hand for silence.

"And then, after everyone has seen the sword for themselves, you will graciously set it aside, and compete with an ordinary blade."

Arthur's stomach flipped.

"But I'm no champion swordsman," he protested. "Not against the best knights in the realm."

"That's of no matter," said Lord Agravaine. "You'll have a distinct advantage."

"And what advantage is that?" Arthur asked.

Lord Agravaine's grin was as sharp as a knife. "Why, that scabbard, of course."

Arthur quietly choked.

"You were clever to keep its power quiet in front of the court," Lord Agravaine went on. "And now, you can use it without appearing to cheat."

"But, Father—" Arthur began.

King Uther swept his drink to the floor, the foul liquid splattering everywhere.

"I believe I made myself clear," growled the king, his voice low in warning. "Any man would be a fool to rise against the crown that wields Excalibur. Your participation isn't a request. It's a command."

Arthur squared his jaw, but said nothing. Once again, his life was being decided for him. And he hated it.

"Of course, Father," he murmured with a bow.

◐ ◐ ◐

Arthur felt sick as he left his father's chambers.

He hated that he was expected to cheat against his own knights in front of every noble in the kingdom, and visiting royals besides.

And he didn't see a way out of it.

He knew his father feared King Yurien, and with good reason. When Yurien had seized control of Lothia, the kingdom's coffers were nearly empty from paying tribute to Alba. Keeping the peace with the northern kings—three fierce brothers who ruled as one enemy—came with a heavy price tag.

And it was one that Yurien refused to pay. Instead, he had turned his army on neighboring Northumbria, burning and pillaging every unsuspecting town just across the border until their king begged for peace. And when he did, Yurien had gladly granted it—so long as Northumbria paid the Albans' tribute on their behalf.

In the months since, Northumbria had withered under the financial strain, while Lothia had flourished. King Yurien was obviously strengthening his army. And it was anyone's guess whether he would move west, to seize the kingdom he had already weakened, north, to wage war against the brothers who made such impossible demands, or south, toward the once prosperous Cameliard, in pursuit of an empire.

And if Cameliard fell to Yurien, then Camelot was as good as doomed, and Cornwall along with them.

So Arthur didn't blame his father for wanting to keep a close eye on Yurien. The trouble with this plan lay squarely on Arthur's shoulders.

If he were a better swordsman, he'd have no trouble flashing around Excalibur, then picking up an ordinary sword and trouncing his opponents. It all fell apart because he was no great talent with a blade. And he had no one to blame but himself.

The skill had never seemed important.

Perhaps his father's advisors had been right when they had declared him utterly lacking. Yet instead of doing something about it, he had stewed, and wasted time in the wizard's workshop, and sulked in the library.

No wonder Guinevere saw him as such a disappointment. No wonder everyone did.

Arthur paused on the staircase, wondering how he had been so shortsighted. It was so obvious now what he should have done, not that there was much chance to remedy it in the coming weeks.

Perhaps, if he practiced morning and night, he could avoid the humiliation of coming last. It wasn't as though he needed to win the competition. And if he did, he was fairly certain there'd be whispers that he had cheated.

So he didn't have to be the best swordsman. Just . . . a better one.

He glanced out the window, where the guard was training on the lawn, as they always did in the mornings. Captain Lam stood to the side, watching critically as the men crossed swords, and barking corrections.

Lancelot's words floated back to him then, from weeks ago in the armory, before the rest of the castle was awake.

You should come train with the guard. That'll whip you into shape.

Well, Arthur decided, *better late than never.*

CHAPTER 27

Emry was still fuming the next morning. She sat at the battered wooden table in the wizard's workshop, by all appearances working on a poison antidote. But in truth, she was waiting for Arthur to walk through the door so she could tell him exactly what a spoiled, entitled ass he was.

She couldn't believe he'd made her apologize to Guinevere, yet had insisted *she* was the one being ridiculous.

You forget your place, apprentice.

Ugh. The way he'd said it. Like he could be her friend one moment, and her prince the next, and she was somehow supposed to know the difference.

She heard a noise and glanced up, hoping it was Arthur. But the sound was simply Master Ambrosius adjusting his chair by the fire.

"Have you managed it already?" he asked, raising a bushy eyebrow.

Emry made a face, glancing down at the eight—no, nine—dead snails scattered across the table. She was supposed to be changing a tincture of monkshood into an antidote for the deadly poison. But no matter how many times she tried, she couldn't get the spell to work.

She was running out of snails. And patience.

"No." Emry sulked. "This spell is impossible!"

"Your father didn't think so," Master Ambrosius said. "Now focus and try again."

Emry scowled at the poison, trying to concentrate. Once more, she fixed her attention on the tincture in the small glass vial.

"*Edhwierft,*" she whispered, willing the poison to reverse its deadly properties.

She felt the magic release, and watched the poison fizz. Carefully, she tipped a few drops onto a hapless snail, and waited.

The snail twitched and fell over.

"Ughhhh!" she groaned. "Why isn't it working?"

"Have patience," Master Ambrosius advised. "There's no shame in encountering magic beyond your capabilities."

"If it's beyond my capabilities, then why did you assign it?" Emry grumbled, wondering if he was trying to teach her a lesson. She wouldn't put it past him.

"I was curious if you could do it," said Master Ambrosius. "I didn't try your father on antidotes until his second year at the castle. And he struggled with it for weeks."

"He did?" Emry said, feeling slightly better.

That wasn't so bad, then.

"He did," Master Ambrosius confirmed. "This spell is beyond me. It is beyond almost every wizard I have ever met. But I think, with time, it will work for you."

He went to the bookshelves and took down a slim volume, sliding it onto the table in front of Emry. "How about we give those poor snails a break and try a hiccup-curing draught?"

Emry mumbled her agreement. Yet as she measured out the ingredients for a hiccup cure, her attention drifted back to the antidote she hadn't been able to manage. It had been a long time since she'd been bested by a piece of magic, and she hated it.

◑ ◑ ◑

Emry woke up early the next morning still annoyed about the poison antidote. Perhaps, she thought, she could sneak up to the wizard's workshop a little early and practice before her lessons. As she got dressed in the pale gray dawn, she was distracted by some commotion down in the training yard.

She crossed to the window, wondering what was going on with the guard.

Arthur was out there, dressed in a pair of tight linen trousers and a close-fitting tunic. He had a bow and arrow raised, and appeared to have challenged his own guards to some target practice. His first arrow had hit the very edge of the bull's-eye, hence the shouting.

Dakin, meanwhile, had landed his arrow high, missing the inner ring.

Emry watched in fascination. She'd never seen the prince shoot before, and was annoyed that he wasn't half bad. Lance stood off to the side, looking smug. Arthur endured some good-natured backslapping after he hit the edge of the bull's-eye a third time in a row, and said something that made the nearby guards double over with laughter.

He was such a maddening, infuriating boy.

If he wasn't coming back to the workshop, he at least could have had the decency to say so. But no, he'd left her to discover it on her own, which was somehow worse.

Oh, she *hated* him.

She fumed as she watched the captain assign the guards a lap around the training field, and as Arthur dropped his equipment and joined in. He jogged alongside Lance and a tall, handsome boy with a wide grin, dark brown skin, and some of the thickest biceps she'd ever seen. They were quickly joined by a stocky stocky, freckled, ginger-haired lad who struggled to match their brisk pace.

Ugh. Arthur was clearly trying to impress Princess Guinevere, because she'd caught him moping around the wizard's workshop.

Well, fine. He could go swing around a sword and shoot arrows and be a dumb boy if he wanted. At least now she'd be able to study without his constant interruptions.

And with that, she gathered her books and stomped off to the workshop, where she wouldn't be distracted by her view of the training field.

◑ ◑ ◑

By the fourth day of Arthur's absence from the workshop, Emry had to admit that she missed his company.

Her mornings felt empty without the prince smirking at her across the table as they worked. So she threw herself into her studies, glad for the distraction. And at the end of each day, drained and ravenous from all of the spellwork, she fell gratefully into bed, too tired to dream.

That Friday evening, Emry was walking back to her room from the kitchens, devouring a cheese sandwich and running over a new, complicated piece of spellwork, when she bumped into Gawain.

The prince's cousin was dressed more restrained than usual, in a dark green jerkin and matching boots. A slightly shabby wool cloak and hood hung from his shoulders, which she wouldn't have guessed he owned.

"Lord Gawain," she said, hastily swallowing a mouthful of sandwich.

He considered her, and then his face broke into a grin. It made him look far more approachable. "I don't suppose you're free at the moment?"

"Why?" she asked warily, wondering what he wanted.

"Come and have a drink with me."

Whatever she'd expected Gawain to say, that wasn't it. "A drink?"

"I'm not Arthur," Gawain said with a wry grin. "I can leave the castle quite easily. When I wish."

"And you wish *me* for company?" Emry asked skeptically.

"We did fight bandits together. By my estimation, a drink is long overdue."

Emry bit her lip, considering.

"Say yes," he urged. "It's depressing to go alone."

She knew she should refuse, just as she knew Gawain was trouble. But she was bored. And lonely. And she'd seen so little of London in the weeks since she'd come to the castle. And she knew it would infuriate Arthur. The last one clinched it.

"All right," she agreed, stuffing the rest of the sandwich into her mouth. "One drink."

The gate guards let them through easily, and even called after them to have a pleasant evening. What a difference Gawain's presence made, Emry thought bitterly, remembering how she'd needed to conjure a pass from Master Ambrosius just to meet her brother.

"I know a great place," Gawain promised.

He led the way through the market square and turned onto the Strand.

The wide lane was flanked with brick mansions and regal townhouses that had private landings on the Thames. Some were palaces in their own right, ensconced behind walls and gates, and boasting guards in their own livery. Emry tried not to let her jaw drop.

"What prompted the expedition?" she finally asked.

Gawain lifted one shoulder in a shrug. "I'm heartily sick of babysitting my brother," he confessed.

"But he seems so nice," Emry deadpanned.

Gawain snorted. "He has no regard for anyone but himself," he said darkly. "His horse is on box rest this week, yet he keeps sneaking down to the stables and riding her anyway. I had to bribe the stable boys to tell me when he does it." Gawain grimaced. "Our mother has always indulged him, but I don't understand why our father doesn't reprimand him."

"Fathers always have soft spots for sons," Emry said, thinking about how her own father had been so much more forgiving with Emmett.

"And blind spots," Gawain added with a bitter smile.

"You mean Lance?" Emry said, surprised he would mention it.

"There's no shame in following your heart," said Gawain. "But my brother needs to watch where he steps while doing so. And on whom he steps."

"I take it there's a reason he came back from boarding school," Emry guessed.

"He burned down the scriptorium." Gawain shook his head. "With help from his roommate. Who, by the way, is a minor Flemish royal. Apparently they were both naked and drunk at the time. In a *scriptorium*."

Gawain stopped himself, loosening the tension in his shoulders.

"You better not tell Arthur, he'd have a fit over all those burnt manuscripts," Emry said.

Gawain started to laugh. Once he started, he couldn't stop.

It was the kind of laughing, Emry realized, that you did instead of screaming.

Perhaps Gawain really did desire nothing more than a drinking companion and a sounding board for his troubles. It was possible she had misjudged him. His anguish was certainly real enough.

"Come on," he said, ducking down a narrow lane. "It's this way."

He paused outside an unmarked red door next to a hat shop, knocking a quick rhythm, a grin on his face.

A small opening slid aside, and a a pale, heavily rouged woman's face peered out from behind the door. She was old enough to be his mother, though she was certainly no countess.

"Milord Gawain!" she said with a French accent.

"Madame Becou," Gawain purred.

The door swung open, and the woman ushered them down a dark hallway and into a dim, lavishly decorated sitting room with velvet chairs and a crackling fire.

Diamond-paned windows looked out onto the Thames. Wherry boats drifted past, their lanterns lit against the fog. A rosy-cheeked blonde girl in a gauzy ephemeral gown sat in the corner, plucking at a harp, which gave the room a pleasant atmosphere.

A group of well-dressed young gentlemen had a card game going, their shouts a bit too loud, their table littered with empty goblets. An ample-figured brunette in a gossamer gown poured wine from a silver jug, and one of the men drew her close to press a kiss against her neck. Emry's eyes widened, expecting the girl to protest. But she flashed a seductive smile instead, and led the man up a staircase.

Suddenly, Emry had a very bad feeling about what sort of establishment they were patronizing.

"Is this a—"

"Brothel?" Gawain finished, a flicker of amusement crossing his face. "Well, *technically* it's a bathhouse with extremely loose morals."

Emry choked. "I thought we were going for a drink," she said, horrified.

Gawain quirked an eyebrow. "We are. They have excellent wine. Amongst other things."

"I believe I'll pass on the other things," Emry said, feigning lightness.

"Suit yourself."

Gawain stepped to the side, conversing warmly with the woman who ran the establishment, and kissing her briefly on either cheek.

Emry watched them warily, wishing she'd never agreed to this. She'd been so desperate to leave the castle that she hadn't stopped to worry where she'd end up. And now she knew. A bathhouse full of drunken gentlemen. With loose morals.

The worst part was, knowing what she did of Gawain, she had only herself to blame. He'd sounded so upset about his brother's misdeeds that she'd forgotten he was no angel himself.

Madame Becou showed the two of them to a small, cozy table lit by the rosy glow of a small, ornate lantern. It was a lovely space, Emry grudgingly thought, not that she had much experience with brothels. But she wasn't about to admit it.

She glared daggers at Gawain, who was watching her discomfort with unabashed amusement.

She felt a momentary flicker of panic at his attention but shoved it down. There was no reason for alarm. Perhaps he simply wanted to watch an inexperienced country lad squirm.

Emry knew that her brother wouldn't squirm. That, in the same situation, he'd be delighted. But she realized that somehow, she'd stopped pretending to be Emmett a long time ago.

"Something the matter?" Gawain's brows knitted together in mock concern.

"I don't spend my coin on company," she said, lifting her chin. "A wizard gets no pleasure in paying for illusions."

Gawain threw back his head and laughed. "You surprise me," he said.

"In all the best ways, I hope," she replied with a ghost of a smile.

"And in many others," Gawain said, with a look that she couldn't quite read.

A willowy, dark-skinned maiden with golden leaves pinned in her curls set down a bottle of wine and two silver goblets with a knowing grin.

"Permettez-moi de vous charmer, mes seigneurs," the girl murmured.

With an elegant sweep of her wrist, she poured them each a glass. Her hand lingered around Emry's goblet, and she raised a finger to her soft lips to taste a stray drop of red wine.

Sard. Emry knew she was blushing. And that Gawain was watching.

"Plus tard, peut-être," Emry said with studied disinterest. "If you wish."

"I will hold you to that, milord," the girl said, with a lingering glance at

Emry, and a private smile as she reached across the table to adjust a candle-stick, her bosom brushing inches from Emry's face. It was, Emry noted, a particularly lovely bosom.

Her eyes met Emry's, and she winked.

Emry let out a sigh of relief when the girl left.

"You are surprisingly adept with women," Gawain observed.

"In a brothel?" Emry's lips quirked. "I can't imagine that's any great accomplishment."

"It is here," Gawain said, leaning forward with a wicked grin. "Madeleine is particular about whom she takes to her bed. A night with her is said to bring good fortune. So long as you kiss the heart-shaped birth-mark on her left thigh."

"Are you trying to shock me, Lord Gawain?" she asked.

"Yes. And it isn't working." He raised his goblet in a silent toast.

Emry drained hers in one insouciant gulp, as she'd seen her brother and his friends do countless times.

Gawain watched her appraisingly. "Very good," he said. "You even drink like a lad."

Emry choked. "I don't know what you mean."

She pushed back her chair and rose from her seat as if insulted, though her heart was hammering with alarm. She felt as though she was about to be sick.

"Oh, I think you do," said Gawain, with a slow smile. He was watching her again, his gaze sharp and his insinuation clear. Emry stared back, the whole world narrowing as he accused, "You switched places with that twin brother of yours. Temporarily. But then he refused to change back."

Emry's eyes went wide. How could he possibly know that?

"The night we met," she said, realizing what had happened. "You were at the Crooked Spire."

"Et voilà," Gawain murmured, gesturing for her to take her seat. "Sit. People are beginning to stare."

Annoyingly, he was right. "Why haven't you told anyone?" she asked, slouching back in her chair.

She remembered all of the times she'd caught Gawain's watchful gaze from across the Great Hall. And the times she'd encountered him in the library.

He lounged in his seat, taking an appreciative sip of wine as though her future didn't hang in his grasp.

"I already have enough sins to answer for," he said with a shrug. "Besides, it's been amusing to watch you get away with it for so long."

"Just like it was amusing to bring me here? To a—" Emry lowered her voice to a whisper, "a *brothel*?"

Gawain's grin stretched wider. "A bathhouse," he corrected. "With extremely loose morals."

"And when it stops being amusing?" Emry asked nervously.

"Is that how you think of me?" he asked, putting a hand to his heart. "Like some villain lurking in the shadows?"

Emry didn't say anything. She didn't have to.

Gawain grimaced. "I'm not my father," he said. "I have no desire for a position in Uther's court, nor do I want one in Arthur's. To be honest, I would prefer *less* of a position than the one I'm granted, currently."

"Yes, it must be tiring, wearing such expensive coats and keeping such expensive company," Emry said lightly.

"Oh, I think we both know how to play a part when it best serves us."

"And what part are you playing, Lord Gawain?" Emry smiled sweetly.

Gawain took another slow sip of wine. "In London? The faultless second runner-up to the throne. In Paris? Well, my father insists I keep an eye on things."

"What sorts of things?" Emry asked.

Gawain's eyes met hers and searched her face, as if he wasn't sure how she would react.

"As a royal, I'm received at court. What I overhear while I am there is my own business. And, if I wish to share it, Camelot's."

So he was a spy. It made sense. As did the fact that he reported to his father.

"And my secret?" Emry demanded.

"Well, I could blackmail you," Gawain suggested. "If you'd like."

"I could turn your nipples into garden slugs, if you'd like," Emry returned.

Gawain laughed. "I should inform the king of your deception," he said, suddenly serious. "Masquerading under a false identity at court is a serious crime."

"You think I don't know that?" Emry retorted.

"I think you have no choice but to see it through," said Gawain. He took a sip of wine before adding, "Your deception is foolish, but endearing. I like you. I have a terrible feeling that my cousin does, too."

"Not currently," Emry said with a sigh.

"I've seen similar lovers' quarrels blow over easily enough," Gawain said innocently.

"It's not—" Emry stopped herself.

"Yes?" Gawain asked, leaning forward.

"Any of your business," she finished, annoyed he'd almost drawn a confession out of her. She folded her arms across her chest. "So, you'll keep your mouth shut?"

Gawain traced his finger along the rim of his goblet. He had to know he was making her squirm. "I do have one condition," he said with a wide smile.

"Which is?"

"That you stop avoiding me," said Gawain. "As I said, I could use some company."

"You seem to have plenty," Emry pointed out.

"Ah, but with them I have to play a part. There's no pleasure in paying for an illusion. But there's little pleasure in maintaining one, either. With each other, we can drop the pretense and just be ourselves. How does that sound?"

It sounded wonderful, actually.

"Deal," said Emry, "but no more brothels."

"It's technically—" Gawain started to say.

Emry cut him off with a glare. "No bathhouses, either."

◑ ◑ ◑

Lancelot stared out at the quiet London night through the narrow slit in his helmet, willing his nose to stop itching. He tried scrunching it, but it was no use. The itch was a fierce thing, and it wasn't going away on its own.

He leaned his halberd against the gate and wrenched off his helmet, sighing in relief.

Percival hesitated a moment, then removed his helmet as well. "I won't tell if you won't."

"Believe me, I'm not so eager to face the captain's wrath," said Lance.

He stared out at the abandoned market square, slouching back against the stone bastion. The night air was still and warm, and if anything interesting was happening in London, it was happening elsewhere.

"You've been requesting gate duty a lot," Percival observed. "And no one requests gate duty."

Lance shrugged and adjusted his grip on his halberd. Percival was right.

It *was* one of the worst patrols in the rotation, along with the guard tower and the dungeons. Although personally, the assignment he hated the most was the east wing.

His old room had been on that hallway. Now it belonged to Sir Kay's tow-headed squire, who frequently practiced the lute off-key. Lance hated walking past it. But not so much as he hated walking past another set of doors.

How dare you assault me so, page? I merely asked for help unclasping my cloak.

Lance sighed. At least the gate was quiet, and far away from the castle.

"He's not like I thought," Percival said, breaking the silence. "The prince. He doesn't flinch when he takes a hit. I figured he'd be too precious to get his boots scuffed."

"Arthur?" Lance chuckled. "He'd jump in the lake if you told him you'd accidentally dropped a book in."

"Aah, no one would believe I was readin' a book." Percival grinned.

Lance smothered a laugh. "About as likely as Tristan winning at cards?" he suggested.

"Or you missing the archery target." Percival shook his head. And then he chewed his lip a moment before adding, "I never thanked you for what you said to the princess."

Lance shifted uncomfortably. "It was nothing," he mumbled.

Percival snorted in disbelief. "It wasn't nothing. We all heard you make her swear no guard would be punished for that stray arrow." Percival cut him a serious look. "Why'd you do it?"

"What do you mean?" Lance asked.

"You don't seem to like us all that much. You're always keepin' company elsewhere. And when we go to the tavern, you never come."

Lance stared at Percival incredulously. "I'm never *invited*."

"Who needs to be invited? If you have the night off, you go."

Lance blinked in surprise. It hadn't occurred to him that the other guards saw *him* as standoffish. "I didn't think anyone wanted me around," he admitted.

Perce gave him a meaningful look. "It's no secret Lord Jereth's a nasty piece of work. Treats the staff terrible and the horses worse."

For once, Lance was grateful to be a guard. To hear the simple truth, unadorned by courtier's flattery. He watched as Percival adjusted his grip on his halberd.

"I knew a boy like him back home," Perce went on. "He'd kiss me drunk and punch me sober." Perce shook his head. "Tell you the truth, I don't know which hurt more."

"The hangover, I'd imagine," Lance joked.

Perce's dark eyes flashed in the torchlight. "I *am* a lightweight." He shot Lance a grin. "Which you'd know, if you ever came to the tavern."

Lance was about to say something cutting when he spotted two figures staggering across the square. "We've got company."

"Trouble?"

One of the approaching figures laughed, high and clear as a bell. Lance knew that laugh. "Nope. It's just the apprentice wizard."

As Merlin got closer, Lance saw that he was unsteady on his feet, as though he'd been drinking. His arm was slung around someone's shoulder. Lance couldn't quite make out who it was, and then—

"Lord Gawain," Percival said with a hasty bow.

"Helmets on, gentlemen," Gawain ordered, stumbling through the gateway. His doublet was unbuttoned, and his voice slurred.

Lancelot frowned. Surely Merlin had no business with Arthur's cousin. Yet it looked as though they'd been out *drinking* together.

"I'm desperate for the privy," Lance lied when they'd passed, and then, as quietly as he could, he followed after them.

"You going to make it back to your room, wizard?" Gawain asked. "Or should I carry you?"

"Don't you dare," Merlin protested. "Besides. You can't *say* things like that here."

"Then we'll just have to go out again," said Gawain, a teasing smile on his face.

And then Merlin *giggled*.

There was something odd about the young wizard, Lance thought. And he was beginning to formulate a theory on what that something was.

CHAPTER 28

Nearly finished, Your Highness," the royal tailor promised.

"You've been saying that for the past fifteen minutes," Arthur grumbled. He ached all over from training, and he was starving besides. He'd been standing still for the better part of an hour, having new clothing pinned with painstaking precision. The outfits were all for the king's upcoming birthday festivities, and they were designed to impress.

Arthur stared at his reflection in the mirror. The current suit was black with gold buckles, and elaborate swirls of embroidery at the cuffs. Its high neck was banded with crimson velvet, and boots of soft black leather stopped just below the knee, the toes tipped in hammered gold.

He hardly recognized himself. He looked regal. Intimidating. He looked like a prince.

Which was, of course, the desired effect. Especially since King Yurien had accepted the invitation to attend the festivities.

"I'm worried I might have pinned this too tight," said the tailor. "Can you lift your arm?"

Arthur experimentally raised his right arm, and a spasm of pain shot through his shoulder from where he'd rotated it badly during training.

"Are you well, Your Highness?" the tailor looked concerned.

"Perfectly," Arthur said, shrugging out of the half-finished garment. "The jacket is a masterpiece."

And then, before the tailor could protest, he left to visit the wizard's workshop to see if there was anything that might help his shoulder.

"Ah, Arthur," said Master Ambrosius. "I'd been wondering when you'd come and visit."

"It hasn't been *that* long," Arthur admonished. But when he tried to remember his last visit, he realized that it *had* been a while. He'd been so focused on everything to do with his father's birthday celebrations—and the sarding sword-fighting contest—that he'd abandoned everything else.

And *everyone* else.

He looked around, hoping he'd spy Merlin slouched in a chair by the fire, or coming out of the storeroom with an armload of herbs.

"Merlin isn't here," Master Ambrosius said wryly, "if that's who you're looking for."

Arthur was about to protest, but the old wizard silenced him with a look.

"Take this," he said, pressing a small jar into Arthur's hands. "And tell me what's in it."

Arthur grinned at the challenge. He removed the lid and gave the contents a sniff.

"Tallow," he said. "With lavender. And something else. I'm not sure about the spice."

"Magic," the old wizard said. "It's a healing salve. For your shoulder."

Arthur wondered how the old man knew. "Thank you." He pocketed the jar. The old wizard had given it to him only once before, cautioning him that it was in short supply, the ingredients rare and the spellwork difficult.

"It will dull the pain, although it won't be nearly as much help to you as my apprentice," said Master Ambrosius.

Arthur sighed.

"I've seen you in the yard, taking hits from men twice your size," the wizard went on. "My abilities aren't what they used to be, but Merlin's grow by the day."

"Along with his ego."

"Perhaps it isn't what you think," said Master Ambrosius.

"What isn't?" Arthur asked.

The old wizard smiled. "You should pay Merlin a visit. And bring some food with you. Healing magic works up an appetite."

◖ ◖ ◖

An impatient knock sounded on Emry's door.

It was late, and she was lounging across her bed, practicing a summoning spell on a deck of playing cards.

The knock sounded again, breaking her concentration. The knave of spades dropped to the floor, and she looked up, annoyed at the interruption. Whoever was there wasn't going away.

She flung open the door, finding herself face to face with Prince Arthur for the first time in over a week. He was elegantly disheveled in that careless way of his. And he held a plate of bite-sized cinnamon cakes. The smell of them alone was enough to make her stomach rumble.

Oh, she wanted to kill him. And hug him. And yell at him. Preferably all at the same time.

"May I come in?" he asked.

"Why bother to ask, since I'm just a lowly apprentice?" Emry retorted.

Arthur winced as his words came back to him. "That wasn't my best moment," he allowed.

"I hope you're here to apologize," she said.

"I hope you're volunteering to go first." He offered her the barest edge of a smirk.

Insufferable.

"Just—get inside," Emry said.

She watched Arthur lower himself gingerly onto the edge of her bed, as though every bone in his body ached. There were dark smudges beneath his eyes, and he looked exhausted.

He offered her a cake, and her fingers hovered over the pastries until she found the one with the most icing. Dear god, it was good. And still warm from the oven.

Arthur popped one into his mouth, then reached for another, absently licking the icing from his fingers.

"Just so you know, I'm only tolerating your presence because cake," she said.

"You're angry with me." He said it as though he was only now discovering this fact.

"Of course I'm angry with you," Emry replied in exasperation. "You treated me like—like a *servant*. And then you just . . . abandoned me without a word so you could flex your muscles with the guard."

Arthur frowned. "I'm not 'flexing my muscles,'" he retorted. "I'm training for the sword-fighting competition my father is making me enter in front of every sarding noble in the kingdom!"

"Wait, *what*?"

Arthur shrugged. "I thought you knew."

"How on *earth* would I know that?"

Arthur put his head in his hands.

"I didn't tell you," he mumbled. "In my defense, there's been a lot going on."

Emry ate another cake so she wouldn't have to reply. It was so annoying how he could just . . . make her feel awful for being annoyed with him. She shouldn't care, yet she did. Far too much.

She watched as the prince rotated his shoulder like it pained him. "Show me," she said with a sigh.

"Show you what?" He blinked at her, feigning innocence.

"Whatever injury you're pretending you don't have from training with the guard."

"I don't want to bother you," Arthur protested.

"Right." Emry snorted. "Which is why you're here. To not bother me."

"And to not apologize," he reminded her.

Arthur gingerly slid off his jacket and untied the laces on his tunic. He groaned as he wrenched the fine linen fabric over his head.

Emry's cheeks flamed. She'd been so caught up in teasing him that she hadn't realized she'd asked him to undress.

And now he was shirtless. In her bedroom.

And they were completely alone.

It was almost too much to bear, how much she wanted to close the distance between them and press her lips against his. How she knew that, if she did, his mouth would taste of icing sugar and cinnamon.

"Well? Will I live?" he teased.

Emry realized she'd been staring. She gave the prince a quick assessment: a large purple bruise spread across the side of his rib cage, and he held one of his shoulders stiffly. But she was more distracted by the hard, defined muscles of his chest. She glanced away.

"Unfortunately," she retorted.

"I know, I should have worn my scabbard," Arthur said with a sigh. "But I wanted to do it without training wheels."

"Who got in the lucky blow?"

"Only about four different guards. I believe they meant to see if I'd quit."

"Well, you didn't." She was staring at a spot over the prince's shoulder, which seemed safe.

"Can't. Otherwise I'll embarrass myself in front of everyone."

"You'd do that far less painfully if you just wore your scabbard."

"So noted." Arthur scrubbed a hand through his hair. "Do you mean for me to stand around with my shirt off all night?"

Emry coughed. "Oh, right," she said. She rolled her sleeves and reached for her wand.

"*Angsumnes*," she whispered, feeling the magic flow between them.

It was different than with Lance. She hadn't cast a healing spell on Arthur before, and she was shocked how easily the magic flowed. How quickly his bruises faded. How she only lost her breath, not her balance. She was barely even dizzy.

Without thinking, Emry brushed her fingers over the place where, moments before, there had been an angry bruise. Arthur's skin was warm. And soft. He smelled of cinnamon and coffee and old books. They were standing so close together, and her heart was beating so fast and—

She jerked her hand away.

Arthur cleared his throat. "Fascinating," he said, staring at the place where his bruise had been. "I didn't realize it would be painless."

"It's not medicine, it's magic," Emry reminded him, reaching for a cake. She popped it into her mouth whole. And then she reached for another. The spellwork might not have made her fight to stay upright, but it had certainly made her ravenous.

Arthur watched her with a strangely protective expression. "Hold on," he said, tugging on his tunic and disappearing into the hall for a moment. She heard some quiet talking, and then footsteps. Arthur poked his head back in. "I'm having more food sent up. Hope you don't mind. I'm starved from all of the training."

He offered her a small smile, and just like that, they were okay again.

☾ ☾ ☾

Arthur wiped the sweat from his brow and adjusted his grip on the sword. It was late, and he was alone in the armory, trying to clear his head. The padded practice dummy stared blankly back at him, but no matter how many times he lunged in attack, his thoughts remained just as tangled.

They had almost kissed twice now.

He was sure of it.

First in the workshop, and again, just last night, when he'd gone to the wizard's bedroom and had somehow stayed for hours, confessing his troubles over platters of leftovers and a jug of ale.

He pressed forward, delivering a feint to the dummy's left side and a strike to the right, his heart pounding from the effort. Sweat beaded his brow, but he didn't stop to catch his breath before he tried the move again.

He didn't understand what it was about the sarding wizard that got to him like this. Perhaps it wasn't Merlin in particular, but the feeling of someone in his arms.

Maybe, if he spent more time with Guinevere, he'd start to dream of pressing his lips against hers, too. Although he doubted it. He found the princess beautiful, but ice cold. Like a sword worn too long in the snow. Whereas Merlin was a glowing blade, one he ached to hold.

No. Stop, he told himself forcefully, trying the feint again. The practice dummy wobbled at the force.

So he had feelings for the lad.

He'd get over them. He had to.

Because the last thing in the world he needed was to feel the way he did about that smug, insufferable wizard. Or to feel so indifferent about the girl who was going to become his wife.

Arthur sighed, wishing he knew what was going on. His head had never turned at the sight of another lad before. And when it came to beautiful women, he wasn't without experience.

There had been the lady-in-waiting who was thrilled to be caught in his bed the next morning. Another girl who'd gathered a flock of courtiers eager to hear every sordid detail. A third who'd seized the opportunity to whisper in his ear about her father's debts, hoping they might be forgiven. A fourth who had come to his room smelling of herbs that increased fertility, and had sworn it was merely perfume.

At sixteen, he'd been too eager to care about the girls' motivations. But with each betrayal, he'd felt more and more foolish.

So he'd begun to make excuses, or slip unnoticed from the banquet hall through the servants' stair. Alone in his room, he'd told himself a story about the girl he'd meet at university. He'd imagined her whenever he felt lonely.

And then his mother had died, and his heart had broken, and when he closed his eyes, he couldn't imagine anything, or anyone, that would make him feel better.

So he didn't understand what it was about the boy wizard that made his heart pound and his trousers go tight whenever the lad got near.

Merlin was on his mind whenever he went riding, or sipped a mug of coffee, or ducked into the library. And he couldn't take his eyes off the wizard at supper. That was the worst. He didn't understand how he was so painfully aware of Merlin's presence, even from the other side of the Great Hall.

Sard, this was a mess. *He* was a mess.

And on top of everything, guests would start arriving for his father's birthday festivities in a matter of *days*.

Focus, he told himself, loosening his stance and trying an overhead pass with the sword. With the pain in his shoulder gone, the move was easier than it had been before. Or perhaps that was all the training. He could feel himself improving, and more often than not, Captain Lam and Master Lionel offered him an approving nod, rather than a correction.

But the training fields weren't the wizard's workshop. And he knew which one he preferred.

You will be a great king with this wizard by your side, the Lady of the Lake had said.

He wished, for the thousandth time, that he'd asked what she'd meant.

Arthur put away his sword, locking the door to the armory behind him. Perhaps he should get a book from the library before bed, to distract from his problems.

Yet when he reached the library, he paused. The doors were ajar, and there were voices inside.

Merlin and Gawain sat hunched over a chess set. Gawain moved a bishop and leaned back in his seat with a smirk.

"Oh, I was hoping you'd do that," Merlin gloated, capturing the bishop. "It's check, by the way."

"*Merde*," Gawain swore, frowning at the board a moment. "I still think you should make the pieces catch fire when you capture them."

"I still think your jacket is ridiculous," replied Merlin. "I could make that catch fire instead?"

"By all means, if you wish to be billed for the expense." Gawain smirked.

Arthur gritted his teeth. The wizard was doing nothing wrong. Nor was his cousin. Yet for whatever reason, watching the two of them play chess together was tremendously upsetting.

He wanted to drag Merlin away and demand an explanation. Even though the wizard didn't owe him one. Even though it was just an innocent game of chess.

Forget the book, Arthur thought angrily. Something in his room would do. When he got back to his apartments, he realized what the emotion was that he'd felt at seeing Merlin with Gawain. Of all the things—it was jealousy.

CHAPTER 29

A pologies, Your Highness," said Lucan, returning pale and hunched from the privy for the third time that morning.

Guests were due within the hour for the king's birthday celebrations, and Arthur's valet was so obviously ill. Yet Lucan insisted on denying it, stubbornly staggering back and forth from the communal easement to the prince's rooms without managing to complete a single task.

Arthur watched as his valet shuffled over to the fireplace, leaning his arm against the mantel and resting there with his eyes closed. The man's brow was damp with sweat, and he looked faintly green.

"Luc—" Arthur began.

"I just need a moment," he insisted. And then he bolted for the window and vomited.

Arthur winced, then went to his bathing chamber to run his own bath. At least the stream of warm water from the tap was good cover for the sound of Lucan's retching.

A knock sounded on the door to his apartments.

"Your Highness?" It was Brannor.

"Yes?" Arthur asked warily, padding over to see what was the matter.

Brannor's uniform was immaculate, in preparation for the royal visitors. His boots were perfectly polished, and even his mustache had been waxed.

Arthur, meanwhile, was still in his nightclothes, his hair a tangle.

The guard's lips disappeared into a thin line. "You're not dressed."

"Late start this morning," Arthur said apologetically.

The guard's gaze went to the window, where Lucan heaved again.

"Can you see that Luc gets to the infirmary?" Arthur asked.

"Right away," Brannor said with a curt bow. "And I'll have someone sent up to take his place."

Arthur padded back into the bathing chamber, noting with displeasure that he'd used too much rose oil. The steam was cloying and sweet, but there was nothing he do could about it now. Other than toss his night-clothes to the floor and step into the fragrant water.

◐ ◐ ◐

Emry had never seen the kitchens so frantic. She'd gone down to see about a cup of coffee and some toast, and instead had been enlisted to knead bread. Thankfully, a flick of her wand had taken care of that loathsome request, leaving her free to lounge against the counter, sipping her coffee and watching the dough knead itself.

Which was what she was doing when Brannor rushed into the kitchen.

"I need a spare page," he announced.

Chef, who was gutting a fish, glanced up and muttered a foul curse in French.

Emry committed the colorful swear to memory, planning to use it to torture Gawain.

"And that means?" said Brannor.

Chef smirked. "No spare pages. A dozen serving staff are sick this morning."

"It was the haddock that did it," a sullen-faced kitchen boy accused. "I *knew* it smelled off."

"Blame my cooking again, and you'll forage from the horses' trough for a week," Chef threatened the lad. "Now get back to chopping."

"An apprentice then," said Brannor, his annoyance growing. "I've been *everywhere*. Surely there's someone left."

Emry tried very hard to become wallpaper.

"Take the wizard," said Chef, pointing his knife in her direction, along with a dark look. "I don't need enchanted food in my kitchen."

"Merlin?" Brannor's eyebrows knitted together in consideration. "You'll do. Come along."

Emry took a last sip of her coffee before reluctantly abandoning the mug. "Where are we going?" she asked, following after the guard.

"To assist the prince."

"Arthur?" Emry said, surprised. "Why? Is something wrong?"

"Yer to step in as his manservant," instructed the guard.

Emry laughed, thinking it was a joke. But when she took in Brannor's expression, her stomach knotted.

"Do you expect the crown prince of Camelot to dress himself?" Brannor said, as though the idea was absurd.

"Um, yes?" Emry replied.

Brannor's graying whiskers twitched in disbelief. They had nearly reached the prince's bedchamber.

"He is the one true king," the guard said, his expression proud. "Serving him is an honor."

Not this again. But she saw the determined set of Brannor's jaw, and remembered how seriously the man took his duties. Especially since Arthur had retrieved Excalibur. She doubted she'd be able to talk him out of it.

So this was actually happening.

"Don't screw it up," Brannor warned, pushing her inside.

☾ ☾ ☾

"Hello? Arthur?" Emry called, glancing around the empty bedchamber. The air was thick with the scent of rosewater, and something else beneath, which was far less pleasant. Perhaps that explained why the window was open.

"Merlin?" Arthur called from another room, recognizing her voice. "What are you doing here?"

"Brannor sent me," she said sourly. "To step in as your manservant."

Arthur's laughter floated through the half-open door, followed by the sound of sloshing water.

"Did he really?" Arthur sounded amused. "Well, hand me a towel."

Emry stiffened. "A towel?"

"I'm in the bath," said the prince, as though it was obvious.

There was that splashing noise again.

"I'm not going to make you dress me," Arthur promised, "but I really do need a towel."

Oh no. She couldn't possibly go in *there*.

Emry sent up a quick prayer, and then positioned herself outside the bathing chamber. She tried a summoning spell, but it was hopeless when she couldn't see what she was trying to move.

"I'm sending you a towel. Is it working?"

"No," he said crossly. "Just get in here and hand me one."

Emry edged into the bathing chamber, her eyes squeezed shut.

The smell of rose was overwhelming. She tried not to think about Arthur, naked, in the bath. Which of course meant that she did.

"What are you *doing?*" he asked.

"Giving you some privacy," she snapped, waving her hands in front of her until she found the wall.

"You're being ridiculous," said Arthur, the water splashing. "We're both men."

Emry bit back a laugh. At least he hadn't guessed the truth.

"*Merlin,*" the prince warned. "I don't have all day."

Emry opened her eyes, her heart racing. She was in a large, wood-paneled room that was thick with fragrant steam. Two flickering candelabra cast a dim glow as they dribbled wax onto the inlaid floor. A marble tub sat at the far end, and hanging over the side of it, wet hair dripping into his face, was Arthur. He looked thoroughly annoyed.

Emry glanced around. A carved basin was set into an alcove, with taps that provided running water. Her eyes widened at the luxury. A stack of linen towels balanced on the edge of the basin, and Emry grabbed one. She took a deep breath, summoning her nerve, and approached the tub.

"Thanks," Arthur said.

She waited for him to ask her to turn around. Instead, he stood up.

Water ran down his naked torso, and the sight of him filled her eyes. She couldn't look away, even if she wanted to.

He stepped from the tub, his gaze dark and amused as he reached for the towel. She let go a moment too soon, out of panic, and the cloth dropped to the floor.

She stared down at it in barely concealed horror.

"I've got it—" she said, scrambling to retrieve it.

"No, it's—" Arthur insisted.

Emry straightened, holding the towel out in front of her as though it was a shield. The steam was making her light-headed. Or maybe it was the heat. And she was staring. She couldn't stop staring. Her eyes kept wandering slowly, hungrily, over the naked prince. And he'd *noticed*.

"You're blushing," Arthur accused lightly, wrapping the towel around his waist. The pale, thin linen was practically see-through, and did little to conceal what was beneath.

"It's the steam," Emry insisted, her throat dry.

"My mistake." A corner of his mouth quirked up.

He was standing so close. She could smell the rose oil on his skin. See the droplets of water caught in his eyelashes. Feel the weight of his gaze on her, searching for the answer to an unasked question. And then his eyes fell to her lips. Before Emry knew what was happening, the distance between them had vanished.

Arthur's lips pressed softly against hers, in a kiss that was sweet and forbidden and dangerous. She melted into it, tasting the salt and heat of his mouth.

The kiss grew bolder, hungrier, and she surrendered into it. Into him. The room spun, and everything inside of her went molten. The world was elsewhere, nowhere, unimportant. All that mattered was the taste of him, and the flutter of his fingers against her jaw.

Heat spread across her skin, and a groan tore from her throat. She arched forward, overwhelmed by the insistent pressure of his warm, wet tongue against hers. And then, by the insistent pressure of something else, much lower.

Arthur released her roughly, the kiss ending as abruptly as it had begun. The look in his eyes was one of total panic.

She stared at him in alarm, her heart skittering in her chest.

How had she let this happen?

"I—" she began.

"I'm—" Arthur said at the same time, his voice ragged.

He turned away, clearing his throat, and took the opportunity to wrap the towel more firmly around his waist.

A knock sounded on the door to the bathing chamber, making them both jump.

"What is it?" Arthur asked roughly.

"The guests are beginning to arrive, Your Highness," Brannor called.

Arthur swore, running a hand through his hair in anguish. "I'm nearly dressed," he lied.

Emry stared helplessly at the prince.

"Do you need—"

"No," Arthur ground out. "Just go."

Emry's cheeks burned from the cold dismissal as she turned and fled the prince's chambers.

CHAPTER 30

Emry hurried through the hall, her cheeks flaming, her heart a wild and skittering thing.

Arthur had kissed her, and she had kissed him back. And what a kiss it had been. Not just a chaste brush of their lips, but an agonizing ecstasy. A tangle of desire and heat and—*sard*. How had she been so foolish?

The king's birthday celebration was about to begin, and the castle had never been more crowded. Master Ambrosius had suspended her lessons so that she might attend the festivities. *Be careful*, he had cautioned.

This had been the *opposite* of careful.

Emry squeezed past a retinue of attendants in unfamiliar livery, headed to the throne room. She'd been looking forward to that evening's banquet and concert, but not anymore.

Just go.

She winced as she remembered the panic and horror that had flashed across Arthur's face after—after he'd pushed her away.

If she stayed in her room all weekend, that would be fine by her.

When she got back to her room, she collapsed onto her bed. Her heart was racing, and she wasn't sure whether she wanted to scream or laugh or cry. Because she had never been so undone by a kiss. When their lips had met, every nerve in her body had lit up, as if by magic. Except the kiss hadn't been magic. It had been better.

And she should have never, ever let it happen.

She'd spent her whole life suspecting that the things other people were feeling, and the way they were feeling them, didn't apply to her. And it wasn't just the magic that coursed through her veins. It was this secret worry that the parts of her that were supposed to be the same as everyone else's . . . weren't. And the fear that, if she tried to explain, no one would understand.

It was so confusing, having feelings for someone regardless of their gender, and realizing not everyone felt the same way. How simple and straightforward it sounded, to like just one gender.

Trying to guess at someone else's feelings was hard enough, but adding her own into the mix was an undeniable path to heartbreak, every time.

First with Kira, the blacksmith's daughter. They had started as friends, but one afternoon in the meadow, they had become more. It had lasted barely a fortnight. Before the wildflowers gave way to autumn leaves, Kira was engaged to a cleric in a neighboring village, and acted as though Emry meant nothing.

Next, there had been the traveling playwright with soulful eyes and ink-stained fingers, who had undressed her in poems, and then in his room at the inn, until she'd discovered he had a wife and son back home.

The blacksmith's boy, who had looked like his sister, but was half as clever, and had stunk like an alehouse besides. All of them mistakes, regrets, scars.

And now, Arthur. The last person in the world she had any right to kiss.

Just thinking about him made her chest flutter, and her heart wish for the impossible. Made her imagine that he was simply a boy, and not a prince. That she was simply a girl, and not a wizard. That she hadn't mistaken his feelings for friendship for so long. Because he *was* interested, wasn't he?

Except how could he be, when all he knew was this frustrating fiction? When he thought her to be her useless, disappointing *brother*?

She imagined their kiss again, except this time he was kissing her without deception. She imagined his hands sliding through her long hair, and then other places. His soft mouth, everywhere. His narrow waist, with just the damp towel wrapped around it. Her stomach tumbled at the thought.

All of the kisses she'd ever had paled in comparison to the one they'd just shared.

A kiss that couldn't happen again. No matter how much she wished otherwise. It was bad enough she was masquerading under a false identity at court, a crime punishable by death. She was already deceiving Arthur. She couldn't bear to betray him, too.

◐ ◐ ◐

Arthur could scarcely concentrate as he stood next to his father's throne, waiting to greet their honored guests.

The royal guards lined the hall, their armor gleaming, their boots polished, crimson cloaks flowing elegantly from their shoulders. Courtiers and nobles drifted about, dressed in their finery, greeting one another and whispering about the guests from afar.

Arthur spotted Lancelot dressed in a handsome suede jacket, though he still wore his guard's sword. He stood at Guinevere's side, smiling and chatting with the girl, who seemed to enjoy the attention.

Arthur had asked the captain to spare Lance for the weekend, since he couldn't bear to have his friend standing at attention in a corner while the other nobles enjoyed the festivities. Still, he hoped Lance never found out that he'd said anything.

King Uther shifted on the throne, annoyed at being made to wait, especially for his own celebrations. Arthur couldn't remember the last time he'd seen his father look so regal or intimidating. The king was dressed in a decadently embroidered velvet suit, a cloak of pure gold spilling from his shoulders, a heavy necklace of jewels draped over the inky black silk of his doublet.

And Arthur was clothed to match, in royal blue silk fastened with endless gold clasps, with a crisp white collar and a golden half-cape knotted over one shoulder. His boots laced up the back with golden thread, and his best circlet was freshly polished, and seemed to be staying put. The royal tailor had truly outdone himself. Though Arthur could have done with slightly fewer buckles.

At least the task of fastening them had helped him get his nerves under control.

But standing here, waiting, they were beginning to fray again.

He couldn't help but picture the wizard's unusually pink cheeks, his blush as deep as any maiden's, and the searing heat behind his gaze.

Something had come over him in that moment, and the worst part was, the kiss hadn't chased it away. If anything, it had invited the something in.

The kiss hadn't been enough.

Hadn't satisfied his hunger.

Had only made it worse.

And now that hunger paced anxiously, a caged thing, growling within him and wanting to be set free.

He thought of what he'd seen on Avalon, the image of Merlin and himself, kissing. Which of course made him think about the other things—the girl on the ship. The child. The dungeons. His own untimely death. And his dream, where he'd been unable to rescue the wizard. A dream that Merlin had shared.

What was fiction, and what was truth? More important, would all of those things come to pass?

He looked out at the crowd of courtiers, searching once again for Princess Guinevere. Her dark, glossy curls caught the light, and her lips were painted a deep, vibrant red to match the elaborate gown she wore. She noticed him looking, and glanced away with a demure smile. No smirk, or wink, or eye roll over the king's impatience. No indication that they were anything to each other at all beyond polite acquaintances.

Why had he done it? Why had he kissed the young wizard? The worst part was how much he had enjoyed it. Followed by the moment—that humiliating moment—when they'd pressed together and he'd realized Merlin wasn't having the same reaction. That the wizard's blush was out of embarrassment, not arousal.

He'd been so sure that Merlin felt the same way, and he didn't quite know what to do now that he'd miscalculated so badly.

Arthur held back a sigh as he stared out at the sea of nobles and royal guests, enjoying themselves.

Of course King Yurien was late.

The others had arrived—his uncle from Cornwall, thankfully without his spoiled, petulant son, Maddoc. The duke's eyes had narrowed when he'd spotted Arthur at his father's side, and at the unmistakable message it was meant to convey.

Next had been King Leodegrance and Queen Isabella, along with Prince Gottegrim, a balding, mild-mannered man in his late thirties, who seemed closer in age to the queen. The king and queen had eagerly embraced their daughter, Guinevere, and presented Uther with a citrus tree from the queen's native Andalusia, its branches heavy with exotic orange fruit.

After that was the Queen of the Isles, with three of her five unmarried daughters, dressed in matching gowns of pink ruffles. The girls hadn't stopped whispering since the moment they'd stepped into the hall.

The queen had exchanged empty platitudes with King Uther, excusing her husband's absence due to illness, and offering a case of sweet wine as a birthday gift.

It looked as though King Yurien wasn't coming after all.

"The hour grows late," said King Uther. "And we have a concert for tonight's entertainment—"

The trumpets blared again.

King Yurien strode into the throne room, a few steps ahead of his wife. Attendants followed behind, their formation making them appear more like soldiers than guards. Arthur had expected a grim warrior, but King Yurien was nothing of the sort. He was a man gone soft, with a ruddy complexion, and a hardness to his eyes that hinted at what would happen if he didn't get his way. His fading ginger hair was extravagantly coiffed, in an attempt to cover more of his head than it should. He looked like an overfed noble, the sort who complained of gout while ordering another tureen of duck liver from the kitchens. His wealth was on display with every jewel-encrusted button and fur-lined sleeve. He wore no weapons, and no crown—of course not, Arthur thought—it would ruin his hair. But even so, there was no doubt that he was a man of great power.

Unlike the king, the queen was delicate and demure, a petite figure in black and cream velvet. As she drew nearer, Arthur was surprised to see that she couldn't be much older than thirty. She wore a gable-hooded veil, which covered her hair with a length of silk. Such things weren't the fashion in Camelot, and Arthur found the style severe, even trimmed as it was in pearls.

Behind her, wide-eyed and fidgeting, was a ginger-haired slip of a boy of eight or nine, who was dressed in replica of his father. He regarded the Great Hall in awe, half hidden behind his mother's skirts.

"King Uther," said King Yurien. "It appears I've kept you waiting. My ship had some trouble putting in at Radcliffe."

"I understood you were to dock at Blackwall," said Uther with a frown. "It is no matter."

Two of Yurien's attendants stepped forward with a large cloth-covered rectangle. A painting.

"A gift," said Yurien. "To decorate your castle. I had it commissioned from the finest artist in my kingdom."

"You are too generous," said King Uther.

The attendants removed the cloth, and Arthur fought to keep his expression neutral. It was a painting of King Yurien's forces invading Northumbria. A painstaking depiction of a blood-soaked battlefield, with a village burning in the distance and a large pile of peasants lying dead in the town square. The painting was exquisite in detail, yet utterly ghoulish in subject.

The gift was an unmistakable threat.

"It would look well in this throne room," King Yurien said, his smile sharp as a blade as King Uther shifted uneasily on his throne.

Arthur matched Yurien's smile, stepping forward. "And even better in the armory," he said, his tone light. "To serve as motivation while training."

Yurien gave a nod of acknowledgment and exchanged a few more empty sentiments with the king. Arthur smiled and nodded at the exchange, feigning interest, yet whenever Arthur looked up, Yurien was staring straight at him.

Yurien didn't stop staring even when Uther stepped from his throne, joining the festivities as he plucked a goblet of wine off a tray.

Arthur steeled himself against the unfortunate task of meeting Princess Guinevere's parents. Drinks were passed around, and music played, and the atmosphere was lively enough, yet it felt more like a chess game than a party.

A hand grasped him on the arm, and he turned, finding himself face to face with the King of Lothia himself.

"I've been curious to meet the boy who pulled the sword from the stone," said Yurien.

Arthur should be careful, he knew. Especially given the hungry way Yurien was studying him.

His earlier remark had been a mistake. But perhaps he could play it off. It was better if the man thought him a silly, empty-minded royal. So he put on his best grin and prepared to act the part.

"It's a favorite tale of my bards," Yurien went on. "But musicians do exaggerate."

"I confess, I rarely pay attention to the lyrics," Arthur said. "Especially when there are lovely maidens dancing."

"The sword," Yurien went on. "I'm surprised you're not wearing it."

"It didn't match my outfit," Arthur said with a disarming smile.

Lord Agravaine joined them. "Pardon the intrusion, Your Majesty," he said. "Do the men crewing your ship have adequate supplies to remain docked for the next few days?"

"They have their rations," said Yurien.

Arthur immediately guessed at Lord Agravaine's aim. "But that won't do at all," he protested, feigning ignorance. "This is a celebration! All of our kingdom's guests should have cake!"

He nearly cringed at how silly he sounded. Yet he kept up the charade, turning to his father's advisor in mock distress at their poor hospitality.

"My lord," he went on. "You will see to it that the men eat their fill. And perhaps a case of wine?"

"Of course, Your Highness," Lord Agravaine said smoothly.

Arthur blinked at Yurien with studied innocence. "Is it just a carrack?"

"A galleass."

That explained why he had put in at the larger port. And if Lord Agravaine was perturbed to hear that a three-mast great ship flying a Lothian flag was docked in London, he hid it well.

"Then we shall need refreshments for fifty," Arthur said with his most princely smile, as though he also saw no reason for concern. "If you'll excuse me."

He backed away from King Yurien, still faking good cheer. Perhaps his father's plan to get a measure of the man wasn't without merit.

CHAPTER 31

Emry stared out her bedroom window at the chaos below. The practice yard had been transformed into a sword-fighting ring, with banners flying and stands lined with cushions for the noble spectators. The stands were packed, though the contest hadn't yet begun.

The oversized royal box flew five banners: Camelot's crimson, Cameliard's green, Lothia's black, Cornwall's gold, and pale blue for the Isles. Only Northumbria's white was missing.

"Merlin!" a cheerful male voice called, knocking on her door. "You in there?"

It was Lancelot. Instead of his guard's uniform, he wore an elegant royal blue doublet with silver buttons. The sleeves weren't puffed and slashed, Emry noticed, as was the latest style, but fitted. His golden hair was slicked back into a bun, and his face fresh-shaven. A signet ring glinted on his pinky, depicting a stag leaping over a fleur-de-lis.

He grinned at her, looking unmistakably like a nobleman's son. Even if he did still have a guardsman's sword belted around his waist.

"You look well," she said.

"I look two years out of fashion," he said wryly. "But thanks."

"Did you need something?" Emry asked.

"I'm squiring for Arthur," Lance explained. "In the sword-fighting competition. You should come down to his tent."

"Did he ask for me?" she said, surprised.

"Not exactly," Lance hedged. "Actually, he told me not to bother you."

Emry sighed. Of course he didn't want to see her.

"But you're bothering me anyway," she said.

"Whatever's the matter between the two of you—" Lance broke off, pressing his lips together in a frown. "I need you to set it aside. Now. Because Arthur's going up against knights even *I'd* be nervous to fight. And I hope nothing happens, but if it does . . ." Lance winced, his meaning clear.

"Lead the way," Emry finished, reaching for her wand.

◑ ◑ ◑

Arthur hurried onto the field, joining at least a dozen other knights and nobles. He spotted Sir Kay immediately—the only one vain enough to wear gold-plated armor—but was surprised to see his cousin Gawain, and Prince Gottegrim of Cameliard, who tipped him a friendly grin. The Duke of Cornwall had joined them as well. Arthur nodded a tense greeting at his formidable uncle, whose prowess on the battlefield was well-known. He hadn't expected the duke to enter the competition, and judging from the whispers in the stands, neither had the crowd.

But Arthur didn't have time to brood about the duke. No sooner had he taken his place than the herald announced them down the line.

Each competitor stepped forward at his name, and then knelt before the king and the royal guests, drawing his sword when he arose. Arthur, who was fourth from the end, waited nervously for his turn, knowing that this was the moment his father expected him to reveal Excalibur. Not just to the lords and ladies of Camelot, but to the visiting royals as well.

No pressure, he thought wryly, as his stomach turned itself inside out in anticipation of the spectacle.

"Prince Arthur of Camelot," called the herald.

Arthur stepped forward, staring up at the royal box, its colorful flags flying, one for each kingdom present. Princess Guinevere peered down at him, dressed more for a ball than a sporting competition. She sat between her parents and the Queen of Lothia, who wore a conical hat and veil, and held a pair of purple-tinted lenses attached to a stick, so she might see every move of the contest. At her side, her young son clapped and cheered. King Yurien looked annoyed at the boy's enthusiasm.

"Your Majesties," Arthur said, kneeling down with his helmet tucked under his arm.

This was it. The moment his father had arranged so carefully.

He pulled Excalibur from its sheath, the sword's glow blinding against the soft morning light. Instead of pointing the blade down, he held it upright.

The nobles gasped, and the stands filled with whispers.

King Leodegrance actually made the sign of the cross, as though the sword was a holy object. The ladies from the Isles seemed confused. Guinevere pasted on a smile and applauded, and after a moment, her mother joined her, along with the confused princesses.

Underneath his black banner, King Yurien leaned forward, his dark eyes glittering, a satisfied expression on his face, as though a mystery had been solved. His wife seemed utterly astonished, and when Arthur met her gaze, her expression was calculating. Their son gaped, tugging on his father's sleeve.

"Papa," he said in a loud whisper. "Why is that sword *glowing*?"

King Yurien shushed him.

Arthur waited, kneeling there, his sword extended, for a moment longer. And then he straightened and looked up at his father with a sheepish expression.

"My apologies, sire," he said. "In my haste, I grabbed the wrong sword. Perhaps you could hold on to Excalibur for me?"

At mention of the sword's name, a gasp once again went through the crowd.

"Of course," Uther said.

Arthur handed his father the sword for safekeeping, its sheath still fastened around his waist.

"Squire!" Arthur called. "My spare sword!"

Lance, who looked uneasy about his part in this, jogged into the ring and presented Arthur with an ordinary blade.

Arthur nodded his thanks, and knelt down properly. "Your Majesties," he said again.

"Rise, Prince Arthur, and compete well for Camelot," said King Uther, as he'd said to the previous combatants.

Arthur rose, tucking his spare sword into his scabbard. He took a deep breath, trying to slow his hammering heart. Next to him, the aging Sir Ban of Berwick was announced, and knelt without incident, but Arthur could feel the crowd's attention still on him, still whispering about Excalibur.

Sir Ban straightened, and without warning, Arthur's scabbard burned hot against his thigh. He grimaced, hoping it didn't get worse. And then, just as suddenly as it had started, the heat stopped.

Arthur breathed a sigh of relief as he watched the final contestant, Sir Olwen, kneel before the royal box.

And then it was over, and the competitors were sent back to their tents to await their first match.

◗ ◗ ◗

Emry stood inside the small crimson tent, fiddling absently with a piece of equipment. Moments earlier, Lance had left her alone, sprinting off toward the arena with a sword under his arm. No wonder he was dressed so handsomely, Emry had thought, as she'd watched him hurry onto the field with Arthur's spare sword.

She didn't know the first thing about a squire's duties, but she knew that it meant a lot Arthur had given Lance the honor. And that he would prove himself more than up to the task.

He'd been right, Emry thought, about the competition being stiff.

Arthur had no place on that field. She hadn't known Gawain would be competing, but he'd never made a secret of his skill with a blade. Standing there in his armor, the foppish, devilish royal had vanished. Gawain was every inch a formidable swordsman. But then, Emry expected no less. It was only Arthur who looked out of place.

She pictured him off to the side, in the small white tent, making sure Master Ambrosius and the court physician had adequate supplies to treat those who got injured. But that wasn't right, either. That's where *she* should be. Arthur would be in the royal box next to Princess Guinevere, a golden crown on his head, applauding the competitors as they knelt before him.

A herald announced that the first match would commence in five minutes, between Prince Gottegrim and Sir Olwen. The stands erupted in cheers. And then the tent flap was pushed aside, and Lance and Arthur ducked into the tent.

Emry had to admit, Arthur did look handsome in his armor and chain-mail, a helmet tucked under his arm, and his hair a tousled mess.

He also looked ill from nerves. And entirely unhappy to see her.

"Um, hi," she said awkwardly.

Arthur's eyes narrowed. "I thought I said—"

"This is what you get for asking me to play squire," Lance said mildly.

"You're not *playing* squire." Arthur sounded as though they'd been over this before. "If anything, *I'm* playing a knight. At least you have the training."

"But not the experience," put in Lance.

"Then it's a good thing you're getting some now," Arthur said. He frowned, holding up his right arm. "Should these pads keep slipping down?"

"I warned you they'd loosen as you moved," Lance admonished, unfastening Arthur's arm and chest plates. He tossed them onto the equipment table along with Arthur's scabbard.

Emry stood uselessly in the corner, next to a table set with a decanter of ruby wine, watching as Lance re-laced Arthur's padding in tense silence.

The two of them weren't cracking jokes, she realized. And they were *always* joking.

"That's as tight as they go." Lance shook his head. "You need smaller ones."

"Well then, squire," said Arthur, a smile ghosting over his face. "You'd better fetch them in a hurry."

Lance cursed, ducking out of the tent, and leaving Emry alone with the prince.

He hefted his sword, studiously ignoring her as he tried a pass.

How annoying. Well, if he didn't want her here, she certainly wasn't staying. She could watch from the stands.

"I'll go, too," she said, edging toward the tent flap.

And then she caught sight of Arthur's scabbard lying on the equipment table, and stopped. It seemed . . . wrong somehow. She frowned down at it, trying to figure out what had snagged her attention. The scabbard looked the same as always, ancient and worn, with fading runes etched into the leather.

She picked it up, expecting to feel the spellwork that coursed through it. But the scabbard felt empty.

Like plain leather.

Like there wasn't any magic in it at all.

"What are you doing?" Arthur snapped. "Put that down."

Emry wondered what she had done to offend him so greatly. Sure, she'd skipped last night's feast and concert, but she doubted that, with all of the important guests, Arthur would even notice her absence.

She supposed he was still annoyed about the kiss. Which, fair. Although he was the one who had kissed *her*. And he was the one who had a . . . Princess Guinevere. So if anyone had the right to be upset, it was her.

Outside, the crowd's cheers reached a crescendo.

"Victory goes to Prince Gottegrim of Cameliard," announced the herald.

A trumpet sounded, signaling that the next match was about to begin. Arthur was up fourth, according to the tournament boards. He pressed his lips together and began strapping on his armor.

"What about Lance?" Emry asked.

"It's fine," Arthur said tiredly. "It doesn't matter if my pads are loose."

The words spilled out before she could stop them. "Does it matter if your scabbard has been stripped of its enchantment?"

Arthur froze. "Explain," he demanded.

"When I picked up the scabbard just now, I couldn't sense any magic in it at all. It's just . . . ordinary leather."

"It seems the same to me," Arthur said, frowning down at it.

"I'm telling you it isn't!" Emry said desperately. "The enchantment is gone!"

"It can't be," Arthur protested. "It was fine this morning. Besides, how does a magical object just stop working?"

"I don't know! But I don't want to see you hurt!"

"It's a little late for that," Arthur said pointedly. "Don't you think?"

"What are you talking about?"

"Yesterday, when we—kissed," Arthur said tersely. "I'd thought—well. If you were enjoying yourself, I certainly didn't notice."

Emry frowned, confused. She thought back to their kiss. To the way it had deepened, and how their hips had pressed together. How she'd felt him—and then they'd sprung apart.

She realized exactly what Arthur meant by his accusation, and her cheeks flamed. She opened her mouth to protest, but the prince silenced her with a glare.

"Don't," he warned. "You'll only make it worse."

He buckled his breastplate with a grimace, and Emry saw that his hands were shaking. He really did mean to go out there. And she had a terrible feeling what would happen when he did.

"If someone removed the enchantment on your scabbard, then they know what it does," Emry pressed. "And they know you're planning to wear it in the ring."

"What would you have me do?" Arthur snapped. "Bow out before the competition has even started?"

"I'd have you know if a hit could kill you!" Emry cried desperately.

Distant cheers erupted from the stands. He considered her for a moment, and then nodded.

"All right," he said, buckling the scabbard around his waist. "We'll test it. Again. Grab a sword, wizard."

Her stomach twisted as she realized he meant for her to stab him. She stared at the prince, with his faint I-told-you-so smirk, so convinced he would come to no harm. And then she stared at the freshly sharpened blades on the table.

She'd never wielded a sword before. Not a real one. Only the blunt-tipped fakes they used in the theater. She was horrified at the thought of striking him too deeply—horrified at the thought of striking him at all.

"I can't," she whispered, staring at her boots.

"Well then—" Arthur began.

"Test it on me," Emry blurted, lifting her chin. "If you're so convinced nothing is wrong, then test it on me."

"Fine," Arthur said coolly, handing over the scabbard.

Emry buckled it on, her fingers clumsy with nerves, and held her arms stiffly at her sides, willing her heart to calm. She was doing this for Arthur. Because she was his wizard. And he was her prince.

The Lady of the Lake's words came back to her then: *Before you shed your disguise, you must protect Arthur from those who would stand against him.*

"This is ridiculous," he muttered, grabbing a sword from the table.

She probably should have closed her eyes.

The sight of him lunging toward her, in full armor, with a sharpened blade, sent her into a panic. Instead of taking the attack, she flinched.

The hit that was meant to land on her forearm slashed across her rib cage.

Pain ripped through her. She gasped, pressing a hand to the wound. When she lifted it, her hand came away red.

Her fingers were sticky with blood, and her legs were shaking. She felt faint, and she wondered distantly how much longer she'd be able to remain standing.

"Merlin!" Arthur cried.

He was at her side in a moment, helping her to a chair.

"I told you," she said, wincing against the pain. "I told you it—wouldn't work."

"I believe you now," Arthur said gravely. "Sard, Emmett, why did you flinch?"

He never called her Emmett. Always Merlin, or wizard. Her brother's name felt wrong as it floated in the air between them.

Emry leaned back in the chair, her hand still pressed against the wound. Her magic was blocked—she was in too much pain—but even if she could reach it, it wouldn't work. Which she should have remembered before attempting such foolish heroics.

She laughed softly at what a fool she'd been, and then groaned at the fresh stab of pain. The wound was more than just a graze. And she didn't know how much more.

"Can you get Master Ambrosius?" Emry asked.

"I assume he's tending to Sir Olwen," Arthur said apologetically, and Emry realized he was right. She was a mere apprentice, and Sir Olwen a knight. She could wait. She'd have to wait.

She swallowed thickly, thinking that she'd never been in so much pain in her life. *Breathe*, she reminded herself. In and out.

She watched dizzily as Arthur rifled through a leather bag, wondering what on earth he was looking for.

"I know it's here somewhere," he muttered. "Ah! Got it!"

Of all the welcome things, Arthur was holding up a small jar of Master Ambrosius's rare healing salve.

He twisted off the lid, and the spicy scent of magic itched at her nose.

"Take off your tunic," he instructed.

That was when Emry realized—he meant to physic her himself.

"No!" she protested, horrified. "Just give me the salve."

"Don't be ridiculous," Arthur snapped. "Let me see how bad it is."

And with that, he lifted her tunic over her head.

Emry couldn't stop him. She could only hunch forward, wearing just her tights and her boots—and the bandage wrapped tightly around her chest.

The world screeched to a halt, her secret spilling out at the worst possible moment.

"What's this?" Arthur asked quietly. He stared at her bandaged chest as though he wasn't sure, and needed to hear it from her before he jumped to any conclusions.

"Don't tell me you've never seen a girl with her shirt off before," Emry joked, and then winced.

"You're not Emmett Merlin," he said. It came out as a question, and he looked to her for the answer.

Not the answer, Emry realized. The truth.

She shook her head.

"I'm his twin sister, Emry," she confessed. "The *other* Merlin."

◖ ◖ ◖

Arthur stared down at the girl—at Master Merlin's daughter—overwhelmed. He didn't understand how he'd missed it. How the thought had never even occurred to him.

And then his eyes widened as he remembered why he had ripped her shirt off.

"I stabbed you," he said, horrified.

"It's not that bad," she said tightly. "Just—pass me the salve."

Arthur pressed it into her hands, and waited nervously as she smeared on a thick layer of the tallow. He worried it wouldn't be enough, but he watched as her cut slowly knitted itself into a tender pink scar. She sighed in relief, some color returning to her cheeks.

"Why can't you magic it better?" he asked, confused.

"Spells can only be cast outward, not inward." She twisted the lid back onto the salve. "So it's lucky you had this."

"It's lucky you knew the scabbard was broken," Arthur returned.

"I'm still a wizard," she reminded him.

"Emry Merlin," he said, trying out her name. It fit her in a way that Emmett never had.

Sard, of course not. Because she'd never *been* Emmett. She'd told him that Master Merlin had both a son and a daughter. That she was a twin. The truth had been right there, from the beginning.

He watched as she reached for her bloodstained tunic and muttered a cleaning spell, an over-strong smell of rosewater filling the tent. She gingerly tugged the tunic back over her head, and Arthur knew he should look away, for modesty's sake, but he couldn't bring himself to stop staring.

It was painfully obvious now that she was a girl. Not a girl—a woman. And she hadn't wanted to tell him.

She hadn't meant for him to find out at all.

Arthur rearranged the past two months in his head, filling in so many things that had puzzled him about the young wizard. And then remembering all of the nights he had turned up at her room unannounced, barging inside. The bed he'd insisted she share with Lance.

She had deceived him. Over and over. He should be furious. He should be calling for his guards to remove her from his sight and cast her outside the city walls, or worse, to drag her before the king.

After all, she'd impersonated a royal apprentice. Lived at the castle. Become his friend. Helped Lance. Journeyed with him to Avalon. Healed his wounds. Made him laugh. Made him furious. Kissed him. Broken his heart. Done everything in her power to keep him safe. That was the part he kept coming back to.

And yet, through everything that had happened, she'd lied to him. Over and over again.

"You could have trusted me," he said softly.

Emry stared up at him, hurt and panic clear on her face. "I couldn't ask you to lie for me," she said.

"Isn't that what you're asking now?"

"Not on purpose," Emry retorted, which made Arthur snort.

He realized he wasn't angry, he was just overwhelmed. It was a lot to take in.

"I'm not excusing what I did," Emry went on, "but if it makes a difference, it was only supposed to be a week. But Emmett refused to change back, so I got stuck pretending to be him indefinitely, which was never the plan." Emry loosed a sigh. "Not that there *was* much of a plan. And if we *had* switched back, it would have been a disaster. Because my brother is lazy, and selfish, and terrible at magic. And the truth is, it should have been me all along."

Her chin jutted forward, and a storm brewed in her eyes. Even now, she was every inch the stubborn, overconfident wizard Arthur had always known.

There was no doubt she was Merlin's daughter. And that she was in over her head. And panicked. And hurt. She stared up at him, her expression a mixture of hope and fear.

"Why didn't you stab me?" he asked. "When you suspected the scabbard wouldn't work, you could have stabbed me."

She bit her lip. "No, I couldn't," she said.

"Why not?" Arthur asked, leaning forward until his face was inches from hers. It was a challenge. A dare. This connection between them—he needed to know if she felt it, too.

"I think you know why not," she whispered, lowering her lashes. "And for the record, when you kissed me, I enjoyed it very much."

Arthur gazed down at her. At the faint blush coloring her cheeks. At the soft pink of her lips. At the way, in just her tunic, her shoulders seemed so slim and delicate. And her legs. Dear god, she'd been walking around the royal court in *tights*.

He knew that if she looked up, she'd see it on his face, how he felt about her. How he'd felt for a long time.

Before she could, the tent flap opened and Lance stumbled inside, out of breath and holding an armload of padded wool.

"Found some," he said. And then he took in the scene with a frown. "What'd I miss?"

◖ ◖ ◖

The trumpets sounded their ten-minute warning, and Arthur sighed, scraping a hand through his hair. What an absolute mess.

"I don't suppose you knew about this?" he asked Lance.

"The scabbard? No." Lance was very carefully not looking at Merlin—rather, *Emry*—who was curled miserably in the chair, arms hugged around her knees.

"But you knew about *the wizard*?" Arthur asked.

Lance's expression turned sheepish. "I had a hunch," he admitted, and Arthur stared at him, betrayed. *Lance* had figured it out? And he hadn't *said* anything? Seriously?

"To be honest, I'm surprised you didn't guess," Lance went on. "You've been acting really weird."

"I have not!" Arthur protested.

Maybe Lance had a point. Arthur sighed. "This is just perfect," he muttered. "What on earth am I supposed to do now?"

"About me?" Emry asked nervously.

"About the *tournament*," he said, as though it was obvious.

"You go out there and act as though nothing's wrong," said Lance.

Arthur slowly let out a breath and nodded, recognizing the logic in what Lance was suggesting.

"There aren't many people who know what the scabbard does," said Emry. "For those who do, Lance can watch how they react."

"And what about you?" Arthur asked.

"If you want my help," Emry said hesitantly, as though she wasn't sure he would, "I'll be there with my wand out, ready to stop anyone who tries to . . ."

"Kill me?" Arthur suggested quietly.

". . . do violence to your person with the sharp end of a sword," she finished.

Lancelot laughed. "It's so much better now that she's a girl saying these things," he said.

"I was *always* a girl," Emry reminded him.

"Well, sure, theoretically. But—"

"Finish that sentence and I really *will* turn your nipples into garden slugs," she threatened.

Arthur groaned. Apparently some things were exactly the same. Like the way the wizard never knew when to keep her mouth shut. As charming as it was to listen to his friends bicker, he really didn't have the time.

"Squire, my armor?" Arthur said sternly.

Lance picked up a gauntlet, and expertly buckled him into the rest of his armor in record time.

CHAPTER 32

Arthur staggered back into his tent, drenched in sweat, his heart pounding. He could hardly believe it. He'd just won his match against Sir Ban of Berwick. The knight was forty-five if he was a day, and Arthur had almost underestimated him, until he'd seen the fire in the man's eyes, and the knight's thirst to prove his mettle against men half his age.

Thankfully, Arthur had also seen a weakness on the man's right side, where he held his shield just wide enough to admit the clever thrust of a blade.

Which meant that Arthur advanced to the next round. He didn't know whether to laugh or to cry.

"I told you training with the guard would whip you into shape," Lance said, thumping him on the back.

"That remains to be seen." Arthur pulled off his helmet and ran a hand through his sweat-dampened hair. "How do you breathe in this thing?"

"You don't," said Lance.

Arthur collapsed into the chair, unscrewing his water pouch and drinking greedily. He shook the last drops onto a linen cloth and draped the wet fabric across his neck.

"Well, anything?" he asked.

Lance shook his head, his expression grim. "Sir Kay looked pretty annoyed when you won, but that might just be his face."

"I'm not looking forward to fighting him," Arthur said, reaching for his water pouch, and remembering too late that it was empty.

With a grimace, he unstoppered the decanter of ruby wine, pouring himself a glass. "Plenty for two," he offered.

"A squire doesn't drink while attending to his duties," Lance replied.

The tent flap lifted, and Emry stepped inside. She looked pale, and had one hand pressed to her rib cage. She smiled at him, and his stomach flipped a little.

"I won," he said, pleased.

"Yes, I saw," she replied. "Huzzah."

It was impossible, now that Arthur knew the truth, to remember that he'd ever believed her to be a boy.

Sard, she'd seen him *naked*. She'd kissed him while he wore nothing but a towel. And *he'd* been the one to pull away. He studied her, hoping they could do it again. The kissing part. Not the pulling away.

"I thought you wanted a squire, not a chaperone," Lance grumbled, looking back and forth between them.

"No one *wants* a chaperone," Emry pointed out. She helped herself to Arthur's jar of healing salve, lifting the hem of her tunic and exposing her bare stomach. And the waistband of her tights.

Arthur cleared his throat. Sard, it was warm in here.

"It hurts," she complained. "Don't be weird."

"I'm not being weird," Arthur said, even though he was.

"We've shared a room before," she pointed out. "Lance and I shared a bed."

Arthur quietly choked on a sip of wine.

"That's right," said Lance, amused. "And you—oh. No wonder you raised such a fuss about it." His expression turned horrified. "But—you shared a room with four men. You—we—"

Lance looked as stricken as Arthur felt. She was a *maiden*.

"I promise, I've seen it all before," said Emry. Both boys went red in the face, and she snorted at their discomfort. "Oh my god, like either of you are virgins."

"Of course not," Arthur protested. "But that's different."

"How so?" Emry asked with a sharp smile.

Wasn't it different? Arthur frowned and had another sip of wine.

Ugh, the wine really was terrible. Acidic and bitter, with a bouquet of musty herbs.

He grimaced and pulled at the collar of his armor. It was boiling in the tent, and he wondered why he was the only one who'd noticed.

"You all right?" Lance asked.

"Fine." He squinted, wondering if it had always been so bright.

"Lance is right," said Emry, peering at him nervously. "You really don't look so good."

"I—" Arthur said, and then he looked down at the cup in his hand. He gave the wine a sniff. When he tilted the cup, he spotted a small cluster of black seeds at the bottom. Seeds that he'd mistaken as sediment.

He had been a fool.

He knew someone had tampered with his scabbard. He had sent Lance and Emry into the crowd during his match because of it, leaving the tent abandoned.

He hadn't checked. He hadn't even thought to check. And now he was—he could barely even think the word.

The room spun, and his heart thundered in his chest, and he felt panic deep in his bones.

"Arthur?" Lance asked, his voice low in warning. "What's going on?"

"The wine's poisoned," he mumbled woozily, as the goblet fell from his hand.

◑ ◑ ◑

Emry stared at the ruby wine puddled on the floor like blood. *Poisoned.* No. That couldn't be true.

Yet when she looked at the prince she had no doubt. He had gone white, sweat beaded his brow, and his breathing was labored.

"Should I get Master Ambrosius?" Lance asked, eyes wild with panic. "Or the royal physician?"

"What can they do?" Arthur rasped. "I'm already feeling the effects."

No, Emry thought. She couldn't lose him. Not like this. Arthur wasn't supposed to die in the middle of a conversation. She had *protected* him like the Lady of the Lake had foretold—and she had the stab wound to show for it.

"There has to be *something*," Lance insisted. "A unicorn horn. Don't those cure poison?"

"Probably, if they were real," Arthur said tightly.

Suddenly, Emry knew what she needed to do. Or maybe she'd always known. She took a shaky breath, trying to sound confident as she promised, "I know how to magic an antidote."

Arthur's eyes met hers. They were glassy and feverish. "You do?" he asked, with a flicker of hope.

Emry swallowed nervously. "Of course I do."

Never mind that she'd never managed it before. Never mind the bucket of dead snails Master Ambrosius had tossed into the fireplace. Never mind that, if it didn't work, Arthur wouldn't be drinking an antidote—he'd be drinking even more poison.

She *had* to do this. For Arthur.

She took a deep breath and reached for her wand, focusing all of her attention on the contents of the glass decanter.

"*Edhwierft*," she ordered, willing the poison to reverse.

She gasped as the magic released and the wine bubbled. The churning liquid stilled, and Emry stared at it, unsure whether the spell had worked. It looked the same as before. Sard, she wished the spell changed the drink's color or something.

She poured a generous glass and handed it to Arthur. "Drink up," she insisted, hoping he didn't notice the tremble in her voice.

He stared down at it, his hands shaking as he raised the goblet. Emry blanched, unable to bear what would happen if she was wrong.

Lance, meanwhile, was pacing the tent and muttering obscenities.

Arthur took a sip of the drink and coughed. "Is it supposed to be spicy?" he asked.

Emry almost laughed in relief. Spicy was a very good sign. "Yes," she insisted. "Keep drinking."

Arthur drained the cup.

Please work, Emry thought. *Please.* She peered anxiously at the pale, sweating prince.

"Well?" she asked nervously. "Anything?"

Arthur closed his eyes and took a deep, unlabored breath, color returning to his cheeks. He carefully set down the goblet, sagging back in his seat, and Emry noted with pleasure that his hands were no longer shaking.

"It worked," she whispered, hardly daring to believe it.

"It worked," Arthur confirmed. His liquid brown eyes found hers, filled with gratitude and with something else that might have been pride. He didn't glance away, not for a long while. And she didn't want him to.

She had saved him. Her prince. Except she didn't know if she was still his wizard, or if the truth of who she was would change everything between them.

Arthur cleared his throat, glancing away.

"When did you learn to make a poison antidote, wizard?" he asked.

"Just now," Emry admitted.

"Just now?" Lance echoed, horrified. "As in, you didn't know whether or not it would work?"

"Nope," she said brightly. "To be honest, I've never successfully managed that spell before."

"You've never—" Arthur spluttered.

"You're welcome, by the way," Emry said.

The trumpets sounded outside, signaling the end of a match.

"Victory goes to Prince Gottegrim of Cameliard," the herald announced.

Arthur sighed. He looked exhausted. Purplish bruises stood out beneath his eyes, and he was more slumped in the chair than sitting on it.

"When am I up?" he asked Lance.

Lance looked stricken that he'd forgotten about his squire's duties. "I'll check."

Before he could leave, Gawain pushed open the flap of the tent. "We're next," he said, looking annoyed. "Why aren't you ringside?"

Arthur grimaced.

Gawain cocked his head. "What's going on?" he asked. "Lance looks ready to pass out. So do you, actually. *Did* you pass out?"

"Arthur was poisoned," Emry blurted.

Gawain's mouth fell open. And then he frowned. "*Was?*" he asked. "As in, past tense?"

"Thankfully, Merlin concocted an antidote," Arthur said. "Was there a decanter of wine in your tent?"

"Ale." Gawain made a face. "As though I would drink such swill."

"Lucky you didn't," Lance murmured.

"Merlin will examine your drink, to determine whether it's safe," Arthur instructed, in that annoying way of his.

"Um, right," Emry said. She hadn't even considered the possibility that others might have been targeted as well.

The trumpets sounded again, and Arthur pushed to his feet, reaching for his sword. He staggered a little under its weight, gritting his teeth from the effort.

"Well," he mumbled, "at least I'm not still poisoned."

"You're in no shape to fight," Gawain protested.

Arthur mustered a thin smile. "I have to," he said. "Someone went to a lot of trouble to cause me harm. Or worse. And I'll never find out who—or why—if I withdraw."

Emry could tell from the set of Arthur's jaw that he meant it. She remembered how he hadn't flinched when he and Lance had tested Excalibur. He had the same quiet steadiness now.

Gawain gave the prince a long, searching look. And then he nodded, as though he'd decided something important. "Then you won't withdraw," he said. "I will. At the first 'en garde,' I'll sheathe my sword, and they'll announce a draw."

"That's very noble of you." Arthur sounded surprised. "Considering what happened the last time we crossed swords."

Gawain grimaced. "Don't remind me. My father should have punished me for striking you while you were down. When he didn't, *Queen Igraine* marched me to the kitchens and insisted I work off my pride. For a month."

"I didn't know that." Arthur frowned.

Something important passed between them, although Emry wasn't sure what it was. Perhaps it had something to do with the reason Arthur had always disliked his cousin.

"I wish she'd done the same to my brother, and saved us all a lot of trouble," Gawain said.

"You and me both," Lance put in.

The trumpets sounded again.

"Well," Arthur said with a shaky grin. "I guess we should get moving."

"Come on." Gawain clapped him on the shoulder. "Let's go disappoint everyone who wanted to watch us fight."

◖ ◖ ◖

Gawain steeled himself as he caught sight of his father stalking the perimeter of the arena, the man's sharp mouth pressed into an angry line. Dressed all in black, with an unfashionable, gloomy cape fluttering around his shoulders, he looked less like a viscount and more like a dangerous bird of prey.

"What happened?" Lord Agravaine demanded.

"I withdrew," Gawain said, not wanting to get into it.

His father dragged him behind the wooden stands. Gawain waited for the lecture. But none came.

Lord Agravaine merely crossed his arms and ordered, "Explain."

"Explain what? My lack of interest in swinging around a sword for the entertainment of day-drunk nobles?"

Lord Agravaine studied him carefully. "You looked weak, refusing to face Arthur in combat."

"Maybe," Gawain allowed. "Or maybe I gave Arthur the opportunity to withdraw with his honor intact, now that I have done so first. No one expected to fight the Duke of Cornwall."

"There are plans in place that you don't know about," Lord Agravaine growled. "This competition is—"

"A thinly veiled excuse for my cousin to flex Excalibur in front of our guests," Gawain snapped. "Otherwise it would have been a joust. Or archery. Or *anything* besides sword-on-foot."

"That much is obvious," said Lord Agravaine. "But you still haven't explained—"

"I will not explain myself to you!" Gawain retorted. "Jereth gets away with everything. Am I not allowed even this?" He stared at his father, chest heaving, wondering if he'd gone too far.

"Careful," Lord Agravaine said, a sharp smile touching his lips. "Your anger betrays you. You're hiding something. And so is the prince."

"What on earth could we be hiding?" Gawain said nonchalantly.

"Perhaps it has to do with why that infernal wizard has been hovering around his tent all morning," his father guessed. "An area out of bounds to anyone except competitors and their squires, let me remind you."

Gawain's stomach twisted. He had only to reveal Emry's secret to re-direct his father's wrath. He saw it immediately, how he could sacrifice the wizard to save himself, returning to his father's good graces once again.

"Merlin—" Gawain began.

This was it. The ugliness coiled within himself that he'd always known he would have to face. He'd avoided it—barely—by withdrawing from the match against Arthur. But it had caught up with him again.

He was sweating inside his armor. His father glared at him, waiting. And then he thought of the way Emry always made him laugh. How she'd fought bandits twice her size without flinching, and matched him drink for drink in a brothel, and been at the prince's side when he was in need.

"Merlin—" Gawain said again, and then he shook his head.

He couldn't do it. Because when it came down to it, he didn't want to spend his life gathering secrets and using them as steps to gain greater power.

"Merlin was obviously ordered to do so for good reason," Gawain finished. "And if you think I know Arthur's mind, you clearly misinterpret our relationship."

"I told you to get close to that wizard," Lord Agravaine accused.

"And to enter this tournament, and to mind my brother. Am I to have no time to breathe between your constant lectures and assignments?"

The slap, when it landed across his cheek, stung like a fierce thing.

Gawain took it without flinching.

"I'll find out what you're keeping from me," his father threatened. "I always do."

And then he turned and walked away, cape billowing.

Gawain raised a hand to his stinging cheek, watching his father get smaller and smaller until he was swallowed by a crowd of drunken revelers.

It had felt good, standing up to his father. Today, when it had truly mattered, he'd chosen to do the right thing. And really, it hadn't been a choice at all.

CHAPTER 33

Arthur stood at his bedroom window, looking down on the final match of the tournament. Excalibur was belted at his waist, and he was fairly sure the sword was the only thing keeping him from collapsing of exhaustion.

In those horrible moments after he'd felt his throat go tight and his vision blur, he'd thought he was done for.

The poison, he now suspected, had been henbane. Not deadly, but humiliating. Amongst other nasty things, the drug caused extreme hallucinations. He would have looked a right fool if its effects had kicked in while he was in the ring. He could just picture the dark whispers that he was unfit to be king if he'd begun raving and screaming in front of half the nobles in the kingdom. Or worse, if he had fallen to the ground writhing in agony before his opponent had so much as touched blade to his armor.

And he had a theory about who was responsible for such a vile concoction: his uncle, the Duke of Cornwall, who would stand to inherit the throne as regent with Arthur out of the way. It would have been easy enough for him to dispatch his squire to Arthur's tent unnoticed.

But the one thing Arthur couldn't figure out was how the duke had managed to tamper with his scabbard. Or how he'd known about the enchantment at all.

"Who's winning?" Lance asked, glancing up from the plate of fruit and cheese that he and the wizard were demolishing.

Far below, on the castle lawn, Sir Kay bested the furious Duke of Cornwall, to the delight of the spectators.

"Your uncle," Arthur said.

Lance groaned. "He's going to be even more insufferable now."

"At least he defeated the duke," said Emry, through a mouthful of cheese.

"I'm not sure that's such a good thing," said Arthur. "My uncle doesn't like to lose."

He leaned back against the windowsill, offering his friends a thin smile. They didn't smile back. If anything, they looked as grim and serious as he felt.

"At least no one knows you were poisoned," Lance pointed out. "Other than Gawain."

"Excalibur does well to hide the lingering effects," said Arthur. He nodded at Emry. "Thank you, by the way, for retrieving it."

"Always happy to burst into the royal box and demand that the prince needs his sword back," said Emry dryly. "Besides, you didn't look as though you'd make it back to the tent without it."

Arthur hated that the wizard was right. "You try walking in full armor," he grumbled.

"You try concocting a poison antidote after being run through with a sword," Emry returned, smiling sweetly.

"Speaking of which, we need to figure out who has it in for the prince," said Lance.

"Other than the duke." Arthur grimaced as he said it. His uncle was the most obvious culprit.

Except for the scabbard. It simply didn't add up.

"I can talk to the guards who've been down in the vault," Lance suggested. "See if anyone was sniffing around."

"Do that," Arthur instructed. "Whoever did this has access to magic, and knew what the scabbard was."

"The big question," Emry said, "is whether they simply removed the enchantment, or if they were able to somehow *transfer* it."

Arthur stared at her. That hadn't even occurred to him. "Is that possible?"

"I'm not sure," Emry admitted. "When you cast off a spell, it's not like snuffing a candle. You're essentially freeing the magic. But maybe you don't have to. Maybe you can redirect it somewhere specific." Emry bit her lip. "Master Ambrosius might know."

"But he wouldn't be able to do it himself," Arthur guessed, plucking her unspoken sentence from the air. "Cornwall and the Isles have court wizards of their own, neither of whom are present. There are some old wizarding families in Camelot, but the last time my father checked, none of the Ninianes or Dulacs had much in the way of magical talent."

"You mean none of the *sons*," Emry corrected.

Arthur nodded slowly, processing that. "It's possible Camelot has some powerful sorceresses that we don't know about."

"Just say wizards," Emry instructed. "'Sorceress' and 'witch' always feel like accusations."

"Wizards, then," Arthur said with a wave of his hand. "You know what I mean. And based on the poison in my wine, it stands to reason that they had a particular goal in mind."

"Could it be an act of war?" Lance asked.

"If someone wanted me dead, they would have used nightshade. Or hemlock."

"Not if they were hoping for a terrible accident in the ring," argued Lance. "One that they couldn't be tied to."

"And if anything happens to you, the duke has a clear path to the throne?" Emry said uneasily.

Arthur nodded. His cousin Maddoc was only thirteen.

"Whoever did this doesn't think we know," said Lance. "That's the important part. And they probably think the poison didn't work. So if they're going to strike again, their best chance is tonight, at the ball."

"And if they have the enchantment from your scabbard, they'll be unkillable," said Emry.

Arthur winced, realizing she was right. The question of what someone would do with that ability was troubling.

There was a knock at the door, and Gawain poked his head inside.

"I tried the library first," he said, which might have been a joke.

Arthur waved him in, noticing the fresh bloom of a bruise against his cheek.

Gawain caught him looking and shrugged. "Courtesy of my father," he said curtly.

"You need to put something cold on it," Lance said. He deliberated before adding, "I've used plate armor before, in a pinch."

"I know something better," said Emry.

"No!" Lance said, at the same moment Arthur said, "You're injured!"

"I *meant* the healing salve," Emry said, sounding annoyed. "Stop fussing."

Gawain cocked his head and frowned, as though working something out. "And you said no one knew," he accused.

Emry shifted in her seat. "It's been an eventful day," she muttered.

"Hold on, *Gawain* knows you're a girl?" Arthur demanded.

That was entirely unfair.

"Really, cousin, it's obvious," Gawain drawled. "And you should note that I've said nothing. For weeks."

"It's true," Emry agreed. "He didn't even blackmail me."

"And I could have," Gawain added. "I *did* take her to a brothel, though. Just to watch her squirm."

Arthur's mouth fell open. Lance chuckled.

"I didn't *squirm*," Emry replied, rolling her eyes.

"It was terribly disappointing," Gawain reported.

"What's next?" Arthur grumbled. "Is everyone secretly hanging out with Guinevere?"

"Of course not." Gawain bristled. "And I notice she's not part of your little war room, either."

"This isn't a war room," Arthur protested.

"My apologies, then, for crashing your ménage à trois."

Arthur turned red.

"I came looking for you for a reason," Gawain said. "You know I've been Camelot's eyes and ears at the French court."

"A spy, you mean," said Lance.

"If you'd like," Gawain said impatiently. "So whatever it is you're planning, I want to help."

"Who says we're planning anything?" Lance asked.

Gawain shot him a look. "What have you got so far?"

Arthur filled his cousin in. After he'd finished, Gawain was quiet a moment, and then he said, "I have an idea. But I'll need the wizard's help."

◑ ◑ ◑

Arthur approached the corridor that led to his father's private chambers, his stomach churning with dread. It never got easier, facing the king's displeasure. And he suspected withdrawing from the sword-fighting contest was cause for displeasure enough.

He tried to gather his nerve, and found his thoughts once again snagging on Emry. He'd never met anyone with her talent for magic. Even Master Merlin hadn't been able to cast spells by *thinking* them. Yet somehow Emry had that ability.

Lancelot had always been his best knight, no matter what sword or uniform he wore. And Emry felt like his wizard. No matter that she wasn't her brother, a lad Arthur had never met, and from the sound of it, was better off not knowing. But he knew without a doubt that it would matter to his father. Which was why the king couldn't find out.

Arthur adjusted his cuffs and nodded to the guards.

They flung open the doors, and there was King Uther, in the midst of preparing for that evening's ball. He wore only a pair of velvet breeches, his chest bare, and was sipping a goblet of wine.

A valet was fussing over the rest of his ensemble, while a serving maid added logs to the fire. Lord Agravaine and Lord Howell stood by the window, scowling deeply.

"What were you thinking?" Uther demanded, apparently deciding to dispense with pleasantries.

Arthur looked wearily to his father's attendant, the maid, and the two advisors. "Must we have an audience for this?"

The king motioned for his attendant and maid to clear the chambers, and Arthur wished he could go with them.

"That wizard of yours is a menace," Uther accused, looking upset.

"How so?" Arthur asked nervously.

"He blundered into the royal box and took Excalibur!" Uther roared. "In front of King Leodegrance—and King Yurien!"

"He was acting on my orders," Arthur replied tersely. "The sword is my business."

"We had a plan," accused the king. "One that you agreed to."

"You wanted me to show off Excalibur, and I did," said Arthur. "You wanted me to compete, and I did. There was no mention of my having to fight the Duke of Cornwall in front of every noble in the kingdom. And I wasn't even the first to withdraw."

Lord Agravaine's expression soured at that.

"You defy me at every turn," said the king. "And making Lance your squire!"

Arthur's eyes flashed with anger. "It's about time *someone* did," he snapped. "I believe this pretense of a scandal has gone on long enough."

Arthur arched an eyebrow at Lord Agravaine, issuing a challenge.

"He *is* of noble birth," Lord Agravaine said grudgingly.

"There, Father, you see?" Arthur said. "Your own advisor agrees with me on the matter."

That wasn't what Lord Agravaine had said, and they both knew it. But Arthur offered the man his most princely smile, daring him to object.

"Give me the sword," his father demanded.

Arthur's stomach twisted. He'd been afraid something like this might happen. "I thought I would wear it to the ball," he said casually.

"We're not allowing any but castle guards to carry weapons this evening," said Uther. "Give it to me."

For the first time, Arthur realized how easy it was to say no. To do what he knew was best, rather than give in to his father's demands. His hands didn't go to his waist to unbuckle his scabbard, and everyone noticed.

"That's an order," said the king.

"It's one you should rethink," Arthur said coolly. "Someone removed the enchantment from my scabbard before the tournament. I'm not letting this sword out of my sight until I'm confident it won't come to any harm."

It seemed wise not to mention the poison. He didn't want his father putting *him* under guard for the rest of the evening, or insisting he miss the ball entirely. And he *really* didn't want his father knowing that Emry was capable of producing a poison antidote.

King Uther and his advisors blinked at Arthur in stunned silence.

"How do you know about the scabbard?" asked Lord Howell. "It looks the same to me."

"Merlin spotted it," Arthur said. "As to the nature of magic, I'm afraid it's beyond my comprehension."

"The wizard could be lying about the scabbard," said Lord Agravaine.

"A reasonable assumption," Arthur agreed, "which is why we tested it before the tournament. If you require a demonstration, you're welcome to try it on and see for yourself."

"That won't be necessary," Lord Agravaine said coldly.

"We must find out who did this—" the king began.

"I already have that covered," Arthur assured him. "If Gawain, Merlin, Lance, my guards, or I find out anything useful, you'll be the first to know." He paused before adding, "And of course I'll have my guards return Excalibur to the vault before tonight's festivities, where I'll be stationing them as extra security until Captain Lam can rearrange his men's assignments. I trust that will be all, sire."

Arthur strode from the room before his father could dismiss him, or get in another word edgewise.

CHAPTER 34

Emry couldn't believe she'd let Gawain talk her into this. Dressing up as her brother was one thing, but pretending to be a courtier at a royal ball was quite another.

"Well?" Gawain called from the sitting room. "Can I see?"

"Not yet!"

Emry stared in the mirror in Gawain's dressing room. The girl who gazed back was an impossible, improbable version of herself, all dark eyes and dark hair and mysterious glamour.

Her dress's neckline plunged almost to her navel. A black lace bodice hugged her curves and skimmed over her waist. Layers of pale gray silk cascaded from her shoulders, darkening to almost black at the bottom. The skirt was studded with swirls of crystal that took the shape of tangled branches. The effect was both terrifying and beautiful. Like an enchanted forest filled with thorns.

She had never worn anything so fine. A couple of spells had taken in the waist and lengthened the hem. She only wished she had something stronger than Master Ambrosius's salve to take care of the still-tender wound across her ribs. Well, he could show her what to do in the morning. At least she had plenty of spare bandages to wrap it.

Emry gave her wig a tug, settling the glossy dark waves over one shoulder.

She looked like someone who *belonged*, and she couldn't help but think how much easier everything would be if the girl in the mirror was real. If she was attending tonight's ball as the daughter of the court wizard. Or as the court wizard herself.

"Does the dress fit all right?" Gawain called.

"It's fine," Emry said, smoothing a wrinkle from her bodice.

She hadn't fully thought through what it meant, shedding her disguise for the first time in months. And how it would feel to put on another, with no chance to be herself in between. It was disorienting, seeing herself with long hair and a ball gown. The speed at which she was expected to be someone else, yet again, was dizzying. Especially when all she wanted was to be herself.

Someone pounded heavily on the door to Gawain's apartments, and Emry's heart thudded in alarm.

"A word, before the festivities," a familiar voice called. Lord Agravaine.

"I'm undressed, Father," Gawain protested, frantically motioning for Emry to hide.

Emry pressed herself behind the wardrobe, heart pounding. And she was just in time. Lord Agravaine ignored Gawain's warning, pushing open the door.

"You seem perfectly dressed to me," he observed coolly.

Emry's heart pounded against her rib cage like a frantic, wild thing. She could just make out the corner of his dark coat, and the edge of his sleeve. She hoped he wouldn't walk past the flimsy screen that separated the solar from the dressing room. Her clothes were strewn across the floor, and the man was bound to notice. But then, she hadn't had much warning.

"Well?" Gawain said impatiently. "You needed something?"

"The prince was poisoned," Lord Agravaine accused. "*That's* why you withdrew from the contest."

"How did you find out?" Gawain asked.

"I have my ways," Lord Agravaine said silkily. "It's strange that Arthur forgot to mention he'd been poisoned when he spoke with the king. Wouldn't you agree?"

"Not really. He's recovered now."

"And I wonder why that might be," said Lord Agravaine. "It really is convenient, the way Merlin keeps turning up whenever there's trouble."

"So does Jereth," Gawain shot back. "Yet he's presumed innocent even when he's guilty."

The room went still and cold. Emry remembered the bruise on Gawain's cheek, and his terse explanation of how he'd gotten it. She squeezed her eyes shut and tensed her shoulders, waiting.

"In regard to Jereth, I don't believe it prudent to keep your brother at the castle much longer," said Lord Agravaine. "There was an incident with his horse—"

"I warned you about that."

"One of the grooms had to be paid off. I've arranged for him to spend some time studying at a monastery outside Paris. You'll accompany him there, see him settled, and return to your responsibilities overseas. You'll leave within the week."

"But, Father—"

"If Princess Anne is betrothed to King Yurien's son, it could spell disaster for us all. You will make sure the boy is not considered a suitable option. At any cost. You have your orders. I expect you to follow them without complaint."

"Anything else?" Gawain asked sourly.

"Not at the moment. But if there is, I'll certainly let you know."

"I don't doubt it," Gawain muttered.

Emry heard the door close, and Gawain loosed a sigh.

"Hi," she called. "You okay in there?"

"Just contemplating garroting myself with my cape."

"That poor cape," Emry replied. "Thought it was going to a ball, but instead it's a funeral."

Gawain snorted. "All right, I'm coming in," he insisted. "You better be dressed by now."

He was in the doorway in a moment, dressed as elegantly as any prince, resplendent in deep purple velvet. The bruise under his left eye made him look gallant, and a little dangerous. His expression startled as he saw her.

"Oh," he said softly.

Emry made a face. "Is that all you've got? I was hoping for 'putain de bordel de merde,'" she said brightly, repeating the foul thing she'd heard Chef mutter in the kitchens the day before.

Gawain swallowed thickly. "You look, um . . ." He cleared his throat. "Beautiful."

"Just wait until I open my mouth and ruin it," she warned.

"You mean you hadn't done that yet?"

She wished he'd stop looking at her like that. Like *this* was who she truly was, instead of yet another disguise.

"I'll admit, I wasn't expecting such a dramatic transformation," he said, considering her. "Perhaps I should have borrowed a different dress."

"Borrowed?" Emry asked.

"Don't worry about it."

Gawain offered his arm. Emry took it, feeling ridiculous. It was hard to cast off the small but constant adjustments that she'd used to make everyone believe she was her brother. Especially since now she was playing yet another part. It was so strange, going from strutting boy wizard to elegant court lady. She supposed the real Emry was somewhere in between.

"You'd make a good spy," he said as they walked down the castle corridors.

"I hope that's a compliment," Emry said.

"It is," he promised.

They passed a group of giggling courtiers, who curtseyed to Gawain. He offered them a brief bow in return, placing his hand on the small of Emry's back. She stiffened, surprised.

"Curtsey," he hissed.

She did, and he steered her away.

She took a deep breath, reminding herself once again why she was doing this: She could move through the crowd unnoticed, and who knew what she might overhear—or what someone might confess. She could cross-examine the duke, under the guise of dancing with him. And of course, she would be near Arthur, should disaster strike again.

They reached the doors, and Gawain turned to her, a half grin playing over his face.

"What?" she asked.

"I'm trying to figure out where you put your wand," he mused.

"Oh, shut up," Emry muttered as two liveried guards threw open the doors, revealing candlelight and music and dozens of fabulously dressed nobles, courtiers, and royals enjoying themselves.

Even the suits of armor had been draped with festive garlands. Emry spotted grand tables of sumptuous sweets, and cakes that were carved and iced to look like sculptures. It was lavish and lovely and overwhelming all at once. Next to her, Gawain looked both used to this kind of thing and exhausted by it.

"Steel yourself," he warned.

And with her hand on his arm, she stepped into the Great Hall.

☾ ☾ ☾

Arthur was dancing with the Queen of Lothia.

She and King Yurien had approached him the moment he arrived, peppering him with an onslaught of questions about Excalibur. Where had he gotten it, and how long ago, and was it true that the blade only glowed for those it deemed worthy? Arthur had answered their questions as politely and as vaguely as he could, twisting around to look for anyone who might rescue him.

But there was no one.

"I'd love a dance," the queen had proclaimed, resting a pale, slender hand on his arm.

And before he knew it, they were on the dance floor, where he was hastily trying to remember the steps to the Basse. Every time he tried to cheat by seeing what anyone else was doing, he could sense the queen's amusement.

"Are you enjoying yourself, Your Highness?" she asked, as the dance brought them together palm to palm.

"I am, Your Majesty," Arthur lied. "I'm just a bit, er, tired from the contest."

Tired was an understatement. He wanted nothing more than to collapse into bed and sleep for a week. Instead he was here, at his father's grand birthday ball, with the Queen of Lothia and no idea whether their next dance step lasted six counts or eight.

"I wasn't aware the Duke of Cornwall intended to enter," she said.

"Nor was I," said Arthur.

"I admire a man who knows what he wants," the queen said silkily. "But somehow, I find that very quality abhorrent in the duke."

Arthur bit back a laugh. "Then we are in agreement," he pronounced.

Their palms were inches apart, held aloft as they circled one another. A large emerald ring glittered on the queen's finger, and a matching stone swayed on a long golden chain around her neck. Her veil was a similar shade of green, embroidered with silver to match her gown. And her eyes were rimmed with thick smudges of dark makeup that flicked up at the corners in a way that was almost catlike.

"Was your journey to Avalon very difficult?" the queen inquired.

"I did have some trouble with the boat," Arthur allowed. "Luckily, I had our apprentice wizard Merlin with me, or else I might have arrived soaking wet."

The queen's eyes glittered with interest. "I've heard of the wizard Merlin," she said. "I expected him to be older."

"This was his, uh, son," said Arthur.

The queen looked surprised. "I didn't know he had children."

"Twins," Arthur said absently, trying to remember the count. Were they supposed to circle twice or three times? He glanced at the couple on their left, who was no help, unless he was looking for instruction on where to place his hands should he wish to be slapped. "A boy and a girl."

It was three times, Arthur realized, completing the final round. The dance floor burst into applause for the minstrels, and he clapped politely as well. He really hoped he didn't have to dance with her again. There was something a little unsettling about the queen.

Arthur never thought he'd be relieved to see King Yurien, yet as the man approached, he truly was.

"Come, Morgana," said King Yurien, extending an arm, "I must show you the gardens."

The queen inclined her head at Arthur. "A pleasure," she said.

Arthur bowed in return. When he straightened, he caught sight of Emry in the doorway and nearly lost his balance.

He wasn't prepared for it. For her. For this beautiful girl in a dark, glittering dress, her neckline plunging dangerously low, revealing assets he hadn't known she possessed. Long black hair cascaded over one shoulder, and her whole face lit up as she laughed at something Gawain had said. He wondered why the entire room hadn't ground to a halt, why every courtier in the place wasn't staring.

He couldn't reconcile the fact that this impossibly lovely creature was the shabby apprentice he'd sat across from in the wizard's workshop for weeks.

He waited for her to turn and notice him. He knew he looked well in his black jacket and best crown, and that the weeks of training had broadened his shoulders and improved the width of his biceps. Still, he wished there weren't dark circles under his eyes from that day's trials. That his hair had cooperated with combing, and that a stray lock hadn't snuck itself loose, dangling over his right eye.

But Emry hadn't noticed him at all.

"I've been looking for you all day, Your Highness," a girl said at his elbow. He turned hopeful, and came face to face with Princess Guinevere.

She was exquisite as always, her lips perfectly rouged, her hair expertly curled, her emerald gown tightly fitted. She wore a tiara to match, and jewels glittered at her throat and earlobes.

"Princess." Arthur bowed. "You're the loveliest girl at the ball."

"Thank you, Your Highness," she replied dutifully. "How handsome you look as well."

Neither of them sounded the least bit convincing.

The minstrels began to play once again, announcing the Black Almain.

"Would you care to dance?" he asked, realizing there was no way out of it.

"I'd love to." Guinevere beamed.

Arthur tried to match her enthusiasm, even though all he wanted to do was slip away and find Emry.

"You fought well this morning," she said. "I was most disappointed that you didn't wish to continue."

"It seemed prudent to follow my cousin's example and step aside."

"Perhaps my brother should have done the same." Guinevere nodded toward an alcove, where Arthur noted with surprise that Prince Gottegrim's right shoulder was tied with a sling.

"Is he badly hurt?" Arthur asked.

"The wound will heal. I told him your wizard might be of help. But he doesn't approve of magical healing. He believes suffering is an act of penitence."

"And you don't?" Arthur asked.

Guinevere's smile tugged higher in one corner. "I believe getting bested in a sword fight by the Duke of Cornwall is suffering enough."

"I believe you're right."

Arthur caught sight of the duke, his dark hair slicked straight back from his temples, his posture rigid as he clutched a drink and glared at Sir Kay. And then he tried not to choke as he saw Gawain and Emry approach the duke, or as his wizard bobbed a low curtsey that made the duke leer.

"You missed a step," Guinevere pointed out, and Arthur dragged his attention back to their dance. She was right. They were facing the wrong direction from the rest of the dancers.

"My apologies." Arthur corrected himself, wishing they could dance as they pleased, and not have to follow the same pattern as everyone else.

When he glanced back at the duke, he saw the man leading Emry to the dance floor. *This is the plan*, he reminded himself, even though his stomach curdled at the sight of the duke's lecherous grin. Even though he could hardly tear his eyes from the pair as they moved through the familiar dance steps.

"The weather was nice today," Guinevere said politely, and Arthur suppressed a sigh.

◑ ◑ ◑

"Are we supposed to pretend we don't know each other?" Arthur asked, joining Emry next to a table of lavishly displayed sweets.

"I believe so, Your Highness," Emry murmured, dropping into a bow.

A smile traced over Arthur's lips. "And *I* believe you meant to curtsey, my lady." His eyes danced with amusement at her misstep. She blushed and hastily corrected the error.

"Bowing's easier, with a wand strapped to my thigh," she muttered.

Arthur bit back a laugh.

"Don't tell Gawain," she went on. "He's been pestering me to tell him what I've done with it."

"I'm surprised you didn't make something up, just to torture him."

"Oh, the mystery is torture enough." Emry reached for a piece of marzipan, popping it into her mouth and absently licking the sugar from her fingers.

Arthur watched, his throat going dry. "So," he said. "How was the duke?"

"Handsy." Emry made a face. "And he certainly thinks highly of himself. You might be right about the poisoning, but he was absolutely clueless about Excalibur."

"You're sure?" Arthur asked.

Before Emry could answer, they were set upon by the three princesses of the Isles, all of whom were dressed once again in frilly pink gowns. What wretched timing. If he had to dance with all three of them, he thought he might scream.

"My apologies, princesses," Arthur said with a bow. "My—er—companion and I were just bound for the dance floor."

Emry startled, but took Arthur's hand nonetheless. A warmth spread through him at her touch, and he wondered if it was magic, the way he felt when he looked at her, or if it was something else.

"What happened to not knowing each other?" she asked as they crossed the ballroom.

"Three pink princesses," Arthur said tightly. "I hope you don't mind."

"Actually, it's you who should be wary," Emry warned. "I'm a terrible dancer."

"Oh, I'm worse," Arthur promised cheerfully.

They joined the others on the dance floor. It seemed a wonder that he was allowed to hold her. He had never much cared for dancing, but pressing so close to Emry made him reconsider.

"So, the duke," Emry prompted.

Right, the duke. That was what they were doing. They were dancing merely to avoid being overheard. Still, Arthur couldn't help but thrill at their closeness. At how Emry seemed to grow prettier with every moment, a blush coloring her cheeks, her dark hair shining in the candlelight.

"What about the duke?" Arthur asked, staring down at her.

"I believe his exact words were, 'Only a poor swordsman needs an enchanted blade. My reputation on the battlefield is worth at least ten Excaliburs.'"

"Not that I wanted it to be him," Arthur said with a sigh.

"I know." Emry smiled ruefully. "But it would have made things a lot easier. We still have no idea who tampered with your scabbard. Or why."

The dance grew more complicated, and Emry bit her lip, fumbling slightly at the steps. Arthur held back a grin.

"Oh, shut up," she mumbled.

"I don't believe I said anything." Arthur smirked.

"But your silence speaks volumes." Emry sighed and admitted, "I only know the steps from the theater. I've never been to a ball before."

Across the dance floor, Arthur watched as Lance fell out of step with the rest of the dancers, twirling Guinevere so she could show off the folds of her dress. Guinevere seemed delighted, and Arthur couldn't remember the last time he'd seen Lance so pleased.

"You're doing fine," he promised. "But whatever you do, don't look at Lancelot and Guinevere."

"Why not?" she asked curiously.

"They're putting everyone to shame."

Emry looked anyway. And then she shook her head, holding back a smile. "So that's what enjoying yourself looks like. I'd wondered."

"And here I thought it looked like this." Arthur's hand slid lower on Emry's back. She gasped slightly.

"What are you doing?" she murmured.

What *was* he doing? Sard. Thankfully, the song slowed and ended, and he bowed before taking his leave. She was right, they really *shouldn't* have danced together. It was lucky Lance had borrowed Guinevere, giving him an excuse.

Arthur looked around, hoping there was somewhere he might disappear for a moment.

He passed King Yurien and Queen Morgana, who smiled wolfishly in his direction. And then he caught sight of one of the pink princesses heading toward him and hung a sharp left. He snagged a goblet of wine from a passing tray, though the last thing he felt like doing was drinking, but at least it was something to do with his hands. And his attention.

"Your Highness," a voice purred at his back. "And here I thought you'd dance with the princess all night."

Arthur turned and found Lady Elaine fluttering her eyelashes. He nearly groaned. Her ivory gown was covered with pearls, the waist cinched far too tight. It looked horribly uncomfortable.

"Guinevere may dance with whomever she chooses," Arthur said. "Lance is far more adept on the dance floor than I."

Elaine wrinkled her nose.

"She's a *princess*. He's a *guard*. They'll cause a scandal, the two of them."

"Then perhaps you should cut in," Arthur suggested.

Elaine went pink at the insult. "I don't recognize the courtier you were dancing with," she said, attempting to change the subject. "How do you know her?"

"Oh, she's a guard, too," Arthur said with a straight face.

"You're making fun of me." Elaine pouted. "To make up for it, you'll dance with me."

Arthur stared at the girl, who was practically gloating at her own cleverness.

"You know," he said, "I don't believe I will."

And with that, he walked away.

◐ ◐ ◐

Emry ducked into an alcove of the ballroom, hoping to avoid the duke's notice. He had sought her out for a second dance, and she wasn't about to allow him a third. Vile man. He'd offered to fetch her a drink, and she was fairly certain that if he did, it would come laced with sleeping tincture.

The duke wasn't a man with access to magic. Of that Emry was certain. Or else he would have revealed his hand long ago. Which meant there was someone else. Someone Emry was missing.

She glanced around, noticing that two of the pink princesses had cornered a horrified Prince Gottegrim. The duke was dancing with Lady Elaine, who wore a pained look on her face, although that could be due to the tightness of her bodice. Where was King Yurien?

Emry shifted, trying to find a better vantage point. And bumped into something.

No, *someone.*

"Hi," a boy's voice said.

It was Arthur. He was leaning against the wall, half cloaked in shadow, and he looked exhausted.

"Hi," she said. "Sorry, I didn't realize I'd found your hiding place."

"I'm willing to share," he said, a smile tugging at his lips. "I believe they're meant to accommodate two."

Emry glanced at the other alcoves and blushed at the amorous couples.

"So," Arthur said. "How goes your night of spying? What have you observed so far?"

"Jereth is a shockingly good dancer."

"What else?"

"Sir Kay has eaten four slices of cake. Which doesn't seem the thing if he was up to anything nefarious."

"What else?"

They stood so close. Eyelash to eyelash. Lip to lip. Emry's breath caught.

"Have you observed," breathed Arthur, "how badly I want to kiss you?"

Oh, she wanted to kiss him, too. But not here. He took her hand, rubbing his thumb in slow, maddening circles against her palm.

"You *are* being rather obvious about it," Emry murmured.

"Do you object?" He arched an eyebrow.

"Not at all."

Her heart pounded as Arthur led her through the castle, darting into a servant's stair, and then through an unmarked door behind a tapestry.

He pulled her through the labyrinthine stone corridors and stopped at an ancient wooden door, pressing a soft kiss to her mouth.

He pulled away, a questioning look in his eyes.

"Don't stop," she whispered. "Not when we're finally getting to the good part."

His lips met hers again, more insistent this time. Her mouth opened to him, and she lost herself in Arthur. In his smell, his taste, his arms.

He fumbled a hand behind her back, and she tilted her head with a frown, wondering what on earth he was trying to do.

"Shortcut," he explained as the door swung open.

☾ ☾ ☾

The candles burned low in the sconces, and the balustrade was entirely in shadow. Narrow rows of books stretched up on either side of them. They were in the library stacks.

Emry laughed, because it was so entirely *Arthur* to duck out of a ball and bring her to the library. But her laugher was cut off as he pressed another urgent kiss to her lips. They became a tangle of hands and mouths, and caught in his embrace, Emry realized just how much she had wanted this, and how much it had hurt to believe it would never happen.

Arthur trailed warm, slow kisses down her neck and onto her shoulder, pushing her dress aside. Her skin tingled from his touch, and all the hairs on her body stood up. She arched herself against him, and he groaned.

Her name escaped from his lips like a prayer, or maybe a spell, and she murmured his back, her breath caressing his collar. Here, in the cool quiet of the library, he was just Arthur. Just a handsome, dreamy-eyed boy, who wanted nothing so much in that moment as to kiss her. And she was just a girl who was eager to kiss him back.

She grabbed a handful of his hair as his hand found its way underneath her impossibly full skirts. Slowly, wickedly, it slid up her thigh, and then stopped.

"This has to go," he said with a grin, tugging her wand from its makeshift holster.

"If you insist," Emry said raggedly.

"Oh, I do." Arthur's warm brown eyes met hers as his fingers traveled higher, and a delicious ache bloomed in her belly.

Arthur brushed the space between her legs, and his touch nearly undid her.

"Clothes off, wizard," he demanded, tugging at the laces of her dress. "That's an order."

"Right away, Your Highness," she teased, mumbling a spell that she'd used countless times backstage at the theater. She stared into the dark pools of his eyes as her dress fell to the floor.

She wished she didn't have that infernal wound across her rib cage, wrapped tight with gauze. But Arthur didn't seem to notice. His throat bobbed, and his breath hitched as he took in the sight of her.

"That was quick," he breathed.

"Magic," she replied.

They crashed together, his breath hot and urgent as it fanned across her ear. She yanked his tunic loose from his trousers, and he shucked off the rest of his clothing while pressing rough, insistent kisses against her lips.

His clever fingers found her again. She raked her nails down his back as everything within her went taut, until she could barely breathe for wanting. She was going to come undone in his arms, in the sarding library, and he knew it. His mouth pressed hungrily against hers, and she gasped. She broke apart into a million glittering stars. And then she reached for him and made him shatter, too.

☾ ☽ ☾

Arthur stumbled from the library, straightening his jacket. He had better get back, he knew, before he was missed. It had been a risk to slip away, but ever since Emry had walked into the ball looking like *that*, everything had emptied from his mind except her.

It seemed impossible that the ball was still going, that courtiers filled the dance floor and sipped from their drinks.

"Where were you?" Lance demanded when Arthur returned.

"The library. What? It's the truth."

"Where's Merlin?" Lance asked, and then muttered, "No doubt also in the library."

"At least I was safe," Arthur protested.

"Were you?"

Arthur chose to ignore that jab. "Well," he demanded. "Any developments?"

"I'm afraid not," said Gawain, joining them, as the king rose from his throne and signaled for everyone's attention.

"Friends and guestsh," said King Uther, slurring his speech. "I am honored to have all of you gathered here in celebration."

Sard, Arthur thought, taking in his father's glassy eyes and unsteadiness on his feet. He wasn't the least bit sober.

"Yet one of you has betrayed me," the king went on. Gasps and whispers echoed through the ballroom. "As you no doubt know, my son has recovered the lost blade Excalibur. Today, someone has tampered with the sword's scabbard."

Arthur winced, desperate for his father to stop. But there was nothing he could do but stand there with the rest of the crowd as the king motioned for silence.

"Rest assured, the culprit will be found," said King Uther. "And they will be gravely punished. I command anyone who has knowledge of this crime—"

"A question, Your Majesty," said King Yurien, stepping forward.

Uther went red at the interruption, but waved a hand in Yurien's direction.

"You speak of the scabbard that Prince Arthur was wearing this morning?"

"Yes," said Uther. "It is a highly rare and magical object."

"I see," said Yurien, in a tone that made it sound as though he didn't see it all. "So you accuse everyone in this room of committing an invisible crime, while admitting that your son intended to cheat in your contest."

Arthur's stomach twisted. Yurien wasn't wrong. Yet to hear it phrased like that—it made him sound pathetic. Weak. Unworthy of leading a kingdom.

"What's more," Yurien went on, holding up a hand for silence, "you invite us to accuse each other of this offense, while your guards slink about the castle and pass amongst us in secret, dressed as royal guests?"

He meant Lance, Arthur realized. Somehow, he knew Lance was a guard. Arthur remembered seeing Yurien speak with the Duke of Cornwall at supper the previous night and thinking little of it. But now, recalling how targeted and precise the Lothian king had been with his questions about Excalibur, he knew the man had been doing his homework. And that he had likely dispatched his wife to do more of the same.

"The only guests at this celebration are members of the nobility, I assure you," said Uther coldly. "And as for my guards, you see a threat that does not exist."

The room went quiet, and ice cold.

"Perhaps," said Yurien, "you accuse us of a crime that does not exist."

There were some murmurs around the hall.

"Your son is no warrior," Yurien went on, gesturing toward Arthur. "One need only glance at the boy to know that. His own cousin withdrew to advance him in your little contest, sparing him the embarrassment of defeat. A shame he was too cowardly to continue."

"How dare you speak so about my son?" King Uther roared.

"I merely give voice to what everyone is thinking," said Yurien. "The true king of England is whoever can pull the sword from the stone? How convenient, when the sword and stone are in your own kingdom. You pretend to keep the peace, Uther, but you march us all closer to war."

King Leodegrance scowled, coming forward. "You know not of what you speak, Yurien. There is only war between kingdoms that share no friendship. Cameliard and Camelot stand together."

King Leodegrance stepped to the dais beside King Uther, and an unspoken agreement passed between them.

"Our kingdoms are indeed joined," said Uther. "As my son Arthur is engaged to marry Princess Guinevere of Cameliard."

No.

His father couldn't—not like this, here, now.

And yet, as he stared all around him, at the overwhelming press of courtiers cheering at the happy news, he felt frozen in place. Guinevere looked equally shocked. She drifted to his side, wearing an impossibly fake smile, and Arthur saw that she was trembling.

"I hope you will all join us in congratulating the happy couple, and in wishing peace and prosperity to our two kingdoms." King Leodegrance beamed.

Guinevere's trembling grew even worse. Arthur touched a hand to her shoulder, to try to still her. The watching courtiers mistook it for a sign of affection and smiled.

"Did you know about this?" Guinevere hissed through clenched teeth.

"No," Arthur whispered back.

"I don't—I never—" she began.

"Same," he told her.

And then Prince Gottegrim clapped him gamely on the back. "I'll look forward to hearing the banns in church tomorrow," he said.

"I—er—" Arthur spluttered.

"No spending time together unchaperoned until your wedding night, little sister," Prince Gott said with a teasing wink.

Arthur went cold at the thought. Not the thought—the memory. Of a different girl in his arms. One he actually had feelings for.

This wasn't happening—and yet, it was already done.

He looked up, and there she was. His wizard. She stood in the doorway, eyes wide, face pale, looking for all the world like her heart had been smashed to pieces.

◑ ◑ ◑

He tried to go after her, but the crowd swallowed him up, a hungry thing, eager to bestow congratulations and well wishes on their future king and his bride-to-be.

Everything had gone horribly wrong. He ducked into the hallway, his heart hammering, needing this cursed day to end.

"Arthur."

His father had followed him.

"Happy birthday, Father," Arthur said, coldly furious. "I would have appreciated a warning that my gift to you is an arranged marriage."

"Don't be a fool. You must see how necessary this was."

"You made it so!" Arthur accused. "I told you I had everything handled! Yet you insisted on using a party as a weapon. And I'm the one who staggers away wounded."

"I've been patient with you thus far," said Uther. "But let me be clear: King Leodegrance and I have already agreed to the terms of the arrangement. This marriage is not up for discussion."

"Especially now that you've forced her hand in front of half the kingdom," Arthur said bitterly. "Am I such a disappointment that you needed to strong-arm my bride?"

"When have I ever called you a disappointment?"

Arthur toed a rough spot in the stone floor, saying nothing. It was true his father had never spoken those exact words aloud, but his thoughts on the matter had always seemed clear.

"I'll admit I was hard on you. But my actions were necessary. Had I

behaved otherwise, you would have seemed a threat to the crown," said
Uther. Arthur stared at his father in surprise. "I didn't want my court to
split favor amongst my children. For my sons to fight over the crown. So I
acted as though you were nothing to me. A mistake. A spare. How could I
say differently, after the scandal surrounding your birth?"

Arthur couldn't believe what he was hearing.

"After your mother died, I couldn't very well take it back."

"You could have told me this sooner," said Arthur.

"What would it have changed? You have always been stubborn.
Foolish. Determined to remake the world into something different than
what it is."

"Is that so wrong?" Arthur asked.

"It is no way to rule a kingdom," said Uther. "Now, more than ever, we
need to protect Camelot."

"Not this again." Arthur sighed.

"Yes, this again," Uther insisted. "Excalibur paints a target on your
back. You need an heir whose lineage is beyond dispute. King Leodegrance
assures me his daughter will breed. You'll see to it that she does. Quickly."

Arthur stared at his father in disbelief. "Let me see if I've got this
right," he said sarcastically. "Marry someone I don't love, and immediately
have children? Is that all, or is there anything else you'd like me to do before
I turn twenty?"

Rage flickered across King Uther's face. He stepped forward, grasping
Arthur roughly by the shoulder. Arthur could smell the drink on his father's
breath, and see the yellow film gathered in the corners of his narrowed
eyes.

"Accuse me of being unreasonable again, and you'll find out just how
unreasonable I can be," growled Uther. "Now act happy about your bride.
Or I will personally dismantle your precious library, triple your guard, and
order them to accompany you *inside* the privy."

CHAPTER 35

E mry didn't know how long she'd been lying in bed, her faced pressed into a pillow that had gone wet and salty from her tears. She'd told herself not to catch feelings for the prince. She'd warned herself what would happen. And now it had.

Smart as spades, but foolish as hearts.

And she had been so foolish. Arthur had told her himself that his father intended for him to marry Guinevere. What happened in the library hadn't changed anything. It only made the inevitable heartbreak worse, knowing that he burned for her, too. And of course she'd found out moments before King Uther and King Leodegrance had announced the royal engagement.

Arthur must have known it was coming. That was why he'd led her away where no one would see. Why he'd been in such a hurry to return to the ball.

Every time she gave her heart to someone, they chose someone else. She was the unwanted one, the twin who was an afterthought when her father taught them magic, the girl whom no one ever picked.

Her shoulders shook, and her throat felt raw, and she realized belatedly she was still wearing the borrowed dress. Her clothes were in Gawain's chambers. Well, her brother's clothes.

She'd retrieve them in the morning.

All she wanted was to be alone with her misery. Earlier, she'd felt as if she was filled with stars. Now the stars were gone, and there was nothing to light her way back from this dark and empty void.

There was a tentative knock on her door.

She didn't move. She couldn't move. It had been foolish to come back here dressed as she was.

She waited for whomever it was to give up, but the knock sounded again.

"Go away," she called. She didn't want to talk to anyone. She just wanted to be left alone to cry and have feelings.

"It's me," Arthur said.

"I repeat, go away," she called.

Instead, he opened the door.

There he was—a prince dressed for a ball. The jeweled circlet shining in his dark hair, the fine silk jacket clasped with silver and gold. The handsome curve of his jaw, and the way he smelled faintly of roses and steel. The heir to the throne, engaged to marry a beautiful princess. He wasn't the boy from the library at all. And maybe he had never been.

Sard, she wished she'd mumbled a locking spell at the door.

"I guess congratulations are in order," she said sourly.

"Emry, don't," he ground out.

"How could you do that to me?" she demanded, crawling out of bed and attempting to smooth the wrinkles from her dress.

"I didn't know my father was going to declare it like that!" Arthur winced, but didn't apologize. Which was just so—ugh.

"What am I to you?" she asked.

"You're my wizard." Arthur didn't hesitate.

"Did you propose before we snuck away to the library? Or after, while I was lacing my dress?"

She glared daggers at him, hating that he'd put her in this impossible position. That he had acted as though she was more to him than just his wizard. That he had destroyed everything without so much as a warning.

"Emry, you don't understand," he said. "I don't want to marry her."

"Don't want to, or aren't going to?" she demanded.

His silence spoke volumes.

"May you have many sons," she said. "Isn't that the blessing you be-stow on a member of the royal family?"

"I don't love her."

"May you have many illegitimate heirs, then," Emry said wretchedly.

"Emry—" Arthur began.

"I've heard that royals bed whomever they please, but I never thought they snuck out of their own engagement parties to do so," Emry snapped.

Arthur's mouth opened, and then closed. "It's not like that," he said finally.

"It's exactly like that!"

"I'll be more tactful, going forward," Arthur promised. "But I need you by my side."

"Disguised as my brother. Forever."

"Maybe just until after the wedding," Arthur said.

Wrong answer.

It was as though he'd stabbed her, and there was no magic salve to heal the wound.

"And then what?" she demanded.

Fight for me, she pleaded silently. *Tell me that I matter to you more than your father's approval.*

"I don't know," Arthur admitted. "My father isn't making this easy on me."

"If there was ever a time to stand up to him, this is it."

"You don't understand what it's like! I *have* to do what's expected."

Emry couldn't believe it—couldn't believe him. "I absolutely under-stand what it's like to have a father who makes all the decisions and expects them to be obeyed without question. Mine used to teach my brother magic and bring *me* hair ribbons! But I challenged him because I knew he was wrong. I thought that's what you were doing, visiting the wizard's workshop and making Lance your squire. Was all of it a lie?"

"Of course not," Arthur snapped. "But you have to understand my position. I don't have the luxury of putting myself first. *Ever.*"

Arthur's expression was one of pure misery. Emry wanted to shake him by the shoulders and scream that he had it all wrong. Before she could, he took a deep breath and composed himself.

"I want you to be my court wizard. Isn't that enough?" He gave her a long, searching look. "Tonight, in the library, I forgot myself. I'm sorry."

That's what he was apologizing for? Oh, she wanted to kill him.

"You're *sorry*?"

Her anger overwhelmed her. She could feel herself losing control. Magic crackled at her fingertips, and everything started to warp. A stack of books levitated on her desk, and the fire in the grate, which had been a low smolder, surged with sudden strength.

A flick of her wrist was all it would take for that tension to snap. For the room to go up in flames. For a moment, she *wanted* it. But then she took a deep breath, steadying herself. It was almost a shame when the books dropped, and the fireplace returned to normal.

"Do you know how risky it was for me to go to the ball tonight? Dressed like *this?*" Emry accused. "I'm terrified every day that the wrong person will discover I'm Merlin's daughter, and not his son. That I'll find myself dragged before the king as a traitor for what I've done. I didn't sign up for this! It was only supposed to be for a week!"

"Then why did you stay?" Arthur asked.

"For the same reason I let you stab me with a sword. Because I thought you were someone you're not. And I thought *we* were something we're not. Now get out."

"Emry—"

"Get out!"

Arthur's mouth pressed into a thin line. And then he left, slamming the door behind him.

☾ ☽ ☾

Morgana watched as her husband paced the length of their ship's cabin, his face blotched with anger. He had been seething ever since King Uther's accusation at the ball earlier that evening.

"You said no one would notice the scabbard," Yurien growled.

"No one was supposed to. I didn't account for their apprentice court wizard."

She'd felt as though she had seen a ghost, watching Merlin's boy burst into the royal box. Especially when Excalibur had leapt into his hand as if summoned by mere thought. And as it did, she'd recognized the silver mark upon his palm.

He had opened a door to the Otherworld. Somehow, for him, it had *worked*. No wonder the prince had Anwen's scabbard, if their apprentice wizard was capable of such rare and impossible magic.

"The apprentice wizard?" Yurien sounded incredulous. "You're talking about that scrawny teenage boy?"

"He is a *Merlin*," Morgana hissed. "Perhaps even more powerful than his father."

She ripped the dark veil from her hair, tossing it to the floor. Even if it had been amusing to wear such an outlandish costume, her disguise had proven wholly unnecessary. She had thought the king might recognize her, with how strongly she resembled her mother, but he hadn't thrown her a second glance. No one had.

"And the prince is no fool," Morgana went on. "You forget that he recovered both the sword in the stone *and* Excalibur."

"I forget nothing," said Yurien, coldly furious. "And it would serve you well to remember that I *covered for you*. You neglected to consult me before you took that enchantment."

Morgana shot her husband a look. If only he knew all the things she neglected to consult him before doing. "There wasn't time," she said impatiently. "You don't know how many years I've been after a piece of Anwen's magic."

"And now we have one." Yurien admired the emerald ring on his forefinger, the stone glinting in the candlelight. "It worked well enough earlier. I gave it to the boatswain before I slit his throat. He's already back to his duties."

"I can't believe you let Mordred see that," Morgana admonished. "He's just a boy."

"He's strong, like his father." Yurien's eyes lit with pride.

But Morgana knew better. Her son was sensitive. Clever. Curious. He might have Yurien's fair coloring, but if he took after anyone, it was her.

And then, as if he had overheard them, Mordred appeared in the doorway, in a linen shift that had grown too short for him. He blinked, rubbing his eyes.

"What's the matter, my love?" Morgana asked. "I thought you were asleep."

"I had a nightmare," Mordred complained. A worn poppet shaped like a dragon dangled from one hand, its tail trailing on the floor.

Morgana threw an accusing glance at her husband. "It's late." She placed a hand on her son's shoulder, steering him back into the hall. He was so small, she couldn't help but thinking. So breakable. "Go and have your nurse tuck you into bed."

"She's asleep," Mordred complained. "And she smells funny. Can't you do it?"

Morgana sighed. "All right," she agreed, walking him back to his quarters.

Belowdecks, the galleass was more of a warship than a residence, its corridors spare and weathered. They would have been much more comfortable staying in the proffered guest quarters at the castle. But Yurien refused to sleep under another king's roof, especially when he wasn't allowed his own armed guards.

Morgana pushed open the cabin door and wrinkled her nose at the smell. She pointed accusingly at the balled-up bed linens in the corner.

"*Mordred*," she scolded.

"It was an accident!" the boy wailed.

She dug her wand from her sleeve and muttered a cleaning spell. "Did you even try to fix it yourself?" she asked. "It's a simple incantation."

Mordred lifted his chin. "Father says a prince shouldn't use magic."

Her lips pressed into a thin line. "Your father is just jealous because he *can't* use magic."

"That wasn't what it looked like today when he slit the boatswain's throat. You should have seen all the blood. It was like a *fountain*." Mordred climbed eagerly into his bunk, pulling up the covers. "May I have a bedtime story? A really quick one, and then I promise I'll go straight to sleep."

He stared up at her, his expression pleading. Morgana sat down, smoothing the covers. She had never been able to refuse him.

"Once there was a little girl whom everyone had forgotten," she began.

"No, I hate that one! It's stupid and boring. Tell me one about pirates. And make them slit each other's throats."

CHAPTER 36

Emry made her way to Gawain's chambers the next morning. She was once again dressed as her brother, and the binding felt tight and constricting against her chest. Or perhaps that was the heaviness in her heart over what had happened with Arthur.

One of the friendlier guards, Tristan, stood outside, his helmet under his arm, his ginger hair a mess. Emry had often seen him in the yard, trying to match pace with Lance during laps.

"I didn't realize Gawain—" she began, wondering when he'd started stationing guards outside his door.

"I'm only here to run an errand," Tristan confessed. "Actually, I volunteered. There's a very impatient, very pretty French girl at the servants' entrance, asking for Madame's gown back." Tristan gave her a conspiratorial wink. "Anyway, go on in."

Emry made a face. If she was going to interrupt Gawain in flagrante, she might as well get it over with.

"Thanks," she said, pushing open the door.

"You can set the coffee on the table," Gawain said grandly, and Emry snorted.

"I'm not your breakfast," she called.

"A pity. I'm starving." Gawain appeared in the doorway that led to his bedroom, knotting an absurd green silk dressing gown embroidered with acorns. "Well, don't just stand there looking like you're afraid to interrupt."

"Isn't anyone else here?" Emry frowned, taking in the table set for two.

"Do you really think I let my conquests spend the night and stay for breakfast?" He made a face at the thought.

"You're such a rake," she accused.

Gawain shrugged, neither accepting nor rejecting her insult.

"I believe Madame Becou is expecting her gown back," he said, holding out a hand.

The brothel. Of course that's where he had gotten the dress. Emry dutifully held out the bundle, shaking off the enchantment that had disguised it as laundry. Gawain gave an appreciative snort before vanishing with it into the hallway.

"So," he said, sweeping back into the room. "That was quite a party."

"I don't want to talk about it," Emry grumbled.

"Then you're the only one in the kingdom," said Gawain.

He motioned for Emry to join him as he poured himself a steaming cup of mint tea. "That breakfast is for you," Gawain said. "Figured you'd stop by for your clothing. There was only tea, so I had to send Amilde back for coffee."

Emry was touched that he remembered. "I can't stay," she said, and then she spotted the bacon and eggs and amended, "Well, I can't stay long."

"Nor can I," said Gawain with a sad smile. "I'm bound for France this week. As my brother's minder, and then back to Saint-Germain."

"You could refuse," Emry said.

Gawain sighed, leaning back in his chair. "My father's right that I'm needed overseas," he said. "Besides, I'd prefer not to watch the whole castle get swept up in my cousin's wedding preparations."

"You don't have to rub it in," she said, angrily chewing a piece of bacon.

"Rub what in?" Gawain asked with a frown. "The fact that our prince is marrying a perfectly acceptable princess from a perfectly respectable kingdom, with whom we just happen to share most of our northern border?"

When he put it that way. Still. Emry sunk down in her chair.

Gawain studied her. "I *knew* there was something between the two of you!"

"There's nothing between us."

"Anymore," Gawain finished.

"He's really going to marry her." Emry shook her head in disbelief.

"Of course he is. Because when it comes down to it, all my cousin wants—all he's ever wanted—is his father's approval. Even at the expense of his own happiness."

"And what about you?" Emry asked, nibbling a piece of toast. "What is it you want?"

"When I figure that out, you'll be the first to know," Gawain promised.

"Same," said Emry. "I just . . . don't know what to do. I can't stay disguised like this forever."

"I have an idea." Gawain's mouth quirked up at the corner. "You could come to France with me."

He was joking. He had to be joking. Yet there was a sincerity in his face that made Emry wonder just how much he really meant it.

"Very funny," she said.

"I'm serious," Gawain insisted. "You speak the language. And I wouldn't mind some company. Wear a nice dress, and I'll introduce you at court as my fiancée."

Emry choked on a sip of tea. "Your fiancée," she repeated, incredulous.

"Why not?"

"I'm a wizard!"

"So?" Gawain asked.

"And a commoner."

"That hardly matters. I'm no prince."

"Just his cousin."

"Arthur and I are *not* the same," Gawain protested. "Obviously, I'm far more handsome." He smirked, and Emry rolled her eyes. "Listen, I know what it's like to pick up the endless slack for a brother who never gets it right. To be desperate enough to run away, and naive enough to think my problems won't follow me. To prove myself a hundred times over for something that I'll never have the chance to be. I'm not saying we should call for the bishop tomorrow. But, for the record, I wouldn't mind a wife who conjures fire, and matches me drink for drink, and gets herself stabbed to protect the heir to the kingdom."

Emry wished a different boy was saying these things to her. And yet, staring across the table at Gawain, more handsome than he had any right to be in his dressing gown, his eyes bright and his expression hopeful, she wondered how she had ever thought him a villain.

It was strange to realize that he saw her so clearly. That they had so much in common. Stranger still to remember that he had pulled a knife from his boot to protect her before they had even met. That he had kept her secret, and been silently in her corner from the beginning.

He was right. They could go to France together, and when they returned, she could stay at the castle, and study magic with Master Ambrosius, and not have to lie or pretend.

It was an elegant solution. But as tempting as it was, it wasn't what she wanted. And Gawain seemed to realize that.

"Or not," he said, grimacing into his teacup.

"I'm sorry," Emry apologized uselessly.

"Don't be," he said, suddenly all business. "It was an absurd idea."

He stood, pushing back his chair. And Emry had the strangest sense that she'd disappointed him. That he'd hoped she might say yes.

"It wasn't your worst idea," Emry said.

"What a terrible compliment." Gawain shot her a rueful grin as he walked her to the door. "Before I set off for the continent, I don't suppose you'd want to pose for one of my portraits? Give me something scandalous to remember you by?" He quirked an eyebrow.

"Your naked portraits?"

"I would allow a tasteful drape of linen," he said. "For the sake of my lady's modesty."

"Hard pass."

"A shame. I promise it would be fun."

"Good*bye*, Gawain." Emry shook her head, smiling. And then she headed to the wizard's workshop.

Lady Elaine pressed her back against the wall, a hand over her mouth at what she'd just heard. When Gawain's maid had told hers that his lordship had requested breakfast for two that morning, she'd been intrigued.

The girl he'd brought to the ball—the black-haired courtier in the gloomy dress whom no one had known—surely she hadn't stayed the night in his chambers?

Elaine was the daughter of a minor lord, and at court, that made her little better than a lady's maid, trotting along eagerly after Princess Guinevere. She didn't want to be another girl's attendant. She wanted girls attending *her*. Curtseying to *her*.

Gawain was of royal blood, and with Arthur now spoken for, he was her best shot at becoming royal herself, and possibly—if she was so fortunate—queen. But she'd lost track of him for one moment, and somehow, he had arrived at the ball with a mystery girl on his arm.

Certainly Arthur knew who she was. He had danced with her, and he didn't dance with just anyone. And when she'd asked, he'd insulted her and acted as though it was a secret! Well, secrets were delicate things. Poke at them long enough and they unraveled into shocking truths.

The door opened, and Elaine beat a hasty retreat to the end of the hallway, where she hid herself on the far side of a tapestry, barely daring to breathe. She stared in disbelief at what she saw. Not what—whom. Gawain, still in his dressing gown, was beaming at that infernal wizard as though the lad was the most beautiful girl at the ball.

The ball. The mysterious courtier on Gawain's arm, who had seemed so familiar with Arthur. It couldn't be . . .

"I would allow a tasteful drape of linen," Gawain murmured, "for the sake of my lady's modesty."

His lady.

Merlin was a *girl*! Elaine studied the shabbily clothed apprentice, imagining that darkly glittering dress, and that long hair—wigs were quite in fashion, so Elaine hadn't thought much of it at the time—and oh! The wizard *was* the girl from the ball!

Why, Prince Arthur had traveled to Avalon with her by his side. Elaine had been in the throne room the day the girl had arrived, and had been as shocked as any courtier at the insouciant way she had conjured snow with a mere whisper. This girl was clearly a powerful sorceress.

And she'd been in the prince's tent at the tournament! Elaine had seen the wizard with Excalibur—and then, at the ball, King Uther had said someone had enchanted the scabbard. Obviously it was this evil, scheming girl, who had weaseled her way close to both Arthur and Gawain.

How had no one else seen it before now? Elaine's heart raced with excitement. She'd been hoping for something like this. It was why she'd cozied up to Princess Guinevere, waiting for the girl to reveal a secret that would make her an unsuitable bride. And of course, if Elaine was the one to have saved Arthur from making the mistake of marrying the girl . . . well, all the better.

She hurried down the hall, her heart hammering excitedly as she considered her next move.

◗ ◗ ◗

Emry slouched in the wizard's workshop, chopping herbs for a healing salve. Master Ambrosius hadn't been lying when he said the ingredients were complex. A single jar would take nearly a month to produce. And she'd have to feed it. Daily. That was almost as bad as a sourdough starter.

Still, she supposed it was better to lose herself in her work than to drown herself in everything that had happened over the past few days. So she chopped, and mashed, and diced, and prepared the alembic over boiling water.

"You're awfully quiet," Master Ambrosius accused. "Perhaps you're tired from dancing at the ball."

Emry winced. She hadn't realized the old wizard knew about that.

"I take it Arthur wasn't too upset when he found out," the old wizard went on, raising an eyebrow.

"Well, I did save his life," she reminded him. "Told you I'd master that poison antidote."

"Smug is a terrible look on an apprentice," Master Ambrosius chided. "But well done."

The water under Emry's alembic began to boil, and she hastily released some steam.

"I wanted to ask," she said, "is there a way to move spellwork? Like the spell on—"

"Arthur's scabbard?" Master Ambrosius finished with an approving nod. "There is. The trouble is making it fit."

"Making it fit?" Emry asked, taking a dropper of rose oil and carefully adding two drops to her water bath.

"Could you move the contents of a bathtub into a wineglass?" Master Ambrosius asked.

"What would happen if I tried?" she asked curiously.

"Nothing good, that's for sure. Magic doesn't like to be moved. You have to force it. And there's no guarantee that it will work as it did before."

Emry mulled this over. "So I'm guessing it's not an easy spell," she said.

"It makes your poison antidote look like lighting a candle," Master Ambrosius said. He nodded toward her apparatus. "You better watch the temperature on that!"

"*Calesco*," she mumbled, flicking her finger at the flame.

She was about to ask him how you *forced* magic when there was a deafening clatter of footsteps on the stairs. Four royal guards burst into the workshop, swords drawn.

"May I help you gentlemen?" Master Ambrosius asked. His voice was polite, but his eyes were bright with warning. He'd taken out his wand, Emry noticed. And had put on his pince-nez.

"Apprentice Merlin, you're to come with us," ordered one of the guards.

Emry recognized him vaguely from the training yard. Morian, she thought he was called. He always had a slight sneer to his mouth, as though he enjoyed ordering people around.

"What's all this about?" Master Ambrosius demanded.

"'S none of your business, old man," said a thick-necked guard with a piggish face.

Two guards seized Emry roughly by the shoulders, and she stumbled after them, a deep panic clanging in her chest.

What was going on?

The guards marched her to the throne room, no longer festooned with flower garlands and cheer. The shades were drawn, the fire a low and menacing hiss. The space seemed enormous, devoid as it was of courtiers.

Emry swallowed nervously, looking around the room. Were there always so many guards? And none of them looked the least bit friendly.

At the far end of the hall, King Uther sat on the dais, fingers pressed to his temples, looking as though he'd rather be in bed sleeping off last night's drink. Lord Howell stood at his side. Strangest of all, Lady Elaine hovered just behind her father, looking pleased with herself.

"Your Majesty," Emry said, bowing low. "You sent for me?"

"Well?" the king demanded, looking to Lord Howell. "Will someone tell me what's going on?"

"Gladly, Your Majesty." Lord Howell stepped forward, an accusing finger pointed straight at Emry as he said, "We have all been deceived by this wicked *girl*!"

The chamber went completely still. Emry's heart froze.

"Girl?" King Uther stared haughtily down from his throne, peering skeptically at Emry.

"I saw her, Your Majesty!" said Lady Elaine. "She was at the ball last night! And she seemed on *very* intimate terms with the Duke of Cornwall!"

No. Emry wanted to scream. Or drop through the floor and disappear. She felt as though she might faint.

"Is this true?" demanded the king.

"No!" she protested. "I was only trying to learn if the duke posed Arthur any threat—"

"That is not what I meant!" growled the king. "And how *dare* you refer to His Royal Highness as 'Arthur'?"

Emry blanched. "I'm sorry, Your Majesty," she said. She looked up at them all, her voice shaking as she confessed, "Yes, I am a girl. But please, you have to let me explain. I came to court in my brother's place—"

"See?" Lady Elaine insisted. "She admits to impersonating a courtier!"

Emry's stomach twisted. "No!" she said. "Please, let me—"

"She lost her father in service to the crown," accused Lord Howell. "And it's clear she's come seeking revenge against the royal family!"

The room felt like it was spinning. This couldn't be happening. Surely, if she could only wake up, she'd be back in her bed, with the guard practicing noisily outside her window.

The king raised his hand for silence. "You have done well to discover this girl's treachery," he told Lady Elaine, and the girl preened. Emry had always known Lady Elaine was spiteful, but this was a new low. And then the king leveled a harsh glare in her direction. "And you," he said, his voice cold and hard as ice.

Emry winced. She had really done it. She'd been so worried about Arthur discovering her secret—and so relieved when he had taken it in stride—that she'd forgotten to worry about the king.

"Do you take me for a fool?" King Uther demanded. "You lied to me. You lived in my castle, enjoyed my hospitality, accompanied my son and *sole heir* to Avalon—all under a stolen identity! I have never *imagined* such treachery and deceit could happen under my roof!"

Emry cringed. "Please, Your Majesty," she begged. But she doubted an explanation would make a difference. The king was furious, a vein throbbing at his temple, his face gone ruddy and his eyes ablaze.

The door to the Great Hall flung open, and Arthur entered. He was out of breath, as though he'd been running. Emry's heart twisted at the sight of him.

"Father, this is a mistake," he pleaded. "The wizard has committed no crime."

"The wizard is a *woman*!" growled the king.

"Yes, I know," Arthur said calmly. "I understood the term 'wizard' to be gender-neutral. Surely such a small matter could have been handled more discreetly."

"But she stole—" Lady Elaine began.

"No doubt Lady Elaine indulged overmuch at last night's festivities, and has painted a story of events that never took place," said Arthur.

"I am not mistaken!" insisted Lady Elaine. "The girl is out for revenge!"

"Against me?" Arthur said with a frown. "Whatever for?"

"Against the entire royal family!" insisted Elaine.

"The girl is a liar and a witch," said Lord Howell. "Many have been hanged for less."

"Are we hanging witches now?" Arthur shook his head in disdain. "What a shining example of progress Camelot will be."

"Enough!" bellowed the king. "You increase my headache by the minute." He waved a hand. "Guards, take the girl to the dungeons. She is to be executed in the morning."

Emry felt as though the ground had opened up under her. As though she was falling, and there was nothing to grab on to. Her knees went weak, and she could barely breathe.

"Father, please. Be reasonable," warned Arthur.

The king's jaw clenched, and his eyebrows knitted together. "You accuse me of being unreasonable?" he asked, his voice dangerously low. "This is *my* castle. *My* kingdom. And if you continue to question my authority, you can spend your days in the dungeon. Perhaps young Maddoc will come of age in the meantime."

"You wouldn't dare," said Arthur.

"Do *not* test me," growled the king. "Guards, the girl!"

Two guards seized her again. More roughly this time.

"Arthur!" she called.

"I'll fix this," he promised, his expression grim.

But she could see the panic in his eyes. And as a guard pushed her roughly forward, she knew her fate was sealed.

CHAPTER 37

Emry stared bleakly at the rough-hewn stone walls, trying to figure out how everything had gone so wrong. She was locked in the dungeons. And she stood accused of treason. Accused of using a false identity at court. Accused of trying to hurt Arthur.

She'd known the risks. She'd known what Uther might do if he found out who she truly was. And now he had, and she was here, awaiting her execution.

She felt too hollow to cry, like sobbing would only rip open the ache in her chest even more, until it was too big to ever close.

She shifted, trying to get comfortable, the irons heavy across her wrists. They contained the same spellwork she'd noticed on the castle wall her very first day. And whatever spell was on them had clamped down on her magic. No matter how much she reached for it, or tried to summon even the smallest, most innocent spell, her power remained just out of reach. It was a maddening stretch, and one she couldn't hold for long without gasping for breath.

Time warped and bent. She wasn't sure if she had been in the dungeon for hours or minutes. How much longer did she have left? She could feel her entire life slipping away, just like her magic.

She wished she'd have the chance to say goodbye. To Emmett, who was no doubt up to his usual mischief. To Gran, whose shaky-handed letters pressed with lavender from the garden never came frequently enough. To Marion, whose friendship had made their small town seem big enough, whenever they were together.

To Master Ambrosius, who had believed in her, even knowing the truth. And Lance. And Gawain. And Arthur. She had done what the Lady of the Lake had told her. She had protected Arthur from those who stood against him, so that he might one day be a great king.

The Lady had said they would return to Avalon together, one day. But clearly she'd been wrong, because the only place Emry was going was the executioner's square.

And she only had herself to blame. She should have come to the castle as herself and explained what had happened to her brother. But she'd taken Emmett's spot instead, and told herself that she deserved it more, even though their father had been right—there was no place for her in Uther's court.

She wished she'd been content at home, with the theater troupe and Marion and Gran. It may have felt small, but at least that life had been hers for as long as she wanted it. And now she couldn't even have that. She couldn't have anything. There wasn't enough time.

There were so many things she hadn't done. She could feel the press of them on her chest, of a life she wouldn't live, a future she wouldn't be around to see. And she really, really wished she could see it.

A tear trickled down her cheek, and she let it continue its tortured slide down her jaw. What was the point in wiping it away? She had every reason to cry. Yet she doubted crying would make her feel better. Nothing would.

Dull footsteps thudded on the stairs, along with the familiar clink of guards' mail. She looked up, anticipating the same guards who had been so rough earlier. Come to bring her some bread, perhaps, and some ale.

"Emry," a voice whispered.

It was Lance. For a wild moment, Emry's heart leapt, hoping to find Arthur behind him.

"It's just me," he said, removing his helmet. "How are you holding up?"

"I'm not holding up, I'm falling apart."

"Been there," Lance said, passing her the tray of food. "Well, not to this extent, obviously."

It wasn't prisoner's fare, but fine white bread with roast beef and cheese. There was a silver goblet of wine as well, which he handed her through the bars.

Emry stared at it curiously. "Did Arthur . . ."

"I lied to Chef." Lance shot her a small smile.

"I did wonder at the lack of reading material," said Emry. She took a sip of the wine, tasting none of it.

"Arthur's been in his father's rooms for hours," said Lance. "For that matter, so has Gawain." Lance leaned against the bars, as though they were nothing but a decoration.

"The king can't honestly believe—" Emry began.

"Oh, I'd never start a sentence like that," said Lance. "It doesn't matter if the crime is false, or unfair. It only matters that Uther maintains the precarious balance of his court. You were accused by a noble, and so you must be punished. We're not all equals here, and he doesn't pretend we are. If you had the impression that your word, your honor, or your life was worth as much as anyone else's, you got that from Arthur."

Emry sighed. Lance was right. "Is it all just hopeless then?" she asked.

"I have hope," said Lance carefully. "Just not in King Uther."

Solemnly, Emry raised her goblet and drank to that.

It seemed a very long time since she had come here, and seen the rumpled boy bent over his books, mistaking him for a librarian. A long time since they journeyed to Avalon and jokingly referred to Excalibur as Aunt Matilda.

She wished they were still there. In the clearing behind the inn. With Lance vowing to slay Arthur's nipple. She wished they were in the prince's bedchamber, sharing plates of food sent up from the kitchens. Or back at the ball, twirling across the dance floor in their finery, pretending just for a night that they truly belonged to that world.

This couldn't be it. Not just the end of her time at court, but the end of everything. She didn't want to die. But if she had to do it over again, she wasn't sure if she'd choose any different.

"It shouldn't matter that you're a girl," said Lance. "Things like that— your gender, or who you love, or where you come from—they shouldn't matter."

"Yet somehow, they matter the most to the wrong people," Emry said. "And I'm out of time. I can't keep waiting on the world to change."

"Which is why we're going to change it ourselves," said Lance, holding up a ring of keys.

☾ ☾ ☾

It was late, and the castle was silent. Emry followed behind Lance, her heart hammering at the thought of being discovered. He'd promised he had taken care of the guard, and that his friends had swapped for gate duty and patrol with anyone who might sound the alarm. But still. She was a traitor. A prisoner. And the risk Lance was taking to help her—she didn't know how she'd ever repay him.

She'd thought Lance's loyalty extended only to Arthur, and was surprised he included her in his inner circle. It made her heart ache at the thought of leaving.

"This way," Lance whispered, nodding toward a dark, echoing corridor. His footsteps squeaked against the stone floor, and he winced.

Thankfully, it wasn't much farther. Lance lifted the corner of a decorative tapestry, revealing a door built into the castle's paneling. Emry stared in surprise at the hidden passageway.

"When you grow up in the castle, you learn things," he said, ushering her inside. The door clicked shut, plunging them into absolute darkness.

"*Ignis*," Emry muttered, making the passage glow with a pale, silvery fire. She staggered, nearly losing her balance from the spell.

"Oh, um, Master Ambrosius said you shouldn't work any magic for at least an hour after having those handcuffs removed," Lance said.

"Should have led with that," Emry grumbled, wincing at her sudden headache.

Lance signaled for Emry to follow him, and she did. Their footsteps seemed to echo strangely, or perhaps that was just the pounding in her head.

The passage let out in the gardens, and they crept past the dark shadows of the hedge maze until they reached the servants' entrance. There were three other guards up ahead.

Emry's stomach clenched, but Lance nodded at them, and they nodded back.

"They're friends," Lance promised.

"Of yours?" she asked.

"And Arthur's," said the handsomest one with a merry grin. "Besides, rescuing a maiden from the dungeons is a lot more interesting than standing in front of a door."

Emry shook her head.

Uther exerts no will at all. Soon he will fade into obscurity. But Arthur is destined for greatness.

She tried to forget what else the Lady had said.

You will be a great king with this wizard by your side.

Too late for that now.

One of the guards pressed a bundle into her arms. Her things. Emmett's clothes, her father's books.

And then Lord Agravaine stepped out of the passage behind them, his dark cloak billowing.

No. She'd been so close. She stared down at her shoes, willing herself not to cry.

"You're surprisingly hard to track down for a prisoner who's supposed to be locked in the castle dungeon," said Lord Agravaine. He cut a dark look at Lancelot.

Lance winced. And then he reached for his sword. "I released her," he said, his knuckles white as he gripped his blade. "And you'll—you'll have to go through me if you mean to sound the alarm."

Lord Agravaine held up a hand. "If anyone learns the girl has escaped, they won't hear it from me," he promised.

"They won't?" Emry asked, hardly daring to hope.

"Your father was a good man. We didn't see eye to eye on most things, but he risked his life in service to the crown on many occasions," said Lord Agravaine. "King Uther forgets he owes your family a debt. And he forgets he owes you one as well, for protecting his son and heir." The man offered her a thin smile. "Go. Before anyone else discovers your absence."

Emry stared at him. "Thank you," she said simply.

Lord Agravaine only nodded, then turned to the guards. "You men better get back to your posts," he warned, an edge to his voice. He stalked off through the castle gardens, and Emry drew a long, steadying breath.

"That was close," said Lance.

"I know." Emry bit her lip. "Can you tell Arthur . . ." There were so many things she wanted to tell him. But it hardly mattered now. "That I'm sorry. And that I wish things were different?"

Lance nodded. "For what it's worth, you'd make a great court wizard."

"For what it's worth, you'd make a great knight," she replied.

With a heavy heart, Emry squared her shoulders and walked away.

CHAPTER 38

Brocelande was just as Emry remembered. She didn't know whether to laugh or to cry as she took in the chickens pecking in the yard, the pigs in their wattle-and-daub enclosure, the neat rows of vegetables and herbs in the garden.

It looked like so much less now that she'd seen so much more of the world.

At least the money she'd sent home had been put to good use. She could see the fresh thatch on the roof, and thick panes of new glass on the windows.

Emry hesitated at the front door. Should she knock? No, this was home. And with that, she went inside.

Everything was still here: the blackened hearth, the sturdy wooden furniture, the curtained bed that had once seemed like her own private room. Had it really been a lumpy mattress stuffed with straw, pushed into a corner of their cottage?

It was as if time had been holding its breath. As if her entire adventure at court had taken place in the space of a moment.

Gran was asleep by the hearth, knitting bundled on her lap.

"Gran," Emry said, going to the old woman.

"Emmett?" she said, frowning. "Back so soon?" Then she raised a hand to Emry's face, and understanding dawned.

Emry threw her arms around her grandmother, breathing in the familiar scent of her, the herbs and wool and the faintest traces of the mists of Avalon.

Emry frowned. Had Gran always been so frail?

"We weren't expecting you, child. Was there a letter?"

Emry shook her head. And bit her lip.

"Oh, my poppet," said the old woman. "My dear. What on earth has happened?"

The tears—and the story—spilled out of her. Gran listened quietly, and when Emry was done, she simply nodded.

"Well," Gran said. "That can't be the end."

"It can't?"

The old woman gave a decisive shake of her head. "So there's no sense crying, if you don't know how the story ends."

Emry laughed despite herself.

Somehow, without her noticing, it had gotten late. She stood, brushing herself off. "I suppose I had better make supper," she said, inspecting the bare shelves of the larder.

It was just dawning on her that she wasn't going to be able to stomp down to the castle kitchens to demand coffee and fresh rolls. That once again, *she* was the kitchen.

"There's pottage from yesterday," said the old woman.

Emry flicked her fingers toward the hearth, and the fire crackled to life.

And then Emmett bustled through the door, carrying a fresh loaf from the baker's. "I went too late, they only had oat left," he called. Then he spotted Emry and frowned. "What are you doing here?"

She didn't answer, but pressed him into a hug instead.

As they ate, she gave him the short version, but even that took a long time to tell.

"Better than I would have done," Emmett said with a shrug, reaching for more wine.

Emry's fingers twitched. The bottle slid across the table, into her hand, and she smirked. "How's Jane?" she asked.

Emmett grimaced. "Oh," he said, looking embarrassed. "That. It was a false alarm."

"The girl certainly took her time admitting it," Gran said sourly. "Had your brother halfway to the church before she confessed she'd been mistaken."

"We weren't *halfway to the church*," Emmett corrected.

"Well, you should have been," scolded Gran. "She'd certainly climbed into your bed enough times, insisting you were near as wed."

Emmett coughed into his wine.

"So there's no baby?" Emry said. "That's wonderful."

"That's what I said," Gran sounded smug. "The girl is barely sixteen. And of no ability to run a household. Her other abilities, I'll leave your brother to comment on, should he wish his mouth washed out with soap."

Emry laughed. "No," she said. "I mean, it's great because now Emmett can go to the castle. They need an apprentice court wizard. Badly."

"I already told you—" he began.

"You're selling yourself short," Emry argued. "You wouldn't believe how much I've improved under training."

Fleoges.

Emry smiled as the wine bottle floated into the air. With a flick of her hand, she refilled Emmett's glass. "They serve a different wine with each course at supper," she said innocently.

"Each course?" Emmett asked, intrigued.

Emry merely smiled.

"Someday soon, Camelot's going to need a wizard. A good one," she said.

Emmett's eyes met hers with a hint of amusement. It was what he'd said to her, back at the Crooked Spire. But she could tell Emmett wasn't convinced.

"Arthur will make a great king," Emry went on. "He's brave, true, clever, and kind. And if you've been waiting to use your magic for something important, Arthur *is* that something."

Emmett stared at her, considering. And then he drained his wineglass in one gulp. He sighed, scrubbing a hand through his hair. "Will you leave me alone if I say yes?"

Emry's only answer was to throw her arms around him.

◐ ◐ ◐

Two days later, Emry watched her brother leave, her heart aching.

It was never yours, she reminded herself. But that wasn't true. It hadn't been hers at first, but the castle—and the people in it—had become hers.

Losing them felt like a constant, painful reminder of a world she'd been allowed to visit briefly, a world that had closed its doors in her face while welcoming her father and brother.

There's still Gawain, Emry remembered. But he deserved to be more than someone's back-up plan. And anyway, she doubted Gawain's offer to accompany him to the continent still stood after the king had declared her a traitor to the crown and ordered her executed.

So she tied a kirtle over her dress, did the best she could with her hair, and went to the theater to see if Marion needed help.

◐ ◐ ◐

"Emry! Pay attention!"

Emry startled as Marion waved a hand in front of her face. They were backstage at Brocelande Hall, assisting with a performance of *The Faerie King.* Ordinarily, it was the kind of thing Emry loved, yet she was somehow bored by it. She had drifted off, thinking once again of Castle Camelot, and of Arthur.

But, judging from Marion's panicked expression, she'd missed her cue. "Sorry," she said, flicking her wrist.

Rain fell onto the stage, soaking it. The actors stopped in place, shocked as water drenched their costumes.

"Emry!" Marion hissed.

"What?"

"It's supposed to be an illusion!"

Emry's eyes went wide as she realized what she had done. "Oh, right!" She waved a hand, and the rain stopped. A twitch of her finger had the water cleared from the stage, and the actors' costumes made dry.

"Sorry," she apologized again, casting the illusion properly this time.

"It's fine." Marion smiled reassuringly, but Emry could tell her friend was worried about her.

She hadn't meant to lose control like that. To cast the real thing instead of the illusion. But the truth was, every day since she'd come home, she went out to the woods behind their cottage and practiced magic. Everything Master Ambrosius had taught her, and more.

Because whoever had taken the spell off Arthur's scabbard was still out there, and she had a bad feeling about what they wanted.

She couldn't forget how powerless she'd felt that night in the alleyway, when the thieves had stepped from the shadows, and she'd saved herself with an illusion that had barely held. How weak she'd felt before the king. She needed to be able to defend herself. She needed her magic to be better. *More.*

Yet every night when she returned home ravenous and bone-tired, she wondered why she was doing any of it. Emmett was the apprentice wizard now. She was back home where she was supposed to be. Except she couldn't help remembering a life she didn't know how to forget.

CHAPTER 39

Arthur slunk from his father's council meeting with the beginnings of a headache. He'd promised to take Princess Guinevere for a stroll through the gardens, and he didn't think he could stomach her company with the pounding in his temples. He needed something to steady his nerves. And soothe his headache.

Still, as he rounded the corner to the old stairwell up to the wizard's workshop, his heart hurt at the knowledge that Emry wouldn't be there. That she was gone.

He had fought for hours to make his father see reason. And after the king had grudgingly agreed to spare her life, Arthur had snuck down to the dungeons to tell Emry that it was going to be all right. But he'd found her cell empty, the door wide open.

He only wished he'd gotten the chance to say goodbye. Or to help her escape.

Instead, Lance had been the one to do that. He'd even enlisted some of the guards. Arthur caught them exchanging meaningful looks in the hallway, as though they wanted him to know they'd taken part. As though his approval mattered more to them than the king's.

Things like that had been happening more and more. Especially after Uther's drunken outburst at the ball.

A few months ago, Arthur hadn't been able to imagine what it would be like to become king. Now he was impatient for it. Because leading the kingdom wasn't about being bowed to and respected. It was about fighting for a future that was more forgiving and more open-minded than the past. And that was a future worth sacrificing for.

At least, that's what he told himself. But still, sometimes his heart raced, and the walls felt like they were closing in when he thought of how much responsibility he would have to shoulder. And how much he'd have to sacrifice along the way.

He didn't know how he was supposed to do any of it without Emry. Sitting around the table in his apartments with Lance and Gawain and Emry, strategizing what they should do, he had felt, for the first time, like he didn't have to face the future alone. But Emry was gone, and Gawain was headed back to France in a matter of days, and Guinevere was his inevitable future.

He climbed the stairs to the wizard's workshop, knowing the room that awaited him would be thick with memories. The quiet joy of her laugh. The glint in her eyes just before she made a joke. The feel of her in his arms, in the library, when he'd forgotten for a few blissful moments that his future wasn't his to spend as he pleased.

And then he stepped into the workshop and there she was, slouched at the old wooden table. His heart leapt at the sight.

"Merlin!" he cried, pleased.

The wizard turned around.

It wasn't her.

The resemblance was uncanny: the boy had the same wide mouth and dark eyes—was wearing the same shabby burgundy doublet even—but there was an undeniable smugness about him, as though he always got his way and saw no reason why that should ever stop.

The boy's eyebrows went up in alarm, and he gave a hasty bow, along with a mumbled "Your Highness."

"My mistake," Arthur said. "I thought you were someone else."

"Emmett Merlin. I arrived last night." He paused before adding, "My sister said you were in need of an apprentice wizard."

"She knows me well," said Arthur.

"So I've heard." There was unmistakable heat behind the young wizard's reply. "If you weren't the crown prince, I'd have a lot to say about that."

"Don't hold back on my account," said Arthur.

They regarded each other coolly. How unlike his sister Emmett was. Arthur could feel the barely caged pride that seeped from the edges of the boy's smirk.

"Arthur!" Master Ambrosius said brightly. "Are you joining us this morning?"

"No time," said Arthur. "I just needed some feverfew." He helped himself to the wizard's stores, pouring a mug of water. "Heat this up for me?" he asked Emmett, an edge to his smile as he slid the mug across the table.

The young wizard suddenly looked nervous. "Um," he said, taking out his wand. He rolled his shoulders, taking a couple deep breaths before whispering, "*Calesco.*"

Steam curled from the mug, and Arthur noticed the wizard breathe a sigh of relief.

"Thanks," Arthur said, steeping his headache cure in the boiling water.

It was a simple spell. The kind Emry would have mumbled under her breath, without even glancing up from her book. Or saying nothing at all, but slanting him a smirk as the mug scalded his hands.

Well, at least her brother had managed it.

"If you still have that headache this evening, you might want to try butterbur," said Master Ambrosius.

"I'll remember that," Arthur said. He gulped down the infusion and went to see to Princess Guinevere.

◐ ◐ ◐

The sarding castle was enormous. Emmett didn't know how he'd ever find his way around it. Not that he needed to, what with his private room, and servants who would fetch him anything he requested. And he spent most of his time in the wizard's workshop anyway.

Annoyingly, Master Ambrosius had started him on the simple household spells he'd found so tedious back in Brocelande.

"Can't we do something more exciting?" he'd begged.

"Such as learning to erase someone's memory?" Master Ambrosius had asked with a pointed look, and had sent him to the library to track down a copy of *Introductory Magical Theory*. It had taken him damn near an hour to find the dusty copy—how was he supposed to know the books on magic were alphabetical by title?—and he'd almost missed supper.

After three days, the castle was beginning to feel less like a confusing hedge maze and more like a city, whose rhythms he was starting to understand. He could do without the guards making noise beneath his window at dawn, though.

The first morning, he'd been so horrified that he'd clamped a pillow around his head and accidentally slept until noon. Which hadn't been his fault, as he'd explained to Master Ambrosius.

Of course his sister had conveniently forgotten to mention that he needed a pass to go into the city most days. He'd been planning to spin some pennies into gold by playing cards at the city's alehouses, with the help of a little magic.

Instead, he was stuck in a pungent attic reciting Latin and Greek from morning until night, and proving to the old court wizard the distance from which he could ignite a candle. How dull. The spells he preferred were ones that dazzled and impressed—or at the very least, things that weren't shortcuts for servants' tasks.

Arthur had literally asked him to heat up some water for his tea. True, he probably shouldn't have goaded the prince about kissing his sister. But the way Emry had looked when she'd returned home, as if all the light and happiness had gone out of her . . . And with a stab wound besides! He couldn't very well say *nothing* to the boy responsible for Emry's misery. Even if, knowing his sister, most of it was likely her fault.

At least the food was excellent. And he didn't have to trek outside to use the jakes. But he was *bored*. The other lads his age were royals, squires, or guards, and they all seemed to take their positions so *seriously*.

And the women—sard, they were beautiful. But their eyes slid right past him in the halls, searching for wealthier, more impressive fare. He saw the problem immediately—he didn't *look* like an elegant courtier worthy of their attention. Well, he could fix that. He needed better clothing. A silk doublet or two, and one of those fine half-cloaks that clasped at the shoulder. A pair of suede boots wouldn't hurt, nor would an embroidered jacket with silver buttons. His wages, when he received them, would just about cover the expense. Perhaps a tailor would give him credit, seeing as how he was in the king's employ.

With his lessons finished for the day, he was merely wandering. He'd discovered a weapons training room, but didn't know if he was allowed to use it. And after the mess with his sister, and the king's displeasure when he'd turned up unannounced, and months late, he didn't want to risk it.

Idleness was a much safer pursuit. So he sent a servant to fetch him a bottle of wine and some sweets, and then he went out to the castle lawn to feel sorry for himself.

◐ ◐ ◐

Guinevere hadn't truly lost an earring back in the gardens. She'd only said as much because Lady Elaine's company was starting to feel smothering. Still, it was a wonderful excuse, and as she hurried away from her overeager shadow, she felt a delightful sense of calm.

So long as she didn't remember the part where she was stuck here indefinitely, engaged to a boy who hadn't asked her to marry him. But why would he, when it turned out his dear friend Merlin was a girl in disguise?

Guin had sensed there was something strange about the young wizard from the beginning. And the look on Arthur's face when he thought no one was watching, gazing across the dining hall at Merlin as though imagining the two of them alone, at a candlelit supper. She didn't know whether to be relieved or annoyed that the wizard had been a girl all along.

Relieved, because she didn't want a husband who pursued boys right under her nose. And annoyed, because actually, she'd quite enjoy having a female court wizard. It was progressive. Modern. And would provide for some interesting company. Unlike the hideous Lady Elaine, who was responsible for nearly having Merlin executed.

Honestly. The first thing Guin would have done was drag the young wizard to her rooms and hear what the castle boys were *really* like when they thought no girls were around.

Guin wound through the gardens, making a good show of searching for her earring, even though she hadn't been through this section, which featured a large hedge maze and was shaded by ancient oaks. But appearances were important, and Guin always tried to keep up appearances.

"Lose something?" a boy's voice asked, with just a hint of amusement.

She hadn't been expecting anyone, and she glanced up in surprise. The most glorious boy was sprawled beneath a tree. He was pale, with a mop of dark hair and a pirate's grin, and he wore just his shirt and hose, his jacket spread beneath him like a blanket. Even his posture was handsome; he had one leg propped up, with his arm resting upon it, and a goblet of wine caught lazily between his slim fingers. A book sat by his side, open to the first page. He smiled at her, looking up through long, dark lashes.

"I'm sorry?" Guin replied. She couldn't stop staring. She felt drawn to him, as if by magic.

"Perhaps I can be of assistance," he said smoothly. "What is it you're looking for?"

Her heart sped up at the cool, mannered charm of his voice. "A lost earring," she admitted, "that doesn't exist."

His grin stretched wider. "Why then, I've already found it," he said, holding up an empty palm. "How lucky you came this way."

This, Guinevere thought, as she mimed plucking the object from his hand, *is how I've always wanted to be courted*. She pretended to fasten it on, though she already wore emeralds in her ears.

"It looks well on you, my lady," he said seriously.

"Your Highness," she corrected.

The boy's lips tugged up at the corners. "I'm no prince," he said. "But I'm deeply flattered by the mistake."

She threw her head back and laughed. Not the fake giggle she used at court, but her real laugh, deep and unrestrained.

"Do you have any more of that wine?" she asked, even as she could see there was still half a bottle.

The boy tipped back the contents of his goblet. She watched his throat bob as he swallowed, and decided that, as far as jawlines went, his was a weapon that could win tournaments.

"Would you like to see a magic trick?" he asked. He reached beneath his jacket and pulled out a length of wood—no, a wand—and with a deep frown of concentration, he tapped the rim of his cup and spoke a word of Ancient Greek. At least, she thought it was Greek.

The cup hovered in the air above his hand, and then he spoke again, and it *sparkled*.

"A clean cup, for Your Highness," he said, offering it to her. "Since I wasn't sure you'd wish to share mine."

So *this* was the new court wizard. Definitely another Merlin, judging from his dark hair, wide grin, and tall, thin frame. Well, Guinevere thought, eyeing him, he'd *certainly* do.

She joined him under the tree, to hell with ruining her skirts.

CHAPTER 40

L ance never should have gone into the royal stables. He'd already tried the prince's rooms, the wizard's tower, and the library. But when he pushed aside the barn door, it wasn't Arthur he found. It was Jereth.

The lad sat on the floor of a horse stall, a bottle of wine at his feet, and his head propped heavily in his hands. Behind him, a spotted palfrey nickered for his attention. Her head was down, her coat matted with dirt and slick with sweat. She was still tacked, iron stirrups hanging low at her sides. She looked miserable.

Jereth glanced up at the interruption, his contemptuous gaze raking over Lance. "Well?" he said. "What are you doing here?"

"Looking for Arthur." Lance winced. He'd done so well at avoiding Jereth for weeks.

"How disappointing, to find me instead," Jereth said, daring Lance to deny it.

"If you say so," Lance replied blandly.

A beautiful gray mare nosed forward in the nearest box, and Lance gave her a pat. It had been a long while since he'd been permitted to choose his mounts from the royal stable.

He remembered the very last time, a hot summer afternoon when he and Jereth had ridden out to the lake, and shared their first kiss. They'd galloped back with swollen lips and wet hair, stealing last glances at each other as they returned, Lance late to his duties as a page, and Jereth late to his fencing lesson.

Lance watched as Jereth took a gulp of wine straight from the bottle. His riding boots were filthy, and mud splattered the hem of his cloak. He looked a mess. The palfrey wasn't much better. She stamped impatiently, her ears set back.

Lance couldn't take it anymore. "Are you going to untack that horse?" he asked.

Jereth shrugged. "Someone else will, if I don't."

Lance shook his head, disgusted. He hated the way Jereth was looking at him. All dark eyes and haughty jawline, a beautiful boy who loved himself and knew how to make others love him, too. It made Lance suddenly, inexplicably angry. This was all still a game to him, because the consequences didn't rest on his shoulders, and they never would.

"For once in your life, can't you take responsibility for anything?" Lance ground out. "Or must you always get caught in a mess that you refuse to answer for?"

Jereth's eyes burned with resentment. "You groom her then, if you care so much."

"I can't believe you'd ask me that!"

"I wasn't asking," Jereth said with an imperious tilt of his chin. "And you forget you should address me as 'my lord.'" He motioned toward a tack box. "Her comb is over there."

"You can get it yourself," Lance replied, crossing his arms. *"My lord."*

He made the last part sound like a curse, and Jereth's shoulders stiffened. Lance watched nervously as he hefted the wine bottle, threatening to smash it. For a terrible moment, Lance thought he might. But then the fight went out of him.

"I leave in the morning," Jereth said, a muscle feathering in his jaw. "Will you miss me?"

Lance didn't hesitate. "Not at all. You might recall that I was deemed unfit to become a knight because I *assaulted* a member of the royal family."

Lance held his ground after making the accusation, even though his heart was racing, and he wanted nothing more than to back out of the stables and spend the next few hours obliterating the bull's-eye on an archery ring until he was drenched in sweat and his muscles ached.

Jereth winced, suddenly fascinated with a piece of hay. At first, Lance thought he wasn't going to say anything, but then Jereth pushed to his feet and staggered toward him.

"I panicked, okay?" he said. "I was sixteen, and I screwed up. Because that's what I do. I panic, and I screw up."

"That's what you're going with?" Lance said, incredulous. "Two years after completely wrecking my life, all you have to say for yourself is 'I panicked'?"

"What else am I supposed to say? That it was a mistake, and I wish I could take it back?"

"That would be a start!" Lance retorted. "You don't know what it's like—"

"No, *you* don't know what it's like, being the family disappointment!" Jereth accused. "I'm shit at politics. Hopeless at lessons. Terrible with a sword. My father shuffles me around like a burden, hoping to be rid of me. He sent me away *days* after my mother found us together. That's how revolted they are at the thought that, on top of *everything else*, I prefer boys."

Jereth's breath was ragged, and a storm raged in his eyes. And as much as Lance wanted to land an immensely satisfying punch, he remembered how awful it felt, carrying around such a weight, and not knowing how to start the conversation, or how his father might respond when he did.

"It's possible your father sent you away because you caused a scandal," Lance pointed out. "Have you ever tried to talk to him?"

"I already know what he'll say. That I'm a failure in every imaginable way, and the whole family would be better off without me."

Jereth's lip curled with distaste, and Lance wondered why he'd bothered.

"If you really believe that, then no one can help you," Lance said, shaking his head. "Now curry that sarding horse, and clean off your boots before some poor maid has to scrub your mess off the castle floor."

Lance shouldered his way out of the stables, and came face to face with Lord Agravaine. He blanched. "How much of that did you overhear?" he asked.

"Enough." Lord Agravaine regarded him appraisingly. "That night, when his mother found the two of you together. It wasn't the first time."

"No," Lance admitted. "I cared for him very much. And I believed he felt the same, even though he insisted no one could know about us."

"Because he thought we'd disapprove," Lord Agravaine said, looking unspeakably disappointed. "Of his interest in boys."

Lance frowned. "You don't?"

"How could I fault him for being himself? He is my son."

"Then you need to talk to him. Because Jereth believes you sent him away out of disgust."

Lord Agravaine grimaced. "I sent him away because I thought a change of scene would do him good. I went away to school as a child. The discipline helped."

"I doubt you got into much trouble," said Lance.

Lord Agravaine lifted an eyebrow. "You'd be surprised. Jereth's a lot like I was at his age. Stubborn. Angry. Passionate."

"You should tell him that." Lance hesitated before adding, "Before my father passed away, it meant a lot to hear him say how proud he was. He'd always wanted me to follow in his footsteps and become a knight."

Lance looked away, willing his chin to stop quivering. When he got himself back under control, he saw that Lord Agravaine had a bleak expression on his face.

"It hasn't escaped my notice that you've had a curious effect on the castle guards," said Lord Agravaine. "In the face of injustice, they did what they knew was right." he arched an eyebrow. "You're fashioning them into knights."

"I'm—what?" Lance frowned.

"You're teaching them loyalty, chivalry, and honor. I've seen for myself how they follow Arthur's command, as well as your own."

"They do not," Lance protested, even though there was truth to the man's observation. "Well, maybe a little."

"I think," Lord Agravaine said carefully, "that it is more than time to set the record right. I'll make certain Jereth does so, before he departs."

Lance stared at him, barely daring to believe what he was hearing. "I—" He cleared his throat, barely trusting himself to speak. "Thank you."

Lord Agravaine nodded. "Thank you for reminding me that some things need to be spoken aloud, no matter how obvious they might seem."

◐ ◐ ◐

The next evening, Lance received a summons from the king. He brushed imaginary dirt from the front of his uniform, trying to remain calm as he approached the castle's east wing.

And then he saw Arthur hurrying toward him. The prince skidded to a stop, taking a moment to catch his breath.

"I'm coming with you," said Arthur. "For moral support. And to vouch that you made a wonderful squire at the sword-fighting competition."

"Thanks." Lance shot his friend a nervous grin. "But it's probably too late for him to reinstate me. It's been nearly two years since I've had any training."

"I refuse to accept that. Any knight would be privileged to have you."

Lance wished his friend were right. Yet as they approached the king's chambers, all he could think about was how impossible it felt that everything could snap back into place. That the past two years could be erased as easily as if they were a bad dream.

King Uther seemed to be in good spirits, or at least deep enough in his drink not to be irritable. Lance stood rooted to the spot as the king read Jereth's confession aloud, then crumpled the paper into a ball.

An eternity passed, and then, finally, King Uther spoke. "Well?" he said. "What do you expect me to do about this?"

Lance shot Arthur a panicked look. He couldn't bring himself to ask, only to be refused. He stood there, staring at his boots, unable to say a word.

"Come, Father, what else would you do, besides the right thing?" Arthur said. "There's no reason Lance shouldn't be reinstated to his former position. The accusations against him were a lie, and have been formally withdrawn. You can announce it tomorrow, at court."

Lance shook his head in disbelief. It never ceased to amaze him how Arthur would stand up to his father to save his friends, yet never quite managed it for himself.

"I can announce it tomorrow, at court?" Uther repeated, his voice low in warning.

Arthur frowned, pretending to misunderstand. "Unless you feel it would be more appropriate for Lord Agravaine to do so?" he said.

Lance smothered a grin.

King Uther looked annoyed. And then his expression turned thoughtful. "Fortunately, Sir Kay has been complaining of his squire, and has twice come to request a replacement. Do you accept the position?"

Lance nearly groaned. It *had* to be Sir Kay. "It would be an honor to squire for my uncle, Your Majesty," he said.

"I'm sure he'll be delighted when he finds out," said Arthur. "How perfect it is, Father, that you'll be the one to tell him."

Lance barely held back his incredulous laughter at the thought.

He couldn't believe it. He was going to be a squire after all. And after two years, a knight.

He imagined the stands at a tournament, the crowd shouting his name. Imagined dining in the Great Hall dressed in the full-length cloak of a knight. Imagined riding into battle alongside Arthur, a company of men at his command.

It was overwhelming, having everything he'd lost returned to him so suddenly.

And it felt so different now that he'd had to fight for it. Now that he knew how hard it was to stay awake through a night's watch, or to stand all day in the snow guarding the castle gates. Before, even though his page's duties were tough, his had still been a life of chivalry and feasts.

Sir Kay would be a hard master. The knight was impatient and exacting. But Lance couldn't deny that he was the best. And to learn from the best, he'd gladly pay any price.

"Thank you, Your Majesty," Lance said, sinking into a bow. "I can't thank you enough. This is—"

"Leave me," ordered the king, picking up his goblet of wine.

Lance and Arthur beat a hasty retreat, and when the doors to the king's chambers were safely behind them, Lancelot slid down, his back against the castle wall, and put his head in his hands.

"What just happened?" he whispered.

"I believe you've been made a squire," said Arthur.

Lance shook his head, still in shock. "I won't have to sleep in the barracks. Or dine in the guard's mess. Or stand duty at the gate."

Arthur shot him a grin.

"Just think of all the extra time you'll have to hang out with me in the library."

For a moment, Lance thought he was serious. And then Arthur laughed.

Strangely, Lance realized that he was going to miss it. Well, parts of it. His friends. But it wasn't as though he couldn't still see them.

For the past few years, it had seemed that, no matter what he did, he was destined to be left behind. That his friendship with Arthur would only grow more awkward and impossible as time dragged on. After all, what king had a guard as his closest confidant? Yet the thought of Arthur knighting him had always given him pause. He didn't want to be seen as someone who had traded royal favor for a position he hadn't earned.

But this—King Uther announcing his reinstatement, and the opportunity to squire for the king's champion—it was beyond anything he had hoped for. And the worst part was, it was what he should have had all along.

"Sir Lancelot," Arthur said, slanting his friend a proud look. "It has rather a nice ring to it."

CHAPTER 41

A tavern brawl. Arthur couldn't believe it. That good-for-nothing wizard had gotten into a fistfight with a sailor and his crew over an impossible hand of aces. And he hadn't even wiped the smirk—or the blood—off his face before turning up at Arthur's rooms, asking if he had any spare healing salve.

Arthur was still stewing over it as he left his father's council meeting the next day. Master Ambrosius said the lad had potential, but he was a slow study, and lazy besides. Emmett was fast proving to be far more trouble than he was worth, and Arthur found himself missing the young wizard who had sat by his side in the quiet of the early morning.

I want you to be my court wizard. Isn't that enough?

He closed his eyes, regretting those words. Regretting so many things, none of which he knew how to fix.

And then he tucked the legislation he needed to review under his arm, and went back to his rooms, hoping for a moment of calm.

Instead of calm, he found Princess Guinevere.

She sat in his favorite chair, reading one of his books, her skirts tucked up around her. Her hair had come undone from its pins, and she looked more approachable, and less like a painting designed to draw his admiration.

"Princess?" Arthur said, surprised.

"Your guards let me in," she said with a small smile.

"Yes, but what are you doing here?" Arthur asked curiously.

"Occupying myself, especially now that I no longer find Lady Elaine's company pleasing."

Arthur couldn't fault her there. He wished the girl removed from the castle for what she'd done.

Guinevere held up the book. "May I borrow this? I started it while I was waiting, and I'm just up to the part with the shipwreck."

"Be my guest," Arthur said, amused.

"Also, I wanted to speak with you," said Guin.

Arthur smothered a sigh. "We speak plenty at dinner," he reminded her. "And on our walks."

"You mean we speak of nothing, while dining with others, or being trailed by your guards." She motioned toward the chair across from her as though she sat upon a throne.

Arthur inclined his head. "Your Highness," he said, taking a seat. "What's on your mind?"

"Our engagement."

"What an exciting prospect it is," he replied. "Don't you agree?"

"Don't patronize me," Guinevere said, her dark eyes flashing. "It's obvious you don't want to marry me."

Arthur opened his mouth to reply, but Guinevere silenced him with a glare before adding, "And I don't want to marry you, either."

"You don't?" Arthur said in surprise.

"You're more in love with any book in your library than you are with me," said Guin.

"That's not true," Arthur protested. "I—"

"Have been miserable since our fathers hatched this ridiculous plan in the first place," finished Guinevere. "And I don't blame you. This whole thing is . . . how do I even put it?"

"A sarding nightmare?" Arthur suggested, and then muttered an apology for his language.

"Oh, it's precisely a 'sarding' nightmare," replied Guin. "So I have a better plan: we refuse to go through with it."

"Can we do that?" Arthur wondered aloud.

Guinevere tossed her curls. "I don't see why not." Her expression turned wry. "Alliances can work in other ways. Such as, if you don't marry me, I'll be your ally out of sheer gratitude."

Arthur laughed. "Our fathers will kill us," he said, not entirely joking.

"They'll get over it," said Guin. "I love my father, but he's too set in his ways to realize the world is changing. Or to see why that's a good thing."

"Mine is the same," said Arthur. "It's just so *frustrating* to make him see reason sometimes."

He thought of Lance, and of Emry. Of his father's drunken accusation at the royal ball, and the way he'd tried to smother it by announcing Arthur's engagement.

"At least your father doesn't dismiss you as some silly girl meant only to look pretty. Most of the time I have to convince my brother to present my ideas as his own." Guinevere sighed. "And even then."

They stared at each other in perfect understanding, for once.

"The future will look exactly like the past if we don't start making some changes here and now," Guinevere said decisively. "You give up a lot of things, being royal. But I'd like the chance to fall in love, if I could."

For the first time, Arthur saw Princess Guinevere without her polished smile and perfect hair and flawless manners. She was just a girl, and she was just as scared and unhappy as he was.

"So would I," said Arthur.

"That's funny, I thought you already had."

She was right, he realized. And deep down, he'd known it for a while. He'd just filed it under one more impossible thing on his growing list of them.

Guinevere gave him a meaningful look, and he cleared his throat, eager to change the subject. "We can't very well call everything off now," he said.

"I agree, we should pretend we'll go through with it," said Guinevere. "And then at the altar, we'll both say no."

"I'm honored you'd bother to show up at all."

"And give up the opportunity for everyone to see me in a wedding dress?" Her lips quirked into a grin.

"That's a good point," said Arthur. "With everyone assembled, we can announce our intentions at the wedding. And instead of a marriage contract, we'll propose a treaty of aid and alliance, and encourage everyone to celebrate the good news."

"It's perfect," said Guinevere. "My dream arranged wedding."

Arthur snorted. "In which case, I suppose I had better ask you something."

He got down on one knee, and Guin's eyes widened.

"Princess Guinevere," he went on, "would you do me the honor of being my ally? In feast and in famine, in war and in peace, for as long as our respective kingdoms shall stand?"

She laughed. "I will," she promised.

When he rose from his knees, she kissed him on the cheek. Softly. She smelled like roses and mint. Like a different girl, one he had far too many feelings for.

Guin was right. They did need to start making changes. Except it was Emry he needed by his side, not Emmett. He needed her help. Her guidance. Her magic. And more than that, he needed her.

But so much had gone wrong, and when it had truly mattered, he'd hurt her. He'd tried so hard to be the perfect prince that he hadn't realized what he was losing.

And now he had to get her back.

☾ ☾ ☾

Arthur hovered impatiently outside the door to his father's chambers. The king was occupied, his guards had said, as though that might deter him.

"I'll wait," Arthur had replied, slouching against the wall alongside them.

But a few too many telltale noises from behind his father's closed doors later, he was beginning to regret his decision.

Finally, the door opened, and Lady Amiya emerged, flushed and patting her hair back into place. Arthur caught the door behind her and slipped inside.

The poor guards looked horrified.

"What is it?" King Uther snapped, tying his dressing gown closed.

"You summoned me, Father?" Arthur said with a frown.

"I did nothing of the sort."

"How strange," Arthur mused. "My apologies for the mistake. But, seeing as I'm already here, I assume now is as good a time as any to discuss the matter of our apprentice court wizard."

King Uther grunted, reaching for a goblet of wine and sinking into a chair in front of the crackling fire. "What's wrong with the boy?"

Arthur didn't even know where to begin. "He's not the best candidate for the position. But I think you know that."

"The boy stays," said Uther.

"I believe there is another option," said Arthur, meeting his father's gaze.

"If you're talking about his sister," the king growled, "you'll recall I spared her life. At *your* request."

"Here I thought you had pardoned Emry because it was the honorable thing to do," said Arthur. "She saved my life, Father. And she exceeds her brother in every way. I don't see why—"

"BECAUSE I FORBID IT!" the king bellowed, banging his goblet against the arm of his chair. "And I forbid you to mention this matter again, either in my presence or in my court."

Arthur winced at the metallic clang that echoed through the king's bed-chamber. He half expected the guards to come bursting in. When they didn't, Arthur summoned his nerve.

"We should be lifting up those loyal to the crown, not sentencing them to death!" said Arthur. "And if I'm to be king one day, I'll lead Camelot on my own terms. Not anyone else's. Including yours."

Arthur glared at his father, breathing hard.

"How dare you?" his father asked, dangerously calm.

"You've made my decisions for years," Arthur said. "And that stops right now. Tomorrow morning, I'm leaving to get my court wizard back. Lance will accompany me—I'll send my apologies to Sir Kay for borrowing his squire." He let that one sit a moment. "And when we return, I expect you to give her a royal welcome."

CHAPTER 42

Arthur left for Brocelande at dawn. He wore Excalibur, sheathed in a plain scabbard. Lance rode at his side, dressed in a handsome velvet jerkin, his family crest glinting from his gold ring and a new sword at his waist, bearing Sir Kay's emblem in its hilt.

When he'd told Lance to prepare for the journey, his friend had given him a long look and said, "It's about time. What changed your mind?"

"It was something Guinevere said. That the future will look exactly like the past if we don't start making changes."

"Well." Lance offered him a crooked grin. "I, for one, am a big fan of these changes."

And then he'd shown up at the royal stables the next morning dressed in a fashionable new jacket, and had overseen the saddling of Arthur's horse as well as his own.

All was nearly as it should be. Which was a strange notion, because a year earlier, he never would have believed he'd consider Guinevere or Gawain to be his friends, or that he would welcome the day he would be crowned King of Camelot. Yet somehow, over the past few months, everything had changed, and he finally felt ready to face the future.

They reached Brocelande by late afternoon. A babbling river meandered along one edge, and an ornate manor house sat on the hill overlooking the town.

They passed beneath the gatehouse alongside a crowd of carts and wagons that had come from the countryside for market day. Houses and inns with steeply angled roofs lined the road, merchants' storefronts displaying their brightly colored wares. Packhorses laden with goods ambled down the lane, alongside steering carts.

Emmett had assured him that any merchant would know the way to Master Merlin's place, but the directions emptied from his head as soon as he was confronted with the small but lively town.

"Look!" Lance said, pointing to a cheerful inn, whose enclosed yard was attracting quite a crowd. He spurned his horse and rode up to investigate. A moment later, he returned with a wide grin. "The Lord Brocelande's Men are putting on a play."

Arthur grinned. "I guess we're going to the theater."

They crowded into the innyard along with the other market-goers. Arthur couldn't remember the last time he'd been to the theater—a real theater—not a troupe commanded to perform at the king's pleasure, and so terrified to play at the castle that they flubbed half their lines.

The story was one he'd heard before, and the players were of middling skill, but the costumes were fine, and the effects—the first time the fairy king appeared, it was in a cloud of purple smoke. The enchanted goblet seemed to actually levitate, and the part with the lightning storm—the audience gasped as the wind blew back their cloaks, the spray of rainwater misted their faces, and what looked to be real lightning flashed across the stage.

That was Emry all right. Arthur was sure of it.

When the performance was over, he motioned to Lance to follow him, and headed for the doorway he'd seen the players using.

"Excuse me! You can't go back there," a pretty, plump blonde girl scolded, coming toward them with her hands on her hips.

"My apologies," Arthur said, favoring her with a brief bow. "We were looking for a friend who's with the theater troupe."

"Then you can wait out back, at the stage door."

Arthur was about to protest, but Lance mumbled their thanks, and dragged him away by the collar.

Emry was one of the last to leave. She wore a rough-spun green kirtle, and her dark hair fell just past her chin, despite having been as short as her brother's a week ago. She twisted around, yelling something about bloodstains. The reply made her laugh. She was still laughing when she caught him standing there.

"Surprise," he said.

She startled and went white, as though he was the last person in the world she wanted to see.

Arthur frowned. He'd expected a warm welcome. Not this.

"What's wrong?" she asked, her eyes wide with panic. "Emmett?"

"He's fine," said Lance. "Everything's fine."

Emry's shoulders relaxed. And then she crossed her arms and demanded, "Then what are you doing here?"

Arthur swallowed nervously. "I came to bring you this," he said, holding out the letter.

"I already received word of my pardon," she said.

"This is something else," Arthur promised.

Emry frowned and opened the letter. Arthur waited, barely daring to breathe, barely daring to move.

She stared up at him after she read it, her dark eyes questioning, as if she didn't quite understand.

"It's an invitation," he said. "*Not* a summons. For you to come and train at the castle to be my court wizard. If that's what you want. Which I hope it is."

"But Emmett . . . ?"

"There's no reason Camelot can't have more than one court wizard," said Arthur. "I suppose I *could* make it a competition, to see which of you is the most qualified, but that hardly seems fair to your brother."

Emry snorted.

"Emry, I need you," Arthur said. "And I don't want to do this without you. Any of it. Please. You have to come back."

She bit her lip. And then the door to the theater swung open one last time, and the rosy-cheeked blonde girl came out with an armload of costumes and a sewing kit.

"Oh," she said, startled. "I didn't know they were here to see you!"

Emry's eyes narrowed. "You've met?" she asked the girl.

"They tried to go backstage," said the girl, "but I—"

"You watched the play?" Emry asked, horrified.

"Loved the special effects," Lance said enthusiastically.

"And the costumes," added Arthur, with a nod to the bundles of fabric in the girl's arms.

"I'm Marion," the girl said, "and you are?"

Lancelot turned on the charm, kissing the girl's hand and introducing himself with enthusiasm.

Arthur slanted an amused look at Emry, and saw that she was shaking her head in spite of herself. It really was over the top.

"And I'm Arthur," he said pleasantly.

"Emry," Marion said, her voice low with warning, "please tell me the Prince of Camelot didn't just stand through our performance of *The Faerie King*." No one said anything. Marion made a disgusted noise. "What next? Will you be joining His Royal Highness for a drink at the Prancing Stag?"

Arthur shrugged. "I hope so," he said.

"You could come as well," Lance suggested. "And maybe you could bring that dark-haired lad who played the shepherd?"

Marion rolled her eyes at his lack of subtlety. "Are they always this much trouble?" she asked Emry.

"Worse. But I can manage them."

"She can't, actually," said Lance. "The last time she tried, she got stabbed."

"Stabbed?" Marion looked aghast.

"I barely grazed her!" Arthur protested. "Besides, I had healing salve."

"Half a jar," Emry countered. And then her expression softened. "Well, are you coming or not?"

"To the Prancing Stag?" Arthur asked, pleased.

"I'm going to regret this, aren't I?" Emry muttered.

"Probably," Arthur said. He looked to Lance, silently asking his friend for a moment alone with Emry. Fortunately, Lance understood.

"I'll meet you there." Lance grinned. "First, Marion has to introduce me to . . . actually, I don't even know his name."

"Thomas," Marion supplied. She shoved her bundle of costumes into Lance's arms. "Might as well make yourself useful."

◑ ◑ ◑

Emry kept glancing at Arthur out of the corner of her eye as he walked alongside her. She couldn't believe he'd ridden all this way just to ask her to come back to the castle.

That he'd invited her to train to be his court wizard.

King Uther didn't ask, Emry reminded herself. He had demanded Emmett's presence, without considering the implications. But Arthur had come in person, to give her a choice.

He will be a great king, the Lady of the Lake had predicted.

She saw it now. She couldn't stop seeing it. There was a fresh confidence to the lift of his chin, and the square of his shoulder. But she didn't want him to have to carry that burden alone. Not if she could help it. She'd sent him Emmett, but clearly that wasn't enough.

"How's my brother getting on?" she asked.

A muscle feathered in Arthur's jaw. Somehow, Emry wasn't surprised.

"It's been less than a week," she said with a sigh. "How much trouble can he have gotten into?"

Arthur shot her a look.

Emry winced.

"He's got potential," Arthur allowed. "But he's not you."

"Give him a wig and a dress, and I bet he could do a decent impression," Emry joked.

Arthur snorted. "You haven't said whether you'll accept my offer." He glanced at her nervously.

"I'm still considering it."

"My father won't be a problem, I've seen to it," Arthur promised.

"So you're saying that my daring escape from the castle dungeons was a waste?"

"I'm saying you don't have anything to worry about."

"I'm not *worried*," Emry said. "I'm *upset*."

"With me," said Arthur.

"It's my own fault for—" Emry stopped herself, horrified. She'd almost told him how she felt.

How easy it seemed to share the truth here, with this brilliant, beautiful boy by her side.

But this wasn't real, she reminded herself. Princes didn't join peasant girls for a pint at the local tavern. She was just a diversion to him, the same as she'd been at the ball. They were from two separate worlds. And there was no place where those worlds met.

Especially with Arthur engaged to be married.

"How's Guinevere?" she asked bitterly.

"Less annoying, once you get to know her," Arthur admitted, a smile dancing over his lips. "The two of you might even become friends."

"And how would that work, exactly?"

"Oh, easily, I'd imagine. Especially since we're not going through with the wedding."

"You're not?" Emry tried to mask her surprise.

Arthur explained their plan. Emry had to admit, it was clever. And she approved wholeheartedly.

"No one should be forced to make decisions out of fear," said Arthur. "Even to protect the people they love. It only leads to regret. I'd think you of all people would understand that."

"I don't regret masquerading as my brother," Emry protested.

Arthur smiled as though hoping she'd say that. "So you'll come back," he said. "I'm pleased to hear it."

Ugh, Emry thought. She'd forgotten that little trick of his.

"Fine, but I'm going to make you call me Apprentice Wizard Merlin," she warned.

"I look forward to it," he said, closing the distance between them and looking down at her through his eyelashes, "Apprentice Wizard Merlin."

They were in the courtyard outside the tavern, standing there in the cooling darkness. The night air smelled of fresh rosemary and wood smoke, and Emry wanted very badly to kiss him. To feel his arms around her in this garden where no one was watching, and where, for a moment, they could pretend so many things were possible.

She wished he wasn't looking at her like that. Like he'd come here to do more than regain his apprentice court wizard. Like he'd ridden here as plain, wonderful Arthur, because he ached from not having her in his life.

When he leaned in to kiss her, she didn't pull away. Instead, she melted into it, savoring the pressure of his hand against her spine, and his soft lips on hers. She surrendered into his arms, and into this stolen moment she'd never dreamed they would have. The heat from his palm penetrated her clothes, making her knees go weak. His lips brushed her throat and grazed her jaw.

She gasped, and he smiled against her throat, pleased. He pulled away, brushing back a lock of her hair and twirling it between his fingers.

His lips curved into a slow, wicked grin as he asked, with studied nonchalance, "Perhaps we could get a room?"

Yes, she thought. *Yes, please.*

Except she knew it would be a mistake, no matter what pretty lies she told herself. Even if he wasn't actually going to marry Guinevere, they were still engaged. And he was still the crown prince. And the sword that hung at his waist was still Excalibur.

"Perhaps we should go inside," she said, smoothing the front of her dress, "and get a table before the others arrive."

"Right," said Arthur, as though he'd forgotten about the others entirely. "Er—that's probably best."

He offered her a sad smile, and she knew without question that they'd only wind up hurt by the inevitable disaster of who—and what—they both were. Girls like her didn't wind up with a prince, even though she doubted there'd ever been a prince like Arthur. It was better to have him in her life as a friend. Better to deny the feelings that kept drawing them together. Being his court wizard was enough.

It had to be.

◑ ◑ ◑

Emry's heart hammered nervously as she stepped into the Great Hall at Arthur's side. She'd muttered a clothes-cleaning spell as the castle came into view, but they still looked as though they'd been riding all morning and half the afternoon.

She could feel the courtiers staring curiously at her. Although this time, there were familiar faces. Guinevere, looking far less perfect than usual.

Emmett, in an absurd fur-trimmed jacket, as well dressed as any courtier. Lady Elaine, her expression one of barely concealed fury. Percival, on guard at the door, tossing her a wink and a grin.

King Uther sat on the raised dais, on his wooden throne. The last time she'd been here, the king had ordered her locked in the dungeons and sentenced to death. Her stomach clenched, and her pulse thudded, and Arthur shot her a look of encouragement, as if he knew how she felt.

She stopped in the open space before the throne and sank into a curtsey.

"Emry—the other Merlin—has accepted the position of apprentice court wizard," Arthur said, at her side.

She rose awkwardly, trying not to squirm under the king's scrutiny.

"I see," the king said, his expression stony. "As an apprentice court wizard, I trust you'll have no problem providing a demonstration of your magic."

If the king thought he could intimidate her so easily, he was very much mistaken.

"None at all, Your Majesty." Emry grinned. She'd give him a demonstration, all right.

She said nothing and reached for no wand. She gave only the slightest flick of a finger as she cast the spell.

Snowflakes drifted from the ceiling. Real ones, falling in fat, wet droplets onto the shocked courtiers. The hall filled with shocked murmurs, and Emry bit back a smile as a couple of women frantically patted at their elaborately coiffed hair.

Emry flicked her fingers, and the snow stopped. A muttered spell had everyone's clothing and hair dry. The courtiers gasped in disbelief, and the murmurs rose to a frenzied whisper. No one had been expecting such a dazzling display of magic, and for the first time, Emry got some grim satisfaction out of exceeding everyone's expectations, and doing so entirely as herself. A wave of dizziness hit her from the overexertion, but she clenched her jaw and held her stance, waiting for the king's reaction.

She met his gaze, and he stared back at her, shocked into silence.

And then Princess Guinevere burst into enthusiastic applause. The other courtiers hastily followed suit, and the king gave a grudging nod.

Emry's cheeks went pink from the attention.

"Show-off," Arthur accused, nudging her in the ribs.

"You wanted me to," Emry whispered back.

"Of course I did." Arthur tipped her a grin. "But you're still a show-off, Apprentice Wizard Merlin."

She sighed.

"Ugh, fine, you can call me Emry again."

CHAPTER 43

Emry woke at dawn, staring up at the familiar ceiling beams with a grin. From the sound of it, the guard was starting to assemble outside. Oh, she had missed this place. And this room.

It had taken surprisingly little bullying to make Emmett switch rooms with her. If anything, he had been a little too eager to take the frilly pink bedchamber next to Princess Guinevere's off her hands.

Well, he probably hadn't figured out how to cast a muffling spell on the window. Which was his problem, and her good fortune, because Father's old room felt like home.

She couldn't believe that this life she'd envied and dreamed of was truly hers. That Emmett was here as well. That Arthur had ridden all the way to Brocelande to apologize, and had suffered through a rendition of *The Faerie King* in order to do so. That Gran had given her blessing, and had practically shooed Emry out the door when she heard the prince had come in person, insisting she would be fine with Marion to check in on her.

Emry went to the window, looking out at the castle lawn. At the now-familiar guards running perimeter laps for Captain Lam. Lance wasn't out there, she noticed. And neither was Arthur. She supposed everyone was where they were meant to be.

Even Gawain, who had already left for France. She'd looked for him at supper the night before, only to find his seat empty. She was going to miss him, and his ridiculous coats, and his infuriating snobbery.

Emry pulled open the doors of her wardrobe and reached for her best dress, fastening the buttons with a muttered spell. When she peered in the mirror, she looked entirely like herself.

So she tucked her wand into her belt, dabbed some rose salve on her lips, and went to wake her brother.

He was, predictably, still asleep.

"Get up," she ordered, yanking his blankets onto the floor and making Emmett moan in protest. "Now."

"Fleoges." He snapped his fingers, and his blankets slithered back onto the bed, wrapping around him like a sausage casing.

"Seriously?" Emry folded her arms and glared.

"I'm indisposed," Emmett insisted with a groan. "I have a headache."

Emry glanced around the room. No wonder his head hurt; two empty wine bottles littered the table under the window, along with a deck of playing cards, and two very ornate goblets that looked to be made of hammered gold. There was, Emry realized, the faintest smell of orange blossom perfume.

"Did you have *company* last night?" she asked incredulously.

"None of your business." Emmett moaned, burrowing deeper under the covers.

Emry rolled her eyes and pulled off his blankets again. "Must you *always* play the rake?"

"Hey!" Emmett complained, swinging a pillow at her.

Emry dodged out of the way, levitating a pillow and sending it flying toward her brother.

"You're cheating!" Emmett accused as it knocked into his shoulder.

"Magic isn't cheating!"

Emry climbed onto the bed, reaching for another pillow and batting him in the face the old-fashioned way.

"You're acting like a child!" Emmett raised a pillow over his head and prepared to swing it in attack.

Before he could, a piece of elaborate wall paneling clicked open, revealing a hidden door, and Guinevere burst in wearing a thin linen nightdress.

"Emmett!" she cried, looking alarmed. "I heard shouting!"

Emry froze, realization dawning. So *this* was why her brother had been so eager to exchange rooms.

"Um," Guinevere said, looking back and forth between them. "I—well. This is awkward."

"Not nearly as much for you as it is for me," Emry said, gingerly removing herself from the bed. "Since I'm guessing these aren't clean linens."

Guinevere ducked her head, and Emmett blanched at the accusation.

"Em," he said, "please don't tell the prince."

"Wasn't going to," she promised. "I'd prefer never to speak of this again. And we have lessons, by the way, in the tower."

Emmett stretched luxuriously. "I'll see if I'm feeling up to it after breakfast," he promised. "Did you know you can have meals sent up?"

Actually, Emry hadn't known that. But she didn't want to admit it. "You're the worst," she snapped.

And then she left Emmett to his bad decisions, stopped in the kitchens for a mug of coffee, and drank most of it on the way to the wizard's workshop.

When she arrived, Master Ambrosius was bent over his alembic, the lenses of his pince-nez fogged from the steam.

"Morning," she said brightly. "Did you miss me?"

"Two apprentices," Master Ambrosius murmured, shaking his head. "I wish Nimue had warned me."

"I missed you, too," Emry said wryly, taking a seat at the table. "What are we doing today?"

"I thought I might send you to replenish some of my herbs from the gardens," the old wizard said. "And Arthur as well. Supposing he turns up, rather than tormenting the poor castle guard."

"Who am I tormenting?" Arthur asked, leaning against the doorway. He was carrying two mugs of coffee, Emry saw. And he was dressed in one of his elegant new suits, his circlet glinting against his dark hair.

"Everyone, all the time," Emry said. "You're a menace."

"So they tell me." Arthur flashed her a grin, and then noticed her coffee. "I guess this one's for Emmett."

"It might be a while," Emry said.

"Then he can practice heating it," said Master Ambrosius.

"Really?" Emry said, delighted. "*That's* all he's up to?"

"I've switched him to spellcasting in Greek," Master Ambrosius said. "He kept getting the Latin mixed up."

"He's like that with books, too," said Emry. "Takes him forever to read anything."

"The Greek is much easier for him," said Master Ambrosius with a frown. "I'm surprised your father didn't notice."

"Men can be so unobservant," Emry said sweetly.

Master Ambrosius sighed. And then he handed them the list and sent them on their way.

As they walked through the garden path in the first strokes of sunlight, Emry snuck a look at the prince. He had a basket over his arm, and his eyes were bright as he examined a stalk of betony that was just beginning to flower.

"I think this one's going to come in white," he said. "It's very rare."

"Maybe it's from the chamomile," she said, nodding at the cluster of small white flowers around Arthur's feet.

"I bet you're right," he said. "We'll have to keep an eye on it."

Emry knelt down to clip some feverfew, and Arthur held out the basket, his hair glinting chestnut in the rising sun. Her heart ached at how simple it felt, the two of them walking through the gardens together. At how she could pretend they were something other than what they were.

She tried not to think about Guinevere bursting into her brother's room through the hidden passage, and how complicated their whatever-it-was was going to make things.

"Would you look at that," Arthur said with a satisfied grin, nodding toward the distant tilting fields, where Lance was saddling an enormous black destrier as Sir Kay looked critically on. "No more gate duty."

Emry found she was grinning, too. "So much has changed while I was away." And then she bit her lip. "I can't believe Gawain is really gone."

She hadn't even gotten to say goodbye. Or to wish him luck. Or to—well. Something.

"Finally, some peace," Arthur joked.

"You don't mean that," Emry said.

The prince shrugged. "It's not a bad plan, having him keep an eye on what's happening at Saint-Germain," he said. "I did turn down a betrothal to Princess Anne. And King Yurien and Queen Morgana have a son much closer to her age."

Emry dropped her clipping shears. She had to have misheard. That was the only explanation.

"What did you just say?" she asked carefully.

"That King Yurien and Queen Morgana's boy has to be around seven or eight?" Arthur repeated, frowning. "You must have seen him during my father's birthday celebrations."

"Queen *Morgana*," Emry repeated, her blood turning to ice

It couldn't be. Yet she had a horrible suspicion that it *was*. That the Queen of Lothia was the sorceress the Lady of the Lake had warned her about.

"Come to think of it, she asked about you during the ball," said Arthur, unaware that anything was amiss. "She was surprised to learn that Merlin had children."

"And you're telling me this *now*?" Emry stared at him, horrified. "Arthur, how *could* you?"

Oh, she wanted to hit him.

"How could I what?" he asked.

"Keep this from me!" she accused, her pulse pounding in her ears.

Too late, she felt the crackle of magic at her fingertips.

Morgana had *been here*. At the castle. And Arthur hadn't even thought to mention it.

"Emry?" Arthur said, taking a step back, a question in his voice. "What's going on?"

"Morgana's a sorceress. A powerful one. The Lady of the Lake said she killed my father."

Arthur stared at her, his expression a mixture of pity and horror.

Emry felt her shoulders start to shake. She really didn't want to cry. Especially here, in the herb garden, alone with the prince.

"I'm so sorry," Arthur said. "If I'd known, I would have told you. I promise."

Emry took a deep breath, trying to calm her nerves, and her magic.

"I just can't believe she was *here*. That I *missed* her."

She'd been at the ball. Emry must have walked right past her.

"Do you think—" Arthur began.

"That she took the enchantment off your scabbard?" Emry supplied, finishing his thought. "Yes."

They stared at each other, the horrible realization settling around them.

"The Lady of the Lake said she would go to any lengths to gain Anwen's magic," Emry said. "And she's certainly powerful enough to have transferred the enchantment, rather than just destroying it."

Arthur's expression grew even more distressed.

"So King Yurien possesses an enchantment that makes him unkillable in combat?"

This was bad. Catastrophic. The worst possible outcome.

"I could *kill* my father for this," Arthur went on. "The scabbard was never meant to be used in some silly sword-fighting contest. Yet he insisted, because he wanted to show off a sword that wasn't his to boast about. And I *let* him."

"You can't blame yourself," Emry said. "Morgana would have known that scabbard if you'd worn it to supper."

"I suppose," Arthur said, his brown eyes full of despair. "Still, I don't know what to do," he confessed, his shoulders slumping. "I don't even know where to start."

"Me neither," Emry promised, "but we'll figure it out."

CHAPTER 44

Emmett swung the hidden panel aside, marveling at how clever Guinevere had been to discover it. But when he stumbled into the princess's salon, she looked up at him with wide eyes. She had a lady's maid with her, and was practicing her embroidery.

Sard, he'd thought she'd be alone. The maid stared at him, her mouth falling open, and Emmett wished he'd at least thought to knock.

Well, it was too late now. The only thing left was to act as though his presence was entirely unremarkable.

"Er, you wished to see me, Your Highness?" he asked blandly, brushing some invisible lint from his new silk jacket.

"Yes, I require your help mending a—perfume decanter," Guinevere replied, fixing him with a warning look.

"Consider it done," Emmett said with a bow.

"How did you enter through the wall?" the maid asked.

Guinevere gave a gentle shake of her head, as though he might be fool enough to reveal the passage.

"I apologize if the spell startled you," Emmett lied. "But I wanted to arrive discreetly. I wasn't sure of the delicacy of the princess's request. And the guards at the end of the hallway did assure me she was chaperoned."

The maid sniffed.

"Some tea perhaps, Linota?" Guinevere said pointedly.

For a moment, Emmett thought the girl might refuse. But Guinevere—magnificent, brilliant Guinevere—leaned forward and flashed a sheepish smile. "I'm sorry if it sounded as though I was trying to dismiss you. It's only that I worry about your constitution. I've seen an unbreaking spell performed before, and it was so unexpectedly . . . messy."

The girl blanched. "In what way?"

Guinevere bit her lip. "I really shouldn't say."

"I'll just see about that tea, Your Highness," Linota said, making a hasty retreat.

After she was gone, Emmett slouched back against the paneling. "Messy?" he asked, raising an eyebrow.

"Your sister pulled that trick on me, and it was too clever not to borrow."

"Sounds like Emry." Emmett laughed.

Guin shot him a withering look. "I have *attendants*," she said severely. "And they gossip. This can't happen again."

By *this*, Emmett hoped she meant his dropping in unannounced, as opposed to other things.

"Then it won't," Emmett promised. "I'll leave the passage for your use only."

"Good." Guinevere lifted her chin. "I prefer it when things are for my use only."

She let that one sit there a moment, torturing him with a coy little half smile. Oh, she knew exactly what she was doing. And he adored it.

"Aren't you going to thank me?" Emmett asked with a slight pout.

Guinevere tossed her curls. "For?"

"Mending your perfume decanter, of course."

Guinevere choked back a laugh. "Aren't you going to thank me for sending away my maid?"

"I thought you'd never ask."

Emmett's gaze dropped to her lips. He was going to kiss her, he decided, until she was gasping for him. And it seemed Guinevere had a similar idea. With a deeply wicked gleam in her eyes, the princess set down her embroidery.

◑ ◑ ◑

Emry bolted upright in bed, her heart pounding. Someone was screaming.

The scream sounded again, and she realized where she'd heard it before: on Avalon. The Lady of the Lake had told her it was the forest. But she was in London, not Avalon. And there was no magic forest here.

She crossed to the window, curious what was going on. There, on the castle lawn, a hooded figure stared up at her, concealed beneath a dark cloak.

She frowned, wondering why the guards hadn't noticed.

And then the figure reached up to lower its hood, and Emry stumbled back in shock.

It couldn't be.

Her father stood on the castle lawn, looking just as she remembered.

She pressed her hand over her mouth, staring down through the leaded glass in disbelief.

Impossible. Yet it really *was* him. She was sure of it.

She unlatched the window and leaned out, waving to catch his attention. But he turned away, raising his hood, as if he meant to leave before anyone noticed his presence.

Well, too late for that. Emry dressed quickly, grabbing her wand and cloak, and hurried through the silent castle.

Father was back.

Her heart felt impossibly full at the thought. She'd waited and wished for this for so long, even though she'd told herself it was foolish. Even though she'd sometimes felt she was the only one holding out hope that he wasn't truly dead.

Morgana took his life, the Lady of the Lake had said. Clearly, she was mistaken. Master Ambrosius had said the Lady was no oracle, and here was the proof. Emry stepped onto the castle lawn, drawing her cloak tighter around her shoulders. Strands of hair whipped across her face in the wind, and she tucked it back behind her ears, wishing she'd magicked it long enough for a braid.

For a horrible moment, she couldn't find her father, and she worried that he'd already left. Then she spotted him on the far side of the training yard, heading back toward the inner gate.

"Father!" she called. "Wait!"

She had so many questions. Where had he been, and what was he doing here, and why hadn't he sent word that he was alive for so many years? She hurried across the training yard, picturing how wonderful it would be to rush into his arms and breathe in the familiar scent of his coat. To tell him that she was training to be a court wizard, and that Emmett was as well. To catch him up on everything he had missed.

"Papa!" she called again. "It's me!"

But when he spotted her, he didn't wrap her in a hug, or utter a single word. He only glanced over his shoulder to make sure she was following as he led her through the castle gates and out into the square.

The gates had been unguarded. The thought prickled in the back of her mind, and she tried to ignore it.

But no matter how quickly she walked, she could never close the distance between them. And no matter how many times she called out to him, he gave no response.

This wasn't right. She knew it, yet she shoved her misgivings aside as she followed him down the abandoned streets of the dark city. When she saw the piercing spire of St. Paul's Cathedral up ahead, she realized where he had been leading her.

The churchyard was silent, save for the slab of stone that held no sword, but still bore its ancient promise: *Whoso pulleth out this sword of this stone is rightwise king born of all England.*

Her father stopped before the stone.

He didn't turn around. She could sense a lace of magic around her father's cloak, a strange, insistent crackle.

"Papa?" she said uncertainly, her heart hammering so loud that she could barely hear herself speak.

She reached out a hand to tap his shoulder, but it went right through him. And then he vanished.

Emry felt as though her heart had been torn to pieces. "No," she whispered. "Please, no."

It hadn't been her father at all. It had just been an illusion. One she'd wanted very badly to believe, even though she knew better than to go chasing after ghosts.

Her eyes pricked with tears, and her throat felt tight.

"You're very difficult to track down, you know," a voice said.

A familiar woman strode toward her with measured steps, a dark smile curling at her lips. She was pale and thin as a shadow. Beautiful, in a chilling way.

Without her veil, she seemed younger. And somehow more familiar. There was a likeness in the woman's dark hair and the sharp planes of her cheeks that Emry knew she'd seen somewhere before. It was like grasping at a lost memory, one she could almost reach.

"I tried Avalon first," the woman said. "What a waste. I believe I've quite lost my taste for boats."

"Morgana le Fay," said Emry. She should have known. And maybe, deep down, she had.

"You've heard of me." Morgana offered her a smile, sharp and dangerous as a knife. "I thought so. The Lady of the Lake can be such a gossip."

"It was you," Emry said angrily. "The illusion. You didn't have to—"

"What?" Morgana tilted her head. "Show you the thing you most desired, and then take it away, and make sure I saw the look on your face when I did?"

Emry drew a ragged breath, fighting to remain calm. She couldn't let Morgana get to her. Not like this. Her father was such an obvious wound. She couldn't give the woman the satisfaction of knowing how painfully cruel her deception had been.

"I know you stole the enchantment off Arthur's scabbard," Emry accused. "You could have killed him."

Morgana's eyes narrowed. "You mean he could have gotten *himself* killed. Which is no less than he deserved, with that foolish display of arrogance. He gained the ability to beat death, and he used it to cheat at a sword-fighting contest!"

"That wasn't his idea!" Emry protested. "King Uther—"

Morgana flicked her wrist, and Emry fell to her knees. An invisible hand tightened around her neck, choking her. Her pulse thudded in her ears as she gasped for air. She stared hatefully at Morgana, waiting for it to end.

"Don't *ever* mention that man's name in my presence," Morgana warned, removing the spell as casually as if she were swatting away a fly.

Emry coughed, catching her breath, and then climbed unsteadily to her feet. "Understood," she rasped.

Morgana regarded her coolly. "I'll admit, it was clever of you to masquerade as your brother." Her lips pressed into a grim smile. "Why is it that men are so threatened by women with power, do you think? Even your father was the same way."

Emry said nothing, only waited and glared.

"No matter how many times you prove yourself, they will always see you as a witch—or worse, a *sorceress*." Morgana's mouth twitched. "But I didn't bring you here to lament the ways of men."

"Why *did* you bring me here?" Emry asked.

Morgana grinned.

"That scar on your palm," she said. "I've only seen its like once before. After your father opened a door to Anwen."

Emry's heart pounded in alarm. Of course Morgana had recognized the mark, just as Master Ambrosius had. No wonder Morgana had asked after her, tried to track her down, and summoned her here.

"I want you to show me how you did it." Morgana's eyes were bright and eager, and Emry could feel the enormity of the woman's obsession.

"Why on earth would I help you?" Emry retorted. "You killed my father."

"Killed him?" Morgana scoffed. "Is that what Nimue told you? Why would I kill the one person who could show me how to access magic without limits?"

Emry frowned, confused.

"It was an experiment gone wrong," Morgana explained. "Your father got stuck beyond the stones. He's trapped, not dead."

Not dead. For the second time that night, Emry's chest filled with hope. The way her father had disappeared without a trace, without saying goodbye. How she had always felt he wasn't truly gone.

The Lady of the Lake hadn't said Merlin was dead. Not in so many words. Emry had just assumed. She closed her eyes, remembering exactly what the Lady had said.

The sorceress Morgana took his life.

Emry knew the Lady spoke in riddles, but it had never occurred to her that the Lady would do so about her father's death. Technically, Emry had taken her brother's life when she'd borrowed his place at the castle. Taken it, and returned it to him. Perhaps Morgana could do the same.

"He's trapped," Emry repeated. "Beyond the stones."

Morgana nodded, her eyes bright. "Open a door," she urged, "and we can bring him back."

CHAPTER 45

Arthur sat up in bed with a gasp, the nightmare all too real, and all too present. It was the same one he'd had before, of Emry trapped in the block of stone, dying right in front of him. Except this time it had felt different. More urgent. More real.

And for some reason, his room was *glowing*. Then his head cleared, and he remembered he'd taken Excalibur from the vault for safekeeping. The blade shone bright as day against the darkness of his bedchamber. The sword had never done that before.

Something was the matter. He could feel it.

He dressed quickly, pulling on the first boots and jacket he found in the dark, not bothering with the endless clasps and ties. He buckled on his now-useless scabbard and grabbed his sword, hastily preparing what he would say to his guards.

Except when he cracked open the door, both were asleep at their posts. He almost laughed in relief. Instead, he slipped quietly past them and crept down the dark corridors to Emry's room.

He knocked softly, hoping she would yank open the door, her hair a mess, scowling at him for waking her.

Come on, he thought. *Answer.*

When she didn't, he sent up a prayer of forgiveness and pushed open the door.

She was gone.

Her bed was unmade, her cloak and boots missing. There was no sign of a struggle. Wherever Emry had gone, she had gone willingly.

Suddenly, he knew.

He only worried he wouldn't get there in time, and that the terrible events in his dream would come to pass.

London was dark and silent as Arthur hurried through the empty streets, Excalibur at his side. It was past curfew, and at every scuttle or creak, Arthur half expected a warden to emerge from the shadows, demanding an explanation that he didn't have time to give.

His chest ached, and his lungs demanded air, but he didn't slow down. Not until he reached the churchyard.

It had been a long time since he'd last stepped foot in this place, where the odd little tavern sat next to the sword in the stone. And it was strange to see the stone was still there, a forlorn slab rising from the earth.

He had been so young and unsure the last time he came here.

But he wasn't unsure now.

He rushed toward it, his sword drawn, but the stone was merely a slab of pale marble, worn smooth over time.

She wasn't here.

Whoso pulleth out this sword of this stone is rightwise king born of all England

Think, Arthur urged himself. *Prove yourself worthy of your wizard.*

He could see the underground chamber clearly in his mind, just as clearly as he knew he was standing right above it.

He only needed the way in. He looked around, and that was when he saw the ancient wooden door set into the side of the cathedral. It was overgrown with vines, almost as though it was hoping no one would notice it was there. And it had been left ajar.

Arthur drew his sword, its glowing blade lighting his way against the darkness.

◑ ◑ ◑

This was a spectacularly bad idea, Emry thought as she followed Morgana through the crypt beneath the echoing, empty cathedral.

All around her was the smell of packed earth and decay. The walls were stacked high with dusty tombs containing the bones of long-dead men, now forgotten.

Emry's steps echoed, and her heart pounded, and she wanted desperately to turn back and return to the castle. To climb back into bed and pull the covers up to her chin and sleep until morning, when the clatter of the guard assembling in the courtyard would be a welcome wake-up call.

But she had chosen this. She had chased the Questing Beast, and asked the Lady of the Lake about her father, and thrown herself in the path of danger more often than was sensible.

If she hadn't wanted adventure, she should have stayed home in Brocelande.

You can do this, she told herself. *You're Arthur's court wizard, after all.* So she steadied her nerves and watched as Morgana pressed a panel on an elaborately carved wall. Part of the wall swung aside, revealing a passage.

"It's this way," Morgana said, ducking inside.

Emry followed, blinking back surprise as they entered an underground cavern full of clear, bright stones.

Crystalline spikes protruded from the ceiling, and large glass-like boulders leaned against the walls. In the center of it all stood a henge. Or, what remained of one. The stones that formed the henge's doorway were fissured with cracks, and they seemed on the brink of crumbling to dust.

Some of the smaller rocks scattered across the floor of the cave glowed with a bright, otherworldly light.

It reminded Emry of Excalibur, which made her heart twist with worry. If this was a mistake—if she didn't make it back—what would Arthur think, to find she had vanished in the night? What would Emmett think, to have his sister disappear in the same way as their father?

No. She wouldn't worry about that. Not before she had to.

She considered the henge, which was barely standing. At least the one back on Avalon had seemed sturdy. These stones looked as though a gust of wind could turn them all to sand.

"Maybe it would be easier on Avalon?" Emry said nervously. "The wall between worlds is thinner there."

Morgana tensed, and Emry wondered what she'd said wrong this time.

"Avalon is lost to me," the woman snapped. "The mist won't let me pass through again. But this henge will serve our purpose."

She motioned for Emry to approach the altar stone. Emry stared down at it. The stone was freshly painted with familiar symbols and diagrams, ones her father had shown her long ago.

"I made some repairs," said Morgana, tracing her fingers over the symbols. "This one here is for strength. And this one is—"

"συνδέω," Emry said. "To hold together."

Morgana gave her a sharp look, as though she hadn't expected Emry to recognize the marks.

But Emry knew them well. She'd painted them on the roof of their cottage every week for the past three winters, in a frustrating attempt to stave off costly repairs. Even the smallest chip to the design had her scrambling back up the garden trellis with a paintbrush between her teeth, like a pirate climbing a ship's rigging.

"Aren't you clever?" Morgana said, leaning back against the altar. "Your father taught you well."

Suddenly, Emry had an idea. The barest flicker of a plan. "How did you remove the enchantment from Arthur's scabbard?" she asked. "I've been trying to figure it out, but Master Ambrosius refused to tell me. He said it was impossible."

"For him, perhaps," said Morgana.

"Can *you* show me?" Emry asked, trying to sound innocent. "Do you have it here?"

"No." Anger flashed across Morgana's face. "My husband wears it."

So Morgana could be killed. That was good to know. Especially if anything went wrong. Perhaps the sorceress hadn't killed her father, but Emry didn't trust her.

"It is the same with Arthur." Emry made herself sound bitter and jealous. "He wears Excalibur, even though *I* was the one who got us to Avalon. And instead of thanks, I was called a witch and thrown in the dungeons, while my brother was welcomed at court with open arms."

The sorceress tossed her a knowing smile. "A rage burns in you. One that I know well," Morgana said softly. "Let me guess: You were told magic has limits. That you should try only small spells. That magic cannot work on other magic. And you're starting to suspect that isn't true."

"It seems I have a lot to learn," Emry said with an arrogant tilt of her jaw. "From a weak old man who has little to teach."

"Open the door," said Morgana. "And I can show you everything."

Emry bit back a smile. "I'll need a dagger," she said. "For the ritual. It requires blood."

"Very well." Morgana reached into the folds of her cloak and withdrew a small, jeweled dagger. She held it toward Emry with the handle extended.

Emry reached for it, her heart pounding. But at the last moment, Morgana flipped the dagger and grabbed Emry's wrist.

"Allow me." Morgana sliced the blade across Emry's unmarked palm.

The cut was deep. Deeper than it needed to be. Blood welled in its wake, and Emry hissed in pain. Morgana smiled wolfishly.

"I assume that was what you intended to do, judging from your scar," Morgana said.

Emry offered her a watery smile. *It was worth a shot.*

Carefully, Emry pressed her blood to either side of the stone doorway, trying to think. The sorceress watched her with hungry eyes, determined to miss nothing, and Emry had a very bad feeling about what might happen if she showed Morgana how to open a door to Anwen.

"Well?" Morgana said eagerly. "What's next?"

"It takes more blood, here," Emry said, bringing her palm to the altar. Mentally, she traced the Greek letters that she'd spoken back on Avalon to open the doorway. "And that's it."

"But you didn't say any words. You didn't cast a spell," Morgana scolded.

"There isn't a spell," Emry lied. "It's like Excalibur. It works for those it chooses."

Please work, Emry thought. *Please don't make me say it aloud.*

"You're hiding something from me," Morgana accused.

For an awful moment, nothing happened. Then the stone beneath her palm pressed back, and the cave began to tremble. Emry gasped as magic flowed out of her, flooding into the stone. It wasn't like before, on Avalon. It was a hundred times worse. The pain was excruciating as it shot through her.

It felt as though the stone was *drinking* her blood. Not her blood, she realized. Her magic. And by extension, her very soul.

The stone sucked greedily at her power, taking too much too fast, and Emry screamed. For an instant, everything went dark. Then her vision returned, thick and slow, and she bit back another scream, tasting blood.

The air between the standing stones shimmered and lit with a faint glow.

"It's working," Morgana said breathlessly.

All around them, the stones trembled. Emry had the strangest sensation that she had come untethered from the world, and was now tethered to the stone. She felt stuck. Trapped. Spots danced at the corner of her vision again, and when she looked down, she saw far too much blood on the altar.

She felt like she was going to pass out. And she was terrified what might happen if she did.

"I can't—" Emry cried, trying to pull away.

But the greedy stone wouldn't let her.

"*κλείσε την πόρτα!*" she gasped, trying to close the doorway, not caring that she'd spoken the spell aloud.

But it didn't work.

Why hadn't it worked?

And then Emry saw the third symbol Morgana had drawn, at the farthest edge of the altar. The one she'd been hiding, after she learned that Emry knew their meaning.

δεσμεύω.

To bind.

Morgana had bound her to the stones, with no intention of ever letting her go.

CHAPTER 46

Arthur arrived just in time to see Emry collapse to her knees. She was pale, her right hand pressed against a strange stone that was wet with her blood. Her shoulders trembled, and she looked so drained, and so defeated, that his chest tightened with pain at the sight of her.

She didn't glance at him, just gritted her teeth in agony, her head bowed. *She's alive*, he told himself. *That's what matters.*

Arthur tore his gaze away from Emry, taking in the ancient stone arch that shimmered with magic, and the familiar figure dressed elegantly in black.

Morgana's long brown hair was no longer covered with a veil, nor were her eyes rimmed with dramatic makeup. Her mouth twisted when she saw him.

"Hello, brother," she said.

"Brother?" Arthur frowned. That couldn't be right. Yet the resemblance was undeniable. It was there in her dark eyes, in the sharp planes of her cheeks, in the chestnut brown of her hair. "You're Uther's daughter?" he asked, surprised.

"Of course not," Morgana snapped.

Arthur's pulse quickened as he realized what she meant. He knew his mother had been widowed before she married Uther. That the king had held off the wedding as long as he could, for propriety's sake, trying to allow her six months' mourning. And Arthur had suffered because of it.

Bastard. Spare. Illegitimate.

He'd been called so many things. But never *brother*.

"I didn't know." He shook his head. "My mother never said anything."

"That's because Uther had me erased from her memory," Morgana said bitterly. "After he killed my father, he had Merlin take me to a convent and enchant Igraine to forget that I existed." Morgana gave a harsh, short laugh. "I waited for her to send for me. I wrote her letters for years—all unanswered. Then I discovered that she had a new family. A husband. A son. That she had become a queen. I thought she had abandoned me. Do you know what that feels like? To be unwanted by your own family?"

"Actually, I do," he said, cutting a glance toward Emry. She still knelt before the stone, her chest heaving. She stared back at him, her expression one of torment and surprise and fear, and he knew that she'd heard every word. "Uther would have gladly sent me away to be forgotten, if he had produced another heir."

"Yet you stand by his side while he shows himself to be an incompetent old drunk," said Morgana. "How pliant and obedient you are, brother. I wonder who you learned that from."

She tilted her head, studying him. Seeing, Arthur realized, so much of their mother.

"We don't have to be enemies," Arthur said.

"That's where you're wrong," Morgana ground out. "Uther took everything from me. So I am going to take his kingdom. And I am going to kill his son. And when I do, I want him to know *exactly* who's responsible. The little girl he tried to throw away, returned to conquer Camelot."

She turned from him a moment, staring greedily at the scene that was forming between the stones. A faint outline of a forest was taking shape.

Arthur cut another glance toward Emry, who seemed to be straining toward something just out of reach, at the edge of the altar.

"I can't let you do that," Arthur said grimly.

"*Let* me? As if you have a choice. I am not the only one who plots against you. My husband has heard the legends of a High King who will rule over England. And there's no one more convinced he's the rightful ruler of all England than Yurien Vortigen."

"*I* am the rightful king of all England," Arthur insisted. "Excalibur proves it."

Morgana scoffed. "You arrogant little princeling. The sword proves nothing."

Arthur's eyes darted toward Emry again. Her free arm was outstretched, and her eyes went wide, as though she was trying to tell him something. *The sword*, he thought. That had to be what she was reaching for. What she was trying to tell him. She needed his sword.

"When this door opens, I can make a thousand Excaliburs," Morgana boasted, gesturing toward the stones. "A thousand scabbards. What will yours be worth then?"

"If Lothia's army needs a thousand magic swords to defeat Camelot's, I wouldn't go bragging about it," he said.

Morgana's eyes flashed with anger, and Arthur took her moment of distraction to edge closer to Emry.

"I know why you're here," said Morgana. "But you're too late to save your precious witch."

"I don't think I am," Arthur said, hefting his sword. "And for the record, she prefers the term 'wizard.'"

Morgana's expression darkened, her control stretching thin. She didn't hesitate, didn't blink. She waved a hand, and Arthur hurtled backward, slamming into a boulder. Hard. Searing pain shot through his right shoulder and down his arm. He coughed, tasting blood. His sword lay in the dirt, and he scrambled for it on hands and knees. When his hand wrapped around the hilt, the agony in his shoulder receded, and he sighed in relief, pushing to his feet with a groan.

He stared hatefully at Morgana, knowing she had enjoyed herself. Behind her, the trees looked more solid, their fragrant boughs smelling of cloves and winter and tart cherries.

"This won't end well for you," she warned. "You can't fight magic with a sword."

"I can try," Arthur insisted.

Morgana lashed out again. Dozens of crystalline rocks rose into the air and shot straight for him.

He twisted, shielding his face, but the stones tore at him like knives. White-hot pain ripped through his hurt shoulder. He fell to his knees, gasping for breath and struggling to keep his grip on his sword.

A rock cracked against his ribs, and Excalibur dropped from his hands, clanging as it hit the ground.

Morgana grinned. "Shall I keep going? Or have you had enough?"

Arthur's eyes darted to his sword, mere feet away.

"Don't," she warned.

Waves of pain tore through him as he lunged for it.

The relief was instant. He pushed to his feet, pressing forward in attack. Morgana flicked her wrist, and the sword bent back, as if it had encountered an invisible blade.

Arthur gritted his teeth and parried, bringing the sword overhead only to meet an invisible blade again. Still, he pressed forward.

A clap of thunder sounded, and the soft patter of rain filled the cave. Not just the sound, but the smell of it too, soft and damp and earthy.

The doorway to Anwen was open.

Morgana twisted around, distracted by the doorway, and Arthur took that moment to close the distance between them and press the tip of his sword to her throat.

"Let my wizard go," Arthur commanded.

Morgana merely watched him, an amused curl to her lips as his blade dug into her skin, forming a small trickle of blood.

"We both know you won't do it," she goaded, unflinching.

His hands shook as he stared down the length of the blade at Morgana. She had their mother's eyes exactly. Soft brown with the barest flecks of green.

"Yes, I will," Arthur insisted.

After all, she had sworn she would kill him. And his father. She had killed the elder Merlin, and was torturing Emry. But still, he hesitated.

He knew the Lady of the Lake hadn't given him this sword so it could cure hangovers. Excalibur was the sword of a killer. His hand shook, and the blade trembled against her throat.

Do it, he urged himself, but he held back, even as Morgana brought a jeweled dagger out from beneath her cloak.

She plunged it into his stomach with a savage twist.

Arthur gasped as the pain tore through him. He stumbled back, falling to the ground, his sword skittering away. The room spun, and he fought to stay conscious.

"I told you." Morgana tutted.

Arthur coughed wetly, reaching for Excalibur. His fingers scraped against the hilt, and he gritted his teeth, scrambling for purchase. He almost had it. He turned his head toward the altar, toward Emry. She stared back at him, her eyes glistening with fear.

"Arthur," she whispered, her voice not so much breaking as already broken.

He had come to save her. And he wasn't about to give up now.

"Catch," he gasped.

And with the last of his strength, he pushed the sword to her.

CHAPTER 47

Emry braced herself against the pain as the stone sucked greedily at her magic, pinning her hand in place. Her throat was dry, and her heart pumped frantically, and her body felt like a well nearly emptied of water. But she still stretched toward the binding symbol Morgana had inked at the very edge of the altar.

The two triangles, their tips pressed together, bisected by a line.

If only she could scratch off an edge, the spell would release, and she'd be able to use her magic again. To close the door to Anwen.

But no matter how hard she stretched, it was out of reach.

And then, dimly, as if through a fog, she saw Arthur lying on the ground, a dark wound spreading across his stomach. He clawed for his sword, staring at her with an expression she'd seen him wear only once before, after he had been poisoned and was convinced of his demise.

And then his fingers found purchase, and Arthur—brave, wonderful, clever Arthur—pushed Excalibur toward her.

The moment she grasped the hilt, the sword glowed bright as sunlight in her hands, a dazzling thing. She dug the blade into the altar stone, scratching out that hateful binding symbol.

Magic flooded back into her, and she climbed to her feet, pointing the glowing blade at Morgana.

"Tell me," Emry demanded, "how to bring back my father."

Morgana laughed. "You foolish girl! There's an entire world beyond the stones. How should I know where Willyt Merlin is? Or if he still lives?"

"So you lied to me," Emry said, her voice dangerously low.

A clap of thunder sounded from the forest on the other side of the stones.

Emry could sense Anwen's magic calling out to her.

Something you want?

Something you wish?

Something you desire?

She braced herself against the magic's call, but Morgana stared at the doorway, transfixed. The sorceress licked her lips, eagerness blooming across her face as she took a step toward it.

"*κλείσε την πόρτα!*" Emry ordered.

The doorway started to shimmer.

"No!" Morgana screamed, hurling herself through just as the doorway faded.

The altar went still, and Emry stumbled backward. Excalibur trailed from one hand, and she stared down at the other, where she now carried a fresh silver scar across her palm.

"Arthur!" she said, gaping in horror as she spotted Morgana's dagger buried to the hilt in his stomach.

"Hi," he said faintly. "Came to help."

Emry knelt at his side. He looked terrible. His face was white, and his clothes were torn, and a dark, sticky stain had spread across the front of his tunic. He caught Emry staring at it, and then he brought a hand to the wound. It came away wet.

"Lance is going to kill me," she said, her breath catching.

"He'll speak kindly at our funerals," Arthur promised, his voice barely more than a whisper.

He was dying. They both knew it. Blood bubbled from the gash in his stomach and spotted the corners of his mouth.

"Here," Emry said, pressing Excalibur into his hands.

She stared down at him, waiting for color to return to his cheeks. For him to sigh with relief and push himself up. But he merely gave her a sad smile and shook his head. His eyes were glassy with pain.

"Why isn't it helping?" she asked, frantic. "I thought wielding Excalibur means you can't be defeated in battle."

"I'd assume dying isn't the same as being defeated," he said, his voice tight. "Hence the need for a scabbard that prevents death."

He was right, Emry realized. Gran always said death was a beginning, not an ending. And battles always had endings.

Emry stared at the prince, tears spilling down her cheeks. His head was cradled in her hands. When had that happened? When had she drawn him onto her lap? She didn't remember. She bent over his body, feeling as though her whole soul was screaming in despair.

"Got any healing salve?" he joked, his words faint.

Emry's tears spilled faster. That joke was a very bad sign. She'd never see him become king. Or wear that ridiculous sportswear. Or examine an herb in the garden. Or tuck a book under his arm on his way to the library. Or sip a mug of coffee in the morning, his eyes bright and awake as he slipped into the seat across from hers in the wizard's workshop.

She had lost him once, and she wasn't going to lose him again.

"I've got something better," she promised. "Magic."

She was going to save him. She had to.

She dragged him toward the altar, propping him gently into a sitting position. He grimaced, his face white, and Emry tried not to stare at the smear of blood across the ground.

And then she sliced her hand open with Excalibur, laying her bleeding palm on the altar.

She didn't know if she had the strength to reopen the portal, but she had to try. She had to save him. Before she could speak the command, the stone pressed against her hand. Except this time, instead of draining her magic, power flowed the opposite way.

Magic flooded into her, cool and crisp and wonderful. Magic that wasn't hers.

It felt unfamiliar and strange, but there wasn't time to question it.

Emry lifted a hand, picturing the jagged path of the dagger, and Arthur's wound healing itself. Before she could cast the spell, the magic snapped out of her, a bright crackle of light that shot from her fingertips to his stomach.

The dagger came loose, trailing in Arthur's hand. His eyes closed, and he took a deep, shuddering breath. Emry stared down at him, her heart pounding, her throat tight, unsure what had just happened.

And then Arthur opened one eye.

"That was odd," he said. "Effective, but odd."

He groaned, lifting his tunic to take stock of his wound. His skin was still slick with blood, but in the center of it was a bright silver scar shaped like a sunburst.

Emry stared down at her hand, unsure what had happened. She hadn't cast the spell, not even in her head. The magic—not *her* magic, but the strange magic that coursed through her—had done the work itself.

And then the altar stone cracked in half. There was a threatening rumble, and Emry realized with horror that the henge was going to collapse. All around them, large cracks laced across the ground.

There was a shimmer between the stones, as though the door was trying to open from the other side.

"Father?" Emry whispered.

"We have to go," Arthur said urgently. He'd dragged himself to his feet, and Emry didn't think she'd ever seen Excalibur grow as brightly as it did now.

"But my father—" Emry protested, gesturing toward the door.

"There's no time," Arthur insisted as the floor fissured again, revealing a crack nearly too wide to jump across.

He was right. The cavern was going to collapse, and if they didn't make it out in time . . .

Emry let him pull her away.

Rocks tumbled at their feet, and statues tipped, their heads rolling across the floor.

Emry and Arthur scrambled up from the underground crypt as fast as they could, finally tumbling out into the eerie silence of the churchyard.

Alive.

CHAPTER 48

Shadows cloaked the London streets as the two bloody, dusty figures limped away from the cathedral.

Emry didn't know how she was still standing, but she was managing it somehow. And so was Arthur. He hobbled at her side, clutching the hilt of his glowing sword. There was a scrape on his cheek, and a rip in his cloak, and his clothes were sticky with blood. He looked as if he had been through hell, which he very nearly had. Emry suspected she didn't look much better.

She felt shaky and strange, as though there was too much magic inside of her. She could feel it in her blood and beneath her skin, the unfamiliar power humming through her veins. It set her teeth on edge.

Her chest clenched, and everything warped and—

"Hey," Arthur said. "Hey, it's okay."

He wrapped his arms around her and held on tight. She leaned into him, burying her face in his chest. His closeness made the fresh magic inside of her stop churning. Made her feel a little more like herself.

"No, it isn't," she choked out. "I'm so sorry. I did this. I—"

"Of course you didn't." Arthur sounded upset. "Morgana did. The same way she stole the enchantment on my scabbard."

"But it's my fault you came to help," she insisted.

"I had that dream about the stones weeks ago," Arthur promised. "If anything, it was probably *foretold* that I would face Morgana in that cave. Excalibur chose me for a reason. And it wasn't to sit in my father's vault. Or, as much fun as it was, to cure Lance's hangover."

Emry offered him a sad smile. "That's one of my favorite memories," she admitted. "The afternoon in the clearing."

Arthur's expression went thoughtful. "Mine too," he admitted. "That day, it was almost as though nothing bad could ever happen."

"And then it did," Emry finished, pulling away and rubbing a patch of dried blood from her wrist.

They lapsed into silence. No matter that Arthur insisted it wasn't her fault—if she hadn't been so foolish—if she had only stayed at the castle—he wouldn't have needed to come after her. To risk his life.

He had almost died. He *should* have died. She still wasn't sure *how* she had healed him.

Smart as spades, but foolish as hearts.

Oh, her father had known her well. But she hadn't known him at all. What had he done to Arthur's sister? And to his mother? It was terrible, dark magic. A variation of the rotten spell Emmett had tried to use on his debt collectors.

Father hadn't wanted to teach her that kind of magic. He hadn't wanted to teach her magic at all. He was nothing like she had thought. No wonder Master Ambrosius had been so unsurprised to hear what Emmett had done. And no wonder the Lady of the Lake had been so upset when she'd caught Emry opening that portal. *The magic chooses its path*, Master Ambrosius always said. But so did the wizard.

And her path had never seemed clearer. It was just as the Lady of the Lake had said: she was meant to be at Arthur's side. And he was meant to be at hers.

He had been magnificent back there, in the cave. He could have used Excalibur to kill Morgana. Instead, he had sacrificed it to save Emry's life. And she had saved his, in a way she still didn't understand. She felt it between them, an invisible bond of what they'd gone through, together.

"Come on," he said. "We should get back before anyone realizes we're gone."

Emry nodded in agreement, tossing one last glance at the cathedral. The henge had been destroyed. She knew that. But the door had been opening from the other side right before it crumbled to dust. It was possible—

No. She was only fooling herself. She didn't know for certain what she'd seen. The stones had been acting strangely. Perhaps it hadn't been her father, trying to return home. Perhaps it had been Morgana. Or nothing at all.

She had lost her father before, and had kept going. And she'd do the same now. She lifted her chin, and stared at the weary, dark-eyed boy who stood at her side. A boy who had run halfway across London to save her. And a thought occurred to her. The castle had been asleep when she'd left. *Arthur* had been asleep.

"How did you know where to find me?" she asked.

"I had that dream again," he admitted. "And when I woke, Excalibur was glowing."

"Clever sword," Emry said.

"Clever dream," returned Arthur.

Up ahead, Emry could see the warm candlelit glow of the wealthy townhouses on the Strand. She wondered what anyone looking out would make of them, a boy and a girl in torn, bloodstained clothes, with a glowing sword.

"For someone who isn't magic, you sure have an affinity for it," Emry observed. "But then, it does run in families. And your sister—"

"Don't call her that." A muscle feathered in Arthur's jaw.

"I'm sorry," Emry said quietly. "Tonight was a lot."

"Well, we got through it. Together. You, and me, and good old Aunt Matilda." He shot her a crooked grin.

"When your father demands that we explain ourselves, please refer to Excalibur exactly like that," Emry said.

Arthur scrubbed a hand through his hair. "If my father demands an explanation, I'll tell him that now I know what Yurien wants. No more games, or niceties, or pretending we're not enemies destined for war. We should be preparing to outsmart him, not waiting for him to make the first move. That's no strategy, and it's no way to defeat a would-be tyrant."

"Careful," Emry warned. "You're starting to sound like a king."

"Yeah, well." Arthur shot her a sidelong glance. "Probably a side effect of saving your life."

"Whatever, I saved yours first."

"I saved yours better," Arthur insisted with a maddening smile.

"It isn't a contest," she retorted.

They were in the same alleyway, Emry realized, where she and Gawain had faced down bandits after leaving the Crooked Spire. It seemed a lifetime ago that she had been so afraid of two men with mere knives.

Now, she thought, she could destroy them with a twitch of her hand. The realization was both satisfying and terrible. But she had wanted this. To be Arthur's court wizard. To stand by his side as he fulfilled his destiny. And to forge a destiny of her own. She hadn't wondered how it would change her, and what the price might be to lead such a life. But it was too late to turn back. And even if she could, she wouldn't have wanted to. This was her fight now, and maybe it had always been.

"Come along, wizard." Arthur squinted toward the castle gates, where Lance was urgently flinging orders at a collection of guards. "I think they're about to send out a search party."

CHAPTER 49

Arthur stormed out of his father's apartments, wishing he hadn't bothered. He'd gone in with every intention of admitting the truth about where he'd been, and confronting his father about Morgana. But somehow, the words had turned to ash in his mouth.

He had nearly died. He had fought a sorceress, and pressed his sword to her throat, and hesitated because she had exactly their mother's eyes. And the last thing he'd felt like doing after all of that was going toe to toe with his father over events that had happened twenty years ago.

He was so tired. He didn't think he'd ever been so tired. So he'd edited and lied, eager to get his lecture over with, and careful to shield Emry from any blame. The king had listened with increasing disbelief, his face blotching red with anger, especially after Arthur revealed that King Yurien was in possession of the enchantment from his scabbard.

"You mean to tell me that man is unkillable?" Uther had roared, banging his fist against a table.

"So you can see why I did everything in my power to try and fix it," Arthur had explained.

"But you *didn't* fix it. *You failed*. And you could have *died* for your foolishness. Now get out."

Arthur had taken one look at his father's scowl and done so with haste. Perhaps he hadn't needed to fling the doors open with such force, but his father's disappointment chafed at him, especially since it was so unwarranted.

He *hadn't* failed. He had saved Emry, and he'd learned of Morgana's plans, and had discovered the dark and unforgivable truth that his father had hidden from him.

He sighed, scrubbing a hand through his hair as he slowed his pace in the corridor. This mess he was in was entirely his father's doing. His uncle, the Duke of Cornwall, clearly wanted him out of the way so he could take the throne for himself. Morgana wanted him dead out of revenge. King Yurien would stand against him to build his empire, and Morgana would do everything in her power to help him. But despite all of this, Uther still treated him like a child, expecting him to obey commands with no thought of the future.

All Arthur had done—all he had ever done—was to try to fix his father's mistakes.

Somehow, without his noticing, his feet had carried him in the direction of Emry's rooms. He rounded the corner just as Emmett was coming through her door.

The young wizard gave him a withering look. "She's my sister," he warned.

"My intentions are honorable," Arthur promised.

"We'll see about that," Emmett grumbled.

And then Emry appeared in the doorway, making a face at her brother's back. "Ignore him. Come on in."

Arthur hesitated, spotting a girl's nightdress flung over a chair. "He's not wrong." Then, smiling sheepishly, "Want to go out? I could use a drink. And some company."

"Out as in London?" Emry looked surprised.

"Out as in London," Arthur confirmed. He was done playing prisoner in his father's court. If he was going to lead this kingdom one day, he should be able to see it. He said as much, and Emry beamed, reaching for her cloak.

"I know a great place," she said. "The only thing is, it's more of a brothel?"

Arthur held back a sigh. "I think we can do better than that," he promised.

◐ ◐ ◐

Emry surveyed their crowded table at the Crooked Spire, wondering how going out for a drink had turned into . . . this.

The whole gang had come along. Lance, of course. Emmett, who had insisted. Percival, who had volunteered himself as guard, and Guinevere, who had turned up alongside Emmett, wearing a maid's cloak and a fierce expression that dared anyone to object.

The six of them could barely squeeze around the table without bumping elbows.

"This place is wonderful," Guinevere said, grinning into her wineglass. Emry had expected the princess to balk at visiting a tavern, but instead, she'd proven herself an excellent sport when it came to subterfuge.

"Did you know there used to be a sword in the courtyard?" Arthur grinned, slouching back in his seat and looking far too pleased with himself.

Across the table, Lance shuffled his deck of cards with a practiced snap. He started to deal the next hand, and then stopped, glancing out the window with a frown.

"This might sound strange, but does St. Paul's spire look crooked to anyone else?" he asked.

Arthur and Emry exchanged a look, and Emmett let out an accusing cough. Emry gave him a kick under the table.

"I was just thinking the same thing!" said Guinevere.

"Really? It looks the same to me," said Arthur.

Lance raised an eyebrow, and Emry watched a silent communication pass between the two of them. Emry had told Emmett everything, of course. And she'd assumed Arthur had done the same for Lance.

But apparently not, as Lance had barely escaped his squire's duties in time to join them. He still smelled of steel and the stables. Lance finished dealing their round, and Percival went first, grimacing at his luck to draw the low card.

As the game progressed, Emry glared down at her cards, positive Emmett was cheating. She just couldn't figure out how.

Arthur, across the table, chewed his lip, looking equally distressed.

Lance, meanwhile, tossed another coin into the center of the mess.

"Can I bid yet?" Guinevere asked eagerly.

"It's bet," Emmett told her, with surprising patience. "And no, Perce goes next."

"She can have my turn. I'd rather spend my coin than lose it." Percival threw down his cards, sauntering off to the bar for a refill. Emry watched how Lance's eyes followed after him, and how, when Perce returned to the table, he'd bought another round of ale for everyone.

Emry accepted the drink with a smile, though she had barely touched her first.

Her magic still felt wrong. Twisted. Like a blade that had been honed and sharpened so much that it would never quite balance the same. She worried what might happen if she lost control.

Emmett tossed a queen onto the pile and leaned back in his chair with a smirk.

"You promised not to cheat," Lance accused, "but that's the fifth queen in this round."

"I'm sure if you check the deck, you'll only find four," Emmett said innocently. He shrugged and added, "You have to admit, it's more interesting when the cards change."

Emry glared at her brother. "Change them back," she threatened. "Now."

"Okay, okay," he muttered. *"ρέστα."*

She flinched, forgetting that he would use Greek. The sound of it threw her, and suddenly she was back in the crypt, losing herself in the torrent of magic.

"Emry, it's your turn," prompted Arthur.

"Sorry," she said. She stared at her hand of cards, trying to think. When she glanced up, she caught Arthur watching her with concern.

"Sorry," she apologized again, laying her cards on the table. "I need some air."

"I'll join you," Arthur said, pushing to his feet.

They fell into step as they walked into the courtyard. Arthur said nothing for a long while, just remained silently at her side, staring out at the block of empty marble, and beyond, to the cathedral that really did look a little unbalanced. It had rained earlier, and the scent of damp earth filled the air, reminding Emry of being underground.

She breathed deeply, closing her eyes. Reminding herself where she was. Trying to quiet the magic that roiled within her.

"I've been having nightmares about it, too," Arthur said quietly. "Probably will, for a while. Something like that, you don't get over it in a day."

Emry bit her lip. "I don't know how to go back to the way things were," she admitted.

"I'm not sure we're supposed to," said Arthur. "It feels like everything is changing, whether we like it or not."

He was right. Things did feel different. Even the air carried with it a cool, crisp promise of fall. Of change.

"We don't know for sure what happened to Morgana," Emry pointed out. "Or my father." She couldn't explain it, but she felt as though he was still alive.

"And then there's Yurien," Arthur said grimly. "With an army at his disposal, and an enchantment that makes him unkillable."

"We'll fix it," Emry promised. "We'll prevent a war, and unite the kingdoms."

"We can certainly try," said Arthur, bending down to examine a spray of wild foxglove that had sprung up next to the tavern's steps.

He reached into his jacket for a small scrap of linen, and pinched off a flower, carefully wrapping the blossom inside.

Emry's heart ached to see him do that. To watch him transform so effortlessly from the future king back into the Arthur she knew. And she worried she'd never find a way to become her old self again. That the strange magic flowing through her veins would change her into someone she didn't recognize. Or worse, into someone she didn't want to become.

And then Arthur caught her eye and smiled a slow, beautiful smile, and she decided she'd never let that happen, despite the impossible tasks that stood in front of them. They were setting out to make a better world. Together.

"I'm pretty sure this is a terrible idea," Emry said.

"Of course it is," Arthur said, holding back a grin. "But when has that ever stopped us?"

END OF BOOK ONE

ACKNOWLEDGMENTS

This is a book that I've been holding in my heart for a long time. It's one that I spent years writing, sometimes longhand, sometimes in seventeenth-century libraries, sometimes in quaint French villages and bustling London pubs. But mostly, it's a book that I worked on, for a large part, at home during the pandemic. It's surreal to watch it find its way into the world, this story I desperately wish I could send back in time to my younger self.

Instead, all I can do is send it forward in time to you, dear reader. I hope it was everything you needed it to be. Also, thank you for putting up with my extremely dubious reimagining of King Arthur.

But most of all, thank you to everyone who cheered this book on when it was nothing but a crazy idea, a half-finished manuscript, and a copyeditor's worst nightmare (in my defense, I only invented a couple of words and fudged history when it was absolutely necessary). If everyone could line up to the side of the stage until I call your names, that would be great.

First, I'm amazingly fortunate to have found a true champion in my agent, Barbara Poelle, who is nothing short of miraculous. Second, I'm incredibly grateful for my badass editor, Jenny Bak, for believing in this story and knowing exactly how to make it better. Thank you for your guidance and insight, and for only FaceTiming me by accident once.

To my husband, Daniel Inkeles—none of this would be possible without your love, support, and lovingly supportive snark. Thank you a million times over, and sorry for dragging you to all of those castles all of those times and making you take Instagrams of me.

Mom, thank you for listening to me chatter on about characters and plot points and Arthurian legends, and for giving me that copy of *Harry*

Potter and the Sorcerer's Stone when I was twelve, which is really what started me down this path in the first place.

Maura Milan, for always being there to light up the dark times, and for your unwavering belief in this book from the beginning. My ride-or-die publishing confidant, Amy Spalding, for being the first person I text when things get weird, or when I just have a dumb question about copyedits. Thank you to Victoria Schwab, for giving me the best advice at the best possible time: that the stories we write out of anger and frustration are often the ones that save us. Thanks as well to my early readers Emily Wibberley, Mason Deaver, and Kristin Dwyer, for loving these characters as much as I do. And thank you to Sasha Reid, for always believing in me, and to Kerri Maniscalco, for getting on the phone with a complete stranger to convince me I had to sign with Barbara (you were so right).

Thank you to the Bibliothèque Mazarine, for issuing me a reader's card not once but twice. I wrote a significant amount of this story in your reading room, where I felt absolutely transported into the past.

I'm also indebted to the many authors who have paved the way for queer fantasy, and for those writers, agents, editors, librarians, booksellers, reviewers, and readers who are working to lift up and bring more stories into the world that reflect our beautifully diverse reality.

And thank you to my readers, those who have stuck with me since the days of YouTube videos, those who grew up with my contemporary novels, and those who have just arrived at the party. I wouldn't get to do any of this without your continued support and enthusiasm.

Now let's meet back here in a year to discuss the next installment. Deal? Deal.